MIDNIGHT WORLD
VOLUME FOUR

MIDNIGHT WORLD VOLUME FOUR

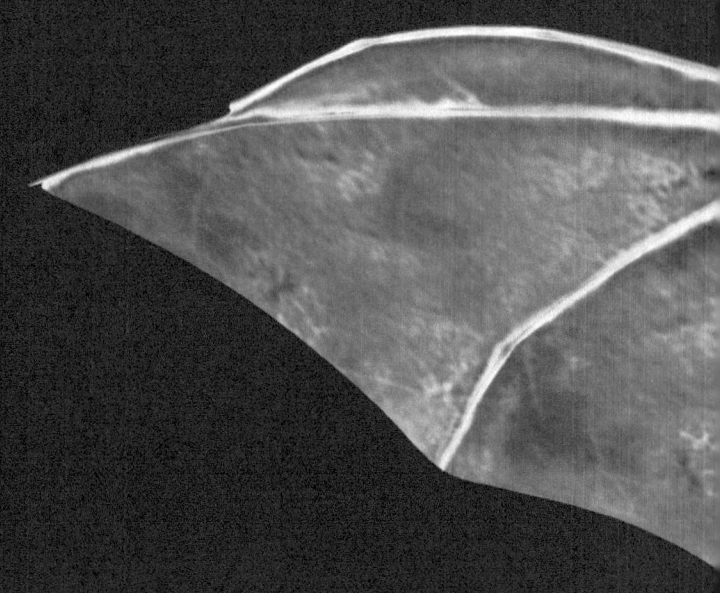

darkness_4.0
OS v. 2.1

DALIVIA PLAUT

DARK PLOT
PUBLISHING

• • •

First Edition, January 2020
Story by Dalivia Plaut
Written by Dalivia Plaut
Edited by Ireland Lelisio

ISBN: 978-1-7344831-0-9
Plaut, Dalivia, 1983—
darkness_4.0 OS v.2.1
I. Title. Fiction. Dark Fantasy/Horror

ISBN: 978-1-7344831-0-9 pbk.

Cover Design by Low Key
Book Design by Dalivia Plaut
Cover Photograph by AndreyPopov/
Yuri_Arcurs (istockphoto.com)

This is a work of fiction.
Names, characters, places, and incidents
are the products of the author's imagination.
Any resemblance to actual persons, living
or dead, is entirely coincidental.

Printed in the United States of America

PUBLISHER'S NOTE
This is a work of fiction. Names, characters, places, and incidents either are the product of the author's imagination or are used fictitiously. Any resemblance to actual persons, living or dead, business establishments, events, or locales is entirely coincidental.

• • •

darkness_4.0 OS v. 2.1

TABLE OF CONTENTS

MIDNIGHT WORLD VOLUME FOUR:
darkness_4.0 OS v. 2.1

"READY *Governor Washington?*"

The pensive governor stared through the tinted window at a mob of news reporters itching to swarm her once she stepped foot outside the town car parked in front of New Way Academy.

Again, the same voice next to the governor: "*Avanti?*"

Finally, Avanti pulled her hard brown eyes from the reporters, in particular, a blonde-haired reporter who had the city buzzing as of late from her fearless reporting and "calling out" politicians, and rotated toward the new aide.

"Yes, Claire," Avanti said under a dark cloud of silence.

The furrow in Avanti's brow ironed out, although both her eyes still remained sharp and snakelike around the beige continent-shaped blotches scattered along her dark cheeks. Once Claire acknowledged that look on Avanti's face—in fact, absorbed the veracity of its raw seduction—Claire immediately backed off.

Sitting in monk-like nimbleness next to Governor Washington: the governor's longtime makeup artist, Violet Odem—or simply "Vye," for short. Vye had been right by Avanti's side well before she ran for mayor of Atlanta; in fact, ever since they met four years before Avanti decided to enter the game of "politricks," the two were pretty much inseparable.

Vye gave one quick eye-turn toward Avanti's gaze; however, like those close to Governor Washington, she knew *that* particular razor-eyed look and definitely knew when not to question such expression.

"Claire," Avanti said again, "What is it?"

"I. . . I have great news," Claire said hesitantly, while skimming through the text messages on her smartphone. "Get this. McCray's ready to come to the table to make a deal."

"Sounds like the lawsuit worked as planned," Avanti said with a half-smirk. "Pawn to e-four."

Inside joke.

"On top of the whole *vamp*-issue," Claire said with a hint of distain, "the media is going to have a field day with us—"

"—I'm well aware, Claire," Avanti said, then trailed off, "Working with ICE to round up thousands of undocumented vamps running around my state fits their narrative. They want to peg me as 'cruel' because that's exactly what their audience wants to hear. It's obvious the media has already chosen their white knight to oust me."

"Don't get me started with Byron," Claire said under her voice. "The woman wants everybody to live in a utopia. 'Save the planet?' That's her solution?" She laughed away the very thought of Bryon. "We can't even save ourselves—"

"—Sure, we've gotten a substantial hit from the movie industry. Companies, like BrainFood and Nikita, are having cold feet about whether or not they should move their headquarters here. The National Basketball League can't make up their goddamn mind about whether or not they want to pull The All Star Tournament out of our state. But, I guarantee you, they'll cave, once they feel the pressure from a party that I do not understand anymore. Which means *no* jobs and no money. But trust me, Claire. Once everything calms down, they'll come running back to us. All of them. They always do. Besides, the *safety*," she emphasized, "of our citizens is more important right now?"

"Of course, it is. *But—*"

"—*But* one thing's for damn sure," Avanti interrupted Claire, "You'll never hear a peep on the news about all the violent crimes these animals committed in the past six months. And I thought wintertime, of all times, was supposed to be the safest time of the year."

The imagery alone of having "untraceable" vamps running loose around her state, from thoroughbreds traveling in packs through late-night hours and devouring anything that had a pulse to lone half-breeds mutilating and committing sexual acts to their victims that'd make wild animals look, dare to say, civil to crossbreeds phantom-flying from one black market blood trader to another in order to whet an endless appetite, caused Avanti to lower head in despair. She ran her palm over the prickly surface of her shaved head, as if she was both stroking for good luck and dissolving any violent thought that manifested in her mind.

"I suggest we propose a strong defensive strategy just in case McCray backs away from the deal," Claire said, her voice distant to Avanti. "If we don't follow through on our end, McCray's going to do everything in his *power* to undermine your campaign for reelection."

One word jumped out at Avanti.

She faced Claire, her eyes narrowing.

"McCray's not the only one with friends in *high* places."

"But don't be fooled," Claire said, not backing away from the governor. "He has a reputation to exploit the weaknesses of those who oppose him. He's sneaky powerful."

"Yeah," Avanti started, "and he'd make a great politician."

Claire's expression—or lack thereof—spoke louder than she could articulate.

Likewise, Avanti acknowledged Claire's change in behavior.

"You have nothing to worry about, Claire," Avanti said, her tone softer. "My constituents know all about my skeletons. Believe it or not, if it weren't for those skeletons, I never would've been voted into office."

"Perhaps you should write a book about them," Claire suggested.

"About who?"

"Your skeletons, ma'am."

The governor ignored Claire and redirected her attention toward the looming storm outside, the chaos-loading. The sight of the mob caused her to take a beat and reflect on the past two weeks, the waves of violence throughout Georgia, bad press, as well as ridiculous conspiracies running wild through the tainted ether.

"Of all the groups out there, no matter what I say or do, I will never win *them* over."

"They can be our friend or our enemy."

"I rightfully disagree, Claire. They're supposed to be neither. Tell me something," the governor said following a heavy sigh. "In this digital age of information where every word that comes out of your mouth is destined to be distorted or taken out of context to merely whet one's own self-glorification, why in the hell do we continue to indulge these people?"

"What people—"

"—Reporters," the governor clarified. "What do they get out of all of this?"

"I guess they're just trying to inform the people."

"Please, Claire," Avanti said sharply, as she held back laughter. "You can't be that naive? Can you?"

"Well, permission to be frank. . . "

"I'd prefer you to be Frank than Dick. That's exactly why I brought you on my team, for your candor."

Claire bashfully cracked a smile.

"The attention," she said, shrugging her shoulders. "There's no surprise here, Governor. Like any Tom, Dick, or Harry who loves being in front of the camera, they're struck on themselves and have been ever since the *Three Stooges* invented the television."

Avanti grinned at Claire's usage of words.

"Yet, there lies the dilemma," the governor said after a slight pause. "People need the media as much as the media needs people. It's all about click bait, *sound bites*, shock-value, likes, and follows. It's one giant circle-jerk, Claire, and everbody's getting off all at once."

Greg the Bodyguard, who was sitting in the front passenger seat, pressed his finger against the earpiece in his ear.

"Ma'am," he said to Avanti, "they're now ready for you."

"Thank you, Greg," Avanti said modestly.

Cue Vye with her fanny pack of cosmetics already out. She zipped open the small pouch, which included a couple of sponges, brushes, puff pads, creams, and powders. She dug through all the cosmetics, sorted through what she needed and what she didn't, for instance, a travel size bottle of sunscreen, as well as foundation, a brownish-beige base to help even out Avanti's skin tone and make her leucoderma—or, best known as "vitiligo," a rare skin disease where the loss of pigmentation created these white-pinkish blotches on the skin—less obvious to the public. Lastly, Vye grabbed two UV cushion compacts, a variety of sunscreen, including sunscreen in powder-form, then, finally, a can of *SunOff* setting mist. Avanti wasn't particularly a "fan" of the sunscreen mist for two reasons: one, the mist provided very little coverage and the only way to get the most bang for your buck was to spray the mist directly into your hand and then reapply the sunscreen onto your skin; and two, if disregarding reason one, reapplying the mist directly to your face, especially those with vitiligo who had extremely sensitive skin, was no different than dowsing your face with Mace, since the inactive ingredient in *SunOff*—and that went for most sunscreen mists—was alcohol and if you weren't careful where you sprayed, even with your eyes closed, then welcome to Burn City.

Since Avanti was already wearing a good base of both sunscreen, which included *Maxfont Coverall* sun protection factor—or "SPF," for short—46 pa+++, as well as foundation, Vye went straight to *Jon Raphael*'s instant mineral broad-spectrum SPF 45 sunscreen, which contained twenty-one percent titanium dioxide and twenty percent zinc oxide powder, which, in essence, was a less expensive yet more effective imitation of the product *SunOff*, and it was also talc-free. Its formula was rich in antioxidants, as well as vitamin A, C, and E; and although it contained silicone, it applied exceptionally well and controlled whatever oiliness was left over from Avanti's base—no cast. Last but not least, Jon Raphael's sunscreen wouldn't show up on darker skin like other sunscreens. The brush was ideal for "on-the-go" reapplication and since Avanti, who normally wore sunglasses while being exposed to the sun, occasionally rubbed off the sunscreen whenever removing the shades from her face, the fine tune-up with Jon Raphael's self-dispensing brush added not only an extra reassurance to get her through the day, but was also gentler on her sensitive skin.

As Vye was just about to make a couple of last-second touch-ups to the governor's face, mainly reapplying more sunscreen to her cheeks, as well as her forehead, she caught the driver—she didn't know his name nor did she care to know his name—staring at her through the rear view mirror.

Vye stared back at the driver until he finally moved his eyes elsewhere.

Once the sunscreen was reapplied to Avanti's skin, she handed her a compact mirror. Strangely enough, Vye ignored the governor's approval and kept her eyes on the driver ahead, as if her poised glare was preventing the driver from moving his eyes in places where they didn't belong.

"I don't know how you do it," Claire said. "I admire your strength."

"I don't look at it as a skin disease, Claire," she said, pulling away the mirror. "I look at it as a gift."

"I never really thought of it that way, I guess—"

"—How do I look?" asked Avanti, as she closed the mirror.

"Beautiful, as always," Claire said.

Avanti glanced over at Vye, flicked her eyebrows, and said, "Showtime."

As Avanti placed the Aviator shades on her face, Claire made one last-second suggestion before she stepped outside.

"And remember to take them off when you look the employees in the eyes," she said. "We need every vote we can get."

Avanti smiled a closed, funeral-like smile.

She didn't say a word to Claire. Didn't need to. Yet, she made a gesture that left her new aide in a thoughtful state of regret.

As assumed, reporters swarmed Governor Washington as soon as she stepped outside the black town car. She immediately recognized one particular face and that face belonged to July August—or better yet, her face belonged to the most watched local network in the greater Atlanta area, WEGT. And yes, the reporter's name shared the same first and last name as two months on the lunar calendar.

With her question locked and loaded, July thrust the microphone inches away from Avanti's face. A plump cameraman, who had a beard that would make Paul Bunyan proud, was standing with a clear shot of Avanti—or what the news industry (and other entertainment industries, for that matter) called the "money shot." Thankfully for Avanti, Greg was there to redirect the microphone from her grill. From behind the mass of flesh, July yelled out exactly what Avanti had expected to hear from Atlanta's "hottest" news reporter on her latest gaffe: "Ms. Washington, do you care to explain what you meant when you said—and I'm quoting—" July read from her notepad, "—'We should send all of them (illegal immigrants) back to Transylvania'?"

Considering only twelve hours had elapsed since her "hot mike" incident, she anticipated that her untimely joke to Congressman Weaver would eventually surface but never so suddenly. From any politician's standpoint, especially one who happened to be on the other and essentially, wrong side of the press, it was fair—in fact, it was beyond satisfactory—to compare "news reporters," even the modern day (wannabe) "journalist" for that matter, to a particular kind of bird that fed mainly on carrion and had a known reputation for gathering with other birds of its species in the expectation of inevitable death.

"When there was one of them circling around a carcass in the air, then surely there were others gathering to pick up the scraps."

Other reporters followed July's lead and joined in on the blistering verbal assaults with follow-up questions based on unfounded evidence.

One reporter: *Is it true you have a bill banning the highborns from Georgia ready to sign on your desk?*

Avanti only caught the words *high born*, but she nearly laughed at the reference used to identify yet, at the same time, oblige an ancient race that survived off drinking the blood of its victims. For the most part, it was the "Millennial" vampires who were offended by the slang word *vamp*.

Another reporter: *Don't you fear your reelection may be at stake after signing a new abortion law that allows women to terminate a fetus past twenty-weeks of pregnancy? Correct me if I'm wrong, Governor, but, to me, is sounds like you just signed your own death certificate as governor of Georgia?*

Then, another: *In a speech last week at the Women Work conference, you claimed you're for the rights of all undocumented immigrants from the Old Country, but you continue to round them up like cattle and lock them in cages. How do you explain this hypocrisy?"*

The reporter's words were strategic.

"Cages" sounded better than "jail."

Made them sound like animals.

And, the governor was in the business of "bad policy."

Then, yet another reporter: *"Can you defend the words of some of the members in your party, in particular, Congressman Lumpkin, about considering some radical high borns as hate groups?"*

Then, another: *"What is your response to late-night comedian, Johnny Crumble, calling you a raccoon?"*

The brazen reporter's words, cold and mean-spirited, were not only strategic, but they were also intended to get a rise out of Governor Washington in order to make for "shock" entertainment. Even the word *raccoon* in itself was a poor attempt to get underneath the governor's skin.

Another reporter followed before the governor had a chance to put the privileged reporter in his place: *"So, Governor. Why did you file a lawsuit against one of the wealthiest men in America?"*

Another: *"Are you a racist?"*

Again, a strategic word, one painted with a broad brush, meant to provoke an audience, to bring about divisiveness.

Like "bigot" or "hypocrite" or "flip-flopper."

Of all the words a politician never wanted to hear uttered from anyone's mouth, it was the label "Flip-Flopper."

Then, another: *"Are you working with the big tech companies to implant each illegal alien with tracking devices?"*

Finally, the governor threw up her hand, removed the Aviators from her face, calmly placed the sunglasses in her breast pocket, and said sternly, "I'm not here to talk about myself. I'm here for the grand opening of the school. That's it."

A high-pitched reporter immediately chimed in: *"But Governor Washington, why do you continue to flip-flop on your stance with undocumented—"*

The governor turned to the reporter and looked her directly in the eyes.

"What did you not understand about what I just said?" asked Avanti, her tone as well as her aura dominating. She explained it carefully for the young reporter, as if she was some three-year-old who recently committed a boo-boo. "I told you that I'm not here to talk about myself, yet you persist on asking me questions regarding myself. Now, if you will, please get out of my way, I'm here to show my support to the good folks at New Way Academy." She called out to Greg, who, in return, made a hole for the governor and then Claire, who wasn't too far behind.

Most of the reporters fell silent. Other reporters looked almost deflated from the governor's unwillingness to provide answers to their questions.

Both camera crews and Greg, who was a few pounds overweight or what his doctor referred to as being "borderline obese," tried to keep pace with the two ladies as they power-walked to the front of the brand new state-of-the-art school, New Way Academy, where the ribbon cutting would take place.

From the corner of her mouth, the governor whispered in Claire's ear, "These people," Avanti said in side-thought, "*Actually, I wouldn't even go so far to call them people. Technically, they're dead.* They're given everything for free. Yet, I make one little joke behind closed doors— which, I will admit, was in poor taste, but that's neither here nor there—then some little rat records it behind my back—by the way, how the hell was that rat able to sneak his phone into the meeting?" For a moment, Avanti moved her cold eyes toward a blushing Greg, who appeared as if he was shrinking in size. "Now," she said, redirecting her attention forward, "all of a sudden, I'm made to look like the enemy here. It's like *people*," she emphasized, "that is, the ones still breathing, care more about the undead than their actual *living* human being."

"After the next month's debate, people will forget all about it," Claire said, as she tried to reassure the governor.

Governor Washington put on a smiley face as she approached The New Way Academy staff, including the principal, Marlin Rowe, as well as the private investors who generously donated to the state-funded school. With cameras flashing away, the governor shook the hand of each staff member of the school. Except for a couple of ballsy reporters, who were hanging out past the barricade and shouting out provocative questions during gaps of silence, the photo-op had gone smoothly so far. No gaffes or blips. The skilled governor had a particular way of not showing any kind of "face" when she was in front of the camera. Only "grips and grins," as she called her public appearances.

Lastly, Marlin greeted the governor with a handshake.

"Governor," Marlin said in his thick southern accent, "it's a honor. It's good to see you out and about for a change. For a second," he said, teasing Avanti, "I thought you only did dinners and speeches."

"And I see you haven't lost your sense of humor."

"Thanks for coming, Governor."

"Please, Marlin," she said, smiling. "Avanti."

"How's Ajax?" asked Marlin. "Brent told me that he didn't like these sort of things."

"So sorry he couldn't make it," Avanti responded. "He was feeling under the weather."

"I heard there was a nasty bug going 'round." Marlin leaned in extra close to Avanti and whispered in her ear, "*Wouldn't surprise me if it came from a vamp.*"

Avanti didn't respond to the insensitive remark. Yet, she faced forward and continued to smile for the cameras.

"Anyway," Marlin said, his voice rising. "Sorry to hear about Ajax." Then, he turned toward the front of a crowd where his son was standing with his mother. "Come on over, Brent. Say hi to the governor of Georgia."

Brent bashfully walked over and shook the governor's hand.

"Hello, Brent," Avanti said, remaining professional despite the awkwardness of the conversation. "I swear, you look bigger every time I see you."

"Hey, Ms. Washington."

"Brent's a late bloomer," Marlin said, clapping Brent's shoulder.

"Where's Ajax?"

"Unfortunately, Ajax couldn't make it," Avanti said. "I was telling your father here that he's at home under the weather."

"What's wrong with him?" asked Brent.

Avanti was taken aback by the question. Still wearing a smile on her face, she turned to the cameramen surrounding her and then faced Brent.

"Stomach bug," she said over a pause. "You know, the kind where it comes out of both ends."

Depressed from the recent news, Brent held his head downward.

After acknowledging the sudden change in the young boy's manner, Avanti leaned in close to Brent and told him to stop by the house and pay her son a visit. "He'd really enjoy your company," she said.

"*But*," Brent returned, "if he sick, I don't wanna be picking up anything."

The governor waved off Brent's concern.

"You'll be fine."

Before he could return with more questions, Marlin shooed him away back to his mother.

"Don't you just love 'em to death at that age?" Marlin said foolishly behind his son's back. "*Question* every single thing you do. I'll give Brent another year or so before he hates my guts."

Trying not to draw too much unwanted attention, Avanti said bluntly, "I think I've already reached that stage with Ajax." With other staff members waiting for the opening ceremony to begin, Marlin escorted Avanti to the pair of giant scissors on the table next to the red ribbon. She eyed the golden scissors and said to Marlin,

"He's gotten to the point where he won't even talk to me anymore."

"They just need space at that age," he said. "Hell, I was the same exact way. Didn't even talk to my daddy until he was an old man."

"Is that so?"

"By then, he was already on his death bed."

"Sorry to hear, Marlin."

"Sons are born to hate their fathers," Marlin said and showed Avanti the pair of scissors, "*not* their mothers." Avanti took a brief moment to absorb the comment. "Give him time, Avanti," Marlin said over a thoughtful pause. "He'll talk whenever he's ready."

"And how will I know when he's ready?" asked Avanti.

"You'll know," Marlin said and held up the pair of scissors for Avanti.

Other members of the press, as well as other staff members gathered around Marlin and Avanti, as if they were two actors on stage.

As he was about to hand the scissors to Avanti, his face went long and slack. Everything about his manner turned solemn. "Listen, Avanti," Marlin said seriously to not only Avanti but also to the sudden crowd that had formed around the two, "I know you have your hands full—Lord! I can't even imagine doing what you're—but I just wanted to tell you that Stew would be proud of you, for everything you're doing and what you've done to our community and all the progress we've made. He'd especially be proud of you for raising Ajax by yourself while trying to govern the great state of Georgia. You are truly one *helluva* woman, Ms. Avanti Washington."

Smitten by the words, the governor replied to both Marlin while, at the same time, making her response clear to the crowd, "Why thank you so much, Principal Rowe. *Marlin.* That means a lot to me. It was Stew who actually inspired me to enter politics; in fact, before Stew lost his battle with brain cancer, I told him that I was going to give politics a shot. At first," she said in a punchy way, "he didn't believe me; in fact, Stew thought

I was the one with the inoperable tumor. Then, over time, as his condition worsened, he started to come around and accept what I was destined to do; in fact, he often joked about me running for mayor of Atlanta. Encouraged me but, at the same time, threw in a couple of jokes every chance he could. There was one in particular. He once said to me, 'What does a baby's diaper and a politician both have in common?"

Marlin was stumped by the question.

"They're changed regularly," Avanti said, leaning in closer to Marlin. "And, for the same reasons," she added.

Marlin laughed, so did the people gathered around; however, it was a forced laugh, as if it was coming from somewhere else inside them.

"There was truth in Stew's joke," Avanti said, more strongly, "and after Stew passed away, I took a vow to prove him wrong. Even today, he continues to inspire me." She tried to laugh away the glumness by bringing in more lightheartedness to the "broadcasted" conversation. "*But*, I'll tell you this, if it wasn't for Savannah helping me out around the house, I believe this job would've taken me straight to the grave."

Another one of those laughs slipped from Marlin, as if he was now laughing on-demand.

Others in the crowd laughed as well.

It didn't matter what the governor had said from this point forward.

She already had them exactly where she wanted; however, the only problem: she was running out of room on her fingers.

Five Years Later.

"WELCOME to the Big Leagues."

The scene was set.

Present day.

St. Gabriel Hotel.

Manhattan, New York.

The characters were all in their designated places like pieces on a chessboard, except for one: Governor Avanti Washington.

Avanti ignored the tweet from across the room and drifted off while rehearsing her lines for the upcoming speech.

Her eyes glazed over as she stared at the softening glow of the phone's screen and the words on it, which started to blur and brighten.

Eventually, the screen faded into sleep-mode, causing the screen to go black.

So, too, did Avanti's spirits.

The sudden change in mood caused Vye to remove the brown puff pad from her face.

Over her trance, she heard the same voice sounding even more farther away: "Avanti?"

Like a ball player imagined winning the big game and whether it be by shooting a wild buzzer beater to win a basketball game or hitting a walk-off grand slam in the bottom ninth of a baseball game or figuratively—or literally, depending on the mentality of the ball player— knocking an opponent's head off in an important football game, or imagining whatever "moment" in whatever sport that often required the least amount of skill, yet demanded a hundred percent determination to hoist that one word up on his or her pedestal, the two-term governor of Georgia imagined herself giving a *winning* speech. Flashes of grit and grace appeared before her. Her speech was deeply profound, historical. The governor spoke a clear "vision" for her future of America and did so with authentic sincerity and compassion: two traits which screamed "Politician!" Or "Not to be trusted!" "A two-face who says what you want to hear!" Or, best, *"Politicians Suck!"* Which was one the governor heard most often. Yet, when she delivered the big speech to the audience, Avanti Oluwaseyi Washington came off as one who walked with them but was not one of them. A true leader, not a follower. She left the audience in a state of hypnosis, convincing doubters and silencing haters. She was a mere vessel for the projected path forward; yet, at the same time, she embodied toughness, decisiveness, and most importantly, *practicality*.

Her mouthy campaign manager, Sonny Mims, who had worked for President Townsend during his campaign against Senator Coats eight years ago and with all baggage aside, including his deep affection for Jack Daniels and his outbursts and short tempers, was considered what those in her close circle called the "people's whisperer," snapped his fingers in front of her face and once more, called out her name.

Startled from airy assault, Avanti pulled herself from her trance-like state.

"Yes," Avanti snapped back.

"Where'd you go?" asked Sonny.

Ignoring Sonny's question, Avanti waked the phone by tapping on the screen.

Patiently, she scrolled through the lines on her NOTES app.

"The part where it says," she read the line from her phone, "'After four years of this administration,'" she turned to the other diverse writers who were scrambling to locate the right page, "on page seven, 'it is clear not only to the people of this great country, but also to the entire world that we do *not* need a businessman running our government.' And," she read, "'when I say *our* government, I mean the *people's* government!'" She pulled away the phone. "It's unnecessary, don't you think? I think we should take it out."

The script readers and writers, who had copies of the speech in their hands, flipped to the "diss" section and followed along with Avanti.

"People want to see you take the gloves off, Avanti—"

"—Haven't heard that one before, Sonny," Avanti said under her breath.

Sonny didn't care much for Avanti's disobedience; in fact, he was two ticks away from lashing out at her.

"And," she said suddenly as she scrolled through her phone once more, "on page—where was it—on page nine, the part about Rhodes' track record on deporting illegal vamps. You really think it's wise to bring up illegal immigration, considering my own record in Georgia? You know exactly what Rhodes' people are going to start calling me—the big 'FF.' I mean, do we really want to start rolling in the mud with these people? We're better than this, aren't we?"

Sonny crossed his arms over his chest in defense.

Avanti's partner, Colin Galloway, a highly respected architect born and raised in Harlem but spent most of his adult life studying in Paris, France, was fourteen years older than Avanti; however, his fluffy, snowy white beard that would've made Santa Clause envious made him look much older than his age and often times, whenever accompanying Avanti at nightly fundraisers or high-stakes dinners, he'd receive compliments and sober nods of respect on his storyteller-like beard. He was wearing a black tuxedo that paired nicely with Avanti's sage green lace maxi dress, which was personally designed by a famous French clothing designer named Claudian Bisset. Along a high, halter neckline was an eyelash lace with a sleeveless, darted bodice, and an open back, which complimented Avanti's toned shoulders. Below the fitted waist, weightless georgette cascaded into a riotous maxi skirt.

In most cases, Colin wouldn't dare stick his nose in Avanti's business or even touch it with a ten foot pole; however, while he patiently waited with his earthy brown eyes targeted on the back of Sonny—the look itself was like an unspoken declaration of disapproval for Avanti's campaign manager and his abrasiveness—he couldn't keep his mouth shut any longer.

"*Go with your gut*, honey," Colin said from the corner of the room.

Avanti absorbed Colin's remark, as if she was filing it away under "Note-to-Self."

In return, Sonny gave Colin a look that shouted "Back off!"

"People want to see you take the gloves off, Avanti," Sonny said again, as if he was finishing a thought. "Even if that means poking *Swamp Thing* every now and then," Sonny threw his hands up in the air, "so be it!" Occasionally using his hands to do most of the speaking for him, Sonny paced around Avanti, as if, by doing so, he was displaying dominance—or simply trying to get inside Avanti's headspace. "Think of this as a warm-up. The American people haven't seen this 'side' of you yet. The *fighter*," he emphasized, "who, I know, can throw one helluva nasty left hook. And trust me, when I tell you this, 'People are *dying* to see that side.' They want that side. Otherwise, Rhodes is gonna do what he does best and he has a bottomless appetite. So, believe me when I tell you that Rhodes will eat you alive during the first debate—"

"—Don't get ahead of yourself, Sonny. We haven't even gotten the nominee yet."

"Croom is a goddamn *gaffe machine*," Sonny argued. "Jett is shrinking in the polls by the hour. Turns out Roundtree is a man-whore. And Bullock, she can't save herself from hot water even if someone threw her a life preserver. You have this nomination in the bag. Which means, if you don't strike first, then Rhodes is going to spit you out like he does with everybody who gets in his way." Sonny paused and faced Avanti. "I can't stress this enough, Avanti. America cannot—I will say it again CAN-NOT—afford to have four more years of this clown. Trust me. All I want you to do tonight is STICK-TO-THE-SCRIPT. Can you do that?"

"Sonny, I haven't slung any mud thus far," she returned. "So why start now? I think you're wrong about people—"

"—Of all the elections I've witnessed, not one candidate has ever run a clean campaign. Not ever."

"And that's exactly why this campaign is so special, Sonny," Avanti said, her voice more stern. "I need you on board with this. . . "

Avanti allowed Sonny a chance to respond.

During the break in the conversation, Vye found the right opportunity to apply a light coat of foundation to Avanti's skin.

"Go easy this time," Avanti said to Vye from the corner of her mouth. "The last time, you made me look like a cancer patient."

"Yes, ma'am," Vye said, dabbing foundation on the sides of Avanti's chin.

With a look of disgust, Sonny looked at Avanti and uttered as if he was talking to himself, "*I need a smoke.*"

He pulled out a cigarette from the pack of Mensticks in his pocket, stuck it in his mouth, and as he was about to light up, Avanti wagged her index finger back and forth in the air like a pendulum.

"No smoking," she said softly.

Sonny's shoulder raised upward in a frozen shrug.

"Serious?" he said with a cigarette dangling from his lips.

"It's a non-smoking room, Sonny."

"So?"

Avanti didn't say a word in return.

All she had to do was give Sonny that "look."

More disgusted in Avanti, Sonny shook his head and stormed from the hotel room. Even slammed the door on his way out.

Claire stepped forward from the back of the room and asked Avanti, "Why'd you even hire that asshole?"

"For your information," Avanti said while Vye continued to apply makeup to her face, "that asshole gets people elected."

"It's not like he's carrying a magic wand or anything. He runs his campaigns on shock and awe. He wants you to be someone you're not."

"And who am I, Claire? Since you know everything about me?"

"A woman who doesn't need to roll around in the mud with all the other pigs, that's who?"

"I can get dirty when I need to—"

"—But like you said, you don't have to."

"You're right," Avanti said and shot her eyes toward Claire, "I don't."

*

SURROUNDED by her entourage, Avanti made her way from the hotel room.

On the way out, she spotted the bathtub in the corner of her eye. She stopped at the edge of the bathroom and found herself staring at the bathtub—and remembering. Four years had past since his death and every single time she found herself looking at a bathtub—any bathtub whether it be the one in the upstairs hallway or one inside a hotel room—she *always* remembered.

Before she could get lost in the red memory, Claire touched her on the shoulder and asked, "You okay?"

Avanti struggled to smile.

"I want your honesty, Claire," Avanti started with a pensive expression worn heavily on her face. "Am I doing the right thing? I mean do the American people really care what I have to say?"

"Of course, they do," Claire said, more tenderly. "You wouldn't have made it this far based on your looks."

Avanti thought more about Claire's comment.

"Believe it or not," she said, as if, all of a sudden, the temperature in the hotel room dropped twenty degrees, "I'm a little nervous."

"There's no reason to be nervous, Avanti," Claire said. "We got this!"

"There's a lot of money at stake, Claire."

"It's just a bunch of old rich people," Claire said, "donors who are ready and willing to sign you the check. Like Sonny said, just stick to the script."

"Right," Avanti said, losing courage.

More thoughtful, Claire said to Avanti, "I've only given like two speeches in front of a large group of people: once in college and then another time at my sister's wedding. Terrified both times. Even at my sister's wedding, despite the liquid courage. Utterly *terrified*—I'm talking to the point where I wanted to just run away people and never look back. I know it sounds silly and all," she said, grinning. "But the only thing that got me through both those speeches was something my dad taught me."

"What's that, Claire?" said Avanti.

"Speak like I'm speaking to myself."

"Really?"

"I know," she said. "Silly. Juvenile, really. But it worked. I mean, who else knows you better than yourself than your *own* self. What I meant to say is, speak like you're speaking in front of a mirror."

"What would I do without you, Claire?" asked Avanti.

AFTER Avanti's entourage exited from room 421, three secret service agents gave Avanti and the rest of her team a go ahead to proceed down the hallway. Her two personal bodyguards, Joel and Kobo, who were roughly the size of refrigerators, led the way while her aide, Claire, and her makeup artist, Vye, walked alongside Avanti, whereas Colin followed close behind.

As the team proceeded toward the elevators, Avanti couldn't help but notice the squishiness of the triangular-patterned carpet. The soft feel of the strange carpet pressed against the ball of her foot, as well as that familiar spongy-sound it made while she walked indicated the dampness of the carpet below. Keeping pace with the team, she glanced downward at the carpet. She grabbed a handful of her maxi skirt and below her sage green stiletto the wet carpet bubbled slightly during each step. Since the mass of flesh, Joel and Kobo, were partially blocking the view of the hallway before her, she decided to glance behind her. There, in the opening of several bodies, she witnessed what looked like the wet imprints of a child's feet dotting the entire carpet.

Curious, Avanti paused in her tracks, causing the rest of the team to pause as well. She squeezed through Joel and Kobo, nudged them aside, and inspected the carpet more thoroughly this time. She found more of those dark outlines of soaking wet feet marks trailing toward the elevators.

"Is there something wrong, Ms. Washington?" asked Joel.

Avanti was more focused on the footprints than the question itself.

"*Avanti?*"

As Avanti turned to Claire, she saw what she thought was a young girl sprinting around the corner at the end of the narrow hallway. The EXIT sign merrily flickered, which made Avanti question whether or not it was really the change in light or some girl who had snuck onto the floor.

"I thought you said the hall was clear," Avanti said to one of the agents.

"Did you see something, ma'am?"

"I thought. . ." she stuttered and turned around to Joel, ". . . it's nothing. It's just my mind playing tricks on me, I guess—"

"—It's nerves, Avanti," Claire whispered in Avanti's ear. "Remember what I told you and you'll be fine. And also, please remember to breath."

Avanti nodded off the comment, did as Claire said and took in a deep breath while straightening her shoulders. Her posture was taller, prouder. She looked as if she was "ready."

Once her team reached the elevators, Avanti and four other members of her team stepped inside the elevators.

Before entering, Avanti asked about Sonny's whereabouts, if he was still off on his "smoke break." However, neither Claire nor the bodyguards had seen him.

Joel hit the number "1" button on the panel.

As the elevator doors began to close, Avanti was drawn to the vacant space in the hallway outside. She continued to stare until her thoughts started to fill in the spaces. The bright colors faded from the memory of her. Before she could visualize that gray, bloated, expressionless face staring back at her through the closing doors, she turned away and embraced yet another deep breath.

"Re-lax, A-van-ti," Claire whispered, more slowly this time as if she was hitting each syllable.

They rode the elevator to the first floor where the ballroom was located. During their descent, Claire pulled out her smartphone and read from an earlier text, "Rhodes is going to unveil his new slogan for 2020 tomorrow night in Michigan. 'Richard Rhodes: Building a *safer* road forward.'"

"He's clearly making it clear for voters," Avanti replied, as she still felt a little off about the upcoming speech. "If there's one thing I do admire about Rhodes, it's his consistency. The man sticks to his message all right."

She took another deep breath and with the back of her hand, patted the top of her forehead, which was glistening with sweat.

Claire tried to lighten up the visual tension inside the elevator by informing Avanti that she had a "quick"—she couldn't emphasize the word *quick* enough— photo-op with a seven-year old girl named Becca Petri. "Friends call her Becky. Becca here," she read from the notes underneath her itinerary, "claims to be one of your biggest fans."

"One of those, huh?"

"Avanti, she's only seven years old."

"What? I can be great with kids."

"Well," Claire said motherly, "just try to be nice. I had to pull a lot of strings to bring her to this private event, considering Adamache basically bought out the entire hotel for the night. Plus, she drove all the way from Locklier, Georgia."

"You know I don't like surprises, Claire," Avanti said, both her face, as well as her tone sharpening. Then, asked: "Was she invited to the dinner?"

"Fifty-thousand dollars a plate?" Claire returned with a hint of sarcasm in her voice. "She'd have to win the lottery to be able to afford to eat here."

"That's not what I asked."

"No," Claire said. "Like I said, it's just a photo-op. Shouldn't take that long. Just be your charming self for the cameras—" Claire paused in mid-sentence, her eyes drifting in a glowing thought. "Why? Do you want me to add the girl as one of your guests? I can do it. It's not too late. I can call Paul from the Financial Committee. Plus, it could leave a good impression on donors."

From the back of the elevator, Vye said coldly, "To me, it sounds like an unnecessary distraction."

Avanti acknowledged Vye's timely yet rare input.

"No," she said over second thoughts. "Just the photo-op," Avanti said, facing Claire. "Besides, I'm not here to win over voters."

"Right," Claire responded and dismissed Avanti's remark. "Apparently, this is Becca's first time in New York. So, be 'extra' nice."

Claire made sure to emphasize the word *extra*.

"You don't think I'm nice?"

"You are. . ." Claire said hesitantly, ". . . when you want to be."

The elevator stopped.

Avanti handed Claire her Bisset rhinestone-covered hand purse.

"Guard it with your life," she said, not referring to the actual hand purse itself but the contents inside the hand purse.

Claire gave Avanti her word, as the elevator doors opened.

As soon as Avanti's team exited the elevator, a horde mostly consisting of the members of the press were ready to pounce on Avanti. Both the bodyguards and secret service agents cleared a tight path for Avanti, who answered only a couple of questions about her "change" in the on-going illegal vamp problem and stated, for the record, that she had, in fact, taken a position to give "all" vamps a pathway to citizenship. After all, she needed each and every vote she could find from the vamp community. Initially, her plan was to answer questions after her speech; however, every now and then, the campaign trail offered its own subtle surprises. After Avanti answered in rapid-fire pace, she walked straight over to Becca's camp: a strategically "diverse" group of supposed neighbors, classmates, as well as distant relatives of Becca, all decked out in purple "Washington 2020" getup, including shirts and hats; one of them in particular was waving around a small purple banner with the campaign slogan that read: "*Look out, Washington! Here comes a new Washington!*"

In the middle of the group, Avanti spotted a little girl, who like the others was decked out in a purple "Washington 2020" baseball cap, a wristband with the initials "WWAWD," and an oversized purple shirt that looked as if it was three sizes too big, reading: "*Where my broom at?*" Since the girl was standing ahead of the group, Avanti assumed that she was Becca Petri. That, and she wasn't quite right. Avanti wasn't so sure about the girl's condition until Claire leaned in and pointed out the spotty-faced girl among the other groupies. Apparently, Becca, as well as her aunt, Nay-Nay, who was now Becca's legal guardian, and her relatives, who, not until Becca's story made the six o'clock news, were all but strangers to Becca, had brought members from their local news along with them.

A reporter and a cameraman were standing anxiously next to the group, as if they were primed to wrap a heart-warming story. However, when Avanti and her team approached Becca, Avanti first realized her story wasn't "heart-warming." And, not only that, from the way Becca was standing in a slouched position, she looked extremely ill.

Before the greeting, Claire informed Avanti about Becca and her recent loss.

"Her mother?"

"Joanne Petri was her name," Claire said closely over the chaos and commotion all around them. "Single-parent—"

"—Why does that name ring a bell?" asked Avanti.

"Before Ms. Petri's life spiraled out of control, she was working two jobs and struggling to put food on the table for young Becca. After they were evicted from their apartment, Ms. Petri got hooked up with a rough crowd. The Gist Brothers. She owed them a lot of money. After Ms. Petri was fired from one job, she and Becca wound up on the streets. Ms. Petri then got involved in drugs. Sent Becca away to stay with her aunt. Eventually, she became homeless."

"She was murdered by a thoroughbred," Avanti said clearly, filling in the rest of Becca's story, "same one who I had deported during my first term. I vaguely remember the story. I do remember, however, that it was all over the news."

"You got it," Claire said and then informed Avanti, "After Joanne Petri was murdered, ICE ended up capturing a vampire named Marian Boboc, *a real bloodsucker he was. . .*"

Once more, Avanti found herself drifting from Claire's words. *She was back in the governor's office, screaming over the phone at the health and human resources secretary for more money for the state while, at the same time, giving her piece of mind about how she really felt about the state legislatures. Claire was in the room as well, heard the cheap jabs and low blows being thrown by Avanti, as she pressed the phone's speaker against the side of her shoulder. After the phone call, the two were going back and forth, arguing about whether or not raising the minimum wage would be beneficial to the state.*

"We raise the minimum wage," Avanti argued, "then employers are going to hire less people. Which means more people are going to be out of work. I've said it from the very get-go. We need to push for more schooling. More schooling and practical hands-on training for higher paid jobs. Who the hell wants to make a living off flipping burgers for crying out loud? And I'll tell you this: I don't give a shit what these protestors—who, by the way, have nothing else better to do with their lives— have to say."

"How can you say that, Avanti?" Claire returned. *"You're a mother and one day, Robert may want to work at one of those jobs in order to pay for college."*

"Ajax can't even lift a finger around the house," Avanti said flippantly.

"Which brings up yet another issue: college," Claire said, pacing around the office. *"How can kids afford college on a minimum wage—"*

"I'm not raising the minimum wage, Claire."

More voices in the commotion clarified.

One particular voice became clearer: Claire's.

"*. . . Somehow,*" Claire said over a sigh, "Mr. Boboc re-entered the states once more and killed another woman who was six-months pregnant. The woman happened to be the wife of an ICE agent. A couple of days after her death, a pile of ash was discovered in a back alleyway. Coroners were able to lift an implant from the remains. It belonged to a one, Mr. Boboc. Investigators never found the person or persons who killed Mr. Boboc."

"If I hadn't taken action sooner," Avanti said, feeling the radiant sting of regret, "then Ms. Petri never would've been murdered."

"Mr. Boboc was quite an evasive criminal, Avanti."

"No," Avanti said, thinking more about her four years as mayor and how she, somehow, won enough votes from the city council to not only relocate a homeless shelter in order to build a new hockey arena, but also gentrify South End. "That's not what I'm talking about," Avanti said, her voice trailing off.

"Then, what are you talking about?" asked Claire.

Avanti finally arrived at Team Becca. In the corner of her eye, she noticed a tiny red dot on the bottom of the camera. After months of being on the campaign trail, no matter where she traveled, she realized the camera was *always* on. Even Becca's relatives had their phones out, fishing for a "like."

Despite Becca's skin condition—"psoriasis," was what the doctors called it— Avanti greeted her with a handshake. The last thing Avanti wanted to do, especially in the middle of a "live" recording, was show the town of Locklier that she was afraid of a red patch, which, by the way, was *not* contagious. After all, during what most would call a pivotal time of the race where it was every candidate for him or herself, every single vote counted, even if it meant reaching out to the seven-year-old who technically couldn't vote for another eleven years or so; however, most of the people standing around Becca were over eighteen, which meant checkmarks for the governor. The sides of Becca's face and neck were also covered with old scars and patches of skin grafts, which had been taken from her legs after Becca developed a serious—near fatal—staph infection that went untreated during that financially uncertain time when she was shelter-hoping and spending a good part of two years of living on the streets with her junkie mother. Her hand was red and scaly; however, Avanti made sure to keep a gentle yet natural grip on it while, at the same time, keep a wide smile on her face for the camera.

"It's nice to finally meet you, Becca," Avanti said ecstatically. "I've heard so much about you."

Star-struck by Avanti's presence, she bashfully rocked back and forth on her heels. She had no words for the two-term governor, only great expectations.

"She's shy," her aunt, Nay Nay, said defensively.

"I was shy when I was your age too, Becca," Avanti said, trying not to look at Becca's scars. "In fact, my parents could hardly squeeze a word from me."

Becca removed her hat, revealing more red blemishes and bare spots around parts of her scalp and forehead. She handed the ball cap to Avanti.

"Can you sign her hat?" asked Nay Nay.

"Why certainly," Avanti said and grabbed the Sharpie from Claire's hand, "It would be my privilege to sign your hat."

As Avanti made out the hat to "her friend, Becca Petri" and signed her John Hancock on the underside of the bill, Becca murmured: "Thank you, Ms. Washington, for all you're doing to help the high-borns. I believe they all have a right to be here just as much as I do."

"I'm so glad you brought that up, Becca," Avanti said to Becca when, in actuality, she was addressing the people who were at home watching her on TV. "I believe, just as you believe, Becca, that high-borns—and *all* walks of life, for that matter—have the God-given right to enter this country whether seeking asylum or education, a job, or even start a new life right here in America."

"*Why the change, Ms. Washington?*" one reporter asked from the back of the crowd. "*Your current position does not reflect your policies in the past.*"

"You're right," Avanti said to Becca, then stood and faced the crowd. "You can call me a flip-flopper, hypocrite, or even your typical politician who tells you exactly what you want to hear. I am all of those things. *But* the truth of the matter is that I have changed. I have 'evolved.' It's only in our nature to *evolve*."

Avanti made sure to emphasize the word evolve for the cameras.

They were known to use strategic words, sound bites taken out of context, as well as catchy headlines. Why not use a play straight out of their own playbook?

"So, I say, 'So what?'" Avanti said. "Over time, people do evolve, especially when faced with tragedy." She looked down at Becca and softly pinched the edge of her chin. "Like young Becca here, a sweet and innocent girl whose mother was sadly taken away from her two years—"

"*Three*," Claire mumbled in Avanti's ear, as if she was a ventriloquist.

"—Three years ago," she corrected, "by an individual named Marian Boboc, a high-born who committed a terrible crime. Now Becca could've blamed Marian and everybody who looked like Marian for what happened to her mother. But she didn't. And till this day, she still doesn't."

Other members of the press gathered around the two-term governor as if she was giving an impromptu speech.

They were holding out microphones and tape recorders. Some of them were jotting down notes on their notepads.

"An 'individual' killed Becca's mother," Avanti said. "Let's remember that, people. An *individual*. Not a group. As long as we are living here in this country, there is only one group—one—and that's American."

Becca's relatives were bobbing their heads to Avanti's every word. Nay Nay applauded Avanti, resulting in other relatives to applaud. By the time Avanti was finished with the photo-op, she had already won over the crowd.

AVANTI hung out with Becca for a couple of minutes longer, mainly taking selfies with her and signing her signature to other belongings and memorabilia and most importantly, embracing Becca and Nay Nay's appreciation for taking the time out of her robust schedule to meet with young Becca.

Once Avanti said her goodbyes to Becca, as well as her friends and family, she was about to join Colin in a large hallway where she had no more than a minute to catch her breath from the chaos in the lobby before Claire pulled her aside for a moment to question her latest comments, which were more than likely going to be discussed and analyzed all over Shane Lowman's *News Zone*.

"What was that back there?" asked Claire. "Flip-flopper? Hypocrite?"

"The crowd seemed to like it," Avanti said, ignoring Claire's tamed overreaction. "Besides, I feel a lot of better. Less nervous. Your little pep talk worked."

"Just remember the earnings at stake here. Six mill—"

"—I know what's at stake," Avanti interrupted before Claire could even utter the big M word.

Claire glanced at her phone and raised her eyebrows from the latest update on Avanti's online fundraiser.

"We have some good news," she said, flattered. "Looks like your latest tweet helped bring in more money."

"Where's it at now?"

"Just shy of eleven *million*," Claire said.

"Looks like the grassroots donations are working better than you thought."

"But it won't be enough to buy our ticket into Iowa—"

"Enough, Claire," Avanti said. "Go find Sonny or something."

As Claire was about to remind her of the whole "sticking to the script" plan, Avanti met up with Colin and together, the two moved their way toward the ballroom where she was going to give her speech to New York's wealthiest—and elite, including investors, hedge fund types, business magnates, yuppies, Wall Street aficionados, even A-listers, celebrities, TV personalities, as well as athletes, and basically those who had pockets so deep that they could fit a country inside them and, of course, those who had Avanti's ear.

Claire sneaked in a comment by making sure to congratulate her for the bump in the donations but didn't waste any time warning Avanti of the host of the fundraiser who was standing directly at her twelve o'clock.

"Alexandru Adamache," Avanti said, eyeing the older gentlemen in the black tuxedo among a crowd of socialites. Standing next to Alexandru were two other men who looked equally as wealthy, if not wealthier. All three of them looked as if they received monthly "touch-ups" to their faces. Not a single one of them had a single wrinkle on their thirty-year-old skin-tight faces, despite being the age of a man where his wrinkles were considered a symbolic yet honest representation of the many hard roads traveled throughout his life. They were a natural yet inevitable progression; and nothing about the whole vibe seemed natural to Avanti.

Maintaining a presidential composure, Avanti discreetly turned her shoulder and searched for Sonny.

"Did you find Sonny?" Avanti asked Claire.

"I thought I saw him wandering around the bar area," Colin pointed out.

"Frankly," Claire said, "I don't think Alexandru Adamache wants to see his dark horse receiving tips from a man who storms out for smoke breaks."

"Just find him," Avanti said quietly, yet, from the darkness in her eyes, came off loud and forbidding.

Claire tracked down Sonny, who was chatting—but more like flirting—with a cocktail waitress who looked twice as young as him next to the bar. And from the way he was "touching" her material, it looked as if Sonny had other intentions for tonight and none of them involved being here.

"*There*," Claire said exuberantly, as if she just spotted Waldo. She nodded in the general direction of the vague shape that was Sonny Mims. He was wearing a shit-eating grin on his face, his mannerisms loose and questionable.

"Go fetch," Avanti hissed to Claire. "And, remind him why I hired him."

Claire said, "I'll try, but you know how he—"

"—Don't try," Avanti snapped. "Do."

"Yes, ma'am," Claire said and parted ways with Avanti, who, in return, became more composed, as she modeled for Colin.

"How do I look?" asked Avanti.

"Ready," Colin said. "You look ready." He glanced over at the sharks waiting to have Avanti's ear. "You want me to join you?"

Avanti thought over Colin's question. Again, Colin was considerate like that. The last thing Colin wanted to do was get in the way of Avanti's hustle—in other words, he wasn't trying to "distract" her from the prize at hand.

"Can you?" asked Avanti, her face cringing as if it was a burden to ask.

"Absolutely," Colin said, grabbing Avanti's hand. "That's why I'm here."

As they made their way toward Alexandru Adamache and company, Avanti was caught off guard by the mayor of New York City.

Surprised, she turned toward the familiar face.

"Mayor Armitage," Avanti said with an open look of surprise on her face.

Nursing a glass of ice in one hand, the mayor of New York City reached out to shake Avanti's hand with his other free hand.

With a grin on his narrow face, he said, "If it isn't the woman who's going to save this country from the Clown in Command."

"Nice to see you, Mayor Armitage," Avanti said, shaking the mayor's hand.

"Please," he replied. "Call me Marcellus."

"I don't think you've met my partner, Colin—"

"—Colin Galloway," Marcellus said before Colin even had a chance to finish speaking his name. The mayor released his grip from Avanti's hand. Then shook Colin's "money-making" hand. "I've read *a lot* about you."

"Hopefully, only the good," Colin said teasingly in return, as he held firmly onto Marcellus hand before, finally, Marcellus let go.

"You designed the new opera house in Chicago. . ."

"That's right," Colin said. "*Maison de Merveille.*"

"You know, ever since I got back from fighting overseas in Iraq, I've developed a deep fascination with art and architecture—"

"—You were in the service?" asked Colin.

"US Marine Corps," Marcellus said.

"Thank you for your service," Colin said and once more, shook the mayor's hand.

"Thank you, Colin."

As Marcellus shook Colin's hand, Avanti noticed a couple of maggots crawling from underneath the cuff of his sleeve and along his wrist.

"Your father was a vet as well, wasn't he?"

Avanti heard the mayor's question, even though it sounded as if it was spoken so far way; however, she was too distracted by the maggots crawling from the mayor's sleeve.

"Avanti," the mayor said, leaning into Avanti's range of vision, "your father's a veteran?"

"Yes," Avanti said, pulling her eyes from Marcellus's wrist. "Vietnam. But he doesn't like to talk about it that much."

"Who does?" Marcellus returned, his voice uneasy.

A petite woman in a powder blue off-the-shoulder dress with a cape, which ran down to the floor, emerged from behind the mayor.

Marcellus introduced his wife, Macy. Then, as he was complimenting Colin and his work on the *Maison de*— "Merveille," Colin corrected—Marcellus shifted the subject to Colin's father, "Samuel 'Shoestring' Galloway was an outstanding baseball player—a legend if you ask me— who played in the Negro Leagues. One of the fastest ball players in the League," Marcellus praised. "Correct me if I'm wrong, Colin, but he could barely even afford to buy a pair of shoestrings."

"That's true," Colin said, bobbing his head. "He struggled like many in—"

Marcellus interrupted before Colin had a chance to clarify his response, "—Sammy Shoestring would always tighten his shoestrings whenever he was about to steal a base."

"Wow," Macy said artificially.

Then, Marcellus said to Macy, as if Colin was no longer a part of the conversation, "It was his way of rubbing it in the catcher's face, so the legend says."

Colin adjusted his red-rimmed glasses.

"He was a character all right," he said.

Before Macy had a chance to respond with a follow-up question about Colin and his father, she was sideswiped by one of her colleagues who worked with her at the firm; however, she didn't at all introduce the husband-and-husband couple to Avanti or Colin. Yet, she said, "Pleasure to meet you." Then parted ways with Avanti and Colin.

"Indulge me, Colin," Marcellus said, bringing Colin back into the spotlight. "How does the son of a legendary baseball player become, of all professions, an architect?

One would think a man, such as yourself, would follow in his father's footsteps."

Colin turned to Avanti, as if she, too, was waiting for an answer.

"Ever since I was a boy," Colin said over the hot silence, "I've always been fascinated with building things." The silence mounted, hard and heavy. "It's fair to say I was a fiend for Legos."

Laughs broke out among the three.

Once the laughs tapered off, Marcellus directed his attention to Avanti.

"And Avanti," he said, stepping in more closely to Avanti, "I truly admire the work you've done in the state of Georgia and also for taking the initiative, as well as providing your own creativity, to fix our broken illegal immigration system. If it wasn't for your resiliency and your imagination, I honestly don't know where we would be." Once more, he shook Avanti's hand. "I want to personally thank you for paving the way for New York." He reached in his pocket and pulled out his smartphone. "In the past two months, we've cracked down on over two-thousand vamps trying to reenter the state all thanks. . . " He clicked on the black *Untitled* app on the home screen of his smartphone, revealing a GPS grid of the entire city, ". . . to our new app here."

Here, a voice said inside Avanti's head. *"Here,"* the voice said again. *She found herself inside the infirmary. The hospital bed was shielded by curtains. Standing next to her was the Head Doctor of Welkins Correctional Facility.*

With a pair of tweezers, the surgeon picked up a tiny tracking device that was the size of a grain of rice from the tray. "And now," he said, as he loomed over the 'subject' who was lying on the hospital bed, "I'm going to plant the chip into the back of his left shoulder."

"Will he know?" asked Avanti, as she stood at the edge of the bed.

"From the way their skin heals faster than ours," the Head Doctor said, "the incision will be closed by the time he wakes up."

All Avanti could do—all she wanted to do, really—was simply agree with the mayor, even though a part of her was rebelling against everything he was telling her.

Then, the violence came at her in waves.

She was sitting in her office, waiting for a phone call while, at the same time, thinking about all the families that were about to be split apart.

As the phone rang, any notion escaped her head.

Everything about her, both inside and out, went cold and dark.

"A good pal Moonlight here led us directly to a colony at Rainwater Cemetery. Two of my men confirmed they counted at least forty-seven of them hiding inside a mausoleum. Maybe more. Shall we proceed as planned?"

"You have the green light," Avanti said. "And remember, leave no traces."

"Yes, ma'am."

As the gunfire flickered in her mind, Avanti pulled herself from the memory. Her eyes were attached to Mayor Armitage's phone. For a moment, she wanted to grab the phone from his hand and smash it on the floor with the heel of her stiletto.

"You can thank TechRight for that one," she said, putting on a smile in order to shield what she was truly feeling inside.

"Can I get you two something to drink?" asked Marcellus, as if it was his attempt to loosen up the mood.

"No," Avanti said, smiling off the kind gesture. "But thank you. I gave up drinking a long time ago."

Marcellus pointed at a bar across the lobby.

"They have non-alcoholic beverages."

"I'm fine for now. Thank you."

"And you, Colin?"

Colin turned to Avanti. She didn't give him any look of approval; however, it was clear to him that she was "ready" to talk to Alexandru and company.

"Absolutely," he said.

"Do you mind if I borrow Colin here?" Marcellus asked Avanti, even though he was going to steal her partner from her anyway. "I'd like to pick his brain for a minute."

"Please," Avanti said. "By all means."

She refocused her attention on the pale face that looked like a shark's fin protruding from the sea of bodies. The billionaire investor, Alexandru Adamache, acknowledged Avanti from the other end of the hallway. So did the two men who were standing to the right and left of Alexandru.

"Mr. Adamache," Avanti said, approaching Alexandru. As soon as she made her presence known, she held out her hand for Alexandru to shake. "So lovely to see you here tonight," she said.

"Why hello, Avanti," Alexandru said queerly, eyeing her sage green dress. "I must say you look stunning as always."

While Colin was away, Alexandru introduced Avanti to his two friends. The first man was Daniel Pugh, like Alexandru, a business magnate, investor, philanthropist, and humanitarian. He was the principal founder of the multi-billion dollar company, Endolink Corporation, which helped spark what was known today as the app revolution. The other, Gerard Fortune—fitting name— was an investor who often made headlines for his candor, as well as never shying away from any stench of controversy. He was a speaker and philanthropist, as well, and had written checks for millions of dollars to other candidates in the past, including her opponent in the upcoming election, Richard Rhodes. Fortune was the chairman and CEO of Heatherman Brocket Inc., a multinational conglomerate holding company which wholly owned dozens of brand names and restaurants. They pretty much owned half the products consumers not only had inside their households, but also the restaurants they ate at every Friday or Saturday night. Fortune had a net worth of eighty-four billion dollars—billion with a b—and according to *Hughes* magazine, was considered the second wealthiest man in the world.

Avanti expected the two men to be glowing. However, besides the work they had done to their faces, up close, the two men looked like any other two old, rich, *white* men. It didn't matter how much a man was worth or how much money he carried in his wallet. Money couldn't rid the liver spots.

Daniel Pugh wasn't much of a talker. He firmly shook Avanti's hand, smiled his toothy, pearly white smile, and wished her good luck in her speech tonight.

Fortune, however, was sizing up Avanti.

"So this is the rising star of Tomorrow's Politics," Fortune said and shook her hand as well. However, the texture of his hand was smooth, his skin papery. His grip was weak, lady-like. "I was completely blown away by how you pulled off that McCray Deal. That man never comes to the table for anybody, yet somehow you won him over despite all of the 'noise' surrounding offshore drilling and harmful effects it has on the environment. Tell me, Ms. Washington," Fortune said, leaning in closer. "What's your secret?"

"If I told you," Avanti said, staring into Fortune's eyes, "then I'd have to kill you."

Fortune was first to laugh, which, to Avanti, seemed like a cue for Alexandru and Daniel, who, surprisingly, offered the most authentic laughs.

"I like this one," Fortune said, laughing while, at the same time, holding up a tumbler of Scotch that had about as much shelf life as his third wife. He took a gulp of Scotch and then placed his free hand over Avanti's shoulder. "Plays close to the chest." He moved his liver-spotted hand from Avanti's shoulder and tactfully readjusted the eyelash lace along the top of the bodice as if the move was his way of primping his surrogate before she hit the stage. "I like to play close to the chest myself."

Remaining calm, as well as professional, Avanti didn't "react" from the indecent move. From the looks of the other two men, who were both acting as if "adjusting" a woman's clothing in order to suit a man's personal needs or desires, the move came off as more so a gesture than an invitation; however, Avanti looked at it much differently. It was a test.

In an unflappable manner, Avanti smirked at Fortune and said seductively, "It looks like we share something in common after all. See you inside, gentlemen."

Avanti excused herself, leaving the three men speechless.

Once she was out of eavesdropping range, Daniel turned to Fortune and said, "Didn't even bat an eyelash."

Fortune followed, "I like her."

Alexandru sipped from his Scotch and said as if he was closing the conversation, "I told you she was The One. And I've heard she's good at tying up loose ends."

Fortune nodded at Avanti's partner, Colin, who was having a drink with the mayor of New York City at a crowded bar.

"How about him?"

"Who? Uncle Tom." Alexandru smiled a devil's smile. "He's harmless."

"Can you imagine? A black man being the First Man?"

"He's got a good story," Alexandru took another sip from his Scotch, "what I like to call the 'American' story. But don't worry. She has him under control, if that's where you were going."

WHILE famous actor Tom Mooney, once Academy Award Actor from the 1970's film *Dust* turned notable animal activist, was speaking behind the podium and occasionally peppering the members of the audience with a routine of topical jokes and horror stories about the film industry, a scrawny waiter with a buzz cut placed an appetizer of wild caught Georgia shrimp, which were said to be caught off the coast of Avanti's home state of Georgia, in front of her, as well as the other elite guests at the table. Alexandru Adamache and a handful of wealthy business magnates as well as their wives—and husbands—happened to be sitting at the same table as Avanti and Colin. However, her main focus wasn't on any of the guests, who were, more than likely, watching her every move. It was solely on the young waiter with red hair and that long pink scar he was wearing along the underside of his wrist. The scar was barely visible underneath the white cuff of his sleeve; however, it caught Avanti's eye, if only for a split second, and she never let it go.

Following Avanti's eye, the waiter made a gesture with his brow, as if he was aware that she was aware of the scar; and somehow, he was left in a state of disbelief by the sincerity of her gaze.

For a moment, only a moment, she witnessed her son and the raw innocence in his freckled face.

Trying not to stare, Avanti looked away. She couldn't help herself. She took yet another glance at the waiter and saw exactly that, a waiter, *not* her Ajax.

The waiter went away.

Despite the nice presentation of shrimp, Avanti had absolutely no appetite; in fact, the sight of the wild shrimp stacked in a cute pyramid made her queasy.

With the other guests watching and waiting for Avanti to eat, Avanti had no other choice than to force herself to eat.

As she carefully ripped off the tail of the shrimp, a stream of black oil suddenly oozed from the insides.

Startled, Avanti recoiled in her chair. She looked up at the other guests surrounding the table. Then, she looked at their plates and the shrimp on them. Apparently, it was only her shrimp that were leaking oil. At first, Avanti thought it must've been some kind of sick joke, a prank by one of the staff members, maybe a cook from Georgia who didn't agree with her policies as Governor. She leaned in closer and smelled the black oil. She nearly gagged from the potent stench.

"*Is something wrong?*" Colin asked closely.

Avanti directed her attention toward Colin.

"Avanti?" another voice said from the other side of the table.

Avanti followed the voice to Alexandru.

"No," she said strangely. "Will you excuse me for a moment?"

Unsure whether or not abruptly excusing oneself from the table was a sign of weakness, Avanti decided to stand anyway. She regretted the very move as soon as she caught the attention of the other guests at the table.

"I need to have a word with the chef," she said sternly.

Somewhat intimidated by Avanti, Alexandru said quietly, "Very well."

When she left the ballroom, she never went to the kitchen to have a "word" with the chef. Instead, she hooked a right and headed straight to the restrooms at the end of the hallway. One of the bodyguards, Joel, caught up with Avanti and made sure she made it to the restroom okay. Before she was about to enter, Joel insisted on clearing the restroom for her but Avanti reassured Joel that she was fine to enter and that he wait outside in the hallway while she "freshened up."

Joel took his post outside the restroom while Avanti stepped inside the restroom. She went straight to the closest stall she could find, closed the door behind her, and pulled out a small vial filled with a crimson red powder. She poured out a smidgen of powder onto the underside of her pinkie fingernail and snorted it up one nostril, then poured out more powder onto her same fingernail and snorted it up in the other nostril. The leftover powder she rubbed onto her thumb, then between her thumb and index finger, and then ran her red powdery fingers along the top of her gums.

More composed, Avanti found herself not drifting but more so slipping into a daydream, as if, one second, she was in a bathroom stall doing bumps of a mysterious red powder and then, the next, she *was in the back of a town car, riding to a workshop called Teachers Teach for the new website TeachersTeach.Org, which was created in order to get more teachers into the classrooms through higher pay and new ways of teaching young students. No more than twenty-four hours earlier, there had been a shooting in a town outside Nashville, Tennessee, which resulted in the death of twenty-one victims. The shooter tragically ended up taking his own life. Which would've made the grand total of causalities to twenty-two victims; however, the media only reported twenty-one victims.*

"Say what you want, Claire," Avanti argued, "mental health has absolutely nothing to do with the shooting in Sislick. We have to draw a line between being emotional and being crazy. The man was angry. Plain and simple."

"Angry, Avanti," Claire replied, her voice more hostile, "is me screaming or throwing a punch, not killing twenty-one 'innocent' people."

"The man had no history of mental illness," Avanti said, trying to lay out her argument, as if she was presenting a case in front of a jury. "No priors. He was a sixty-three year old man who snapped. And don't tell me about being innocent. In today's world, nobody is innocent. Guns kill people. People kill people. Believe me, I want to be the one to get rid of all the guns on the streets. But a fact of reality: that will not happen. It will never *happen, Claire." Her tone sharpened. "You know why? People are good by nature—or at least, they want to be good. But they're also violent. And how do they combat their violence?"*

Claire didn't answer.

Avanti didn't expect her to.

"With violence," she said. Then, she shook her head in disgust. "I want to believe that we can live in a society without guns. But it's already engrained in us, Claire. From the movies we watch to the books we read to the music we listen to, it's here. And it's not going away. Not anytime soon. So, what's the solution? Do we get rid of the guns? It's a good start. But where does that leave us? If we take away the guns, then, if people want to do harm to other people, then they'll find other ways. Don't underestimate people. They can get creative when they want to. Will it be cars or trucks? Will they resort to something else, like bombs or knives? Are we going to start banning knives, too? How else are these fat cats going to cut their filet

mignons? *Let's take away the forks while we're at it and resort to eating with our hands, like the primitive creatures we are.*" She paused for a moment, but left little-to-no room for Claire to retort. "*It starts with the way we treat each other. We are killing each other everyday, if it's the way we talk to one another or don't talk to one another, or the way we deal with our adversaries. The way I look at guns: they're just the cherry on the top. The Big Hush. Do we need them in a civil society? No. We don't. But the only way we're going to get where we need to be starts with taking a good look at ourselves in the mirror and asking ourselves, 'Where does the anger come from and how do we get rid of it without harming those who deserve every right to be here just as the next man?' When we can find answers to those questions, then it'll be the first step to progress.*"

Avanti shook herself from the memory—or flashback or whatever you want to call it—and found herself back in the stall, looking over the red smears of powder along her pinkie, thumb, and index finger.

A single drop of blood splashed onto her hand, leaving behind a perfect circle. Before she realized where the blood was coming from, another drop of blood fell onto her open palm. She ran both her index and middle fingers along the bottom of her nostrils and pulled her hand away. Her fingers were covered in blood.

ONCE Avanti stopped the nosebleed, she exited the restroom where Joel was waiting like a saint next to a water fountain. She caught a small figure darting across the corner of her eye. She turned toward the figure and witnessed the tail end of a girl—possibly the same one as before—rounding the end of the hallway. She instructed Joel to wait at his post. He didn't listen, at first. After all, he had a job to do; however, Avanti told him twice to "stay" put.

She walked toward the end of the hallway, which intersected with yet another long hallway. She heard a strange racket coming from the janitor's closet, which was only a few paces away. The closet door suddenly swung open as she reached for the door handle. Standing before her were Sonny and that same cocktail waitress, both giggling and cackling.

With his face frozen in a gaping stare, Sonny's laugh cut to silence as soon as he laid his eyes on Avanti and her body blocking the doorway.

"Uh. . . " Sonny stuttered, ". . . Avanti? What you doing here?"

"I was gonna ask you the same question, Sonny," Avanti snapped.

"I was showing, uh. . . " Sonny pointed at the waitress and couldn't even remember her name.

"*Novice*," she said for him.

"Right," he corrected. "I was escorting Novice here to the restrooms."

Avanti glanced at a bright red drop of blood on the crease of Sonny's collar. Trying not to draw too much attention toward herself, she turned her eyes upward, back into Sonny's innocent eyes; and in that moment, as soon as Sonny caught a glimpse of Avanti's eyes on his neck, his entire manner changed from imperfect to imperious, as if Avanti was the one, *not* Sonny, who should've been inside the ballroom brownnosing and kissing up to business magnates and filthy-rich investors, *not* wandering around hotel hallways scouting out trouble.

"Why are you not preparing for your speech?" asked Sonny, his tone bolder. "Aren't you about to go on?"

Avanti didn't respond to Sonny's question. She thought long and hard about it. Yet, she glanced him over one last time.

"I hope to see you inside," Avanti said suspiciously, walked off, and met up with Joel, the bodyguard, who hadn't budged an inch from his post.

DEBATING about whether or not to deliver the speech that she was intended to deliver to an audience of potential donors, Avanti eyed over the words on the paper one last time. The words were not hers; in fact, they were far from hers. Yet, except for a couple of lines, they, more or less, belonged to a speechwriter named Bradley Spears, a Harvard grad with a major in political science, who worked as a staffer under Rhodes for two years before his father landed him a job on Avanti's team. Intentionally or not, Bradley borrowed these words from prior speeches, reworded and shuffled the words around and added more emphasis to fashionably tasteful words, which were considered "new," as if, by doing so, he was only rearranging the colors on a palette, instead of changing the final tone of the painting.

With the eyes bearing down on her from all angles, including the beady-eyed audience before her, as well as the wide, nervous gawks of members of her team who were eagerly waiting near the side of the stage, Avanti readjusted her sweaty palms over the podium and peered out into the audience. She could feel the dim spotlight on her face growing hotter and hotter, like a dark cloud gradually drifting from that tiny ball of fire which hung in the sky.

Avanti cleared her throat before speaking *her* words.

"As most of you may already know," she said into the microphone, "I am *not* the right candidate to run this country." From the side of the stage, Claire, as well as other members of Avanti's team, including Sonny, were looking at one another as if they were hearing the same words that they hearing. From their startled reactions, it was clear that the line was *not* in the speech that had been prepared days ahead of the ball. "It's true," Avanti said. "All you have to do is look at my past. *I am not perfect*. But who is anymore? Really?" Avanti looked around the audience, who was equally baffled as Avanti's team. "Who are we to judge people for the mistakes they've made in the past when we live in a society that is constantly changing? If you haven't made mistakes in your life, then I'd say you haven't lived." She shook her head in disgust from the very thought of the mistakes she had made in her life. "No," she said shortly. "We, as a nation, must come to terms that we are *all* a work in progress. *We are not perfect.* I'm aware my past will come up on the trail. Voters are going to want answers to the mistakes that I have made in my past. I'm here tonight to set the record straight once and for all and answer all of those questions, firstly, to dismiss whatever doubts that you may have about electing me for the highest job in office. Like I said, I'm not the right candidate to run this country. But I'm going to prove to you that—of all the candidates who are running against me, including the one who has continually failed to carry out the job that he was elected to do—I am the *only* one who can run this country, even though I am not the right one."

Avanti glanced over at Claire, who was mouthing to Sonny, *What is she doing?* She ignored Claire, as well as Sonny, who looked as if he had an "I told you so"-type of expression on his face, and focused on the words, her words.

"Why?" Avanti asked, not only herself, but also the audience.

Hanging onto Avanti's every word, the audience waited in silence.

"Let's rewind to the beginning," Avanti said. "For those of you who haven't read my book, *Still Intact*—" she said, more casually, as she threw out a blurb from the corner of her mouth for her recent book, "—which is now available at all your major book retailers for twenty-three ninety-nine."

The comment was her attempt at "breaking the ice." The comment was successful by the sound of laughter sprinkled throughout the audience.

"I was born and raised in a small rural town outside Atlanta, Georgia, called Saxmapaw. Growing up, I watched my father come home every night, his hands blistered and bleeding from working long days on the farm, yet, despite how tired or frustrated he was, he still carried not only a sense of great pride for the job he went to everyday, but also a great deal of gratitude for being able to raise a family, regardless of the stress his body had to endure working on the land. We grew up broke, *not* poor. And, there is a difference. One afternoon," she said in reflection, "when me and a couple of friends of mine wanted to go see the movie, *Back to the Future*, which had recently come out in the local movie theatre not too far away from where we lived, I asked my father for some money. I remember looking forward to the movie before its release; but, more so, I couldn't wait to feast my eyes on a young and handsome Michael J. Fox. Whom my friends and I had a crush on. Who could blame us? Who doesn't like Michael J. Fox?"

The comment drew a couple of suppressed laughs from the audience.

"Back then, the movies only cost a couple of dollars," Avanti said. "When he asked me how much I needed for the movie, he could only spare no more than a quarter. I was upset, not only at my father, but also my friends, for their dads had more money than mine. I told him how much I 'hated' being poor and how many friends I had lost over the years for being poor. Like any other father who cared deeply about his son or daughter, my father stopped what he was doing and sat me down at the kitchen table and told me, 'Poor was only a state of mind in which very few people ever recovered from.' He had given me examples of people who were less fortunate than we were, particularly a homeless man, whom my father and I saw almost everyday hanging out on the corner of Fifth and Parker Avenue begging for money to buy himself a bottle of liquor. He emphasized that being broke was considered only a 'financial setback,' a temporary inconvenience, which was fixable, given time. It was what my father said to me that one night in the kitchen that had me thinking more about the homeless man who was always standing on the corner of Fifth and Parker Avenue. One day after school was over, I decided to talk to him. His name was Cameron Limier, but everybody who knew him well called him 'Lemon.' I got to know Lemon, *his story.* Three times a week I paid Lemon a visit. I'd bring him sandwiches, and every now and then, I'd sneak him candy that I pocketed earlier that day. I wouldn't give him money—not a cent— because, even Lemon said so himself, it was money that was enabling his drinking, and worst, keeping him on the streets. So, we just talked. Turns out: all Lemon wanted to do was talk. But was Lemon poor? Yes. He was poor. He was damaged. His family had left him. His children wanted nothing to do with him. Lemon had dug himself a hole that he couldn't get out of. He was stuck in a place, like my father said, where very few ever recovered. One day after school, I went to visit Lemon. It was the week before Thanksgiving and I wanted to invite Lemon to dinner with us. When I made it to Parker Avenue, Lemon wasn't hanging there. Immediately, I knew something had happened. Three days later, I found out what happened to Lemon. A landscaper found him sitting on a bench at a park not too far from Parker Avenue. He was slumped over, dead. Turns out he had been dead for at least 'two days'—that was what the police officer told me. All I could imagine was, for two days, people walked past Lemon as if he didn't even exist. I later found out that he basically drank himself to death because, in a way, that was exactly what society wanted him to do. Society wanted to not deal with him, to ignore him, and, in the end, shut him up by giving him money, "enabling him," as Lemon once told me, instead of getting him the help that he rightfully deserved. But was Cameron Limier to blame for winding up on the streets? Yes—*and* no. The problem wasn't an 'I' problem or a 'you' problem. The problem was an 'us' problem. A 'we' problem. Over thirty years have passed since Lemon's death and 'we' still have the same problems, only 'we' word them differently, soften them up to sound less intimidating. I realized that, in order to fix the problems like Cameron Limier faced—or any person struggling to get by—it started with the way we treated others, by not shunning them but embracing them, despite whatever issues they may be going through,

When my father wasn't toiling away on the farm during those sultry days of Georgia summers, he spent nights working at various jobs in and around Atlanta. It's fair to say my father's drive to provide for us didn't come without its share of sacrifices. It was hard enough for a mother to raise a family of four boys and two girls in the South. It was harder and more difficult for a father, who remained all but a ghost throughout a young girl's childhood,

I lost my only sister, Alicia, to pneumonia at the age of thirteen and witnessed my parents growing farther apart,

Twenty years ago my late husband Stewart and I brought two angels into this world. The first angel we named 'Echo,' and I, like many of the mothers who try to start a family of their own, was grateful to call Echo my daughter. Sadly, Echo was taken away from us at an early age. She was four years old when she died in a drowning accident. I understand why there were so many questions surrounding Echo's death; and if you don't know the story and you haven't read the book, then listen carefully because I'm here tonight to go *beyond* the page,

Before Echo's death, Stewart and I were going through a rough patch as most partners go through. I was thirty-two years old and still, at that age, parenting was 'trial and error.' You can read every book on parenthood, but once you're all the way in it and you are officially a parent, the only real book that can teach you about raising children are the very children you're raising,

I specifically remember the day I laid eyes on Stewart. I had this friend, Lou Myra, who had a friend who knew this guy who was coming up with some weird invention that would allow people to communicate with their pets. I know—odd. But I went with *my gut* and decided to meet with 'this guy' anyway. Despite all the awkward conversations and mixed feelings, the moment I met Stew I knew he was the one. Both of our universes aligned. We were opposites—he was a talker and I was rather shy when it came to the dating scene—yet, after we met, I realized we shared common goals. He was incredibly smart, handsome, compassionate, and most importantly, considerate. He was a gentle spirit, an unselfish man, Stew was, one who'd always put others before himself. But over time, our perfect union started to show its cracks, its blemishes, its imperfections. I can stand here before you and blame Stewart for his infidelity, but such judgment wouldn't at all be fair to neither him nor myself. The fact of the matter: I drove Stew away. My excuse was that Stew was more focused on his work than he was on me. Eventually *that fire*, which brought our universes together, fizzled out; and consequently, when Stewart needed a shoulder to lean on, I was *not* there."

Avanti hung her head in a pause, took a moment to collect her emotions, and pushed on.

Off stage, Claire's eyes widened with bold exclamation marks while mouthing the words *WHAT IS SHE DO-ING?* to Sonny.

In return, Sonny shrugged his shoulders in exaggeration, then folded his arms across his chest, then shifted his weight to one side of his body, as if he was about to watch the world come crumbling down—and he smiled.

"So," Avanti said, more confidently, "he decided to find affection elsewhere and he did so with a troubled young woman who had her own share of demons. I can remember the day as if it was yesterday. Labor Day weekend. The year was 2003. I was spending an ideal afternoon by the swimming pool with my mother and my two babies, my two angels, Echo and Ajax, who were both four years old at the time, when all of a sudden a troubled young woman named Storm McBride broke into our house and attacked me from behind with a bird's beak knife. I tried desperately to defend myself while Ms. McBride relentlessly swung the blade at me by the poolside. She managed to cut me multiple times, mainly around both my arms, as well as my neck. I didn't realize it at first—I figured it was all the adrenaline rushing through my veins—but during her relentless assault, the blade slipped past my arms and caught me several times in my upper and lower abdomen, penetrating my spleen, as well as perforating my right lung. Meanwhile, my mother Farah was in the water with my four-year-old daughter Echo. Bloody and confused, I struggled to stand to my feet; however, Ms. McBride stomped down on my right knee, causing it to bend in a direction that it normally wasn't meant to bend. During this bloody haze, I witnessed Ms. McBride walking over to Ajax, who was reading one of his comic books only a few feet away from me. The first thing—and only thing—that ran through my mind was, *She is going to harm my son, my angel.* Despite my injuries, my broken leg, the stab wounds, I hobbled to my son and tried to shield him from this deranged woman. I didn't even make it halfway. My injuries overcame me. I couldn't put any pressure on my right leg. Crawling inch-by-inch closer and closer to Ajax, I soon realized that Ms. McBride wasn't going for Ajax. She was going for an umbrella base. She picked up the umbrella base, which had to weigh at least fifty pounds; and she walked back over to me. She raised the umbrella stand over her head and was about to 'finish' me off. As she was moments away from striking down, I witnessed both her vacant eyes turn toward the swimming pool to the right of her. I followed her eyes to the swimming pool and noticed something was wrong with my mother. What I didn't realize at the time was that she was having a heart attack and my four-year-old daughter, Echo, unable to swim on her own, was slipping from my mother's grip. The floaters on her arms loosened and eventually came off while Echo was thrashing her arms through the water. Desperate to save my mother and daughter, I begged and I pleaded with Ms. McBride to think about what she was about to do and let me help them. It was at that moment when I looked into Ms. McBride's eyes that I saw the regret inside them. She dropped the umbrella base and ran off; however, my mother and daughter had already gone under. I tried to stand, but I couldn't. I knew that the only way I could reach them was by crawling to them and hopefully rescuing them in time. Such existence, as time, was running out. As the blood started to pool under my body, I soon realized *my* time was running out. Fighting through my injuries, I used every last bit of strength left in my body to save my mother, Farah, and her granddaughter, *my angel*, Echo. It was already too late. I jumped into the pool; the blood pouring from my body caused the water to cloud with red. By the time I pulled Echo from the bottom of the pool, she wasn't moving. Her body was lifeless. Like a doll. The water had already filled her tiny lungs. By then, I was left with a choice: either resuscitate Echo and hopefully, pump the water from her lungs, or swim back under to pull my mother from the pool and try to revive them both. I chose the latter. And till this day, I wonder, if I hadn't gone back under to rescue my mother, even though a part of me knew she was already gone, would Echo still be alive. Would I have rescued my angel in time? And if so, what kind of life would she have lived? *What* kind of person would she have become? Tragically, I lived to see none of the answers to those questions come to fruition. As for my son, my Ajax, he was left in a traumatized state. And I don't believe he ever recovered from what happened on that day,

Days after the police discovered Ms. McBride's body with a fatal stab wound to her neck inside her apartment, a letter was brought to my attention while I was recovering in the hospital. Apparently, Ms. McBride and Stewart had developed an intense relationship over the past few months, and it was—without doubt—out of jealously, that Ms. McBride deemed it necessary to get 'rid' of me, in essence, remove me from the picture. In no way, shape, or form, was Stewart involved in Ms. McBride's actions; however, for months on end, I questioned myself: *How could I ever forgive Stewart for what he had brought into my mother's life, our children's lives, our lives?* No question there was much blame to go around on all sides. Storm McBride was a human first and foremost, and a woman second; and she, like many women out there suffering from depression, faced 'real issues.' I can stand here and point my finger at Storm McBride for what she had done to my family—after all, it was Storm McBride who 1.) Assaulted me and 2.) Left me to die. But I knew just as much as the next person that pointing your finger at someone wasn't going to get anyone anywhere. So, I decided to place the blame onto my shoulders. Me, *I* was the one who abandoned Stew when he needed me the most. *I* was the one who drove Stew away. *I* was the one who forced his hand. *I* was the one who shut him out. I was the culprit.

Was it selfish of me?

Yes. I believe it was."

Avanti couldn't help but turn her attention toward the two people sitting at a bar in the back of the ballroom. One of them was a salt and pepper haired man in his early fifties; however, he had a tall muscular physique and could've passed as a man in his early thirties. The other, a promiscuous dirty blonde-haired woman who was sporting a red sheath dress with silver bracelets that occasionally flickered whenever the woman turned a shoulder in such a coy manner or, on the contrary, leaned in forward to graze the man's hand or, in a form of dominant femininity, straightened her posture and puffed out her chest to exhibit the exquisite shape of her "modified" breasts below drunken angles of canned lights suspended above the ballroom.

After mildly laughing at a side-bar comment from the lone soldier, who was mentally riffling through the best and most strategic lines that would earn him the golden ticket on Underwear Island, the flirtatious woman rested her reddened elbow against the sweaty bar, her mountainous cleavage exposed to the elements as if it was a landscape painting, and with her white glove gripped in her hand like a handkerchief, flagged down the bartender, who was already waiting for her next command before she could even finish the word *bar*—tender. It was there, in the elements, when the stumpy bartender pivoted toward the woman's direction, that Avanti saw the large 10-gallon glass jar beverage dispenser with a spigot next to a pyramid stack of liquor bottles. Inside were fruit about the size of bananas. She cleared her throat and as she was about to continue her speech for to the audience, she couldn't help but look yet again at the jar and *what* floated inside the murky liquid: over a dozen of dead fetuses, swelled and brined like pickles.

Once given the drink order, the bartender grabbed an unwashed tumbler and poured the woman's drink from the fetus dispenser, causing the murky liquid to bubble slightly, then stir each fetus, moving and bumping into one another, revealing much larger, more developed ones inside the jar. The drink was thick and yellow-brownish in color, syrupy. He grabbed a black straw and a cocktail napkin. Placed the straw in the tumbler. Placed the cocktail napkin on the bar before the woman. Then, finally, placed the drink onto the napkin.

The woman thanked the bartender for the drink, took a sip, and immediately displayed a gesture of approval.

Avanti fell into a trance. *She recalled a protest outside her office while signing the new bill into law. Not too far away, protesters were holding up signs like "Baby Killer" and "Murderer."*

Afterwards, once the chaos ended, she remembered her words: "These people care so much about the unborn than they do about the very same people who are struggling to stay alive. Where's the consistency?"

More *words* came to Avanti, chants, shouts, and rally cries, all surfacing like old words that seemed so familiar yet so distant to her. The same words that she had spoken at the "*Women's Choice*" Rally seven and a half years ago while she was running for governor of Georgia.

"*As your candidate for governor," Avanti preached from a makeshift stage to a rowdy crowd of women, "I will make it my duty to provide women with their own healthcare, regardless of their background or economic status. Every single woman in this country has a right, not a privilege, to choose what they want to do with their bodies. And as your new governor, I will make sure that women have access to the services they seek. Even if it means putting a Women's Choice facility on every street corner."*

The crowd lit up in applause, random roars and bellows erupting throughout, including screams of "Hands off our bodies!"

"This isn't just body justice!" Avanti shouted over the lively crowd. "This is our justice!"

The word *justice* resonated through the close-mouthed audience.

Avanti snapped from her trance and found hundreds of beady eyes staring at her, the eyes of donors willing and waiting for what she had to say next. Some of the eyes, however, especially in the front row, were neither round nor beady, yet, sharp and narrow, repulsed.

"*Selfishness,*" Avanti said thoughtfully over the long yet heavy pause, "I was consumed by own pleasure to keep Stew in the dark, hoping that my silence—my distance—would make Stew understand the pain he had put me through. After I lost Echo, close friends of mine would ask me why I didn't leave him. The fact is I was still in love with Stew, despite what had happened. As much as I wanted to punish him, I simply could not. If you've ever been fortunate enough to find *true* love, you already know that it is chain unbroken; however, it comes with a price and in order to keep the chain from breaking, it takes time and effort. That's why I felt somehow responsible, because I got lazy. I no longer put in the *time* and the *effort*; and by not doing so, that chain started to rust, the links deteriorating, loosening,

After Stewart and I worked through our issues, surprisingly, we became closer; in essence, we did what very few ever had the opportunity of doing: we rekindled the *flame* that had brought our worlds together. Then, when Stew was diagnosed with cancer after doctors found a tumor the size of a kiwi, we became even closer. I know a lot of people—friends, family—thought I only stayed with Stewart because he was ill. They were right—somewhat. A part of me thought about leaving, abandoning the warmth of that flame, my one and only true love. A part of me didn't want to deal with the sickness and all the mess that came with it. A part of me wanted to 'move on,' start a new life somewhere else, say my peace with Stew, and be 'done' with it. However, they were thoughts. And thoughts never defined us. It's our actions that define us and our innate ability to act when called upon. Stewart was calling me. And the more I started to think about what friends and family members were telling me, the more I realized how *wrong* they were. I understood why they might've looked at it like that, but me staying with Stew out of sympathy was simply *not* true. I stayed with Stewart because, not only did I love him, but I also saw a side of him that in all my years of knowing him I had never seen. Despite the grim news the doctors had given Stew and how he only had so many months to live, Stew remained resilient and determined to defeat cancer, as if it was his greatest adversary. In those final years, Stewart was a true warrior. Like all warriors, they eventually die. But their fighting spirit lasts forever, living inside each and every one it touches. We must keep that spirit alive in all of us!"

Avanti paused for a warm applause from the audience.

Seated at a table in the middle of the ballroom was her late husband, Stewart Pettaway himself—or so Avanti thought. Stewart had been dead for over a decade; yet, there he was, sitting among a group of investors who were decked out in their Tuesday's best. Among the investors was Jonah Greenberg, a former stockbroker turned celebrity "shark," who contributed most of the funding to Stewart's latest invention called *DogSpeak*^{TM}, a state-of-the-art eTablet that allowed man's best friend to communicate with its human companion through what was known as a "paw-sensitive" screen. The project ended up not being scraped but, more or less, put on hold after the diagnosis; however, a couple of months after buzz surfaced about Stewart's latest invention, other inventors came out of the woodwork, including hardware and software developers who strived to come up with devices and new flavorful apps that shared similarities to *DogSpeak*^{TM}; however, most of the knockoffs were met by one disaster after another: PR nightmares, glitches and virus-resistant bugs, recalls, financial roadblocks, termination.

Jonah and the other investors clapped politely, but *not* Stew. He was clapping hard and slow, elaborate, as if he rubbing it in Avanti's face. Except for the way Stewart was clapping, what stood out the most was his appearance. He was bald and his appearance was much worse than when he later died. On the side of his head was a jagged incision that was sealed close with staples. Stewart was nothing but a skeleton in a leotard of tired flesh, his face pale and haggard with each contour and outline of his skull visible to the eye; and buried deep within the dark eye sockets, two moonlit eyes were pinned on Avanti like thumbtacks.

She looked around the ballroom and saw others—at least a dozen or so, possibly more in the very back—clapping the same way Stewart was clapping. They, too, appeared as if they were plagued by a terminal illness, faces pale and bloodless. When they put their sticklike hands together in that same obnoxious mocking clap, she could hear the *clitter* of their tired bones.

After only a few seconds of listening to that bone-against-bone sound, Avanti attempted to block it out by focusing on the words, *her* words.

But they were still there, those clittering sounds.

As the clapping came in violent waves, Avanti picked out each gaunt, exaggerated clapper from the audience, starting with Storm McBride, whose arms appeared to be moving in slow motion, each one arching outward in synchronization before swinging back inward the same way a bird would flap its wings to display dominance. Storm was graciously wearing "name (fill-in-the-blank)," this custom sleeveless iridescent dress covered in crystal tassels with a silk scarf that matched the color of her dress wrapped tight around her neck to cover a mark or blemish. Avanti knew what exactly she was covering up; however, she was still left baffled from the sight of Storm, who, like Stewart, appeared lifeless. Dead. Yet, here. In the ballroom. Clapping to the equivalent of a stiff soldier's march. She was staring at Avanti with these dark marbled eyes.

The next two to come to her attention were Storm's older brother, Chance, as well as Storm's son, Nicolas—or "Nic"—who were seated at another table across the ballroom. They, too, were clapping. They, too, dead yet *here*.

Throughout the entire audience, Avanti saw many others, all pale and lifeless, their eyes so dark and unnatural; however, of all the causalities who had felt the sharp end of Avanti's "bad side," Chance McBride was the one who stood out the most.

As she had been doing occasionally throughout her speech, Avanti found herself somewhere else other than the ballroom. One second she was standing at the podium. The next, she was sitting at a table stacked with copies of her new memoir in the back of Barley's Bookstore located in the small, predominantly "blue" town of Dire, Pennsylvania.

She was handing a signed copy of her memoir called, Still Intact: The Heartbreaking Journey One Woman Of Color Took In Order To Win Back The Soul Of America, *to a young Reader when the next person in line stepped forward and left Avanti questioning where she had seen his face before.*

After a second study of the man's face, she knew who he was, not a Reader, for sure, but rather a man who had spent hours waiting in line at Barley's Bookstore for other reasons—and they weren't for Avanti Washington's signature. She glanced at her bodyguard, Joel, who, in return, dialed in on the strange man by turning up his already heightened state to a ten. He was two notches away from World War III. The only time he ever came close to twelve was one instance at a trendy roadside diner in Salem called Moe's, which happened to be the same "Moe's" from the cult TV show, Harper's Inn, *when Avanti was abruptly approached by a far-left vamp-sympathizer holding a can of sangria red paint and madly screaming out the governor's previous policy on vamps with a combination of capitalized questions and exclamation marks as she was about to cover Avanti's body in sangria red. With his game face switched on, Joel* sprung into action by grabbing the fanatic's wrist before she had time to dump the paint all over Avanti, slamming her to the ground as if she was a bag of top soil, and putting her in one helluva arm bar that'd make The Jam look like an amateur wrestler. Given the cue which either would've come in the form of a simple nod of the head or even the turning of her eyes, Avanti's right-hand man could've ripped the woman's arm clean off—literally! However, considering the sudden uptick in the latest Morron University Polls, Avanti didn't want a passionate yet "misguided" individual to shit all over her parade. Besides, the woman's amplified I'm-going-to-sue-your-ass type of sea lion screech was loud and piercing enough to publicly announce, "Surrender."

With that same game face switched on, Joel drew his hands down by his side and never took the strange man out of his sight.

As he pulled out his own hardback with a wrinkled dust jacket from behind his back, Joel inched closer to the table, as if, given the cue, he was ready to spring to action. Subtly, Avanti waved off Joel as if she was shooing away a fruit fly. In return, Joel backed away.

The moment the young boy surfaced from the crowd of Readers and potential voters and grabbed hold of his supposed "father's" hand, she realized who the man was based on the stark resemblance in the boy's face.

The sight of the boy's face justified her deepest suspicions. He had her eyes, as well as her nose. However, a part of her wanted to see Stew in his face. Perhaps the boy had his chin or even smile. She looked closer at the boy's face, but he just wasn't there. Her insides coiled up like a snake.

Storm's older brother leaned forward and placed the hardback on the table for Avanti to sign.

As Avanti slowly opened the front cover of the book, a message was written on the first page with a black Sharpie:

I know your secret.

"Make it out to Storm McBride," he whispered and flashed the burner from his jacket pocket.

As soon as Joel heard that name underneath all the background chatter, he made his move.

Before he could grab Chance by the arm, Avanti held out her hand, resulting in Joel coming to a skidding stop. She never signed the book. Yet, she carefully closed it, handed it back to Chance, and smiled. Trying not to draw too much attention to herself, she waved Joel closer, whispered something in his ear, and then after giving the message, Joel approached Chance and mimicked Avanti by whispering something in his ear.

Before Chance and the boy took off, he looked at Avanti with a heated expression on his face, as if the tears that he held in his eyes were boiling hot. She never forgot that look, even months later.

The memory stopped, so, too, did the clapping.

In the dead silence, Avanti looked around at the audience. Each guest waited in anticipation for Avanti to speak.

Before she could continue, she found herself back inside the memory.

As instructed, Chance waited in a narrow alleyway behind Barley's after the crowds died out. Two silhouettes the size of giants emerged from a cloud of dense smoke spewing from the breathing manholes. Chance stopped pacing around a dumpster and redirected his attention on the two silhouettes, which were shrinking into a more humanly form.

Avanti and Joel eventually made their presences known, leaving Chance in a state of uneasiness.

"I read your. . . your little book, Governor Washington," Chance started, his words choppy from the pounding in his chest. "I was particularly moved by the chapter where you talk about your daughter and the vivid details surrounding her death. You made it sound so authentic, except for one major hole in your story."

Avanti nodded at Joel.

Said his name, "Joel."

First, he pulled out a black wand that looked like a metal detector and waved it around Chance's front side first, then his backside, focusing most of the reading around Chance's chest and upper abdomen region.

"My friend here is checking you for a wire," Avanti said.

"What is this?" Chance furrowed his brow in confusion. "I'm not wearing a fucking wire!"

"It's only precaution."

Joel nodded at Chance's arms.

"Raise your arms."

"This is ridiculous," Chance murmured, as he raised his arms upward as if he was being crucified.

Once Joel was finished with his sweep, he patted down Chance's pockets and legs and searched for any weapons. Once complete, he turned to Avanti.

"He's clean," he said.

"The phone?" she asked Joel.

He shook his head.

"No."

"You really think I'd bring my only leverage to a deal?"

"How do I know you're not lying?"

"Right before Storm allegedly 'killed' herself," Chance said, "she left a message on my phone."

"And?"

"And she told me enough to know that you're a lying piece of shit."

Avanti nodded at Joel.

"Off you go," she said and ordered Joel to give them space—not too far from sight but well out of reach.

"You sure?"

Once more, she nodded her head.

Joel did as ordered and stood post halfway down the alleyway while Avanti approached Chance.

"Where is the little one?" asked Avanti, who was calm and collected.

"I took him back to the hotel," Chance said with a tremble in his voice.

"Is he alone?"

"I certainly wasn't going to bring him here," he replied, his voice louder and more strained.

Chance threw his head in a nod at the musclehead towering at the end of the alleyway.

Avanti glanced over her shoulder and then, more amused, faced Chance.

She said, "He's harmless—when he wants to be."

Shaking his head in repulsion, Chance let out a noise from his lips, a cross between a snort and a sigh.

"So," Avanti said, holding out her hands, "does he have a name?"

"Why the fuck you care?" Chance said hostilely.

"I'd just like to know the name of his son," she said, remaining cool. "I have a right to know. I was married to—"

"—No," Chance said, ignoring his previous statement, particularly the comment about Stewart's son. "You don't have the right."

"Okay," she said, surprised by his disobedience—and good acting. "So, why am I here? What do you want, Mr. McBride?"

"Two million dollars," he said bluntly.

"Money?" Avanti returned, her coolness wearing off. "You honestly think I didn't have my people following the money Stew secretly sent your sister every month for child support? Tell me, Chance. What exactly did your sister do with all my husband's money? Because I know she didn't spend a penny on that boy."

"Two million dollars," Chance said again, not missing a beat.

"What the hell do I look like to you, an ATM?"

Chance retorted, "Based on all the money you're making off your book deal, it'd be like pocket chance for you."

"Makes sense, now that I think about it, for someone with a rap sheet as long as a fat man's grocery list to lie to police in order to extort me for money." She paused for a moment and looked over the desperate "little" man standing in front of her. Avanti knew better than anyone else never to trust a man who had nothing to lose. "If it's money you want, Mr. McBride," she said finally, "then so be it. You'll get your money."

"I'll give you the time and the location," he said. "And next time, we meet in public. Somewhere busy. Around people. Not in some sketchy alley where one of your goons can turn me into a hand puppet."

"You really don't trust me, do you, Mr. McBride?"

"Of course, not," he said. *"You're a fucking murderer. Why should a trust a fucking murdering politician?"*

Avanti took a beat.

"Very well," she said, more calmly. *"But promise me that, once you get your money, you're going to disappear. I mean, not a word about what went on here. And if I ever hear from you after you get your money,"* she paused for a moment, her eyes darkened, *"you're going to wish you never came to me in the first place."*

"And what the fuck does that mean?"

"You're a criminal, Mr. McBride," Avanti said, as she raised her left brow in a sharp letter v. *"Use your imagination."*

Avanti cleared her throat and for a moment, held her head down in sorrow.

"We must keep the spirit alive," she said, trailing off under the microphone. "We must," she mumbled. Her eyes fell onto to the speech that Bradley had written for her. She noticed a strange discoloration on the paper underneath the front page. It could've passed as a shadow cast from her arm; however, given the circumstances of tonight's event, Avanti soon realized something wasn't quite right.

More intrigued by the dark stain on the paper, she lifted her gummy arm from the piece of paper. The front page of the speech stuck to the underside of her arm, as if she had a strange adhesive attached to her skin.

With no other choice, Avanti held down the paper with her other hand while she peeled away her arm. First, Avanti noticed the blotches of thick blood, which appeared as if they had been pressed onto her skin by a blood-soaked sponge. She followed the blood to the source: a three and a half-inch incision along her wrist. The cut was deep, too, deep enough to draw enough blood to cover one side of the US letter sized piece of paper.

As soon as Avanti laid eyes on the cut and all that blood on her arm, Avanti immediately shut her eyes, as if by doing so, she was shutting out the memory—the only memory she had left of him.

In the darkness behind the curtains, Claire was wearing a look of concern and confusion on her face. She glanced over at poor ole Sonny, who was neither confused nor concerned; in fact, Sonny was wearing a color on his mug that only suggested anger.

"This has gone on for too long," Claire whispered to Sonny, as if she was shooting darts at him with her mouth. "You have to do something—anything!"

"You're right," he said, unfolding his arms. "I'm going to put an end to this goddamn debacle once and for all."

Sonny was rocking back and forth, ready to storm out on stage to pull Avanti from the podium and make an excuse to the audience that Avanti didn't feel well or maybe she had a bad case of the flu—perhaps picked up the kind of food poisoning that made people talk funny.

Claire's eyes lit up. She grabbed Sonny by the arm. "Wait!"

Avanti embraced a deep sigh and opened her eyes. She ignored the sleeve of blood on her arm.

"Robert—" she started, her voice more clarified, "—Jack was what we originally called him before he rightfully earned the name, Ajax, because he was always getting himself into a heap of trouble when he was little. 'Hey, Jack!' Stew would shout out, as he rushed over to save our curious Robert, who was about to experiment on—or, better yet—test an electrical outlet with a metal fork. If there were two lessons Robert taught us at the very beginning of parenthood, it was to 1.) *Always* childproof a house and 2.) *Never* let him out of your sight. But he was our angel, our *special* angel. It was those mistakes, though, those frequent trips to the ER that made us all stronger. Eventually, 'Hey, Jack!' morphed into the name Ajax. Stew and I shouted out those two words, *hey* and *Jack*, so many times that they blended together. Eventually, the name grew on me,

And so did the young boy behind the name,

Ajax was born on the same day as Echo. Stew and I weren't even expecting twins; however, from the very moment he was born, Stew and I knew he was special, a *gift* that few parents are given. And like most young boys, Ajax was curious about the world and the variety of creatures that lived among it. He was considered what you'd call 'introvert,' and often times, shy. I don't think most of the people who knew Ajax, whether it be from school or camp, saw the side I saw in him: funny, extremely witty, no filter—which, every now and then, got him in trouble—the one in the family who'd always find a way to loosen up the mood. Most people in his class who only saw that quiet, reserved side of Ajax often looked at Ajax's shyness as a weakness, whereas, I looked at it as, not a strength but an invaluable characteristic that very few his age were able to acquire. He was mature beyond his age, an 'old soul' was what my eldest brother called him, who was not only a keen observer constantly absorbing life around him, but also a scrupulous listener—which for a parent, who'd occasionally speak out of frustration in wake of a son's bad behavior or say things that she truly didn't mean, it could've been looked at as a pain in the neck."

The "pain-in-the-neck" comment drew a couple of laughs from the audience, which helped loosen up a reestablished tension inside the ballroom.

"But," Avanti said, more hesitantly, "Ajax was right to call me out, whether it be from recalling what I said or even what I didn't say in the past. And maybe the *greatest* virtue of a scrupulous listener: they are able to show you exactly who you are based on what you say. However, on the downside, they're able to pick up all the terrible things people can say to one another. I understand it has gotten worse over these past couple of years—or so it's made to believe. . . "

Avanti's attention was suddenly drawn to the same waiter as before—the one who looked identical to her son—storming through the back of the ballroom. She noticed that when he pushed open the set of doors and then stormed into the lobby outside he didn't make much of a sound or even noise for that matter, even though his demeanor was hot. Unless the hinges were dripping wet with WD-40 and the door itself was made out of Styrofoam, the waiter would've made quite a disturbance. Strangely, not a single person among the audience turned toward the back of the ballroom.

"Ajax never told me that he was a victim of bullying," she said after a pause. "But, I realize, his actions were telling me a different story. . . ."

"I hate that fucking school!" Ajax shouted out at Avanti while she waited for an explanation as to why he pushed Cory Hart from behind and caused the seventeen year old to hit the side of his head on a jagged rock, resulting in a trip to the ER where he received thirteen stitches.

"You've made that clear that you pretty much hate everything, Ajax! You're lucky Cory's parents aren't going to press charges!"

"I'm lucky?" Ajax repeated hotly from the edge of the kitchen. "That bald-headed fuck is lucky I didn't kill him and every single piece of shit like him at New Way. But you don't get it. You never will. All you see is the aftermath—"

"Like most young men, he was afraid to admit that he was the subject of bullying. My involvement in helping the school's administration develop a punishment system for those who partook in bullying had only pushed Ajax farther away from me. But I was only doing my job as a parent. It is our responsibility to get involved. I failed not only Ajax," Avanti said over the chaos roaring inside her head.

"At the end of the day, though, I not only failed Ajax, but I also failed myself. The name-calling. The *shaming*. The incivility. The discourse," she listed. "To say it's *never* been like this, that there hasn't been as much unrest as there is today, would be a straight up lie. We've *always* been like this. It's a sad reality, but it's a 'true' reality. But why do we continue to let it happen? Ever since our Founding Fathers united the Thirteen Colonies and laid the groundwork what would later become the *United* States of America, there have always been," she held up two fingers like a peace symbol, "two parties.

Two rivals. If you take a magnifying glass and examine the course of our great country, these two parties have changed names throughout time, even changed policies or positions; nonetheless, two opposing ways of governing yet unified under the same exact message: *Life, Liberty, and the pursuit of Happiness,*

After Stew died, I was forced to take a step back and reevaluate my own life; however, in the process, I failed to acknowledge the pain that my son was enduring on a daily basis. I admit that I was a failure as a parent, for not being there for my son when he needed me the most. All of my time spent as mayor, as well as governor, took its toll on my family, on Ajax. A part of me bears the responsibility of what happened to my son. And I believe a part of any mother should bear the responsibility of her child's future because it is her duty to protect them from the dangers of the world. But there lies the double-edge sword: *If we overprotect our children, then we're smothering them. On the other hand, if we don't protect them at all, then it's up to the world to decide our children's fate,*

And that's where I failed, to find the common ground with Ajax, to meet him halfway, in the middle, to *make* compromises,

My slogan reads: 'Look out, Washington! Here comes a new Washington!' What does that actually mean? For as long as I can remember, we have voted in the same politicians who have waltzed into Washington and have failed to deliver on the promises they've made on the campaign trail. Most—if not, all—of you already know my stances on the current issues this country now faces. You know my stance on healthcare, immigration, gun reform, climate. But who said they're written in stone? I look at them as merely a starting point where *both* parties can find room to work together to propose the best, most reasonable solution. The main problem facing Washington today is that we have too many talkers, not enough listeners."

Parts of the audience started to clap and cheer underneath *Avanti's* words.

"It is now time for Washington to finally take us seriously!" Avanti said, her voicing growing in size. "It is now our time to bring back The Power to where it rightfully belongs, to you—the people!"

Half of the audience erupted in applause. The other half—the money—sat in a state of utter silence. Alexandru, who was seated closest to the stage, glanced at another business magnate next to him and discreetly rolled his eyes from Avanti's speech. The only one at the table who was clapping was Colin, despite the looks of sheer gloom and doom all over the other faces.

Avanti pushed aside all the emotion that she had used throughout the speech and savored the moment before it was lost in the fray.

UNCOMFORTABLY seated with the bottom of her dress bunched up into her abdomen inside a cramped bathtub in the hotel bathroom, Avanti replayed the previous speech through her head. She pushed through the words, ones she said and didn't say. The words had drawn her eyes to her wrists, both of them not wearing a single drop or smear of blood, uncut. She ran her fingers across her wrist. Only one person had come to mind. She removed her eyes from her wrists, looked around the bathroom, and wondered what it must've been like in those final moments before he sliced open his wrists and spilled his precious blood out into the world that he scorned. As she sat alone, she couldn't help but feel a great sorrow not for being alone but for being imprisoned by her own flesh. She traveled back in time, replaying events that transpired days before his death and all the signs that he was giving her: the hopelessness and despair, heavy drug use and around-the-clock vaping, filling his body with junk food, becoming a parody of the TV commercials and advertisements shoved down his throat, then the raw fascination with death, constantly watching *movies* or reading *comic books* or playing *video games* strictly revolving around death, afterlife, hell, monsters, demons, the devil, Grim Reaper, skulls and skeletons, and all things morose. A part of him, Avanti knew, wanted to be saved, rather than salvaged. He was implicitly crying out to her—to anyone who gave a shit! However, Avanti thought—or at least, imagined—that another part of him, the lighter, softer part that settled just beyond the darkness, couldn't be saved or even spared from a ravenous world that constantly demanded death in order to fertilize the soil which brought forth more life, a vicious cycle on a never-ending feedback loop. He had already made up his mind, so she thought. He wanted to die, so she thought. And in those final days before he decided that he no longer wanted to contribute to a gluttonous world where social hierocracy was distinctly constructed around the perennial binds of currency, Ajax was, in a fiendish way, taunting his mother, proving to her that, in the end, he stood on the shoulders of his own creation and won that Great War.

She reached inside her Bisset rhinestone-covered hand purse and pulled out a folded-up piece of notebook paper. She opened the letter. She only read through the first sentence before she could no longer bear to look at her son's words.

As Avanti wiped a bloody tear from the corner of her eye, she heard a booming *knock* on the door!

Startled, Avanti immediately lifted her heavy head from its dangled-state and snapped her attention toward the door. A shadow of legs appeared below the narrow crack of the doorway. She pushed her body from the empty bathtub and with one hand bracing the side of the tub and the other balling the bottom of her dress against her waist, she stepped out. She placed the hand purse aside, picked up her stilettos from the top of the closed toilet, and holding them like a weapon, inched toward the closed door.

"Hello," she said, listening for a reply but receiving only cold silence.

Avanti readjusted her grip around the toe-sides of the stilettos and made sure that, if there was someone who intended to do her harm at the door, he *or* she would feel the sharp end of her heel first.

As she approached the door, the shadow behind the door remained.

Once more, Avanti called out to whomever—or *whatever*—was waiting behind the door.

No response.

"I'll be right out," Avanti said mysteriously, as if she was trying to catch the knocker off guard. "Give me a minute—"

As soon as she uttered the word *minute*, she swung open the door.

What Avanti thought was the shadow of a person—or *thing*—happened to be the luggage that belonged to one of the aides. The handle was fully erected upright, which, considering her current state, could've passed as a stubby person.

Cautiously, Avanti stepped out of the bathroom, looked around the hotel room, which was vacant, then noticed the hotel door, which was wide open. She walked from the hotel room and like passing a busy intersection, checked each side of the hallway.

On a second pass, Avanti caught a glimpse of that same girl from earlier darting around the corner of a hallway. Every inch of her body stilled. Her eyes were clouded with memory.

A sequence of images came to Avanti, old, yet fond images. *She was chasing after Echo in a game of 'Tag! You're it!' She ran after a cackling Echo who was breathlessly darting around the kitchen island, then around and under the kitchen table, then, once out of the kitchen, around the living room sofa and she'd occasionally stop by a safe area, like behind the corner of the wall or the closet door, to pinpoint the sweaty-toothed, branch-limbed, Cyclops-eyed MONSTER teetering after her.*

With emotion flooding over her, she blocked out the images as quickly as they came to her and focused on tracking down the girl.

After walking down a stretch of desolate hallway, Avanti found the stairwell door slowly closing, as if the girl was leaving behind subtle yet obvious clues for Avanti.

In a heightened state of anxiety, Avanti called out to the girl, but the girl had already taken off. This time, Avanti quickened her pace and as soon as she made it to the stairwell, the girl was already four flights ahead of her. Running over the edge of the landing were wet footprints, which were about the size of a girl who could've been about four years old. She tracked the footprints down the stairs. Curiously, she leaned over the railing and glanced down at a small, dark figure spiraling around the flight of stairs. The girl came to a sudden pause as she made it to the base of the stairs and shot her pallid mien upward at Avanti.

"Echo?" muttered Avanti.

She hadn't seen her baby girl in sixteen years. Yet, Echo looked the same as she last remembered her. She was even wearing that same exact wavy-patterned one-piece bathing suit that she had on when she drowned.

Before Avanti could call out Echo's name, Echo took off down the stairs.

And Avanti chased after her.

*

YOUNG Echo led Avanti to the lobby where Chopin was playing. She pinpointed the music to the ballroom. Occasionally glancing over her shoulder to see if her mother was still following her, Echo darted directly toward the closed doors outside the ballroom. Before opening the doors, Echo stopped and once more, turned toward Avanti, who slowed down her pace.

"Echo," she said, catching her breath, "is that you, baby?"

Echo stared at Avanti with a blank, lifeless expression, as if whatever Avanti once knew of her baby girl and the once timeless beam of a smile that harnessed a supernatural power to cleanse even the most damaged of souls or that cackle of a laugh she would—more or less—expel whenever being chased around dangerous corners of the house or the simple yet astute observations she pointed out during times of pause was nevermore. Her baby girl was gone, and all that remained was a shell of a four-year-old girl staring back at her.

Echo turned her shoulder before Avanti had a chance to speak her mind. She pushed open the two doors with a loud grunt, as if they were the massive, arching doors of a castle. Chopin's ever-so delicate *Nocturne op. 9 No.2*, which was playing inside, suddenly became louder and clearer.

Adamant about confronting Echo, Avanti followed her into the ballroom.

When Avanti stepped back into the ballroom after being away for a couple of minutes—it might've been longer—she witnessed some of the guests of the fundraiser slow-dancing on the dance floor next to the dining area. A young, bouncy DJ, who remained tucked in the shadows behind a rat's nest of flashing samplers, turntables, and a laptop of pre-cut jams, was perched on top of a raised booth between two line array speakers, which seemed incredibly odd to Avanti, considering the song playing. Perhaps the DJ was taking requests? Regardless of choice in music, Avanti continued to pursue her daughter—or the body of her daughter—but couldn't find her, or "it," anywhere, which made Avanti question herself whether Echo had led her to where she needed to be, as if the whole speech and everything building up to the big speech was all a brutal façade, including the guests, as well as the donors, which were nothing more than background props, a moving background, and the flaunting and secretions of power, suits and modish dresses, a meek interpretation of "Who Owns Who"; and the real *meat and cheese* of tonight's event had yet to begin. It all became crystal clear to Avanti as soon as she saw herself dancing with Colin on the dance floor. Her head rested against the side of his shoulder. Both of her eyes, closed.

All of a sudden, the ballroom dimmed and then darkened while the spotlight on the stage brightened and brought forth a "new" speaker.

Behind the podium stood Ajax. He was dressed in a holey, wrinkled, oversized *Mobocracy* T-Shirt. His face littered with nose and eyebrow piercings. She hated that shirt, hated that band, and most importantly, hated that look—a "punk band for a punk kid," she'd always say. But Avanti knew it was him, her son, *her* Ajax. He was giving a speech to the audience; however, as soon as Avanti turned toward the dining area, the seats and the tables, she realized the members of the audience all looked the same. Seated at each table was a version of her son, Ajax; unlike the other Ajax on stage, these other Ajax's were wearing suits and ties and even dresses. Avanti took her eyes away from the audience for a moment and as soon as she tried to make sense as to what her eyes were looking at, the audience was no longer present; in fact, the rest of the ballroom was left in pitch black. She turned to the dance floor. The dancers, even herself and Colin included, were no longer there either. Yet, all that remained was pitch black. She brought her attention to Ajax, who was speaking behind the podium—or at least mouthing words. She couldn't hear a word that came out of his mouth. Hoping her son was speaking through a faulty microphone, she stepped closer to the stage for a closer listen. Avanti couldn't hear a word that came out of his mouth. Even though she wasn't a lip reader, she tried to make out her son's words, as if she was deaf yet unable to read or understand sign language and faithfully relied on the translator's over-the-top punctuation or expressive facial gestures. Regardless, Ajax was the kind of kid who was only "punctual" when he needed to be. He often mumbled or spoke under his breath or trailed off in a humming rant. Yet, inside Ajax's dome, he was a master storyteller, respected and at times, adored for such poised eloquence. The only time his words were clear— that is, outside his head—was when he'd yell at her.

And, you certainly didn't need a translator for such an event.

As the music softened yet continued to play in the background, Ajax continued to talk not to Avanti, but, more or less, *through* Avanti.

"I can't hear you, Ajax," she said to him. "What are you trying to tell me?"

She asked but, for some reason, she already knew the answer to her question.

While Ajax continued to speak without sound, she inched closer to the front of the stage.

She pleaded and begged for Ajax to speak up, to make sense!

He didn't—at least, to Avanti.

Ajax was having his moment on stage.

Talking.

Reading from a letter, *his* letter.

Frustrated by the lack of sound coming from her son's mouth, she rushed toward the stairs along the edge of the stage and as she was about to climb up the first couple of steps, Ajax pulled himself from the podium and turned to stage-left where his mother had come to a sudden halt.

"Ajax," Avanti said, holding out her arms, "you can talk to me. Please. . . "

Ajax stared back at his mother, as if he wanted to say something but couldn't. He opened his mouth to speak but immediately closed it once the moment passed. Disgusted with Avanti, he shook his head and proceeded through a closed curtain behind the podium.

Determined, Avanti followed Ajax through the curtain. She stopped and saw Ajax walking into the darkness with a strange seven-foot tall creature by his side.

Avanti called out, "Robert!"

Ajax stopped, turned his shoulder, and glanced at his mother.

In the darkness, a scaly clawed hand reached out for Ajax.

Hand-in-hand, Ajax and the upright creature walked away from Avanti until they both faded into the darkness.

Still determined for answers, Avanti followed Ajax into the darkness but only made it a couple of feet before a glass barrier prevented her from passing; in fact, she ended up bumping the top of her forehead so hard against the glass that the sudden impact of the blow forced her backward a few feet.

Stumbling away, Avanti managed to regain her balance. Startled and somewhat shaken up, she eventually recovered from the unexpected blow by taking a moment to find her bearings. Once Avanti was okay to move, she inched closer to the glass. She held her hand out and touched the glass. She walked along the edge of the glass, running the palm of her hand in a wax-on wax-off motion. She cupped both hands around her eyes like goggles, pressed her sore forehead against the glass, and peered through the darkness. She squinted her eyes, as if, by doing so, she was able to tap into a higher range of vision with incredible definition.

In her scan, Avanti *sensed* two figures, her son, Ajax, and another much taller figure with a strong yet a type of magnetic Panglossian-vibe—possibly that same creature from before—walking farther and farther away. Their presence started to dim, leaving behind only a gray film.

Avanti screamed out to Ajax numerous times but didn't receive any response.

Eventually, the figures vanished.

The confusion soon melted away, leaving behind nothing but primal rage.

With her hands curled into fists, she proceeded to BANG on the glass, hoping to break it. She banged until both her fists ached. Then, she banged some more. No matter how hard Avanti banged or pounded, the glass was impenetrable.

Behind the pounding, Avanti heard a man's voice calling out her name; however, she continued to throw her fists against the glass.

"I'm sorry for not being there," she confessed, as that raw emotion started to get the best of her.

As the pounding weakened and slowed, a hand touched her on the shoulder.

Startled, she rotated around, only to find Joel standing behind her. The lighting was less dark.

Baffled, Avanti looked around and wondered how in the world she wound up back in her hotel room.

"Are you okay, Avanti?" asked Joel.

Once more, Avanti faced the glass and found herself standing directly behind a window. The glass was perspired with raindrops. She looked out at the distant cityscape and witnessed the streaks lightning randomly flickering throughout the dark clouds. Then, she moved her eyes downward at the streets below and was left in a state of deeper thought—*Ajax*, he was here, *wasn't he?*

"I was knocking on the door," Joel said, turning toward the general direction of the door—or what was left of the door. Two of the three hinges were dangling on the side of the doorway like loose teeth. Pieces of wooden debris were scattered on the floor. The doorknob looked as if it had been eaten, chewed, spat out, then poorly screwed back into the door. "I heard a noise," Joel said finally, as he caught his breath. "Banging," he said.

"I'm fine," Avanti stuttered, acknowledging Joel's swollenness. "I just. . . " Once more, she faced the window. "I'm fine now."

She looked over Joel's shoulder and saw Colin entering the hotel room. He, too, was flabbergasted by the damage Joel had caused.

Mindful, he tiptoed over shards of door on the floor and tended to Avanti.

"You can go now," Avanti said shortly to Joel as Colin examined her for any injuries on her body.

Joel was hesitant to leave. Eventually, once he saw that Colin had everything under control, he stepped into the hallway outside.

"What happened?" asked Colin, as he consoled Avanti.

Still left in a state of confusion, Avanti's eyes drifted downward as if she was combing through thoughts and straightening out each one.

"I. . . I don't know, Colin," Avanti said unsteadily.

Colin's eyes flicked toward the thumb-sized knot on the top of Avanti's forehead.

"Geez Louise," he said, as he carefully touched the knot. "Did you hit your head on something?"

As soon as his finger grazed the knot, Avanti hissed with pain.

"I must've accidentally hit it on the doorway," she said with a grimace.

Colin walked over to a bucket of ice in the bathroom, placed a handful of ice cubes into a paper towel, and held the cold towel against Avanti's forehead.

"Are you not feeling well?" he asked while recalling what he saw happen with his own eyes as if he was a sports broadcaster breaking down play-by-play coverage. "You left in a hurry, Avanti," he said. "I thought maybe something had happened. Maybe you saw someone you wanted to avoid. An old fling perhaps. . . "

Normally, the comment, albeit innocent, would've been considered a "strike one" for Colin. However, Avanti was more intrigued by the word *left*.

"Left?" Avanti uttered. "Left where?"

"Yes," Colin said, his voice drawn out. He eased his hand from her forehead. "We were dancing, remember?"

"Yes," she said over the mental gap. Then corrected herself, "Of course."

"Here," Colin said and escorted Avanti to the bed. "Have a seat." Avanti did as Colin suggested and sat down on the edge of the bed. Over a comfortable silence, Colin said mindfully, "You're *not* like them, you know that right?"

Avanti let out a sigh.

"I don't know anymore." She rotated her head toward Colin and struggled to find his eyes. "Maybe I am. I'm just good at hiding it."

"Forget about them," Colin said clearer. "The money will come. Just give it time—"

"—I saw him, Colin," Avanti interrupted Colin.

Colin removed the balled-up paper towel of ice from Avanti's forehead.

"Saw who?"

"Robert," she said, holding Colin's hand. "I saw him."

"You saw Ajax?"

"Earlier," she nodded, "when I was giving my speech. He was there, Colin. Somehow, I don't know, it's like I can still feel him with me."

Colin held Avanti, who was still tender, closer to his body.

He didn't question her sanity. In all the years he had known her, he knew not to.

As the two embraced one another, another presence made itself known by the doorway: Sonny, who was standing with both his hands planted on his hips like a flamboyant drill sergeant.

Once he collected Avanti's attention, he stormed into the hotel room.

Only a couple of steps in his march, Joel reached out at the last second and said, "I wouldn't do that, if I were you. . ."

Sonny ignored Joel, who shared subtle eye contact with Avanti before easing back into the hallway.

"I hope you feel better," Sonny seethed, as he planted himself a couple of feet away from Avanti and Colin. "Once this whole. . . fiasco is finally over, you can kiss your chances at getting the nomination goodbye."

Colin glanced at Avanti, who, in return, told Colin to give them room. He looked yet again into Avanti's eyes. She had already made up her mind what she was going to do with Sonny. And there was no stopping the hunger.

"Okay," Colin said submissively and let out a heavy sigh. He stood from the bed and touched Sonny on the shoulder. "By the way, I thought it was a wonderful speech."

Avanti said, "Thank you, Colin."

"I bet you did, Colin," Sonny said rudely over Avanti.

Colin turned toward Avanti one last time and gave her a wink.

Then, he exited the room.

Once the room was clear, he began his verbal assault on the governor: "You want to tell me what the hell that was back there? I mean, are you trying to blow the nomination? All you had to do was stick to the fuckin' script. I mean, you honestly think those old fucks out there give a shit about your life story?"

"Some of them seemed to like it," Avanti said coyly.

"Some," he said. "Maybe. But *not* the ones we needed to convince. All they needed from you was a two-dimensional candidate, a yes-man able to follow orders, to speak when spoken to, not some. . . ." Sonny pointed at Avanti and as he searched for the right word to use, eyed her once over as if she was spoiled meat, ". . . some 'damaged' woman who everyday people could relate to. Whether you like it or not, two-dimensional presidents are what separates leaders, those who are willing and ready to make the tough decisions, from the peons—"

While Sonny was going on a tirade, Avanti peered beyond Sonny, beyond his mouth, beyond his words, and witnessed *the thing* controlling him. These words that Sonny was speaking were not his words but something else's. Somewhere, in a dark room using the dark gift, Avanti saw a glimmer of a pale face speaking the same grating words as her campaign manager was speaking. A narrow beam of artificial light was worn like a mask, bringing forth the shadowy face of tonight's host, Alexandru Adamache.

"—*The American People don't need a friend in the White House. They need a fuckin' leader*," Sonny and Alexandru said simultaneously.

Avanti sorted through Sonny's usage of words.

A half-grin crept onto the corner of her face.

"So," Avanti said suspiciously, "is this Sonny Mims talking? Or, is it Alexandru Adamache?"

Fooled by Avanti's intuitive nature, Sonny thought very carefully about his next words.

"Let's just say he didn't like the speech."

"Too bad."

"Avanti," Sonny said patiently, "you're making a big mistake."

"I'm not a cartoon character, Sonny," Avanti said, her voice trembling as the heat started to rise inside her. "I breathe the same air you breathe."

Once more, he looked over Avanti, but this time with a Witch's brew of feelings etched into his face: confusion, anger, and most importantly, disappointment.

"Forget it," Sonny said loosely over the hot silence and then waved his hand in disgust. "You're on your fuckin' own."

Sonny stormed out of the room, muttering the words *fuck'n' hopeless*.

Meanwhile, Avanti stood from the bed and turned to Vye, who was stealthily sitting in a chair in the darkest corner of the room. Her face was cold and distant like the dark side of the moon. Her presence alone, unnoticed and yet untouched, as if she was no darker than a midnight's shadow.

More shadows came forward, stretching from the hotel room and *filling up a bustling street in Philadelphia. Daylight blazed. People and cars materialized: a bench made of cast iron, a park, a woman dressed in black, a street, a town car, a face. Action!*

Sitting inside the back of a black town car parked across the Riverwalk Park along the Delaware River, Avanti watched Vye take a seat at the bench under a dense canopy of oak trees hidden from the street cameras.

After a couple of minutes of waiting, Vye spotted Chance wandering around the park. She threw a broad stroke of a nod his way. Acknowledging the gesture, Chance was hesitant to walk over and from his overage insecurity, which was obvious to anyone who noticed, he appeared as if he had two angels, one good and the other bad, waging a war on his shoulders. Privately reveling in Chance's diminishing state, Vye remained seated at one end of the bench while Chance, who appeared more skittish from his fidgety behavior, as well as constantly looking over his shoulder by the time he tottered up, eventually took a seat at the other end of the bench.

"You have the burner?" asked Vye, looking forward and watching two labradoodles sniff each other's butts next to a veteran's memorial.

"Where's Avanti?" asked Chance.

"I'm sure you're aware that she has a busy schedule, Mr. McBride. She told me to tell you that she sends her best wishes."

" The arrangement was for me to meet her," Chance argued, as he started to make a scene. "Not some woman whom I don't even know—"

"—So, the phone?"

"You have the money?" asked Chance, more aggressively.

"First, you show me yours," Vye said, "I'll show you mine. . . "

Chance thought over the perverse comment.

"And," Vye noted, "don't get any ideas."

Eventually, he caved and did as Vye instructed and pulled out the flip-phone from his jacket pocket.

"Hand it over," she said.

"I want to see the money first," Chance said, raising his voice.

Vye grabbed the briefcase next to her knee-high boots, brought it to the middle of the bench, popped it open, and revealed the perfectly organized rows of clean, crisp hundred dollar bills, each perfect stack held together by a mustard yellow currency strap. Chance didn't bother to count the money. All he could see were all those faces of Benjamin Franklin. In all his years of living—or better, yet—scraping from one job to another, he'd never seen so many damn Benjamins. She pinched the corner of one bundle and with one hand, gave it a dealer's dovetail shuffle as if she was giving the poor man a quick tease. Then, not wasting anymore time, she closed the briefcase.

"Nice," Chance said, his eyes wide and filled with what could've been money signs. He handed Vye the flip phone. "Here," he said, as Vye, in return, quickly slid the briefcase toward his body.

Vye looked over the flip phone the same way a dog would look at its master after a strange command.

"This is the only copy?" asked Vye.

"The message is in the voicemail."

"You didn't answer my question, Mr. McBride."

"Yes," Chance said, his voice trembling. *"It's the only copy."*

Vye made a contemptuous noise with her mouth.

"Ballsy, might I say," she said arrogantly. *"But I'll take your word for it."*

"Pleasure doing business with you," he said, grabbed his briefcase of money, held close to him like a baby, and stood to his feet.

He had only taken two steps away from the bench before Vye said from behind, "Money's not going to bring back your sister."

Vye's words were cool and sneaky, as if she was slipping a knife between his shoulder blades.

Chance stopped, carefully thought over his next few words, and finally faced Vye with tears worn heavy in his eyes.

"Let me ask you one last question before you disappear, Mr. McBride," Vye said nonchalantly. *"Do you believe your junkie sister was capable of the crimes she committed?"*

"Well, it doesn't really matter what I believe," Chance said, his voice trembling. *"My sister is dead, all thanks to you people."* Heavy emotion came over Chance, like a flood. He clenched his teeth, curled his fists tight; he even strangled the very handle of the briefcase, as if he was trying to choke out the life from inside. *"One day, you people will answer for what you did. And the world will know the truth about what you people are."*

"You're one to talk about honesty, Mr. McBride," Vye said, hiding a smile behind her face. The disguised smile was worn carefully for Chance, just barely visible enough for Chance to see the truth behind it. *"Besides,"* she said, holding back the smile before it could grow on her face, *"how's that boy doing?"*

As soon as Chance witnessed that look on Vye's face, he knew he was in it—neck deep in shit. His skin flushed. Beads of sweat formed on his forehead nearly the size of raindrops.

"Sooner or later," he said, swallowing, *"the world* will *know what you—"*

"—And what are we exactly, Mr. McBride?"

Chance paused, held back his words.

"*I have nothing else to say to you,*" he said with tears in his eyes. "*The way I look at it. . . you people are already dead to me.*"

Chance tried yet again to walk away from Vye, but, somehow, she managed to reel him back in with her softly spoken words: "*Across the street, there's a donut shop called Sweet Tooth. They have these raspberry puff turnovers that they make once a year, which I've heard are to die for. Perhaps you should try one.*"

Once more, he stopped and thought about his words, what he could say to put her in her place.

He acknowledged Vye, this time more squarely. She was no longer wearing her sunglasses. Instead, she was staring directly at Chance with hazy, red eyes.

With his brow furrowed in stupidity, he turned back around and walked off.

"*Chance,*" Vye whispered.

Once more, he stopped but didn't turn around.

Once more, he thought about not his words, but this time his actions, what he wanted to do to Vye. A strange sensation came over him, causing him to stagger. He pinched the brim of his nose and shook his head, as if he was shaking away a dizzy spell.

Once more, he turned to Vye, who was no longer sitting on the bench. Instead, he witnessed a familiar man sitting in her place.

He looked closer.

The man was light skinned, thin, yet fairly built, wore clothes that one would only find at a big box store. He had a scar the shape of a lightning bolt running down the side of his face. He was wearing a turtleneck of tattoos.

"*Stache?*"

The familiar man, whom Chance thought was a man name Stache, stood up from the bench.

"*Sup, Chance,*" he said.

His voice was deep and distinct, Stache's voice. Chance looked over Stache and once he realized that the man was, in fact, Stache, he walked over to him. He hadn't aged a day. The last time he saw Stache was at the Bawkin Correctional

Facility in South Carolina where he was finishing up the last stretch of his five-year sentence for assault and battery. Stache, on the other hand, was supposed to be carrying out a twenty-five year sentence for armed robbery—or what he liked to call a "stretch."

"What are you doing here? You're supposed to be. . . "

"Locked up," Stache finished Chance's sentence. "Yeah. I know," he said, approaching Chance. "They let me out earlier on good behavior."

After an awkward silence between the two, they embraced one another. What Chance didn't realize was that he was hugging Vye, not Stache. She gently whispered in his ear, "You can still redeem yourself. Mr. McBride."

Chance leaned back, revealing Stache once more. He looked at Stache, who, in return, flicked his head in a nod at a homeless man hanging out in the shade of a bridge. Chance followed Stache's eyes and noticed the bearded man who was dressed like the street and clinging onto a damp cardboard sign that read, "Help! Hungry, homeless, and hopeless."

Chance didn't say a word to Stache, not even a goodbye or see ya later.

With a vacant expression on his face, he robotically walked over to the homeless man under the bridge and set the briefcase on top of his overstuffed shopping cart that was packed with all of his belongings. Chance didn't utter a single word to the homeless man, who, despite the minor intrusion, couldn't be more thankful once he opened the briefcase and saw all the green faces of Benjamin Franklin inside. Overwhelmed, the homeless man could hardly stand upright for the sight of money nearly caused him to faint; however, Chance didn't care about what the homeless man had to say to him nor did he even acknowledge his reaction. Yet, Chance walked back through the park and spotted the glowing pink sign across the street that read: Sweet Tooth. Even though he had eaten a cheese steak an hour before the meeting with Vye and wasn't at all hungry, he could hear his stomach growling. Driven by the sugary smell of tasty pastries in the air, Chance walked to Sweet Tooth. He didn't even bother to stop for traffic. Yet, he kept on walking through the busy street. He didn't budge or flinch a muscle from the cars swerving around him. His eyes were mesmerized by a display case behind the front window of the bakery. All those beautiful-looking pies and cakes presented to onlookers, walkers, joggers, bikers, drivers, and riders.

"Forgive me, Storm," he said tearfully, as if he was speaking, not to Storm, but the bakery itself.

As Chance crossed the yellow line and proceeded directly toward the bakery, a sudden horn blared out beside him! Before he could even turn his head to acknowledge the horn, as well as the screech of tires skidding to a stop, Chance's blood was decorated all over the truck's windshield, as well as the street. The truck had struck Chance so hard and violently that his blood had even made it to the bakery where it painted the brick walls and window front like graffiti.

From the unlit corner of the hotel room, Vye nodded her head at Avanti, who, in return, flashed a smirk.

As Sonny made his way from room 421, Avanti said from behind, "Let's make it official, shall we?"

Huffing with anger from Avanti's mild "suggestion," Sonny came to halt by the doorway before walking into the hallway and faced Avanti, who was already inches away from him.

"You know," he said, startled from Avanti's presence, "I was rooting for you, Avanti. I thought you had a chance. I really did. Black woman with a bright future in politics. What better time than now for someone like you to come along and reshape the vision of America?" The anger back over him, this time holding him tight like a fist. "Turns out that you're no different from any idealist who has her head stuck so far up her own ass she doesn't even know shit from Shiloh." He leaned in with his teeth barred. "I tell you what, *Avanti*." Sonny spoke her name with a black girl's sass. "Do yourself a favor and come back to reality where the big boys play. Then, maybe, we can talk about the future of your campaign, huh? Until then, you can go right ahead and find yourself another campaign manager to replace me because, frankly, I don't give a shit."

"Is that how you feel?" asked Avanti.

Sonny looked over Avanti with derision.

"I swear, you women," he said, his eyes flicking toward her swollen breasts, "and you're fuckin' feelings. I was a fool to actually think that a woman could be qualified to run this country."

Sonny let out an airy snort from his mouth before storming away. He made it a few feet down the hallway before Avanti called out his name from behind.

Once more, he stopped and faced Avanti.

He had no other choice than to listen—and listen well.

"You want to know where I get my strength from, Sonny?"

"You call that nonsense that I had to listen to for the past two hours you displaying strength? You looked weak. Thankfully, the press corps wasn't allowed inside; otherwise, except for a couple of sympathizers, the entire country would be writing you off right about now."

"Ever since I was a girl, my mother engrained in me a sense of resiliency. It was my mother who raised me to be the woman I am today and if it wasn't for her words, then I probably wouldn't be standing here. She made sure to tell me that I 'could do anything I put (my) mind to.' And 'just remember,' she'd emphasize, 'one man's shit don't smell no different than another. It all stinks the same.' I've used those words throughout my life; in fact, I've learned to embrace those words. Then," she said, as she took a step closer to Sonny, even though he was standing much farther away, "life—or better yet, death—came along and it bit me where I was most vulnerable. When I was in my early twenties," she pointed to the white blotches on her face, "I developed a skin disease. I didn't want it. I knew I could *thrive* without it. Even till this day, people stare. People look at me funny. But I don't—and didn't—let people stop me from being where I need to be—"

"—And where do you need to be, Avanti?"

"Despite what you heard tonight, Stew was a good man," she said, narrowing both her eyes, "a *faithful* man who wouldn't dare harm a single hair on my head. He knew what I was capable of. And, unlike most of the people who have come and gone in my life, Stew was the one man who accepted me for who I was. He embraced me. He held me the way any woman should be held. But most importantly, he understood me," she said, starting to drift off. "When he became sick, I couldn't control the cancer spreading inside him. It was too deep." Avanti drifted in deep reflection, visualizing his skeletal face during those final moments of his life. The thought alone of Stew going out caused her skin to burn. More poised, she said to Sonny, "But overtime, I've realized that every *living* thing dies."

"Huh?" Sonny said sarcastically. "You just now figured that one out." With a sense of superiority, he looked over Avanti as if she was beneath him. "Good luck to you, Avanti."

The words *good luck* were spoken slow and carefully. Yet, they rang out like a symphony triggering a memory.

Disguised among pedestrians, Vye stood across the street from former Vice President Croom's political campaign headquarters that was located in Fairwell, New Hampshire and watched Sonny Mims having a secret conversation with the former veep. After Sonny was finished talking with Croom, the two of them shook hands as if they were making a deal.

Croom winked at Sonny and said, "Good luck."

By any means, Vye wasn't a lip reader, but she didn't have to be. After all, it wasn't hard to read the words good *and* luck.

Once more, Sonny tried to walk away—more like, flee—but couldn't.

Once more, he stopped but never turned around. Couldn't. Yet, he continued to face the other end of the hallway while Joel stood outside the hotel room.

"You underestimate us," Avanti said, as she removed the contact lenses from her eyes. "But maybe that's the whole point," she said while creeping up behind Sonny. "You already have us figured out. Which, to your advantage, makes us predictable. And if there was one trait that voters look for in his or her candidate, it's predictability. Am I right? Or, am I wrong?"

"Save your breath," Sonny said, not turning around. "It's too late—"

"—You're right," Avanti said, standing directly behind Sonny. Her eyes fell onto the pulse on his neck, which was beating like a kick drum. She pulled down the collar around his neck, peeling away the Band-Aid covering the two fresh bite marks directly above his collarbone. Her eyes were different, her irises crimson red, her pupils opening like black holes. "It is too late," Avanti said softly, as she loomed over Sonny. "*For you.*"

Before Sonny could turn his shoulder, Avanti had already sunk her two fangs into his neck. The blood squirted from his neck like a perforated water hose.

Except for a couple of swings of his arms, he didn't put up much of a fight.

Meanwhile, Joel stood guard as Avanti continued to suck the blood from her former campaign manager's neck. Joel kept his attention directed at a painting of Emaneul Leutze's masterpiece, *Washington Crossing the Delaware*, on the wall before him, not even turning his head an inch to acknowledge the violence taking place only feet away from him. By the time Avanti was through with Sonny, she released her fangs from his flesh, which retracted to normal canines. Her mouth, as well as her chin was covered in blood. Sonny fell from Avanti's grip the same way a tired man would fall into a cool, nourishing bed and hit the floor with a soft *thud*. He made a desperate attempt to crawl away from Avanti, but his hands and knees slipped over his own puddle of blood and left him floundering on drenched carpet. Since fleeing was a futile endeavor, Sonny resorted to his last option—his only option—which was plugging the two massive punctures along the side of his neck with his hands; however, like before, it was a futile attempt to salvage whatever life—or what little life—he had left.

As the flow of blood started to slow and Sonny's life started to fade, Avanti loomed over his dying body; and with an air of solemn reverence, she watched his wide, panicked eyes start to glaze over.

She tilted her body into frame for she had one last thing to say to Sonny before he checked out.

As Sonny took his final breaths, Avanti said like a boss: "Consider this your resignation."

With her feet kicked up on the edge of a desk in a dark office above the Convention Center where she was soon going to hold a rally for thousands of supporters, Avanti pushed the up button on the TV remote to flip the channel from the Phillies baseball game to Channel 9 News where a news reporter was reporting a breaking news story on the sidewalk outside Antonio's Pizzeria in Center City.

"Later this afternoon, workers at this pizzeria behind me discovered the body of a white male in an alleyway. Investigators have yet to identify the body, but they believe he was homeless. As far as the cause of death, investigators are certain the man died from a fatal bite mark on his neck by what they're claiming was a wild animal."

TALORA was making her rounds with a tray of hors d'oeuvres, including cucumber and caviar bites, as well as escargot in garlic butter—which were deliberately positioned at the end of the tray closest to her neck and shoulder and acted as her own repellent for vampires-in-disguise—when she witnessed the red eyes staring at her from behind a congested crowd of well-off socialsuckers in the lobby of St. Gabriel Hotel.

Instantly blindsided by the toll of fear, Talora instantly started to spiral out of control as if she had no clue as to what she was doing, where she was going, and why she was even here. She stopped by the bar and collected her thoughts before she lost control. Talora mentally questioned his presence but could come up with only one reason as to why he chose her.

With more direction, Talora rerouted through the lobby as if by doing so he'd fly off—or phantom jump or whatever they did—and find some other fresh, warm meat to bother. In that moment of climbing suspense, Talora could only imagine what it'd be like to wind up on the national news, her tragic story on the tube, her body covered with a white sheet, another statistic, a "victim;" and surprisingly, it was the thought of her baby brother that had brought on such grim reality. All of those pulses, she thought, beating like a cheap techno song throughout the entire lobby, and if this blood breath was here to party hardy, then he wouldn't have a hard time finding another beat.

Talora shot yet another discreet glance toward his direction. His pale sunken face was drifting in and out of the crowd, those crimson eyes attached to Talora like crosshairs. The man carried a certain hunger in his eyes.

Then again, Talora reminded herself that he was no man.

But something far worse.

A creature spawned from nightmares and forged by daywalkers.

Bloodied and bestowed.

She kept a close eye on the strange creature and with each subtle glimpse of his razor-sharp face, it became clear to her that he most definitely didn't belong at The Governor's Ball—and from the crafty way he tracked her every movement with his blood-soaked eyes, it was even more evident to her that she was his prey. His eyes, magnetic—it was *the gaze*, she realized, the one of an animal, *not man*. His intentions, cold and calculated. That, and the simple fact that not one guest or donor inside the hotel's lobby feared him or, even worse, pegged him as an "outsider," considering the strict dress code and most—if not, all—of the socialsuckers were wearing tuxedos that cost as much as a car opposed to the outsider's informal attire: a raggedy black leather jacket that looked as if it had been handed down by three centuries, a pair of black leather gloves with metal spikes over the knuckles, heavy nose and eyebrow piercings and all that twisted steel on his face, as well as a turtleneck of foreign tattoos along his pallid skin. She figured he was a member of the notorious Vampos gang from those ancient Romanian symbols along his neck and face.

He—or what Talora assumed was an "it"—moved behind one guest the same way a skilled hunter would use a tree or even high grass to conceal its cover from its vulnerable prey. Talora's senses heightened, especially her hearing, as well as her sight. She checked for exits. There was one not too far away. The sight of a glowing green sign that read EXIT in bold lettering showed her the way.

The flash of lightning brought out the two shadowy individuals standing inside a dusty, unlit living room of an abandoned house along the jagged New York coast.

One of the individuals, the taller, wide-shouldered one, a light skinned man with tight cornrows who was wearing a flashy coat that looked as if it was covered in gold glitter, took a drag of a vape pen. He exhaled diabolically. Thick clouds of vapor oozed like smoky snakes from both his mouth and nostrils and trailed around the popped *collar of the Bubblegum Pop-inspired coat.*

Another flash of lightning flickered through the living room in a strobe light-like pattern.

"Promise me," the tall man said, as vapor followed his every syllable, "they won't turn her. . . "

"I can't promise you they'll be nice to her," said the voice of the other individual, a short woman with her dark hair pulled back tight in a ponytail, a smooth operator. "I'm afraid their actions are out of my control." She stepped closer to the partially shattered window, her glossy eyes glowing. "But if you want them to scare her, then, that, you can be sure of."

Talora handed off the tray of hors d'oeuvres to another waitress, who was in the middle of taking a drink order, and shouldered her way through the crowd.

She glanced over her shoulder and saw the creep closing in on her.

His prowl was faster, creepier, deadly.

"I have to ask you, Mr. Japhy," the short woman said, as her pallid face lit up from the flash of lightning, "what exactly did this girl do to you in order for her to receive such. . . horror?"

The tall shadowy man, Mr. Japhy, said quietly over a thoughtful pause, "She stole something that belonged to me. Something I'll never get back."

Three Months Ago

INSIDE a sold-out Madison Square Garden arena, the fueled-up crowd headbanged to the final song, "Recycle Your Pets," by the band Stuffed Animalz.

Riding the choppy, impulsive riffs played by sword-wielding Japanese guitarist, Dexter, aka "T-Rex," real name Akemi Tanaka, lead singer, Japhy Warchild, screeched through his patent pink microphone, "*Razor-Rrection! Razor-Rrection! Razor-Rrection!*"

Concertgoers acted like parishioners hanging onto Japhy's every lyric.

The front of the crowd screamed along with Japhy while these random pockets of mosh pits broke out along the violent tidal wave of flesh like water ripples.

"*Razor-Rrection!*"

"*Razor-Rrection!*"

"*Razor-Rrection!*"

The set ended with a hellish display of pyrotechnics.

After the song finished in a blaze of glory, Japhy caught his breath and took a moment to acknowledge all of his "disciples" shouting out—even chanting—his name. Young teary-eyed women, who were desperate to carry his baby, reached out to him from the very front of the stage.

Japhy couldn't help but laugh at it all.

If they only knew. . .

He pushed the madness aside and thanked the hometown crowd.

Then, he dropped the microphone on the stage.

The lights dimmed.

The entire stage went black.

"WHAT a way to end the tour, my brutha!" the bassist, Product, said, as he slapped hands with Japhy, who was lounging in the middle of a couch where he was surrounded by at least a dozen of bikini-wearing, apple-bottomed Instagram models.

"I'm ready to hit the road again," Japhy said smoothly.

"Shiiit," Product slurred. "That was probably the longest three months of my life. Here-here!"

Product toasted a Pabst with Japhy, who, in return, took a sip of beer and then secretly spat the mouthful of beer back into the can. Japhy hid his disgust for the taste of beer with a smack of his gums.

While Product chugged the rest of his Pabst, one of the bosomy women who was clinging to Japhy's side, leaned in closer and said to him, "Nice move."

"She talks," he said back.

"She does a lot of things."

Japhy swallowed, but it wasn't the beer.

Instead, it was a lump in his throat.

More seductively, she asked, "If beer's not your poison, then what is?"

The Instagram model brushed her shiny brunette hair from her chest, revealing her fake, perfectly round D-cup breasts. She even gave them a jiggle for Japhy. In return, Japhy's eyes moved at a seizure's pace as he followed her swollen breasts. He wanted to play with them.

He looked around the backstage and couldn't help but acknowledge the other band mates who were flirting with other women. He turned back to the Instagram model and not wasting anytime, touched the strap along her lime-green bikini. He didn't realize—at least not until his eyes fell on his fingers—but his hand started to tremble.

"I can think of a couple of things," Japhy said closely and set his hand down by his side before the Instagram model could notice the tremble.

In the back of his mind, he was wondering the whole time when she'd brandish her phone from wherever she was hiding it—and he couldn't find too many places where she could hide it—and snap a quick selfie or make her own "Me and Japhy" highlight reel.

Phones have literally *ruined everything.*

"You know, for a man who's worshipped like a god, you're pretty shy."

"I like to refer to myself as more introvert—"

The Instagram model giggled from the comment.

"I like shy guys," the model said, as she opened up Japhy's trademarked coat. The glittery gold coat sparkled from the overhead light raining down from above. At times, the coat was bright enough to light up the entire backstage.

Immediately, Japhy grabbed the model's boney wrist.

"*Don't* touch the fuckin' coat," he said all god-like, his voice deepening.

Startled by Japhy's abrupt change in demeanor, the Instagram model leaned back a couple of inches and said timidly, "Okay."

"What's this about shy guys," another much blonder model said as she cozied up to Japhy's other side. "I *luuuv* me some shy-on-the-fly guys." She started to play with the curly hair along his chest. While the two Instagram models primped and pampered Japhy, like a god, he spotted a woman in her early twenties—fully dressed—between the sea of flesh.

Intrigued by her presence, Japhy squinted his eyes and peered closer. One of the bodyguards allowed her, as well as a friend ("Lacey," he concluded) past the gates and through the backstage where they were talking—or better yet, hitting it off with keyboardist/DJ, Pacen, who stage name was DJ Pac-Attack. However, Pacen appeared more interested in the other girl, the one whose name wasn't Lacey.

Pacen was considered the backbone of band, provided leadership for the each member of the group, was known to give strong rally speeches whenever the band mates needed rallying or just a pep talk; also gave their sound that needed "edge." It was fair to say DJ Pac-Attack was Wizard in *Wizard of Oz*, the man behind the curtains.

When Japhy saw Pacen talking to her—of all people, *her! What is she doing here? She hates heavy metal!*—a flash of anger came over him, causing his skin to burn. His eyes went cold, dark. Even the feel of a woman's soft touch felt like knives cutting through his chest.

What made matters even worse: Japhy witnessed Pacen taking her to the tour bus. And he knew exactly what happened on the tour bus.

Lacey stayed behind, found one of the stagehands, and started talking to him.

In a heap of rage, Japhy pushed aide the starfuckers and stood to his feet and despite the complaints coming from all directions, such as "You friggin' jerk!" or "That is no way to treat a woman, asshole!" he kept his eyes on the lucky lady as she walked away with Pacen.

Before they exited backstage, Pacen secretly slipped his hand into hers and the two held hands, as if they were now a hot item.

✝

ONLY two months after the Counting Sheep Tour wrapped in New York City, the band reunited at the drummer, Tommy Bango's lakeside cabin, which was located outside Syracuse.

When lead singer, Japhy, arrived at Bango's rehearsal studio, the band was already there... all except for one member, Pacen.

With only three weeks away, the band was scheduled to play for an upcoming festival called Fall Frenzy Festival. Eventually, after much worry and complaint, Pacen finally showed up with, of course, his new fling, Talora. However, to Japhy, the two lovebirds looked as if they were officially "official" from the way they couldn't keep their hands off one another.

As soon as the band geared up, it was clear, not only to Japhy, but also the other band mates, that Pacen didn't want to be there; in fact, Talora was an obvious distraction, making her own little gestures while the band was rehearsing, like winking at Pacen or blowing him kisses. Pacen missed his cues. Couldn't get the beat down correctly. It was like he had other things on his mind and none of them revolved around preparing for the upcoming concert.

Finally, after wasting the entire night rehearsing, Product spoke up and questioned Talora's presence, but did so in a manner that didn't sit well with Pacen.

Product asked something along the lines: *"What the fuck is she doing here?"*

T-Rex interjected: *"My boy here is pussy whipped."*

Defensively, Pacen came back: *"You're one to talk."*

"You, Pussy," T-Rex said under his breath.

Then, Pacen returned wittingly, *"Hey, man. You are what you eat."*

The comment didn't sit well at all with Japhy; in fact, he did everything in his power to keep himself from lashing out at Pacen. Later that next day, when Pacen had gone off with Talora for "a quick hike," which was the excuse he used, Japhy arranged an emergency meeting in the living room to make a vote on the decision whether or not to keep Pacen in the band. Which had made matters worse. The band was split; and those who rebuked the very idea had questioned Japhy's reasoning behind the suggestion. Which created more unwanted tension and division among the band. After all, DJ Pac-Attack was the backbone of Stuffed Animalz!

For Japhy, it felt as if it was the beginning of the end of Stuffed Animalz.

And all fingers pointed at a woman named Talora Katz.

TWO days later after the trip to Lake Oneside, Japhy visited Talora's house, which was located in a small suburban neighborhood in a small town called Ballpointe located in upstate New York. Across the street, Japhy waited inside the passenger seat of his Mustang, while his driver Broot kept the engine warm. The sight alone of Pacen's brand new Escalade parked right next to the burgundy crossover in the driveway pissed him off something awful. *They would never allow it,* he thought. Yet, Pacen and *his silver tongue must've won them over.*

As Japhy opened the passenger door, Broot grabbed him by the arm and said doubtfully, "I wouldn't do that if I was you, Japh."

Simmering with anger, he glared at Broot's chubby, catcher's mitt of a hand touching the sleeve of his coat.

Japhy didn't have to say a word.

His eyes were doing most of the talking.

Broot released his hand from Japhy's coat.

"Think about the consequences. Think about what your parents will do if they find out about you—"

"—Well, Broot," Japhy said over Broot as he hung over the passenger door, "that's the thing. You're *not* me. And you'll *never* know what it's like to be me."

Broot fell witness to a motley crew of emotions shrink-wrapped around Japhy's eyes.

Disappointed by Japhy's actions, Broot ran his finger over the gold W.W.J.D. (*What Would Japhy Do*) wristband around his meaty wrist and then hung his head in despair.

Primed for confrontation, Japhy stepped outside the Mustang and closed the door behind him. He only took one step away from the car before he was greeted by these three neighborhood kids who looked as if they were up to no good. Each one was walking along the sides of their bicycles. Each one leaned in closer for a closer look, as if they were either fans of Japhy or something else—perhaps enemies?

Japhy rolled his eyes once he noticed the three kids, particularly one scrawny kid in the middle, whom his friends called "Lee."

"What do you want now?" asked Japhy, as if he knew the kids.

"What do we want?" Lee returned, as he turned his head to the others. "What are *you* doing here?"

"I can't talk about it right now," he said, the anger coming through his voice.

"Yeah, right. You're too good to talk to us—"

"—It's not like that," Japhy kept an eye on Pacen's SUV, "you know that."

"You know, he's been hanging around here a lot more," another thicker kid boldly said to Japhy.

"Who's been hanging around here?"

The kid nodded at the house across the street.

"Your boy, Pacman—"

"—It's DJ Pac-Attack, you moron."

"Whatever."

More engaged by the comment, Japhy faced the three kids.

"A lot more, how?"

Another more bashful kid said, "Like boyfriend-girlfriend."

"Yeah," Lee said, "like, one day, like in the near future, he's going to be joining the family, if you know what I mean. . ."

"Go fuck yourself, kid."

"Kid?"

"Hey, who do you think you are?"

Lee said over the other kid, "We want Nathan back."

Japhy paused and swallowed his words.

"Nathan's dead," he said to the kids.

Japhy heard the *squeak* of a screen door behind him!

Both Talora and Pacen exited the house, leaving Japhy with no other choice than to react.

Startled by their whereabouts, he ducked behind the Mustang and took cover while, at the same time, the three other kids shooed away Japhy and peddled away on their bikes.

From behind the Mustang, Japhy watched Talora walk Pacen to his Escalade where the two embraced one another. He watched the two kiss before Pacen drove away. Then, he watched her wave Pacen goodbye.

For the first time, Japhy questioned what he was doing back in Ballpointe.

And he didn't the answer.

Not one.

Present Day

AS the creature whom Talora thought belonged to the Vampos gang pushed aside a couple of guests, knocking one of them, a frailer man, to the floor, Talora raced through the exit doors and cut through the parking deck.

Not once did she ever look back.

Instead, she ran as if her life depended on it. She knew that if she could make it to her car, then she'd have a chance to survive the night.

However, her chances were slim—considering what she was up against.

Even though Talora's car was parked on Level 3, she didn't bother taking the stairs. The last place she wanted to be, especially if he caught up with her, was in a confined space like a stairwell.

In her escape, the life around her was turned down. The ambience of traffic outside the parking deck was not as prevalent. The chorus of *honking* horns and background chatter, softened. Surprisingly, she never heard the sound of the door opening or closing behind her. Surely, he was right on her tail when she exited the hotel. Which, for a brief moment, made Talora question whether or not he had ended the pursuit.

Running up the incline of the first level, Talora glanced over her shoulder and confirmed that the door was, in fact, closed. And not one person—or thing—had followed her into the parking deck. She was momentarily struck by a glimmer of hope; however, she kept running, never slowing her dash to safety. She ran up the next level and then, the next. From the sharp U-turn, she spotted her white Honda Civic parked at the other side of the parking deck. She ran about halfway toward the car before she slowed in her tracks from the pungent odor of what reeked of a corpse. The odor was like a wall and once Talora walked right through it, she was completely submerged in it. She pinched the tip of her nose and breathed through her mouth. But even then, Talora could taste the smell on her tongue, as if, during each breath, she was taking small nibbles at it. She increased the speed of her run and hurried to her car. Only three strides in, she heard a high pitch sound coming from a car, possibly her car.

She slowed down her run to a loose jog. Which had given her enough time to catch her breath. She listened closer and pinpointed that chalkboard-like scratching of a screech: a sharp claw crookedly running along the side of a car.

But not just any car. . .

Her car!

Stepping out of the warped shadows at the front of her Honda Civic was the mayor of New York City, Mayor Armitage.

"You wanted to see me, Ms. Katz?" said the mayor.

She was struck by a momentary dizziness. She heard of such effects. Once, her friend, Lacey, had told her about a vamp who used the power of seduction on her. She thought they called it a "lure."

For a moment, Talora was convinced it was the mayor.

But then again, they had the ability to shapeshift.

And, why in the hell would the mayor meet her in such a dark place?

Talora stared at the mayor as if she was looking at an autostereogram painting and focused yet unfocused her eyes. She aimed for the center of his face and angled her eyes along the horizon. His true face slowly started to surface like one of 3D image. Behind the mayor's face was the same exact pale face that she was running away from. Talora reminded herself that he was *no* person.

"Nice try," she said.

The creature stepped through the mayor's vanishing body.

As the red-eyed creature stepped forward and revealed himself entirely under the hazy amber light, Talora heard the same screeching sounds all around her.

Out from the shadows around her emerged more of them. She counted six of them; however, she had heard rumors and stories on the news that they traveled in much larger packs—some close to a dozen or even more.

Before the gang could circle around Talora and leave her no room to escape, she turned around and ran back down to the 2nd level where she was greeted by yet more of them emerging from the dark shadows around parked vehicles. She looked for exits. Behind her was an opening in the deck. The drop was two stories. The fall wouldn't kill Talora—that is, if she didn't land directly on her head; however, at the very least, she'd more than likely break a leg. And, Talora knew she wouldn't be any good if she couldn't run on two legs.

She checked her last option, the more doable option, a stairwell behind one of the gang members. Talora had no other choice. She pulled out her car keys from her pocket and as she balled her hand into a fist, she placed each key in the cracks of her fingers—her car key, apartment key, bike lock key.

Make sure to *aim for the eyes*, she told herself.

"Nowhere to run now, bitch," the same creature from before, whom she assumed was their leader, said from Level 3.

As the gang surrounded Talora, the engine of a car suddenly turned on!

The *clah–clah–clunk* of gears switching echoed throughout the parking deck.

Then, the blistering skid of tires!

As the supposed leader of the gang exposed the fangs in his mouth and revealed himself for not who but *what* he was, a beam of headlights shone upon his pale face. The vampire's attention snapped toward the speeding SUV on his left, putting a new definition to the expression: a "vamp in headlights." Both his red eyes widened, jaw slackened, his entire face stretched out in cartoon-like fashion.

While others jumped out of the way, the alpha remained in the crosshairs of the grill. His body violently rolled along the front hood of the Escalade, his upper body taking the brunt of the hit. He crashed into the front windshield, leaving behind the fractured dent of a body in the glass. His body was flung over the top of the Escalade.

Left in a state of bafflement, it took Talora a couple of tense seconds to recognize the vehicle. Then, as Talora's suspicions came true, the back door behind the driver's seat flung open. Pacen waved Talora inside.

"GET IN!" he shouted out.

Talora looked around, as if she was reevaluating her options. The other gang members were standing to their feet. She couldn't find the other one, the leader.

Pacen shouted out again, "GET IN, TALORA!"

Talora quickly leaped into the backseat and closed the door before one of the gang members could grab her leg.

Once Talora was secured inside, Pacen switched the gear in reverse, backed up into another car parked behind him, and lastly, switched the gear back in drive. He floored the SUV around the gang and managed to drive away in one piece.

As Pacen sped from the parking deck and onto a bustling midtown Manhattan Street, Talora looked behind the SUV.

She couldn't help but sniff the inside of the vehicle.

That funky smell was back.

Death.

"The other vamp," she said, frantically searching for the one who was struck by Pacen's Escalade, "he's gone. . ."

She heard a *thud* coming from the ceiling.

Her eyes slowly moved upward. . .

She cried out, "Pacen!"

All of a sudden, a hand with claws the size of steak knives burst through the ceiling of the SUV. The claws came inches away from cutting Talora's face.

Thinking of the weapons at hand—except for the one he was driving—Pacen pushed in the car lighter below the dashboard.

Talora ducked and dived and dodged each swipe of the hand. Keeping as low as her body would allow, she crawled toward the passenger seat; and as she was about to slip into the seat, her head suddenly jerked backward. The vampire had grabbed a handful of Talora's hair and was tugging her body toward the ceiling. Fighting off the hand by throwing wild punches, Talora cried out for help.

Help arrived in the sound of a *click*.

The car lighter sprung outward. Pacen grabbed the hot lighter from its socket and while steering the vehicle straight with the insides of his legs, he rotated his body around the driver's seat, gripped the vampire's wrist to keep it steady, then pressed the scolding orange coil against the back of the vampire's hand, leaving behind a perfect black circle along his cold flesh.

The vampire released its grip from Talora's hair.

Once she was free, she climbed over the passenger seat.

Pacen told her to fasten her seatbelt.

As soon as she buckled herself in, Pacen slammed on the brakes, flinging the vampire toward the front of the Escalade.

The vampire rolled onto the street; however, from the way he bolted back up on his feet, he looked as if he could do this sort of bat-and-mouse type of thing all day long and not break out in a sweat.

Once more, Pacen floored the vehicle; however, this time, he *embraced* the soon-to-be collision. In a split second, right before Pacen rammed the vampire, a strange smile crept onto the vampire's face.

On impact, the vampire's body suddenly exploded with blood!

Except for the bloody mess, the front of the grill didn't withstand much damage at all; in fact, she was ninety-nine point nine percent sure the vampire's flesh had somehow turned to putty. Not once did the SUV jolt or skid.

Which Talora found was incredibly odd, considering the massive dent he left in the windshield the first time he was struck by Pacen's SUV.

Attempting to wash the blood away from the windshield, Pacen switched on the windshield wipers; however, the dent in the shattered glass was preventing the wipers from properly working. He rolled down the window and poked his head outside for a better look at the street ahead.

"You good over there?" asked Pacen as he continued to drive well beyond the speed limit.

"Apart from some vamp that exploded all over your car," Talora said, trying to relieve the tension. "Yeah," she said shortly. "I'm fine."

"You're welcome," said Pacen.

Talora's mood deflated.

"Thank you," she said finally.

The fact that Talora was riding with Pacen created more unnecessary tension.

"What were you doing at St. Gabriel?" Talora asked over the break.

"I should ask you the same thing, Talora," Pacen returned, his tone bitter. "I could've told you that place was going to be crawling with parasites who'd suck anything with two legs."

"You just always have to turn everything on me, don't you?"

"*Whatever*," he snapped. "What were doing there?"

"I asked you first."

"What you mean?"

"I mean, what were you doing at St. Gabriel?" Talora asked again, her voice keen. "Were you stalking me?"

"I just saved your ass from a ruthless pack of vamps," he said, insulted. "I'd think you'd be a little more appreciative for what I did."

"I am," she said after a moment of pause. "Sorry. I'd just like to know what you were doing there. That's all."

"I know it's weird, Talora," Pacen said. "But trust me, if I wasn't there, then something worse would've happened."

"Worse?" she parroted. "As in what could be worse than getting jumped by a gang of vamps? Pacen, what are you not telling me?"

"It's Japhy," he said.

"Japhy? What the hell does he want?"

"*You*, apparently. I overheard him talking to a highborn. Maybe you don't know it, but you did something to him. And now, he wants you dead. The man's lost his fuckin' mind—"

"—Dead? You're serious?"

"Those animals back there were going to kidnap you, Talora," he said. "And we all know what happens when they get together in packs. So, again," his voice turned more bitter, "you're welcome."

Talora shook her head in disgust.

"I still don't get it, Pace," she said, raising her voice. "What in the hell did I do to that man?"

"I dunno, Talora," he said back. "You ask me."

"I don't know, Pace! You play with him. Surely, you two talk."

"Not anymore," Pacen said depressingly. "He's changed. To be honest, ever since I started hanging out with you, he hasn't been the same."

"What?" Talora argued. "Don't you dare put this on me, Pace. I wasn't the one who got all. . . ." Talora searched for the right word to use, a softer word that wouldn't offend Pacen. She could only find the one that had been on her mind for the past couple of days: "*Obsessed*," she said.

"Right," he said resentfully. "Obsessed. That's cruel, Talora."

"Whatever," she said with more attitude. "You, Pace, *you* even said so yourself that you weren't looking for a serious relationship when we first started seeing each other. What exactly did you expect? Why couldn't you just be content with the way our relationship was going? I mean," Talora said, shaking her head, "why would you want to take our relationship to the 'next level' when you and I both know there is—and was—no next level?"

Pacen removed a vape pen from his pocket and took a puff.

"Would you please roll down a window?" she asked, repulsed from the sight of the vape pen. "I don't want to be breathing in that garbage."

"It's mint flavored."

"Exactly."

"Whatever."

Silence built between the two.

Pacen took yet another puff before pocketing the vape pen.

"I quit the band for you," Pacen said finally.

"What?" Talora snapped. "Why?"

"So, we can see each other more," he listed. "So, we can be together—"

"—Did you ever stop and think that maybe I like just hooking up with you?"

"So, that's all I was to you, a fuckin' booty call?"

"Don't be so melodramatic," Talora said, her tone drawn out. "Correct me if I'm wrong, but aren't you musicians the ones banging groupies in every town you play at?"

"You really got the stereotype down pat, don't you?"

"Pacen," Talora said, as if she was saying her *final say*, "I'm not going to be responsible for ruining your career. That's on you, not me!"

"The band was falling apart to begin with," he said dismissively. "It's only a matter of time before we broke up."

"But isn't that what bands do? You breakup and then, you get back together. Then, you breakup yet again.

Then, you get back together for a reunion tour some thirty years later."

"You watch too much TV," Pacen said, trying to loosen up the conversation.

"Is that why Japhy wants me dead?" asked Talora.

"What do you mean?"

"*Us*," she said, pointing at Pacen. "For some reason, he's getting back at me because he thinks 'I' sabotaged the band?"

"Talora," Pacen said soberly, "I know this is the last thing you need on your mind right now, especially with what your family has already gone through, but I promise you nothing is going to happen to you."

For the first time during the drive, Talora flashed a smirk.

"You're going to protect me?"

Pacen reached over the center console and opened his palm.

"What other choice do you have?" asked Pacen.

Eventually, over some thought, Talora interlocked her hand with Pacen's.

✟

THEY headed north of midtown Manhattan toward East Harlem where, after long deliberation, decided to buy a room at a cheap, shady-looking hotel along the Harlem River in Sugar Hill. The hotel was called The Panorama Inn and was known for its picturesque view of Yankee Stadium at night. After Pacen was given a key to his room, he parked the damaged Escalade in an unlit parking lot behind what appeared to be an abandoned building.

"Are you *trying* to get us killed?" Talora said with sarcasm.

"This car sticks out like a sore thumb," he said. "The last thing we need to do right now is draw any attention. Remember what we're dealing with here?"

"Yeah," Talora said, as if the idea of *what* they were dealing with hurt her. "I know, right? It's crazy. I can't believe we're being hunted down by, of all things, vampires. You hear stories about other people, but you never expect it to happen to you." Talora pulled out her smartphone and scrolled through her Twitter feed. "Feels like I'm stuck in a nightmare. But," Talora said, snapping a selfie on herself, "it'd make for a cool story on social media, wouldn't it?"

Pacen grabbed Talora's arm and lowered it down by her side.

"Let's lay off social media crap for right now," he demanded. "We don't want to ring the dinner bell, do we?"

"Sorry," she said and switched off her smartphone. "You're right, I guess."

As soon as they stepped outside the Escalade, it started to downpour. Which, for Pacen, worked in his favor. "Beats taking the car to a car wash."

The rain washed off all the blood from vehicle, including the windshield, making the Escalade less conspicuous.

In a dim, flickering floodlight, Pacen couldn't help but watch the streaks of blood running down the side of the Escalade. The blood was not only thicker than any other blood that he had ever seen before, but it also appeared as if it was moving, not from the falling rain but actually moving on its own, as if, in a vampish sort of way, the blood was alive.

Curious, he followed the trail of blood to the concrete below and with a sense of inevitable doom, watched the blood mix with a stream of rainwater, which was flowing into the storm drain along the curb.

"What is it?" asked Talora, shielding her head with a jacket that she found in the backseat. "I'm getting soaked out here—"

"—Ah," Pacen stuttered, "*the blood*. It was. . . never mind. It's nothing."

Talora looked at Pacen funny.

Pacen nodded toward The Panorama Inn and together, they kept their bodies low and darted toward the overhang.

✝

AS the rain came down harder, the sides of the streets overflowed.

A stream of rain and blood poured down into a sewer below.

Out of the shadows of the corridor surfaced an emaciated rat that was looking for a drink of water. The rat came across a puddle of the rain-blood mixture along the edge of an overhang.

Drawn to its foul odor, the skittish rat licked from the puddle.

A couple of seconds passed before it reacted to the blood. Its body violently twitched. The muscles in its feeble body started to spasm. The convulsing was so great that its bones broke and shattered. The twitchy rat rolled over onto its side. Jagged bones protruded from its flesh and tangled hide.

As the violence roared in the harsh sounds of *snaps* and *pops* followed by the tearing of flesh, the rat grew into the size of a human; however, it still carried the traits of a rat, although each trait was more exaggerated. During its wicked metamorphosis, a pair of wings suddenly emerged from its back.

Once the rat transformed into its new body, it spread its fleshy wings outward and kneeled downward. The creature launched itself through the narrow opening, its body zipping like a bullet through the grate of the storm drain.

The creature flew away into the night sky.

✝

ONCE Talora was safe inside the hotel room, Pacen made sure to double-lock the door behind him. Even grabbed a chair and wedged it underneath the door handle as a precaution. Talora walked to the bed and examined the shiny floral patterned comforter. She was extremely skeptical about her skin touching the comforter—after all, it was the shine that gave it away. No fabric was that shiny.

With her head stirring with doubts, she grabbed the other chair from the table and sat down while Pacen fetched two bath towels from the hallway closet. Pacen handed a towel to Talora, who didn't waste any time drying her hair.

Out of curiosity, Pacen switched on the TV and flipped through news channels. He came across MTV where Karla Fouler was giving her daily BREAKING NEWS report. In the report, Fouler stated that "Japhy Warchild of Stuffed Animalz was ousted from the band, resulting in the official breakup of Stuffed Animalz. Their manager released a statement earlier tonight, which can be read online. In other news, Teesha Whitehouse was arrested and charged for public intoxication. Rapper, Mo Vega, was shot twice early this morning in what investigators are calling a drive-by and is currently recovering in Burlington Memorial."

"You weren't lying, huh?" Talora turned to Pacen. "If it makes you feel any better, he did need a new look—if you know what I mean."

Pacen switched off the TV and plumped himself on the edge of the bed.

"Not now, Talora," he said, slumped over. "Please. . ." He tried to take his mind off the "BREAKING NEWS" and inspect the shady room. "It's not much, but. . ." Pacen sighed, ". . . it'll make due, I guess."

"Till when?"

"Till we can figure out a plan—"

"—Plan?" Talora placed the damp towel in her lap. "Surely, there has to be someone out there who can help us."

"What? Like the cops?"

"Well," Talora said, thinking, "no. But somebody! What about that cousin of yours. . . Harland?"

"Harland's dealing with enough issues as I speak, and adding two people who are on the run from a gang of killer vamps to that list would be the death of him."

"Okay, so. . . " Talora said, her voice suspended in *dot, dot, dot.*

"So, we hang out here," Pacen said. "Wait it out till sunrise. I've heard they normally don't come out in sunlight. You know with their sensitive skin and all."

"But shouldn't we just keep moving?" She looked around the hotel room. "I feel like I'm just waiting for them to show up—"

"—We will."

"Will what?"

"Keep on moving," he explained. "We have to know where we're going. We can't just drive around. We need a place to go. And," he pointed out, "we can forget about going to the cops. They won't do shit."

"Maybe so, but we can try. Right?"

"It's pointless," he said more decisively. "For all we know, they're expecting us to go to the cops, which very well means that they'll already be influenced—or *lured* or whatever the hell those fuckin' vampnecks call it."

"That's bullshit, you know that right? They do come out in sunlight."

"You've seen them during the day?"

"All the time," she said. "Ever walked down 42nd Street? You can spot them a mile away. Feeding off the rats. Shunned by society."

"All I know is that they're more vulnerable in the sun," Pacen said, checking the clock. "And," he said, reading the time, "it looks like we have at least another six hours until daylight."

Despondent by the lack of options, Talora hung her head in misery. "I've always wondered what it'd be like to be one of them," she said, hanging her head, "to be treated differently. I feel bad for them. In a way, I envy them."

"Envied them? Why?"

Talora shrugged her shoulders.

"I dunno," she said. "Just seems like they've all been stereotyped into something they're not. You only hear about the bad ones, not the good. I mean, there has to be decent vampires out there, right? There has to be good vampires, maybe ones who can help us?"

"Good vampires?" Pacen shook his head the same way her dad would shake his head in disappointment when she was a little girl bringing home a bad grade from school or giving her little brother a bloody nose for acting out of line. "Do you hear yourself, Talora? What world are you living in?" Pacen asked, his nostrils flaring. "They're *savages*. When they find us, they'll kill us in order to survive. And why the whole change of heart? You hate them as much as I do."

"I never said that," she argued. "I hate what they've turned us into."

"Face it, Talora. They've exposed us."

"What makes you any different?"

"What do you mean?"

"How do you survive?"

Pacen didn't have a response for Talora.

"Exactly," she said.

"Talora," Pacen emphasized, "do you know what's going on here? Do you? 'Cuz I really think you don't. We—*you*—have been chosen. You have a price on your head!"

"But why?" Talora cried, waiting for a response from Pacen but only receiving the look of a shrink who was willing and ready to listen to Talora "unburden" herself. "What the hell did I do, Pacen? For once in my life, I finally feel like I could actually have fun again and not worry about all of the bullshit attached to a relationship that is being forced to turn into something that both you and I know it's not. I *liked* seeing you after one of your shows. I *liked* feeling as if I was part of something. I *liked* being. . . adored. I *liked* the way you use to look at me, as if you were carrying this wonderful light in your eyes.

Most importantly, I *liked* feeling like I didn't need *more* than I wanted." Once more, she dropped her head in misery. "I guess," she mumbled, as the words began to crumble in the back of her throat, "I dunno. I just—I just thought I met someone who was unselfish. But it turns out, you're just like the rest of them—"

"—You don't feel safe whenever you're around me?"

"I felt," she corrected, "I feel as if I'm being *watched* by you. Like I'm some sort of. . . I dunno, child who eventually started to wander off too far."

"If I ever made you feel uncomfortable, Talora, I'm sorry. Believe me, it was never my intention to push you away from me." He kneeled down in front of Talora, as if he was about to propose to her. He cupped her cold hands in her lap. "I am so sorry, Talora. After all of this is over, I promise you that I will leave you alone if that's what you want—"

"—And what do you want, Pacen?" she asked, sniffling.

"*You*," he said. "I want you."

"But you can't have me," she said.

"I know," he said. "And that's what makes being with you right now so hard, Talora—I'd do anything to win you back. Anything."

Talora wiped away the droplets of rainwater from the side of Pacen's cheek. Her hand slid upward and ran alongside his face until she reached his scalp. She brushed back the wet hair from his eyes. Pacen closed his eyes, savoring Talora's touch as if it was the last time he'd ever feel her again. As soon as Pacen cracked open his eyes, Talora was leaning forward to plant a kiss. Pacen immediately recoiled from Talora's advance, which had caught her by surprise.

"Don't," he said, fighting off that tingling urge to kiss Talora.

"What's a matter?" asked Talora. "Isn't this what you want?"

"No. . ." Pacen stuttered, ". . . I mean, yes. It is. I just—"

"—Just what?"

Pacen thought about all the rights words, yet once they reached the tip of his tongue, they felt like gibberish.

Talora couldn't withstand Pacen's sudden indecisiveness. She stood up from the bed and told Pacen that she was going to hop in the shower.

"Good idea," he said as if the change in subject was a necessary distraction to his epic failure. "To wash away your scent, right?"

"Excuse me," Talora said, her voice laced with frustration.

"They have your scent," he said, "which means you can easily be tracked."

Talora looked over Pacen as if he was speaking a different language.

"Right," she said, furrowing her brow.

Shaking her head from Pacen's strange behavior, she walked off.

Once Talora stepped inside the bathroom, she closed the door behind her but not all the way. She undressed and placed her waitress outfit on the top of the toilet and hoped in a steaming hot shower.

Pacen spent the next couple of minutes pacing around the hotel room, mentally condemning himself in a heated quarrel while, at the same time, going back and forth, back and forth, his good and bad angel replaying all of the lines that he should've or shouldn't have said to Talora. He couldn't take the internal anguish any longer, that seesaw effect of regret, inevitably the "bad" angel getting the best of him. Determined to prove himself worthy, Pacen marched to the bathroom and noticed the door was cracked open.

Which, for Pacen, was nothing more than a glaring invitation.

While washing her hair, Talora heard a *creak* outside the shower. She turned toward the noise and behind the beige shower curtain, witnessed a dark and lanky figure creeping toward her. She suddenly paused in suspense;

her heart pounding against her chest from the dark figure whose eerie presence still remained unannounced. . .

Pacen slid open the shower curtain; however, his face was the last part of his body that Talora's eyes had settled on. She took a step backward and made room for Pacen, who, in return, closed the shower curtain behind him.

✝

EIGHT out of the nine members of the Vampos gang made it back to the colony, which was currently residing underneath the Old Delaney Bridge over the Hudson River in a disease-ridden slum called Tent City. The bridge had been shut down for over six years, the cracked road above crawling with vines and an overgrowth of vegetation. Some New Yorkers—particularly those who had a fetish for being "owned," which was a common term used by vampires who leeched onto a host in order to bend a human against his or her will—were fully aware of the danger that surrounded Tent City. Most referred to it as a "breeding ground for bitters."

Inscribed along the concrete columns of the bridge were symbols of the Vampos gang: the dark silhouette of a stick figure-like vampire named Marius Ionescu with thirteen lines protruding outward. The symbol was a child-like depiction of Marius's final moments of sacrifice, the thirteen lines being swords. Each member of the gang had the same symbol along the side of their neck. Over the years, the symbol had been mistaken for a "glowing" man.

While Mihai and another vampire named Andrei fetched themselves, as well as the other vampires, a couple of "drinks" from the main living quarters in Tent City, Fane lead the other six vampires toward their nest, which used to be an old apartment complex; however, after the vampires took over Tent City, converting most of the homeless population, as well as the drug addicts, prostitutes, and bottom feeders into their own personal footstools, the apartment complex turned into a haven for the Vampos gang—"best view in the City," they'd say.

Half-drunk off a couple of ripe frat boys who were riding the haze of last call, five of the six members rode the rickety elevator to the top level of the complex.

As soon as the gang stepped out of the elevator and made their way through the deserted twelfth floor, they were forced into a state of high alert by the sound of shattering glass coming from behind a closed door at the end of the hallway.

They pinpointed the sound to their nest.

Not wasting anytime, the four vampires lead the charge, Fane closely following behind.

As the four vampires swung open the door and stormed into the nest—which could've passed as your typical "vamp cave" (walls covered in the most expensive entertainment system a vampire could steal, including a Playstation, a flat screen TV with surround sound speakers, posters of naked ladies, a billiards table on the other side of the room along with a dart board, a bronze life-sized statue of their messiah, Marius Ionescu, posed in His final moment of being ambushed by thirteen sea monsters, as well as a shrine, and not to mention, limbs, fingers, and random parts of human body scattered around the room like empty beer cans)—they burst out laughing from the sight of the sixth member, Marku, who was crawling his way through shards of broken glass.

He brushed glass from his shoulders and shook off his drunken daze.

"*Holy Marius!*" one of the vampires yelled out with great amusement. "What the hell happened to you, Marku?"

Marku eventually found his bearings and braced himself along the coffee table. Grimacing, he grabbed the side of his head and stood upright.

"Looks like someone missed his landing—"

"—Too much to drink, Marku?"

"Fuck you. . . " Marku said, flashing the bird.

"Cut it out!" Fane snapped. "The both of you!"

"Oh yeah, Marku. Learn how to fly."

"I said, 'Cut it out!'"

Immediately, the laughs tapered off.

The other vampires turned to Fane and froze in silence.

As the tension mounted, Mihai and Andrei returned to the nest with two junkies from Tent City. The vamp slaves were weak and badly emaciated, their forearms riddled with needle marks. Each one of them was swaying back and forth from the heavy drugs in their systems and if it wasn't for the two props alongside them, they'd fall over quicker than a vamp on tainted blood.

Mihai and Andrei walked the junkies into the room and sat them down on the couch where other vampires gathered around as if there were itching for a bite.

Mihai was first to point out the obvious, first the shattered window and then, the tense atmosphere.

✠

CAMPING inside an unmarked van parked outside the rundown apartment complex was a motley crew of four blood traders known as "The Four Horsemen," as well as Izzy Black, a writer who was tagging along with the Horsemen in order to gain firsthand knowledge on a daily life of a blood trader. Izzy Black was known for his over-the-top journalism and was considered by non-fiction aficionados as the Hunter S. Thompson of his time. With the exception that Izzy Black used different names for The Horsemen, all of the information he gathered was going in a book about the black market, which was tentatively called *Black Caps*. The point of the book—because for Izzy, there was always a point—was to bring more attention to the black market and how easily accessible the black market was to buyers and sellers, including the very same pharmaceutical companies who were taking advantage of those who relied on their so-called "drug."

Believe it or not, The Horsemen used to work "normal" jobs, as in cops, lawyers, drug peddlers who worked for big pharma, even doctors. Truth be told, each and every one had witnessed the dark side of corporate America before their very eyes, the shady "under-the-table" dealings: price gauging, pharmaceutical companies buying straight from black markets; selling counterfeit drugs or "knock offs." The real kicker: drugs that secretly contained VP-23, which was an ingredient genetically modified from white blood cells only found in vampires. Drug companies manufactured drugs containing VP-23 and purposefully marketed them to the expendable youth in stylish ads and trendy hashtags—for example, new cream to "make your skin glow," or even a "hot" new flavor of e-cig extracted from the tit of a thoroughbred that would increase virility and enhance sexual drive, or dried vampire blood known on the streets as "red snow," which was meant to give humans "more than human" abilities, depending on its user—even cures for melanoma and other cancers and ailments, or a broad range of improved impairments, such as better eyesight, all for financial or political gain.

But to get to all of that, of course, the vampire blood had to be extracted.

"No question," said The Pale Rider, also known as P.R, who was seated behind a row of monitors, "we enjoy the rush, but you think we want to do this kind of shit for the rest of our lives?"

"I suppose not," Izzy said.

Next to P.R. crouched Wizzle, who was paying close attention to the monitor of his high-tech camera—or better yet, the camera that he had stolen from MIT.

The super slow motion camera with five hundred sensors that triggered at one trillionth of a second and was able to track the movement of photons—the speed of light—which allowed Wizzle to see around corners of buildings or, in this case, walls. As Wizzle once stated, the applications for the camera were "endless" and could be applied to medical technology, in particularly allowing doctors to be able to see what exactly was going on inside a patient's body. You know, "Top Secret Stuff, Man," which happened to fall into the hands of a blood trader.

Expert hacker, Stuntman, was tapping into a signal from the tracking devices that Mayor Armitage had implanted inside illegal vampires.

"Thank you to the great mayor of New York City—"

"—Eight years of O'vampa will do that to you."

"Any activity?"

"They're just hanging out," P.R. said, checking the vampires hanging from the bottom of the bridge. "Get it! *Hangin'* out!"

"Yeah. Funny guy."

"And the Vampos?"

"I count ten of them altogether," Wizzle said, as he watched each one of the vampires' every movement on the monitor. "Each one is tagged, except for two. Their heat signatures suggest that the two are human. More than likely, groupies. Could be half-breeds, though. But I seriously doubt it." He turned away from the monitor for a second and nodded at Izzy, who was scribbling in a notepad. "Hey, Izzy Man, you know the difference between a full-breed and a half-breed?"

"You can't get turned by a half-breed?"

"No," Wizzle said. "They both suck."

Other Horsemen burst out laughing.

Eventually, Izzy mustered a laugh, which looked like an attempt at fitting in.

"A half-breed's blood is useless—that is, if you want to pick up diseases."

"I'm satisfied with eight," Wizzle said, as he redirected his attention toward the monitor. "Thoroughbreds, they are." He checked another monitor—an infrared. "Looks like they just ate. Their blood is *boiling* hot, I tell you."

"Hotter the better," Stuntman chimed in, as he was *typing* away on his keyboard.

"Is the team suited up?" asked Apache.

P.R. heard the two Morose Code-like *clicks* on the radio.

"Suited and in position. They're just waiting for the word."

P.R. knew exactly what Izzy was going to ask before he even asked it.

He leaned in close to Izzy and whispered in his ear, "Remember we're not the only one who's watching—"

"—Wait a sec," Wizzle said, checking a new strange reading. "I just picked up something on the monitor."

P.R. paused what he was doing, pulled out Kevlar neck and cuff from a crate, and handed them to Izzy, who, in return, placed the cuff around his neck, as well as both his wrists.

"They'll protect the vulnerable spots on your body. Think of it like a bulletproof vest against vamps. New age police gear that hadn't hit the market yet."

"Got a new reading," Wizzle shouted out, grabbing the other Horsemen's attention. "It's hard to read on the monitors. Whatever it is, it's fucking *big*. . . "

✝

MARKU plowed through the roof access door and stumbled his way to the edge of the roof where he proceeded to urinate or as he previously mentioned to his fellow Vampos, "drain his snake."

As he started to relieve himself, he couldn't help but look down at Tent City below and all the junkies and vagabonds and all that tainted meat loitering around drumfires like soon-to-be consumed livestock. He honed in on a slender man who was slouching over a shopping cart and sorting through garbage scraps while nibbling from a peach that he had pocketed from a fruit stand outside Hudson Market earlier that day. Thinking about how sweet his blood was going to taste later tonight, Marku's mouth salivated.

During midstream, Marku felt a sudden gust of wind followed by the *swooping* sound of a vampire directly behind him.

Assured that it was either Andrei or Mihai screwing with him, he shook away the leftover urine, zipped up, and casually spun around as if he was ready to tear a new hole—or holes—into the prankster.

"That's it! I've had enough with your games—"

As soon as Marku laid his eyes on the massive winged creature looming before him, he fell to silence. Other features fell, including his jaw.

He peered closer, recognized the eyes.

"Vasile?" said Marku with surprise. "Is that you?"

The winged creature stepped forward, part of its face revealed in the mounted light above the roof access door.

"It is," Marku said jovially. "Isn't it?"

Marku acknowledged its misshaped head and how it was stupidly tilting from side to side the same way a less evolved species would display "curiosity."

The gesture alone filled Marku with a primitive rage.

Razor sharp claws extended from the tips of his fingers.

Fangs exposed in a display of dominance.

"What the fuck are you?" said Marku, as he puffed out his chest and stepped closer to the winged creature. "You missed Halloween, muthafucka—"

Out of the dark shadows emerged Death-In-Waiting.

☨

STUFFED Animalz' electronic, gothic-heavy song, "Witch-Hop," an unreleased track which was recorded on a whim while on tour in a makeshift studio outside Atlanta prior to their recent breakup—or "hiatus," as the hardcore fans who were still living in denial called it—was cranking at full volume.

Despite the blaring music, Andrei was still able to hear the *thud* coming from the roof above. He stopped drinking from the junkie's neck and told Mihai to turn down the music.

"What?"

"You hear that?" asked Andrei.

"Hear what?"

As soon as Mihai lowered the volume on the stereo, the door swung open!

Looming at the doorway, the winged creature rolled a severed head into the room as if it was a bowling ball. The blood, veins, and julienne muscle along the base of the head, which conveyed the appearance of a head being pulled, *not cut*, clean off a neck, all whirled around like a vertical boomerang, leaving behind red splotches where it struck the floor. The head didn't roll smoothly, though. Yet, it unsteadily bounced more like a football along the floor until it finally came to rest next to a coffee table.

The junkie, who had two incisions dripping with blood on her neck, pulled herself from Andrei and inspected the round bloody object next to her. Once she realized what it was, she freaked.

The junkie's scream was contagious.

Not too long after, the other junkie screamed out in bloody horror.

Both the junkies fled across the other side of the nest. One ended up tripping a couple of times during her dazed scramble.

Andrei and the other vampires, who weren't as fazed, stood from their seated positions while Fane, as sound as a saint, remained seated on the couch; in fact, he barely reacted from the sight of Marku's head.

Fane nodded at the Rat-Bat-Man creature and asked calmly, "Do you mind?"

"You boys have unfinished biz'ness," the winged creature seethed, his voice like crushed gravel.

Fane immediately noticed the change in his voice; however, underneath all of the grit, phlegm, and anguish, it was *his* voice—

"Vasile?" Fane said, leaning forward. "Is that you underneath all that. . . " he fished for the right word to use. But then again, he wasn't in the business of caring about whether or not he hurt a vampire's feelings. He said, "Grotesquery?"

"Lupu? Really?"

"Yes," Fane said before the winged creature could respond. He appeared delighted to see Vasile. "It's him all right."

"But how?"

"He did what I like to call a lil' 'body swappin','" Fane said from the corner of his mouth, "I used to be able to do it back in the day. But it's been years since the last time I swapped. 'Least you could've chosen someone—*something*—more pleasing to the eye rather than a giant rat."

"It's more like a mutated bat," another vampire suggested.

"What are you fools doing sitting around here when we're still on the clock?" asked the winged Rat-Bat-Man creature formerly known as Vasile Lupu.

"Says who?" Fane said, sharpening his gaze.

"Says me," the winged creature said.

"As you can see, we've already clocked out—"

"—I know where the girl's hiding," the winged creature said to other Vampos before Fane could finish speaking the rest of his excuse.

"Then, why the fuck do you need us? You look like you can handle two meat sticks on your own."

"We haven't finished our end of the deal."

"Deal? Nah. The deal is off, Rat. Besides," Fane said, glancing around the room at the other Vampos, "we don't some high-born bitch giving us orders."

"That high-born bitch made me who I am today. If it weren't for that high-born bitch, then none of you would be here!"

"The money's not worth the time and effort."

"You've lost your vampness, Fane. . ."

Despite the diss, the other Vampos followed along with Fane—clearly, taking their side.

To seal the deal, they inched closer to Fane's side.

"It's official," Fane said, raising his arms. "I'm taking over as alpha."

"Is that so?"

"It appears that way, doesn't it boys?" Fane acknowledged each member of the gang, only to receive what was perceived as unconfident nods of agreement. "Face it: You've broken law, Vasile. A vamp *never* abandons his hunting party, even if that means catching a beat on his prey in order to make a kill."

Fane was speaking church, and the others were now his congregation.

Minus Marku, there were now seven members of the Vampos gang left in the nest—and that didn't include the freakish hybrid that was Vasile Lupu.

The Vampos gang waited in anticipation, all except Fane, who appeared as if he was accepting whatever challenge Vasile was inaudibly proposing. The Vampos didn't know at it—not at first—but they were about to be smack dab in the middle of a battle for dominance and that all-important alpha title, which, in every pack, was held in solidarity. The winged creature, Vasile, temporary alpha himself, was clearly in no mood to hand over his title to, of all vampires, Fane by the way the claws, which were twice the size as they were before, extended outward from his gnarly fingertips.

"In the name of Marius Ionescu, why don't you come over here and take back your title as Head Vamp?" Fane's eyes reddened, his fangs exposed. "As the lil' kiddies say, I double-dog dare—"

Before Fane even had a chance to finish the word *you*, in the blink of an eye the winged creature had already made the first move and was intimately standing over Fane with part of his esophagus gripped in his hand.

Stunned by Vasile's speed, Fane was left without any words; in fact, the only words that dripped from his lips were not words at all but the wet gurgle of defeat trapped inside tiny bubbles of blood.

As other Vampos backed away, the winged creature finished off Fane with a massive chomp to the gaping hole in his throat and slurped enough blood to temporarily whet his never-ending appetite.

"Who's alpha now?" the winged creature said wetly, as he turned to the other vampires.

"You?" said Andrei. "You are, whatever you are."

"I'm still Vasile, you fools."

"Yeah, but you look so. . . "

Vasile stepped in closer.

"So what, Andrei?"

"I was going to say 'different.'"

"Does my appearance frighten you, Andrei?" Vasile asked and stepped even closer, close enough to taste what was left of Fane.

Trembling from the winged creature's presence, Andrei nodded his head.

The blood spoke.

Fear had an uncanny way of stripping lies from a vampire, opposed to a man, who'd lie about anything or everything to save his own ass.

"Would you feel better if I were someone else?" asked Vasile.

Unsure of his response, Andrei shot a glance at the other vampires, who were secretly nodding their heads.

"Yes," he said, as if he had been holding it in.

"And are you speaking for the pack?"

Once more, Andrei glanced at the other vampires, who remained frozen.

"Yes," Andrei said confidently. "We'd feel more comfortable, if—"

"—Very well," Vasile said and turned to one of the junkies.

Andrei followed Vasile's eyes to one particular junkie, a blonde whose blood was like candy.

"How about someone else?" asked Andrei. "I can find you another human."

Vasile suddenly zoomed Andrei; and before he knew what exactly hit him, he was already rising from his feet. Vasile had his hand tightly wrapped around Andrei's neck and he was hoisting him in the air as if he was an action figure.

"You feel uncomfortable taking orders from a woman?"

"No," Andrei uttered, grimacing from the strong grip around his throat. "It's just. . . " the words tightened from the crushing of his larynx, ". . . she belongs to me. I own her."

"You've made her, huh? I'm impressed. And that would be against the rules for a vamp to steal another vamp's property?"

"Pre. . . cisely," hissed Andrei.

"And you will challenge me if I break the rules?"

Andrei's face changed from red to purple. Veins swelled in his forehead.

"No," he choked.

Vasile eventually released Andrei from his grip, which caused Andrei to fall to floor with a heavy thud. Then, he turned his sights on the blonde haired junkie across the room. As soon as she saw Vasile looking at her as if he wanted to eat her, she backpedaled to the bathroom.

"Please," she begged. "Don't do this!"

Vasile followed the junkie into the bathroom. He was polite enough to close the door behind him. A couple of Vampos struggled to listen to the horror inside the bathroom, the screaming, the tearing, and then the sound of splashing.

A dark blood puddle formed underneath the doorway and as soon as the door opened, the blonde haired junkie whore exited the bathroom.

But she was not the blonde haired junkie whore.

At least not on the inside.

One Vampos questioned: "Vasile?"

"In the flesh," the junkie formerly—and presently— known as Vasile said.

As the Vampos stepped outside, Vasile immediately picked up a familiar smell in the air. He scanned the night sky.

Then, pinpointed the smell coming from the street.

"Keep your eyes peeled, boys," Vasile said. "We have company."

"Yes, sir," Andrei said. "I mean, ma'am."

✠

WIZZLE tracked the Vampos leaving Tent City.

P.R. returned to coms.

"We're moving," he said. "Keep your distance."

"Roger that."

✠

THE rainstorm eventually passed.

Dark clouds parted in the night sky.

A sword of moonlight cut across Pacen's face while he nakedly sat in a chair next to the air conditioner and kept a close eye on any activity outside through the slit of the curtain. Occasionally, he flashed quick glances toward Talora, who was sleeping soundlessly in bed. A few rooms down, he could hear a loud couple arguing outside. He couldn't hear exactly what they were arguing about, but whatever it was, it drew enough passion to wake a few nearby guests. Pacen heard another noise, much closer. He listened to bed sheets rustling. He tracked the sound to the stirring in the bed followed by the subtle *squeaks* and *pops* of a loose, faulty bedspring. Talora's shadowy face emerged from the pillow and revealed itself in the hazy moonlit darkness.

"*Hey*, Night Owl," Talora whispered sharply, "Come back to bed, will you?"

"It's going to be daylight soon," he said.

"Even more the reason to sleep," Talora groaned.

He gave one last survey outside the window and saw that it was safe for him to return to bed—at least, for the time being. In his return, he didn't bother to put on any clothes. Yet, he walked as naked as the day he was born back to bed and slipped under the covers, pressing his warm flesh against Talora's.

"I'm just curious," Pacen started, as if he had rehearsed the lines, "What were you doing at St. Gabriel tonight?"

"Ah," Talora said, her voice sleepy, "making money. What do you think?"

"I thought you gave up waitressing."

"I did," she said. "But I needed the money."

"If you needed the money, I could've given it to you."

Talora lifted herself upward onto her elbows as if his question—or inevitable grilling—had disturbed her to the point where the only resolve was a gesture of good night.

"I'm sure you would," she said with a hint of sarcasm in her voice.

She leaned forward and planted a kiss on Pacen's cheek and then dropped her head back into the cooler side of the pillow.

"I would," Pacen drawled.

"Try to get some rest, will you?" she said, her voice muffled.

"But," Pacen said, brooding, "I just don't get it."

"Get what, Pacen?"

The frustration slightly rose in her voice.

"Why drive all the way into The City to work a crap job with very little pay?" Pacen asked, but he didn't receive a quick enough answer from Talora. "It sounds strange, that's all."

"What are you getting at, Pacen?" asked Talora, as she sat upright against the headboard.

"I just feel like you're not being completely honest with me," he said timidly. "Like you're. . . hiding something."

"What are you saying?"

Talora leaned over Pacen and switched on the lamp on the nightstand.

She let out a groan.

"What exactly would I be hiding, Pacen?"

"I dunno," he said, as he folded the pillows behind his back and used them as a backrest. "Is there someone else?"

"Even if there was someone else—which, trust me, there isn't—it's none of your business, Pacen. Remember," she said, her tone stricter, "*technically*, we're broken up. Which means I can see whoever I want to."

"You're right," he said morosely, as he looked her over. "You should. Honestly, I'd be shocked if you weren't. Any man would be grateful to find himself in the presence of a gorgeous woman such as yourself."

"Stop, Pacen," Talora said, pushing away the flattering.

He continued, "I can only imagine what it'd be like to live your life and having to constantly shoo away men, who only saw you on the outside but never had the privilege of knowing the even more gorgeous woman on the inside. And that, in a way, makes me feel lucky." Pacen struggled to look Talora in the eyes. And even when his eyes managed to cross her path, tears formed in his eyes. "Even as I lie next to you at this moment, it makes feel as if I can die and you know what? I wouldn't be bothered by it because I feel nothing but content for having shared a part of my life with a person like you—if only for a moment because, to me, this moment, as well as the moments I shared with you will last a lifetime."

Talora didn't have any words for Pacen; in fact, she had nothing at all but the sting of guilt: *Guilt* that she had left him hanging out to dry in a breakup that was far from mutual; *Guilt* that he had felt so strongly about her, whereas she always felt as if she was living moment-to-moment with Pacen; and especially, *Guilt* that she had just slept with him.

"Excuse me," she said, her face slackened, "I have to use the restroom."

"Yeah," Pacen said. "Sure. Go."

Talora rolled out of bed.

As she opened the bathroom door, Pacen called her back in the room.

"I didn't mean to lay all that on you all at once," he said.

"No," she said, cracking a smile. "Don't be. I thought it was sweet of you."

"You're scared, I can tell."

"I'm not scared of you, Pacen," Talora said. "I'm scared of the vampires out to kill us."

Talora closed the door behind her and as she was relieving herself, she came across a small glass vial containing a red powdery substance inside the left breast pocket of the navy blue flannel shirt that she had borrowed from Pacen. Immediately, she was intrigued by the red substance. She had heard about that substance on the news, through social media. There had been a wave of reports on the news about teenagers—particularly high school students—winding up in hospitals after snorting dried vampire's blood. Apparently, curious students had gotten the idea from vampires, who were known to carry around vials of dried human blood. She heard somewhere that the vampires called it their "cocaine."

Except for more radical states—none of which involved New York—most of the states in the US, had declared the distribution of vampire blood or consuming vampire blood illegal and was punishable by prosecution. It was only fair that she questioned the man who was sleeping next to her as to why exactly he was carrying around a vial of blood, human or vampire. After all, she had explored Pacen's body—more than likely, knew every inch of his body better than he knew himself—and was aware that he didn't have any bite marks on him. The blood wasn't human. That, she knew.

She placed the vial back inside the breast pocket and after some deliberation, figured it was best to save the argument for later.

As soon as she stepped out of the bathroom, Pacen was racing from the window. He threw on his underwear and then grabbed his pants, which he had tossed across the room onto the TV set. He threw them on next. Then scrambled to find his white shirt underneath, which was lying underneath the bed.

"Pacen, what's the matter?" asked Talora.

Pacen snapped his head toward Talora and immediately placed his index finger against his mouth as if he was indicating for her to be quiet.

She mouthed, *What is it?*

Pacen pointed outside.

Talora listened closer to the footsteps outside the hotel room. She tiptoed to the window and witnessed the shadows moving along the balcony outside.

"What do we do?" she whispered to Pacen.

Every second counted, and Pacen made sure not to waste one second.

He raced toward the bathroom, grabbed the single-serving bottles of shampoo and soap, then hurried back to the hotel door. He squirted the remainder of shampoo from the bottle onto the doorway. He did the same with the lavender soap.

"To cover up the scent," he reminded Talora, who was ready to ask the obvious question.

Pacen scanned the room, his eyes landing on each piece of furniture (the bed, the nightstand, the table, the chairs, the dresser, the TV), as well as each piece of item (the clothes hangers in the closet, the iron board, the iron, the ice bucket, the towels, the basket of goodies on the vanity). He knew he couldn't MacGyver his way out of the hotel room. But he knew if he could make it outside without being spotted, then maybe he had a chance to create a distraction.

His eyes scanned the room once more. His eyes landed on light. He pointed at the lamp on the nightstand.

"Cut the lights," he whispered.

Talora did as Pacen demanded and switched off the lamp.

Together, the two rushed to the bathroom and closed the door behind them.

"What's the plan?" asked Talora.

Pacen remained quiet on the outside; however on the inside his thoughts were deafening.

"The rain from earlier should also help mask our smell, but it's only a matter of time before they track us down."

"Why don't we wait till the sun rises?" Talora suggested.

Pacen shook away the suggestion.

"They'll find us before then," he said. "We need wheels. If I can make it to the car, we'll have a chance."

"Okay," Talora said. "Then, we make a run for it."

"No. They'll be on us in no time."

"Then what?"

Pacen became quiet again.

"Pacen?!?"

Talora tugged on Pacen's arm.

"Distraction," he said, thinking out loud. "We need a distraction."

"Okay, what?"

Pacen slipped from the bathroom and searched through the basket of toiletries on the vanity. He came across a bottle of perfume—which, he knew, was highly flammable. *It could work*, he thought. *Just in case his first option failed. Always have a backup, a Plan B.*

Next, he grabbed a hand towel, as well as a pack of matches from the countertop.

Then, a clothes hanger from the closet.

Lastly, an orange cardboard *Panorama Inn* coaster from the table.

"What's the perfume for?" asked Talora. "Don't tell me," he corrected. "To cover up your scent."

"Well, yes and no," he said. "I need it for backup just in case I can't find any gasoline."

"*Gasoline?*" Talora said. "Why the hell do you need gasoline?"

Pacen replied, "Distraction, remember. I'm going to make a distraction. . . " he pulled the car keys from his pocket and handed them to Talora, ". . . and once you're given the cue, you're going to run as fast as you can to the car."

"And what exactly is my cue?" asked Talora.

Despite the growing tension, Pacen strangely flashed a smile on his face.

Which, for a moment, had brought comfort to Talora.

"You'll know when you hear it," he said to her.

"How do you know this plan of yours is going to work?"

"Because I saw it once in a movie."

"So you're basing this plan off something you saw in a movie?"

"Got any other suggestions?" asked Pacen.

Except for her plan to wait for sunrise, Talora had nothing.

"This is gonna work, Talora," Pacen said, cupping Talora's face. "You have to trust me. Okay?"

Maintaining her composure, Talora nodded her head in agreement.

Without wasting any more time, Pacen walked to the window and peeked outside. He counted two members of the Vampos gang three rooms down. Both of them were walking in the other direction.

"Now," he said, waving Talora to the door, "now's our chance."

Through the crack of the curtain, he showed Talora the staircase, which was about ten or so feet away from their room; however, to Talora, ten feet hadn't felt so much longer.

"Take the stairs," he whispered, "and remember to stay as low as possible."

"Where are you going?" asked Talora.

"I'm going to be right behind you," he whispered.

Talora reached for the door handle.

Pacen grabbed her by the arm.

"As soon as we reached the parking lot," he emphasized, "I want you to take cover next to the ice machine."

"Ice machine? I don't remember seeing any ice machine."

"It was to the right of the vending machines."

Talora widened her eyes and waited for more explanation.

"Forget about it," he whispered. "I'll take the lead. Just follow me, okay?"

"Okay," she responded.

Pacen took one last peek outside before opening the door. He stepped aside, allowing Talora to exit first. He carefully closed the door behind him and spotted the two Vampos with their backs turned to them.

Staying "low," as he instructed, they both scurried to the staircase.

Sure enough, there was another gang member standing lookout at the base of the stairs. Lucky for Pacen and Talora, his back was turned.

Pacen pointed to an opening along the second floor.

Talora tiptoed up the stairs while Pacen followed closely behind her.

"What now?" she whispered.

"Plan B," he whispered.

Frustrated and, at the same time, furious with Pacen's half thought-out plan, she flexed her hands as if she was tempted to strangle Pacen.

"Follow me," he said and scurried in the opposite direction of the two members of the Vampos gang.

Eventually, they made it to another staircase on the other side of the hotel.

From where he was standing, he had a clear view of the Escalade, which was parked across a back road; however, he spotted two more of those Vampos wandering around the sidewalk outside the hotel. In fact, they happened to be directly in their path. Next to the hotel was a fence that could've been scaled. *But* it was way too risky. They'd easily be spotted.

Back to the original plan, Pacen searched for an area that would allow Talora to hide while he carried out his so-called distraction. He caught the red glow of a vending machine in the corner of his eye. He followed the glow to a recess in the wall. Inside were the vending and ice machine.

"There," he said to Talora and pointed to the ice machine. "Remember, once you hear the cue—"

"—I know, run like hell."

"Now, go. . . "

Talora hurried to the noisy recess and took cover behind the ice machine.

While Talora was hiding, Pacen kept low and snuck into the parking lot in the front of the hotel. He looked for the oldest vehicle. He didn't exactly know why he was looking for an older model. He figured the older, the better, and the more likely they were at igniting.

In his frantic search, he happened to find a camel brown 1979 Pontiac Grand Prix in the parking lot.

Not too far away, three members of the Vampos gang were standing guard at the edge of the parking lot as if they were making sure nobody came in or out.

One of the gang members was distracted by another member who was showing him a mirror selfie of a single vamptress on his smartphone.

Pacen ceased the opportunity and dashed toward the Grand Prix. He made it to the rear of the car without being spotted. He set the clothes hanger aside, then pulled out what he needed from his pockets, including the hand towel first, then the coaster, the perfume—just in case—and last but not least, the pack of matches. He uncoiled the clothes hanger and used the end to pry open the lid. Once opened, he untwisted the cap. He ripped off a small piece of the hand towel and wrapped it around the end of the clothes hanger.

Carefully, he dipped the end of the clothes hanger into the gas tank and then, once the cloth reached the bottom of the gas tank, he removed the clothes hanger. Based off the smell of gas fumes, as well as the dampness of the cloth, the hand towel was most definitely drenched with gasoline; in fact, when he gave the towel a squeeze, gasoline dripped over the side of the vehicle, as well as the ground below.

Next, he placed the cardboard coaster around the circular opening the tank.

His confidence started to deteriorate.

"What the heck?"

He decided to dump the entire bottle of perfume on the hand towel. The perfume messily splashed on the side of the car, as well as all over the ground.

Pinching the dry end of the gasoline-perfume soaked hand towel, he struck a match with his dry hand and all in one motion, set the hand towel on fire and then placed it against the cardboard coaster.

As he took off running and sought cover behind the rear tire of another car in the parking lot, he didn't realize at the time but, somehow, part of his foot kicked his vape pen that must've fallen out of his pocket while he was removing each of the components he needed to make the fire—the matches, the hand towel, the perfume. The spinning vape pen slid farther underneath the car.

The subtle noises Pacen had made during his escape, such as the metallic *pop* of opening the gas tank or the sole of his shoes scraping along asphalt, caught the attention of the closest vampire. The member of the Vampos gang signaled to the other member to keep watch while he checked out the noises.

The fire suddenly spread along the side of the car and somehow managed to spread to the ground below.

As the fire licked across the pavement, the vape pen came to rest directly below the gas tank. The vape pen ended up catching fire as well.

The member of the Vampos gang spotted a tiny flame burning along the side of the Grand Prix.

With his sense jacked to kill mode, he hurried over to the Grand Prix while, at the end of the parking lot, Pacen nervously watched from underneath a parked car.

Work damn it, Pacen repeated to himself while staring hard at the weakening flame.

After a couple of tense moments, he realized the plan wasn't going to work.

"Fuck the movies," he said to himself.

Curious of the fire, the vampire pressed his clawed hand against the bumper and kneeled down on the ground.

He immediately noticed the vape pen bathing in a mellowing flame.

As he reached for the vape pen, it suddenly exploded in his face. Tiny pieces of shrapnel buried into the side of his burnt face. He fell backward. Both his eyes fell upon the damage underneath the car. He smelled gasoline. And the vape pen was still burning. . .

Before the vampire could run to safety, the Pontiac Grand Prix suddenly exploded into flames!

A massive ball of hell shot up into the night sky, causing hotel guests to poke their heads out of their doors or windows; however, the guests were immediately forced back into their rooms from the sights of Vampos.

"My cue," Talora uttered while bracing herself against the ice machine from the quake of explosion.

Shocked by the intensity of the explosion, Pacen said, "I meant to do that."

While other members of the Vampos raced toward the raging fire in the parking lot, Pacen found his opportunity to escape. He cut through the north wing of the hotel and as soon as he could smell freedom, a young, once-attractive, blonde haired, fair-skinned woman stepped in front of his path.

Pacen recognized that same grin he thought he witnessed before he ran over a vampire who went by the name Vasile Lupu.

"Going somewhere," said Vasile.

"You?"

"Yes," said Vasile. "Me."

Vasile hissed, revealing the sharp fangs in her mouth.

Halfway toward the SUV, Talora heard Pacen screaming from a distance.

She had no other choice than turn around and run back to the hotel. She crept along a fence and found cover behind a dumpster while two other members of the Vampos gang patrolled the area. Once they were gone, Talora walked around the back of the hotel.

She heard—or, at least, thought she heard—the sound of a man struggling.

Remaining stealth-like in her pursuit, she tracked down the choppy, gurgling sounds to a man lying in a puddle of blood in a hallway. As she kept cover behind the corner of the hallway, she took a couple of glances at the man and determined after a third glance that the man was, in fact, Pacen.

And if, somehow, he survived his injuries—primarily, the deep punctures in the shape of a bite mark around his neck—it was only a matter of time before he changed. And the man whom she once knew as Pacen would no longer be Pacen but a dark copy of Pacen. Either way, he was already gone. Dead or alive.

She raced toward Pacen and tried to stop the bleeding around his neck with a towel that she found on a tray of spoiled food resting outside a hotel room.

"Stay with me, Pacen," Talora said, as Pacen's eyes rolled around in the back of his head.

Pacen tried to speak but his words were choked with blood.

While Talora continued to apply more pressure to the bite marks, dark figures surrounded her. She looked up and witnessed four members of the Vampos gang, including Vasile, approaching her. She didn't hear but more so felt them behind her. She turned her shoulder and fell witness to four more members closing in on her, each and every one of them carrying a queer hunger in their eyes; however, it wasn't a hunger—or even a thirst—to satisfy or quench or, in essence, to maintain survival. Yet, the look held the weight of something much more, the bottomless hunger to breed, a sick sort of "welcoming" to her soon-to-be family.

"Stay back!" she screamed at them.

The Vampos continued to close in.

"I said, 'Stay back!'"

Vasile held out her arms the same way a negotiator would approach a homicidal maniac.

"Relax now, Talora," he said calmly. "This can go two ways: Quick and painless or slow and painful. You have a choice, Talora—"

"—How do you know my name?" asked Talora.

"We know a lot about you, Talora," Vasile said, approaching. "We know where you live, where you work, and where you go to have fun. We know what you like to eat and whom you like to eat with," he listed. "We know all of your likes and all of your dislikes. We even know whom you like to fuck," Vasile said snappishly and glanced at Pacen, who was bleeding out. Then, he corrected himself, "Excuse me, *liked* to fuck. Liked, as in past tense. A part of me, that 'hopeful' part of me, was rooting for you two to get back together—"

"—Stay back!" Talora cried out, as Pacen spat out strings of blood from the corners of his mouth.

"But then again," Vasile said, closing in on Talora, "over these past few years I have realized that *hope* rhymes with *nope*."

The other Vampos burst out laughing.

Their laughs were suddenly cut short from the booming voice of a police officer announcing his presence with authority, "Police! Freeze!"

Talora located the voice coming from a police officer with his gun drawn.

Surrounding the officer were at least a dozen other officers and agents, some of them dressed in uniform while others—the rougher, shadier types—dressed in a more casual getup with the letters ICE across the bulletproof vests. Some of the agents were wearing special neck and arm cuffs, as well.

Despite being boxed in, the Vampos prepared for an offensive attack.

With his itchy fangs, Vasile leaped at one of the ICE agents; however, Vasile was immediately shot by a relatively new lasso gun nicknamed The Snake, which discharged an eight-foot Kevlar ® tether around Vasile's torso area, forcing both his arms to his sides. Another agent shot yet another Kevlar ® tether at the lower half of his body. Now, with both of his legs, as well as arms wrapped up like gift-wrap, Vasile stepped forward but ended up falling to the ground.

Even though the Vampos backed off after witnessing one of their own—most importantly, their Head Vamp, their "alpha"—being lassoed to the ground with a Kevlar ® tether as if he was a stray calf, except for the two members of the gang, Andrei and Mihai, Andrei dodging the Kevlar ® tether, then the second, Mihai, being side-swiped by a faulty discharged, the ICE agents used The Snake lasso gun on the remaining Vampos.

Andrei and Mihai slipped past the ICE agents and darted by a group of police officers, who looked more like background props in a movie opposed to a singular body of justice.

An ICE agent drew The Snake on Talora, who, in return, raised both her arms in surrender.

"Human," she declared, her voice trembling.

She couldn't help but turn her eyes to Pacen, who was already dead, and then toward the vampires, who were wiggling around on the ground like worms after a rainstorm.

"Come with us, ma'am," one of the ICE agents instructed Talora to an ambulance, which was parked outside the hotel.

Talora refused to leave Pacen; however, as soon as the ICE agent gave Talora his word that he'd take care of him and then ordered a medic to the scene via his radio, she walked away with another, much younger ICE agent who looked nothing like someone who worked for the ICE organization; in fact, the ICE agent was P.R., the same blood trader who had been tracking the Vampos all night.

Somehow—maybe it was *his mannerisms* that gave it away or the fact that he was awfully fidgety to be working for an organization that demanded precision as well as a steady hand—a part of Talora had a suspicion that the ICE agent wasn't who he claimed he was; in fact, the whole scene felt like a production.

Left in a state of defeat from the latest Vampos encounter, Talora decided to voice what was really on her mind: "You don't look like a cop."

"That's because I'm not a cop," he said robotically, as if he was reading lines from a script. "I work with ICE."

P.R. walked Talora to the ambulance where two other paramedics—Stuntman and Wizzle—were both waiting to tend to any injuries that she might have on her body.

They passed several guests, who were slowly emerging from their rooms and asking questions like "What's going on here?" or "Who died?" or the most important one, "Where the hell is the fire department to put out the damn car fire?" The guests were greeted by a group of police officers, who escorted each guest away from the crime scene and tried to maintain order before the guests stereotypically waddled back into their hotel rooms, brandished the phones, hit the "record" button, and filmed the strange activity from the cozy confines of their dark rooms.

"My name is Agent Rackley," he said, steering Talora's attention away from the police officers.

As before with the ICE agents, Talora knew a thing or two about police protocol after having been around them for so long, both in reality, as well as the fictional world where they were portrayed as either good or bad, a hero or a villain, nevertheless, a clichéd image of a cop that had been worn down like a nub—even worse, having to watch them firsthand in action, either watching them at search parties or even walking around her house, inspecting for clues. She had picked up a sense of who they were and how they acted, how they talked, how they formally conducted themselves. And "these police officers" were much different, dare she say, just as stinky as the ICE agents.

Talora waited for a following up but received nothing. She decided to let her silence bring out his true identity. Talora watched him carefully. He struggled to look her in the eye. Liars never looked a person straight in the eye. Or, someone who had something to hide. . .

"Aren't you going to ask me my name?" asked Talora.

"Of course," he said. "What's your name, miss?"

He is so bad at this, she thought.

Either that, or he was simply a man who turned all mushy whenever he found himself in the company of a woman.

"Talora Katz," she said, eyeing the ICE agent through the corner of her eye.

P.R.'s jaw slackened, his face expressionless.

"By any chance," he said, more thoughtfully, "you're not related to that missing boy, Nathan Katz, are you?"

Of course, she thought. *He* knew the story. Anybody who hadn't been living under a rock for the past year *knows the story.*

"Nathan Katz is my brother," Talora said hesitantly.

"You mean, was?"

"No," she corrected. "He *is* my brother."

"Right."

Despite P.R.'s poor attempt to strike up a conversation with Talora, P.R. regained his confidence and walked Talora to the back of an ambulance, which was parked along the street in the front of the hotel.

Once Talora arrived at the back of the ambulance, she questioned the speediness of the paramedics' arrival. The only reason that she could find through all of tangled wires of thoughts was that someone, possibly a guest or even employee of The Panorama Inn had called 911 and asked the dispatcher to send an ambulance. What other reason would there be an ambulance at an ICE raid? One of the paramedics—Stuntman—was acting extremely coy and for a moment, she thought she saw him holding a syringe behind his back.

"Don't firefighters usually show up before the paramedics?" asked Talora, as the word *fire* in the word *fire-fighters* forced Talora toward the out-of-control fire that Pacen had started. "Isn't that why they're called first responders? I've never heard of firefighters being *last* responders. What is it that you're not telling me?"

"I can assure you they're on the way, miss."

P.R. paid more attention to Talora, who was displaying all the symptoms of a soon-to-be "problem," including Talora's keen observation of the crime scene and the abundance of strategic inquiries meant to provoke contradictory responses.

With his patience running thin, P.R. placed his hand along Talora's back and nudged her toward the back of the ambulance where the two paramedics were eagerly waiting for her. Talora took the innocent nudge as a push. He was pushing her to the ambulance!

"Excuse me," she snapped. "Get your hands off me!"

P.R. held up his hands as if he didn't want to start a fight.

"They just need to check you for any bite marks," he said.

"But I wasn't bit," Talora argued and pulled down her collar and showed him her bare neck.

"It's just for precaution, Ms. Katz."

P.R. made sure to say her last name with clarity for the other boys.

Wizzle heard that name, *Katz*, and shared a similar reaction to P.R. when he heard the name.

Talora acknowledged the change in expression. Somehow, she knew that they knew that she wouldn't talk. What made Talora so sure? It wasn't what she said. It was what she didn't. It was in her face, her body, even in the way she walked. Most importantly, it was in her eyes. *The eyes never lied.* The eyes never lied.

And Wizzle was reading them like a book.

"Please. . ." P.R. insisted, ". . . it'll only take a minute—"

Wizzle interrupted, "—It's fine. If the woman says that she wasn't bit, then she wasn't bit." He turned his attention to Stuntman and subtly shook his head as if he was giving him a cue to stand-down.

"Are you sure?" P.R. asked Wizzle.

"Positive," he said expressionlessly. "She can go."

"What about Pacen?"

"And who is Pacen?"

"He's the guy back there. He was—he's my boyfriend."

"Right. . ."

Before P.R. could further respond, Wizzle and Stunt-man pulled out a gurney from the back of the ambulance and set it on the street. Wizzle assured her that he'd take care of Pacen. Then he and Stuntman wheeled away the gurney and left P.R. alone with Talora, as if she was now his wad of bubblegum to scrape off the bottom of his shoe.

In the awkward silence, Talora's eyes landed on the ICE agent's badge.

The name read: "FERNANDEZ."

It was uncommon for someone who clearly didn't look at all South American to have a South American name. There was a certain irrelevancy about matching a man's name to his looks; however, Talora couldn't help but real-ize the ethnicity of the man. He was as white as Vanilla Ice.

Talora read his name aloud.

"Fernandez, huh?"

From a distance, she heard the sound of sirens.

P.R. pointed to the sound as if the sound itself was a tangible thing in the air.

"You hear?" he said. "They're on the way. Just as I said."

"Well, maybe you guys can ask the firefighters to give me a lift back home," she lied.

"That's not necessary," he said, as he started to walk away from Talora.

To Talora, it was obvious he was trying to distance himself from her.

Walking away from Talora, he said to her, "You're free to leave."

Talora didn't budge.

Which caused P.R. to pause in his tracks.

"Little advice," he said, more grimly, "If I was you, I'd keep my head down and lay low for a few weeks. Eventu-ally, they'll move onto someone else."

"What makes you so sure they'll stop?" asked Talora.

"Because three years ago I was in the same position you're in. And you want to know how I survived?"

"How?"

"I ran," he said bluntly. "And I never looked back."

"Did you have any family?"

"I did," he said, as the sirens grew louder. "But I had no other choice than to leave them behind, otherwise they would've used them to get to me. Do yourself a favor: *Leave* town while you still have a chance."

"And go where?"

"Anywhere but here."

P.R. walked off.

Then, once more, paused and turned around.

"Think of it as a vacation from your everyday life." He shrugged his shoulders. "Who knows? It could be fun."

After P.R. joined the other ICE agents, Talora walked around the fence along the side of the hotel and checked on Pacen. The members of the Vampos were all gone. Not *one* of them remained. Two coroners were carrying away which she assumed was Pacen's body in the black bag. And all that remained was a puddle of Pacen's blood on the ground. Which, to say the least, was strange. She wondered where the detectives were. She had watched plenty of cop shows in her day to know that they never carried away a body before the detectives arrived or—at least—they'd taken photographs of the body. There was not a damn thing, no protocol, no "What do we have here, Mr. Detective?" It was like they were trying to clean up a crime scene and make it look as if it never happened in the first place.

With the ICE agent's advice at the front of her mind, she rushed to the SUV.

As soon as she arrived at the SUV, a strange feeling came over her. She got inside. Inserted the key into the ignition. Then, she turned the key. Nothing.

Talora reached down below the steering wheel to pop the hood of the car, but the hood was already cracked open.

She stepped outside and opened the hood, only to find a missing battery.

It had been completely ripped out.

"Fucking great," she seethed and slammed the hood.

Left with no other choice than to ride the subway back to her car, which was parked St. Gabriel Hotel, she grabbed a bottle of water and a jacket from the back of Pacen's Escalade and started walking.

As Talora was walking past the front of the hotel, she saw that the ambulance was no longer parked on the street; in fact, she couldn't find the ambulance or the squad cars anywhere on site.

Two fire trucks finally arrived at The Panorama Inn and didn't waste any time extinguishing the car fire.

Which made Talora question what exactly she had just witnessed.

Who the fuck were those people?

Good guys?

Or, bad guys?

THE thought of having two other vampires out there, still hungry, still on her tail, still ready to strike at any moment, left Talora in a more paranoid state while she was riding the subway back to Manhattan. She made sure to stay extra close to the other riders, maybe too close to their so-called "safe space."

When she arrived at her stop, she heard that distinguishable *swooping* noise coming from the train tunnel. A familiar noise of both warning and dread that she had been hearing throughout the entire night. She made sure to quicken her pace.

They're close.

Eventually, she made it to the street unscathed.

TALORA was right about the noise.

Once the train had taken off, Andrei and Mihai emerged from the shadows of the tunnel. As they were about to make their way to the platform and follow Talora to the street, a shadowy man stopped them from behind.

Japhy stepped forward, partially revealing himself to the two members of the Vampos gang.

Andrei instantly locked eyes on the coat Japhy was sporting; and somehow, he could look beyond its gleam and glitter and recognize its "old country" vibe.

"Where'd you get that fancy coat?" asked Andrei.

"Forget about it," Mihai said to Andrei. "We have other more important issues to deal with—"

"—He's not vamp."

Mihai eyed Japhy.

"He's not human, either." He tapped Andrei on the shoulder. "Let's go."

Andrei couldn't take his eyes off the coat. Mihai ordered his fellow Vampos to follow him out of the tunnel and eventually, after more convincing, Andrei did.

Not only that, another train was approaching.

"Hold up," Japhy said to the two vampires, "you must roll with the Vampos."

Andrei and Mihai stopped.

"We are Vampos," Andrei said like a boss, as he puffed out his chest. "Can't you see the tats, fool?"

"Yeah," Japhy said, stepping farther into the light. "I see your tats."

"Who da fuck are you?"

Mihai immediately recognized Japhy's face from TV.

"He's that fool from that band—"

"—Yeah," Japhy said with a strange look in his eye. "That fool."

As the train sped by, Japhy suddenly leaped at Andrei and Mihai.

Before they knew what hit them, they were already dead. In the flicker of the lights, their blood was painted all over the tunnel walls as if Japhy was creating his own masterpiece.

☦

TALORA made it back to the parking deck where her Honda Civic was parked.

Before entering her car, she noticed the long, winding scratch mark along the side of the driver's side door from where Vasile had run his claw along the paint. She checked the backseat, the trunk, and then, once she felt more comfortable, she entered the car and sped away.

✟

WITH her nerves still taunt, she crossed over the George Washington Bridge heading west into New Jersey. Then, she got off on Exit 74. She stayed on Palisades Interstate Parkway until she picked up I-87 North and I-90 West to North Ithacan Street in the town, Ballpointe, which was located in the Mohawk Valley region.

During the drive, Talora debated whether or not to keep her smartphone. She wondered about the "supposed" ICE agents and how they were able to track down the Vampos. Or, instead, were these "supposed" ICE agents tracking her through her smartphone? But why would they possibly do such a thing? Talora figured it was best to ditch the phone than to keep it. When the time came to toss her phone from the window, she backed out. She couldn't let go of it.

By the time Talora made it out of New Jersey, the sun was already starting to come up. Depending on the traffic, the drive was roughly a three and a half hours to her parent's house, which gave Talora maybe too much time to spend thinking about the previous night. Any thought of Pacen—or recalling the time she spent with Pacen—had driven her to tears. She turned on the radio, blasted 80's hottest hits to help steer her red thoughts toward a more optimistic road that she was soon going to be traveling on in her not so distant future.

Throughout the entire drive, she was fighting off sleep. Her eyelids were doing pull ups against her eyes, and each blink grew more strenuous and strenuous. The music helped a great deal while driving through the early morning hours—if it weren't for a combination of Flock of Seagulls, Don Henley, Cyndi Lauper, and Johnny Hates

Jazz, then more than likely her Honda Civic would've wound up in a ditch somewhere or even Hackensack River.

However, the only thing that wound up in the Hackensack River was Talora's smartphone.

Music from the 1980's had a peculiar way of encouraging those who needed a little nudge of encouragement.

✠

IT was late morning when she arrived at her parent's house in Ballpointe.

From the intersection, she saw both her parents, first her mom, who was picking weeds in the flowerbeds in front of the house, then her dad, who was mowing a strip of grass along the side of the house and working his way toward the back. She knew, once he made it to the back, then she'd lose any chance at successfully sneaking inside the house. He'd most definitely spot her if she drove by the house or snuck in through the back of the house. He was good at spotting things, including "things" that were never there. She knew the only way she'd be able to pull it off was if she took Glenmore Street, which ran parallel to an alleyway, parked her car behind the old beech tree, scaled her neighbor The Compton's nearly unscalable fence, crept through The Compton's yard, then, finally, after digging her way through the branches of dying—and soon-to-be dead—forsythia shrubs lining the side of the house, snuck in through the laundry room window on the opposite side of her mom. And that was exactly what she did, minus the sneaking-in-through-the-laundry-room-window part. In the nick of time, she darted toward the front of the house as her dad moved his way toward the backyard with the lawnmower.

She sneaked in through the front door, which—*phew!*—was unlocked.

With a couple of scratches along her hands and arms from her planned "sneak in," she made it to her bedroom undetected.

She packed a duffle bag of clothing for at least two weeks, consisting of more shirts and sweaters than pants. She emptied out most of her sock, underwear, and bra drawer. She made sure to grab her toothbrush, as well as a tube of toothpaste; and then, she grabbed more personal items, such as face creams, lotions, and tampons, and placed them inside a smaller travel-sized bag.

Once she was all packed, she grabbed a map of the United States—yes, that's right. She was going old school. No phones, obviously. No technology. But, for Talora, that was the whole point. To be completely "untraceable."

Before leaving, she couldn't help but stand by the doorway and take one final look at her bedroom. Most of her attention was drawn to her bed—what she'd do to lay down, sink into those cool sheets, wrap her head around her pillow, and shut her eyes for an hour or two!

But Talora thought about the hunt and being the hunted, not the hunter. *They wouldn't stop coming for me*, she thought, recalling the ICE agent's words about not putting those she loved in harm's way and then the two vampires who escaped from ICE. She knew that they were still out there, ready to seek vengeance. Despite the sad reality, Talora tried her best to look at the bright side of her situation. The road trip! Even as she stood by the bedroom doorway, she didn't know exactly where she was going or what waited ahead of her; however, only one person surfaced in her mind and she just so happened to be someone whom, as of now, she hadn't had more in common with than ever before.

The notion alone of visiting her Aunt Dina had, in a way, made the upcoming trip much more exciting.

Talora's eyes moved past a black and white speckled Composition notebook on her desk. She tore out a blank sheet of notebook paper from inside, grabbed a Zebra pen, and wrote a note the old fashioned way.

"Dear Mom and Dad,

First off, don't worry. I assure you that I'm completely fine. The reason—

Talora scribbled through the note. Crumbled the paper. Threw it in the trash.

Then, she tore out yet another sheet of notebook paper and tried again.

"I know things have been difficult lately. And the last thing I would ever want to do is make things even more difficult. It's hard to explain it right now (TRUST ME, ONE DAY I WILL), but there is something much bigger happening to me, and I feel as if it's best for me to make sense of what's happening on my own. That's why I'm leaving. I don't have an exact destination in mind—

Talora paused. She hated to lie to her parents, especially her mom whom she was closer to. She reminded herself that it was only for the best.

But I know the road will take me where I need to be. You may look at my actions as self-ish. Maybe I am being selfish. Please don't be mad—

Again, she stopped writing just for a moment and listened closely to a high-pitched *rustling* sound followed by an out-of-tuned chorus of meows coming from underneath her bed.

P.S. Make sure to feed Bitsy and Bizzy while I'm gone."

— Lora

Once Talora was finished writing, she folded the note in half and addressed it to "Mom and Dad."

In a state of regression, Talora's body buzzed with both eagerness and childish exhilaration from the continuing sounds of two kittens stirring between shoeboxes and old picture frames under her bed. In order to draw the two kittens, she grabbed another sheet of paper from the notebook and crumpled it in her hand.

Talora kneeled down for a closer look.

The *crinkling* sound of paper drew out two small figures from behind a picture frame. Two sets of eyes glowed in the darkness.

Bitsy, who was an orange tabby, and Bizzy, who was black, crawled out from underneath the bed. Their eyes were caked with morning crust and trying to adjust to the brightness of natural light throughout the bedroom. A few months ago, the two wound up on their back porch after their mother, a black longhaired, gave birth to a litter underneath her neighbor's crawlspace. Their neighbor managed to round up at least four of them to give to the cul-de-sac queen herself, Ms. Evans, who had lost her husband three years ago and was in the market for a new pet—or pets. Talora picked up both kittens, gave them hugs and kisses, and said her goodbyes. She told Bitsy and Bizzy that she'd be back soon. She heard somewhere—maybe on the Internet—that cats forget about their owners after being away from them for a month or even weeks. Talora hoped that she was going to be gone for as long as a month, but she knew her future was uncertain. And that was the most terrifying part about all of this. And, at the same time, the most exciting.

TALORA closed her bedroom door behind her to keep Bitsy and Bizzy from following her downstairs and tiptoed her way into the kitchen.

Centered on the kitchen table was a glass vase of angelic white roses, calla lilies, mums, and daisy poms. The moment she saw her mom receiving the spread of flowers from the deliveryman, who, in return, informed the two about the identity of the sender, Talora wanted to throw them directly in the trash. She figured it was his way of trying to win her back by pulling on her heartstrings. However, after Talora read the note, she learned that they were addressed not to her but to her family, the Katz family. Her mom was a fan of Pacen. "Loved him to death," she'd say.

Becoming more emotional from the sight of the flowers, Talora pulled out the card wedged between a white rose and cally lily and read the quote to herself.

"It is not so much for its beauty that the forest makes a claim upon men's hearts, as for that subtle something, that quality of air, that emanation from old trees, that so wonderfully changes and renews a weary spirit. — Robert Louis Stevenson."

She wiped away her tears and placed the note between the salt and peppershakers on the kitchen table. Her attention was suddenly drawn to her mom, who had now moved toward the front of the house and was picking up weeds from the flowerbeds outside the front living room window. Ever since Nathan went missing, her mom developed quite the green thumb. Her mom's garden, once as small enough to hold in one's arms or placed along the windowsill of a cramped one-bedroom apartment, had grown substantially in size and had turned into a beautiful display of flowers, fruits, and vegetables. Talora knew people grieved in their own way, either subtly or conspicuously. Some people took up golf lessons; self-defense training; or even started their own trendy badminton league on the weekends. Some people started new hobbies, such as finger painting or collecting old coins. Her mom, she gardened.

Her dad made his rounds in the backyard and was nearly finished mowing the lawn. She saw that he only had a couple of strips of grass left!

She scrambled around the kitchen, grabbing snacks and bottles of water. And then, she checked the backyard once more.

Anxiously, she waited for her dad to walk the other way with the lawnmower as he cut the last strip of grass. Once he made the U-turn, Talora managed to escape through the laundry room window. She heard the lawnmower shut off behind her as she stepped between two forsythia shrubs. Her daring escape was much louder than her initial entry.

As Talora gathered the rest of her things that had fallen onto the ground, she heard the footsteps behind her. She darted to the neighbor's fence.

Curious about what he thought was a trespasser, her dad decided to check out the noise; and when he arrived at the side of the house, he followed a noise to his neighbor's backyard where he witnessed a bird feeder swaying back and forth on a tree branch. The bird feeder was swaying so violently that it was dropping birdseed all over the ground. He nonchantly shrugged off his suspicion— because that was all it was, a suspicion—and walked back to the lawnmower to empty out the catcher of grass into a garbage bag.

TALORA was in the clear. She didn't waste anytime saying goodbye to the ole neighborhood. In essence, Talora put New York in her rear view mirror and headed toward Soy, Missouri, where her Aunt Dina lived. After all, she had at least a day's worth of driving ahead of her—two, depending on the traffic and how much she stopped to pee, eat, or rest.

SHE stopped to use the restroom at a rest stop in Lakeland, Pennsylvania.

On numerous occasions, several cars pulled out in front of her and nearly ran her over and caused her to wreck while passing through Cleveland, Ohio. Being a recovering road rager herself, she had little-to-no patience with those who didn't have a clue on how to drive or even had little-to-no grasp on the rules of the road; however, it was in the state of Ohio, of all places, OHIO!, where she discovered some of the worst drivers whom she had ever dealt with on the road—and Talora didn't even carry a single ounce of bias against the driver-state relationship. She figured that maybe it was just a bad day. Boy, did she hope so. She stopped in a town right outside Columbus to fill up her tank at a gas station called Seven Heaven. She couldn't help but laugh at the irony of the name. She stopped in Indiana to eat a salad and use the restroom. She ate until her belly was modestly full and then she hit the road again. It was when Talora crossed a town named "Perky" that she came close to losing it. The hit song "Cottonmouth" by Stuffed Animalz came on the radio. She couldn't stand to listen to the radio anymore. She fished out a couple of ancient CD's from the glove box and blasted them on repeat. She drove about another hour or two before she decided to call it a day. She was extremely exhausted from not sleeping the night before, and she knew if she kept on keeping on, then she ran the risk of becoming one of those drivers whom she scorned from the confines of her car while driving through OHIO! She ended up spending a rather cold, uncomfortable night in some sleazy hotel in Nowhere, Indiana. The town wasn't called Nowhere; but, in a way, Talora felt as if she was stuck in Nowhere and maybe that was the gist.

That night, she piled up furniture against the window, as well as the doorway, and masked each entry point with perfumes and lotions to hide her scent from the Vampos. There was a window inside the bathroom, which was just big enough to escape through if, somehow, they found her. During the late hours, Talora sat in the chilly darkness with her nose as cold as an ice cube and listened to each and every sound the night offered. Talora only caught a couple hours of sleep.

The next day, she put all the furniture and whatnot back into its original position in the room and was on the road by first daylight.

161

While driving, Talora ate from a couple of pastries, including an apple Danish and a cinnamon roll that she had pocketed from the continental breakfast at the No-where Hotel. She stopped somewhere in the southern part of Illinois to use the restroom. By lunchtime, she ended up making it to Missouri and decided to stop and eat at Burger Hut outside St. Louis where she ordered, of all things, another salad that tasted as if it was concocted from the remnants of a flood. The lettuce, wilted; the so-called "antibiotic-free" chicken was as tough and rubbery as a tire. She found a dead fly underneath an Iceberg leaf halfway through eating the salad and was tempted to not ask but demand a refund on the salad; however, the no-tion of possibly drawing a scene in the restaurant had squashed any notion of returning the salad, as well as the french fries, which were cold and tasted as if they sat out all morning. She tossed the rest of the salad, as well as the french fries, in a trashcan and swore to herself that she'd never eat salads—or better yet, never eat at a fast food restaurant again.

AFTER three more hours of driving on that never-ending road, Talora *finally* made it to Soy, Missouri—or entering "Rhodes Country," as she put it in her own words—where passing a hardheaded redneck driving a noisy truck with a Confederate flag on the bumper wasn't the least uncom-mon. Despite the "in-your-face" backwardness, the "don't tell me what to do, commie skum" or "how to live" spirit of Soy, Talora never dreaded coming here, even as a little girl. Soy had plenty of country, untouched land that stretched as far as the eye could see, and for a girl who often drove into The City, having a warm slice of country-side at her disposal was nothing short of paradise. She was aware that some of the people of Soy were stuck in their own ways and that some of them, especially the ones who lived in the trailer parks, clung to a bloody past that no longer existed the same way a devout Christian clung to the scripture of a Bible. Of course, Talora didn't agree with any of these people or their beliefs and their ways and the only thing she had in common with them was death itself. In a strange way, she didn't care nor was she the least bothered by them. People came in all *shapes*—Soy had its fair share of shapes—as well as colors. It wasn't like people fell from the sky. After all, they came from similar institutions that she did.

Talora drove through Main Street and caught up on old times. The last time she had seen her Aunt Dina was about seven years ago and despite the photograph from Talora's college graduation that her mom had mailed to her Aunt Dina, Talora reckoned she wouldn't recognize her today. And vise versa. The only image that Talora had seen of her aunt was from a photo that she posted on her Facebook page six years ago.

Dina's house was a ranch style house located on a sixteen-acre lot, which was passed down to her late husband, Grayson, a millwright who was killed while repairing a faulty conveyor belt, which was used in one of the largest cereal manufacturers in the central part of the United States. After a shoddy investigation into Grayson's death, Amel and Sons, the makers of the popular cereal brands, *Berry Bunch*, were ruled to be blamed for the accident, resulting in a two million dollar settlement. Dina didn't waste a penny with the money from the lawsuit. She ended up giving some of the money to charities and fundraisers, including Research into Alzheimer's—before his untimely death, Grayson always talked about wanting to give money to the organization because his mama, who was as close as a mother to Dina, had died from the disease. The rest of it was spent on one of those stay-at-home colleges where she earned her business degree through online courses, as well as her own clothing store called *La Lueur*, which, in French, meant "glow."

It was late afternoon when Talora arrived at Dina's house, which, except for a new paint job—Talora remembered it being a baby blue color, not lime green—the house looked the exact same as she last saw it. Talora primped her hair in the rear view mirror and made sure she looked presentable for her Aunt Dina.

As soon as Talora exited the car, her stomach fluttered with nerves. *What do I even say?* She mentally rehearsed lines on the slow walk to the front porch; and after the truth revealed itself in each thought with words like *Vampos*, *death*, and *runaway*, slipping through the cracks of her memorized dialogue, Talora decided it was best to lie.

She *rang* the doorbell.

She only waited a couple of seconds for her aunt to answer the door before her mind flooded with the negative—and surprisingly, most realistic—thoughts of bringing Vampos straight to her aunt's front doorstep. Talora could only imagine that doorbell being no different than her ringing a dinner bell. The realization of possibly putting her aunt in harm's way caused her skin to perspire.

Talora tugged herself away, thinking it'd be that moment of doubt when her aunt answered the door. But she didn't. She walked around the house and peeked into the garage. Apparently, Dina wasn't home. Which had given Talora time to think over her unannounced visit. Where would she go? She had Nowhere to go. And, they wouldn't find her here. Talora told herself over and over. If she didn't tell Dina the truth, *they'd never know.* She decided to hang out in her car, which she parked farther into the driveway. She waited about an hour until Dina showed up in a black Mercedes, which looked like a stark upgrade from the hatchback she used to drive.

Once Talora stepped out of the car, Dina followed suit. It was dark outside and Talora couldn't quite see Dina's face from the bright glow of the headlights masking her face; however, Talora knew it was Dina.

She heard Dina's voice behind the light: "Talora? Is that you?"

Talora stepped forward.

Dina left the car running and walked in an unsteady manner toward Talora.

The sight of Dina's shadowy face revealing itself brought a sense of comfort to Talora. And terror.

"Hey, Dina," she said, her voice trembling.

"Oh my god, Talora!" She stepped forward, her face becoming brighter and clearer to Talora. She looked over Talora's face, then body. Then, she embraced her niece with a hug. "It's so good to see you—"

"—I was going to call, but I didn't have your number."

"It's okay."

"You sure?"

"Of course, I'm sure."

A bit of laughter trickled from her voice.

Dina stepped back and once more, looked over Talora.

"Look at you!" she said with elation. "You're all grown up!"

Talora bashfully responded by not responding.

"Have you eaten?" asked Dina.

"No," Talora said.

✝

DINA had made an old traditional dish for Talora called "Shakshouka." Her Aunt Dina used to make the dish whenever she would visit as a girl. Served alongside the dish was store-bought pita bread as well as a prepackaged Caesar salad—back in the day, Dina used to make her own pita bread from scratch, as well as her own spin on Caesar salad when Grayson was working, but ever since she started running her own clothing store, she "cheated" a little bit, which, in all fairness, tasted similar to the real deal—almost.

Talora was finishing eating when the doorbell rang.

Immediately, Talora's heart dropped from the *booming* sound of the ring.

Her long face went ghostly pale.

"Oh my god," Dina said in a state of shock. "I totally forgot—"

"—Don't answer it," Talora warned.

"I'm sorry," she said. "I have to. Will you excuse me?"

As Dina broke away from the kitchen table, Talora followed her aunt into the hallway, which Dina interpreted as Talora waving a giant red flag. It started to all make sense to her. She must've had an abusive boyfriend, more than likely, possessive—and, she was running away from him. It was at all true, but Talora could run with it.

Dina stopped at the edge of the living room and turned to Talora.

"Is there something you're not telling me, Talora?" she asked Talora.

"No," she stuttered. "I just—"

"—The City has really taken its toll on you, hasn't it?"

"It's not like that."

"What's it like, Talora?"

"It's hard to explain."

"Relax, okay?"

"But—"

"—Am I allowed to answer my own door?"

The tone in her voice was soft; however, the angle of her eyes was sharp and penetrating.

"Yes," Talora said over a pause. "Of course."

As Dina answered the front door, Talora backpedaled away. She grabbed the poker from the fireplace and was so ready to use it on any member of the Vampos that came barging into the house.

In that moment of great pre-war-like tension, her own prologue to madness, Talora heard another woman's voice coming from outside.

She heard words like *my niece* and then a couple of *sorries*.

Talora poked her head from the living room doorway and saw a woman, who was around the same age as Dina, standing on the front porch with a bottle of red wine in her hand.

"Why don't I call you whenever it's a good time—"

"—No," Talora said from behind. "Please. Join us. There's plenty of food."

Surprised by Talora's interruption, Dina turned to Talora. Then, turned back around to the strange woman outside. She stepped aside and showed her inside.

"After you," Dina said shortly, as if she was hiding her frustration.

Dina introduced Talora to her "new friend" Angie; however, as soon as she picked up the awkwardness between the two, in particular, the way Dina tried her best to justify Angie's untimely appearance by claiming that Angie happened to be in the neighborhood, Talora realized the two were more than just friends.

They had benefits.

✟

AFTER two glasses of Cabernet Sauvignon, Dina was carrying what Talora would commonly refer to as a drunken sparkle in her eye. In other words, her Dina was a lightweight when it came to drinking. Which, in a way, made Talora envious.

She downed the rest of her third glass of wine, set it down against the outdoor table, and smacked her gums.

"Tell me, Talora," she said, as if she had reached enough drunken confidence to state the obvious, "how's the Big Apple treating you?"

"I'm actually not in The City anymore," she said, taking a bird-like sip from a glass of wine. "I'm staying with my parents Upstate."

"Where? Ballpointe?"

"That's right," she said. "Occasionally, I ride into The City for work."

"What kind of work?" asked Angie.

"Nothing in particular," Talora said. "Pretty much anything I can find. I'm still trying to pay off my student loans."

"Don't you just hate that?" Angie said with annoyance. "It took me ten *years* to finally pay off my student loans. I understand why all these young kids nowadays want free college—"

"—And who exactly is going to pay for it, Angie?" asked Dina, the softness gone from her voice. That diehard Republican coming out of her. Alcohol had a way of mining through a person's "personal" political stance and unearthing it via the spoken tongue. Dina didn't even allow Angie, who couldn't have been more opposite in her politics—in fact, she wasn't even across the aisle, she was hanging out in the corner of the room—a chance to respond or elaborate. "That's right," she said shortly. "People like you and me. These kids nowadays," Dina started to shake her head in what Talora could only acknowledge as a deep-seated disgust, "they are nothing short of rotten. *Spoiled* rotten."

"We're all spoiled rotten at that age. Come on, Dina," Angie said, trying to convince Dina, "you know it's true. Fresh out of college. Professors filling your head with culture and ideology. The 'World Is Your Oyster.' Carpe diem. Seize the day! For once in your life, you start to feel as if Your Voice matters. All that, of course, comes crashing to the ground once we're exposed to the Real World, as in the one outside your phone, and that spoiled attitude tends to go away, and the Real World starts to shape the person you're going to be for the rest of your life."

"Yeah, Angie," Dina argued, "but we didn't have phones when we were Talora's age—"

"—Phones aren't the problem," Angie said, not missing a beat.

"Then, what is?" asked Dina.

"People," Angie said bluntly. "People are the problem. We've lost the ability to talk to one another or, dare I say, possess the willingness to accept any ideas or beliefs that are different from our own or, worse, different from what is considered the norm. We're too focused on what separates us rather than what brings us together."

"I agree," said Talora.

"See." Angie raised her glass toward Talora's direction. "She gets me."

"It's the high-borns who want to keep us separated," Dina said coldly over a moment of silence. "The more separated we are, the more vulnerable we are."

"Here we go again with the high borns," Angie said under her breath and followed with a sigh.

More curious, Talora leaned in closer.

"What do you mean?" asked Talora.

"What I mean is that they're the ones in charge now," Dina said. "They control what we watch and soon, what we say and what we do. Eventually, we'll be living under their thumb. Or, shall I say, claw!"

Dina laughed at her own joke.

Talora wasn't laughing so much.

"You're talking about vampires?" said Talora, more seriously.

"Of course," she said. "Who else do you think I'm talking about?"

Talora didn't have a response. Yet, she thought that maybe her aunt had one too many glasses of wine.

"Those who dictate what news to report to the people, TV producers, founders of certain social media, even our own politicians, all high borns—"

"—Vampires?"

"Yes," Dina said. "*Vampires.* Why is that so hard to believe?"

"Well, I dunno Dina," Talora said, stumbling her words. "It just sounds like some crazy conspiracy theory you heard from the Internet."

"I don't go on the Internet," Dina said flatly.

"Everybody goes on the Internet."

"Not this gal," Dina said, pointing her thumb at herself while making a *clicking* noise from the corner of her mouth.

"How about your business. . . La Lure?"

"It's pronounced La Lueur," she corrected by slurring the words *La Lashhur.* Which relieved the tension in Dina's statement, not theory.

"Surely, you have a website."

"I do," Dina said more superiorly. "I have a guy who runs it. I'm not at all tech savvy. Hey! I'm not ashamed to admit it but I'm what I call tech retarded."

"Dinasaurs!" Talora drawled.

"What?"

Angie said, "You're not supposed to use that word."

"What word?"

"The r-word."

"Oh shut up!"

Dina couldn't help but laugh at what Talora had called her earlier.

"You know I haven't been called Dinasaurs in years."

"Old nickname?"

"Way back when, when I wore my heart on my sleeve—"

"—Still do," Angie mumbled from the side of her mouth.

"—Talora used to call me Dinasaurs whenever I'd yell at Grayson. She said I looked like a dinosaur."

"I should've come to his funeral," Talora said out of the blue.

Talora's out-of-the-blue comment created an awkward silence.

Angie excused herself from the back patio by fetching another bottle of wine from the kitchen.

"I wanted to come," she said. "I really did. It's just my dad—"

"—Your dad had his reasons, Talora," Dina said quietly. "It was never a secret to anybody in the family. The relationship between Isaac and I was—how do I say—complicated. He played the overprotective brother who was trying to look after the hard-bitten sister. Over these past few years—especially after Grayson's death—I've learned to accept that. And I'm fine with it. We all play certain parts when we're younger, Talora. Certain roles. You just have to ask yourself: 'What role do I want to play?'"

"Nathan's *still* out there," Talora said, picking up exactly where her aunt was going with the conversation.

"I know he is."

"I even tried to talk to Mayor Armitage—he's the mayor of New York."

"Yeah," Dina said loosely and rolled her eyes. "I've heard about Mr. Touchy Feely."

"I went to the cops," Talora said, keeping serious. "I had no other choice. So I found a fundraiser that he was at. I went there. Tried to confront him."

"And?"

"He was busy."

"Of course, he was."

Talora knew that she was treading a fine line. Knew, if she went further into the story, then the truth would come spewing out like a broken levee.

She left it at that, moved on, and gave no opening for Dina to further question her.

"My mom's already given up," Talora said. "You can see it in her eyes. The defeat."

"Molly is a strong woman, Talora. Stronger than you think. And you take up after her. I mean, look at you, Talora! I never would've had the nerve to confront the mayor of New York City. That takes, pardon my French, balls! And yours, yours are plenty big—"

"—I dunno."

"You might not want to admit it, but you do." In a joking kind of way, Dina sharpened her loosen, drunken gaze on Talora. She touched the bottom of her left eye. "I can *see* it."

Talora hung her head in deep thought.

"What about your dad?"

"I think a part of him wants to believe that Gnat's still out there. But," Talora said, fighting back the tears, "every time I look at him, I *see* Gnat."

Dina scooted her chair closer to Talora's and grabbed her by the hand.

"Everything will work out. It always does—"

Talora didn't want to hear words of reassurance.

She wanted the truth.

Most importantly, she wanted answers.

"What did you say to my dad that drove him away from you?" she asked before Dina could console her.

"It's a long story, Talora," Dina responded, sitting more straight in her chair. "I'd rather not bore you with the details."

Silence crept back into the conversation, the silence forcing Dina to move her eyes elsewhere, such as the kitchen where Angie was standing in reflection by the sink and savoring a new glass of wine all by herself.

Dina sighed, looked over Talora, and witnessed the pain wrapped in her eyes.

"I'm not sure if you were aware, but Grayson wasn't my first husband."

"No," Talora said. "I wasn't aware."

"I was married to a man named Sawyer Hauser. Isaac hated him, in fact, despised him."

"I thought all in-laws despised each other."

"No," Dina said, her voice carrying another sigh. "He *hated* Sawyer, I mean, to the point where he started to get involved in my business."

"Involved? Like how?"

"Like threatening Sawyer behind my back or making up lies about his fidelity. It was not only clear to me, but also Sawyer that Isaac was trying to sabotage our marriage—and frankly, Isaac wasn't too fond of Grayson either." Dina tilted her head to the side in pensiveness. "Now that I think more about it, I don't think he liked any of the men I brought home. Even when I started dating, my brother couldn't stand to see me with another man."

"Why was my dad so protective of you?" asked Talora.

"I really don't have an answer to that question, Talora. I really don't," Dina said, drifting off. "The *resentment*," she snapped back, her voice clearer, "the resentment started to build between me and Isaac after my first marriage. It came to my attention that he was saying all kinds of things about me around the town that weren't true; and *eventually*, those things got back around to Sawyer."

As if she was mimicking Dina, Talora drifted off for a moment as she could hardly make sense of what she was hearing about her own dad.

"What was he saying about you?" Talora finally asked.

"He was telling people that I was being 'unfaithful' to Sawyer."

"Why would he say something like that?"

"He was jealous."

"Jealous of what?"

Dina let out another sigh, as if the truth had a particular way of casting sighs.

"He was jealous because I happened to marry the one man who had a bigger wallet than him."

"You mean Sawyer was rich?"

"*Filthy.*"

"My dad should've been proud of you, right? I mean, you hit the jackpot!"

"He thought I was coasting through life, using Sawyer for his money," Dina said. "After about a year, Sawyer just couldn't deal with my brother any longer—then, Sawyer said he didn't think I was worth the trouble. 'When you get me, you get the brother.' That's how it was and that's how it's always been. High school. College. Sawyer filed for a divorce. I said some things to Isaac that, even till this day, I still deeply regret."

"What did you—"

"—I told him that I never wanted to see him again," Dina said strongly, "and that he was the worst thing that happened to my life, that he'd never live up to our father's reputation. Those were the last words I said to him before I packed my bag and got the hell out of New York."

"I'm so sorry, Dina," Talora said soberly. "I didn't know there was so much bad blood between you and my dad."

"Not bad blood," Dina said. "Just bad memories." She sighed and readjusted her position in the chair. "Let me ask you a question, Talora," Dina said, as if she was waiting for a right moment to change the subject. "And please be honest with me. . . "

"Sure."

Dina asked, "Why don't you want your parents to know you're here? Aren't they going to be worried sick about where you are, especially after everything that they've been through?"

"It's fine," Talora said with hesitation. "I'm fine."

Dina lowered her chin, as well as her voice.

"People who say they're 'fine' aren't really fine."

She didn't respond to Dina, who, in return, took her niece's lack of response as a clear indicated that her niece was *not* fine.

"Talora," she said patiently, "you can stay here as long as you want. You are blood, remember? So, don't you act like a guest. You have a home here. Okay?"

"Yeah," Talora said quietly. "Okay."

With perfect timing, Angie stepped outside onto the back patio. In her hand, she was holding a freshly rolled joint, which happened to be pinkish in color from where her wine-stained saliva had glued the joint together. Angie ran her lighter over and under the joint, which helped dry the saliva.

"How about a cherry on the top?" asked Angie, as she showcased the joint.

"You read my mind," Dina said, more relieved.

"Talora?"

"You like to party?"

Talora finished her glass of wine.

"Yeah," she said loosely. "Sure. Why not?"

✠

TALORA woke in the middle of the night with a ball of fire in her chest.

The combination of four glasses of Cabernet Sauvignon—maybe five or six, she lost track after three—on top of two helpings of Shakshouka had done a number on her stomach. She figured it was all of that acidic food and drink.

She sat up, hoping to ease the burn. When that didn't work, she rolled out of bed and waddled to the guest bathroom in search of any antacids inside the medicine cabinet; however, except for an expired tube of Preparation-H, Dina didn't carry any medicine inside the guest bathroom. Tums was a go-to remedy whenever she had heartburn.

With no other choice, Talora decided to search for other remedies elsewhere, including the kitchen where she scoured through cabinets.

Lastly, she tried the refrigerator.

Dina had a gallon of two-percent milk. In the past, milk helped coat Talora's stomach whenever she experienced heartburn; however, having hopped on the soy milk train three years ago, milk was considered one of her last options to choose from—and since she was in no mood to wake Dina—milk was probably her only option. Trying not to make much noise, she poured herself a glass of milk and did laps around the dark living room while sipping from milk.

Once she finished the glass, the heartburn was somewhat less intense; however, it was still there, like a slow burn.

More awake, Talora left the kitchen, flipped on a lamp next to the couch, and piddled around the living room for a while, mostly checking out all of the knickknacks on the bookshelves and cabinets as though she was browsing through your everyday arts and crafts store.

She came across a shelf of leather bound photo albums tucked underneath a shelf of Mary Higgins Clark novels. She happened to find a photograph of herself after only two flips through the first photo album. The photograph was taken outside near the guesthouse, which Dina had converted into an art studio a few years before Grayson's death. She couldn't tell how old she was in the photograph. If she had to point a number on it, she'd probably say fifteen or sixteen.

In the photo were Talora, who was leaning toward the age of sixteen now that she thought more about it, as well as her younger brother, Nathan, who was about as old as the digits on her hand, her mom, her Aunt Dina, her Uncle Grayson, and, finally, in the middle of the group, was Talora's black cockapoo, Broot, who was a three-week old puppy teething on a toy rabbit. Broot had a specific white patch on his back, very identifiable, in the shape of a heart.

Talora navigated through her memories, specifically recalling her dad and his ill behavior whenever her mom would mention Dina and how he never came with them during the rare visits to Aunt Dina's house and the "off-the-cuff" excuses of having to work that were used commonly whenever any suggestion of driving to Aunt Dina's house for the weekend arose. Pondering over what Dina had told her earlier that night and then examining the photo, the absent father, who, in the case of visiting his own flesh and blood, literally embodied the term "not in the picture anymore," forced Talora to at least try to make sense of the fallout between Dina and her dad.

She skimmed through other photographs for a couple of minutes before walking back upstairs. She passed Dina's bedroom on the way to the guestroom.

With her eyes more adjusted to the darkness, she noticed the door was barely cracked open. She peeked inside and saw two bodies bathing in moonlight. Dina was sleeping next to Angie; in fact, both of their bodies were entangled and not in the friend kind of way, but more so like two lovers. She couldn't believe her own eyes. Her Aunt Dina, once a reserved woman who would talk secretly about men, as well as the comfort and ruggedness of men, her Aunt Dina, the one who'd always whisper a comment to her whenever she either saw a handsome—or as she coyly put it, a "hot" or "cute" guy—on TV or even passed one on the street or in public, was now playing on the other team.

One of the women lying soundlessly in bed—she couldn't tell whether it was Dina or Angie—suddenly stirred around while readjusting position. The woman unhooked her leg from another leg and rolled to the edge of the bed, taking more sheets along with her.

The move revealed more clearly the other woman, Angie, who slowly rotated her head toward the doorway. Her glossy moonlit eyes moved toward Talora's direction.

Immediately, Talora stepped from the doorway and tiptoed back to the guestroom as if she was a teenager again sneaking through the night. Each noise, each *creak* of hardwood, each *squeak* of a door, forced her into a mime-like state, as if she was playing red light-green light.

For the first time in a long time, Talora felt, dare she say, happy.

✙

TALORA concealed her laughter as she made her way back to the guestroom where she fell sight to the open window inside the guestroom. That tension she experienced back in New York City was back. She carefully closed the door behind her and crept toward the window where the curtain was weightlessly floating about the room.

As she tried to recall opening the window—maybe she did before she passed out—the sound of nature outside the house rid any doubt in her mind.

A gentle breeze was blowing into the room; however, it wasn't strong enough to blow open the window. Comforted by the coolness, Talora kneeled down and peered out into the vast countryside before her. She could no longer hear man or his creations. She heard the nocturnal life, a familiar yet almost forgotten life that had been masked by street ambience for years. The sounds filled her ears, a symphony of a hundreds of species all speaking to her at once.

THAT night, Talora fought off the burn of an upset stomach and slept well through the morning.

By the time she woke, the bright morning sun was painted all over the entire guestroom. She woke rested. She rolled out of bed and walked toward the closed window. Waking up to the sight of a vast countryside opposed to waking up to a neighborhood of cookie-cutter houses or even cityscape brought a sort of Christmas-morning comfort to Talora. She heard the *clinking* of dishes downstairs. She made her way into the kitchen where Dina was washing the dishes from last night. She turned her shoulder, saw her niece through the corner of her eye, and stopped what she was doing.

Talora immediately noticed the Russian blue rubbing against Dina's leg.

"Look who's up," Dina said, drying her hands with a washcloth.

"Mornin'," said Talora.

"Good morning," Dina said and slid out a chair for Talora at the kitchen table.

"And who may this be?" asked Talora, as she kneeled down and pet the cat.

"Vladimir meet Talora," Dina said.

"Vladimir, huh?"

"Apparently, he was hiding last night."

"Doesn't like guests?"

"No," Dina said. "He's pretty skittish. But," she said, admiring Talora's nature with Vladimir, "he looks like he's made a new friend."

"Did you sleep well?"

"So, so, I guess," Talora said honestly. "I woke up in the middle of the night with a wicked case of heartburn."

"You know," Dina said, more reflectively, "I thought I heard someone walking around this morning."

More intrigued, Talora asked, "What time?"

"I dunno," she said. "I believe it was around three or four o'clock. It was not long before I woke up."

She specifically remembered waking up three minutes after midnight; in fact, that time "12:03" was seared in her memory. Talora remembered walking around for a while; she grabbed herself a glass of milk to cool off that wicked heartburn, then nosied through a couple of photo albums. Then, headed back upstairs where she went back to bed. All of that took no longer than twenty minutes or so, which meant Talora fell back to sleep around 12:30—1:00, the latest.

"Why didn't you wake me?" Dina asked, more concerned about Talora's well being than her privacy. "I could've grabbed you some Tums."

Dina's question released Talora from a sudden wave of panic.

"No," Talora said, playing off her previous illness. "Eventually, it passed."

"Well, then, you should probably eat light today—"

"—No. I'm feeling better." She perked up. "What do you have to eat?"

Dina looked around the kitchen counter.

"Well, I can make you some eggs."

Talora passed a box of bagels next to the refrigerator.

"Bagel?"

"Help yourself—" she shooed Talora away and walked her to the kitchen table, "—or actually, why don't you take a seat while I make you breakfast."

"You sure?"

"It's no trouble," she said in a motherly kind of way, "as a matter of fact, it'd be my pleasure."

Talora, who had gotten used to making her own meals over these past couple of years, took advantage of Dina's offer and took a seat at the table.

Dina was watching a famous chef sampling different plates of pork at a barbeque contest on the Food Network.

"You can turn the channel, if you like," Dina suggested.

"It's fine," Talora said. "I don't watch much TV."

"I don't blame you," Dina returned with a concealed resentment underneath her voice. "Nowadays, who can? Everything has gotten too political." *Political*, Talora thought, *right?* "It's sickening to watch. For me," Dina said, "I'm pretty much left with either The Food Channel or Animal Planet. Nothing too political about food or animals."

Talora wasn't in any mood to question the one right Dina had left to exercise, which was her opinion. Her stomach did most of the talking.

"So," Dina said, her voice rising, "how do you want your bagel?" She looked in the refrigerator and listed Talora's options: "I have butter, cream cheese, grape jelly, orange marmalade—"

"—Cream cheese is fine."

"What kind? Strawberry or hazelnut?"

Talora pinched her nose.

"Hazelnut?"

"It's good," Dina said. "Wanna try it?"

"No thanks," Talora said. "I'll go with Strawberry."

"Strawberry it is."

As Dina prepared the bagel with Strawberry cream cheese, Talora grabbed a cat mug from the top cabinet above the dishwasher and poured herself black coffee from the pot.

"You read my mind," Dina said. "Pour me a cup, will you?"

"Sure."

"My cup's in the sink."

Talora walked to the sink and found two mugs lying on top of the dish grate. Both were empty. She didn't know which one to grab—and for some reason, she was hesitant about asking Dina which mug belonged to her. One had one of those inspirational quotes on the side: *Life is short. Drink up!* The other one, newer, less worn, with a smudge of red lipstick along the rim. Talora grabbed the mug with the message and poured two cups, one for Dina and then another one for herself.

"This will be my third cup." Talora set Dina's coffee next to a box of bagels. "Thank you," Dina said, pulling herself from the bagel to take a sip of coffee.

"Are you hungover from last night?" asked Talora.

"No," she said in a high, untruthful voice. "Well, a little. You?"

"A slight headache, but nothing coffee can't fix."

Talora raised her mug in a one-sided toast.

"Dat a girl."

"I can only drink two cups, though. Three gives me the jitters."

Once the bagel was prepared, Dina placed it on the kitchen table. Then, she poured Talora a glass of orange juice and brought it to the table as well.

Talora sat back down at the table; Dina sat across from Talora and nursed her coffee.

"When did Angie leave?" Talora asked from the one side of her mouth while chewing the bagel on the other.

Dina cleared her throat.

"She left after you dozed off," she said, looking Talora directly in her eye. "I didn't want her to drink and drive."

"She didn't drink that much, did she?"

Dina smirked, then shrugged.

"She's not much of a drinker."

"She's pretty cool," Talora said after washing down the first bite of the bagel with a sip of OJ. "How long has she lived here?"

"She moved down here from St. Louis after an abusive relationship."

"What does she do for a living?" asked Talora.

"She's a stylist," Dina said. "I thought I told you. She does my hair."

"Oh," Talora said stupidly. "That's right! You told me."

"So, what's the plan for today?" Dina asked in a rather hasty manner.

"The plan?" Talora mulled it over. "I was thinking about maybe driving into town. Maybe checking out the new shopping center, ah—"

"—Regalcrest."

"That's the one."

"It's not bad, I guess."

Talora asked, "How about you?"

"I, my dear," Dina said more eloquently, "have to go to work. The bills don't pay themselves." Dina took a sip of coffee. "I'll tell you what. I might be taking a half-day. Why don't you stop by the store later this afternoon? We can maybe grab lunch, if you're up to it. They just put in this new brewery on South Gates Street. I tell you, Talora, they have an arugula-beet salad with crusted, candied pecans topped with their own homemade raspberry vinaigrette that is to die for."

"Yummy." Her eyes widened. She almost purred. Then, she thought more about the name. She furrowed her brow. "Gates Street? I thought Gates Street was located in a bad area."

"It was," Dina said. "It's in one of these new places that was recently, as the kids call it, 'gentrified.' They've completely turned that whole area around. And, believe it or not, it's brought in more money for Soy. It's even brought out all of the hipsters from the woodwork."

"Hipsters in Soy?"

"Apparently so."

Dina raised her mug of coffee in a toast.

FROM the front porch, Talora waved goodbye to Dina.

As Dina drove the car in reverse from the driveway, she stuck her hand out of the window and waved back at Talora. She stuck her head out, as well, and then shouted at Talora, "Call me!"

"Will do," Talora shouted back and watched Dina drive away.

DINA left Talora a number where she could reach her while she was at work. She also left plenty enough food for Vladimir; however, she left a couple of treats for him in the laundry room and told Talora to feed him if he got fussy.

Only an hour since her aunt left the house, Talora was already contemplating giving Dina a call maybe just to talk, maybe just to find out what she was doing at that particular moment, maybe just to ask her a question about whether or not Vladimir liked to be brushed, maybe just to hear a person's voice—a real voice, that is.

Talora had done about everything she could possibly think of doing, including flipping through TV channels but not really finding anything decent to watch on the tube except for a BREAKING NEWS story on a man named Sonny Mims, a campaign manager for the presidential candidate, Governor Avanti Washington, and how his remains were found outside Tent City—investigators believed he was murdered by vamps—or skimming through one glossy fashion magazine after another or washing a pile of dirty laundry, and then, while waiting on her clothes to wash, going through these old boxes of art junk collecting dust in a tiny attic, and then, once the washer finished its cycle, putting the clothes into a dryer, and then, while waiting on her clothes to dry, redoing everything she did after her Aunt Dina left for work, TV, magazines.

While sitting on the couch, she held her finger in the shape of a gun. Placed the barrel that was her index finger to the side of her temple and cocked the hammer that was her thumb and then pulled the trigger.

Boom!

Brains on a wall. . .

What Talora would do to have her phone back?!?

Talora gave the TV another shot and while flipping through channels, landed on the Cartoon Channel where the trendy cartoon, *Japhy and Friends*, was playing.

The sight of the cartoon caused her to switch off the TV and throw the remote across the living room!

After another hour of piddling around Dina's house, Talora decided to take a walk outside and hoped to fight off the boredom with Mother Nature. Talora was surprised by the drop in temperature. Yesterday felt like a crisp fall day, the kind of day which promoted outdoor activities, such as going for a casual stroll through the neighborhood. Yet, today, it was winter. She was only wearing short sleeves and leggings. She decided to power forward and close the door behind her.

With her arms tucked into her chest, she only took seven steps outside before she changed her mind.

As Talora turned back around and proceeded back toward the house to grab more appropriate attire like a sweatshirt or light jacket, she stopped in her tracks.

The back door was wide open!

Huh?

For a moment, that familiar tension gripped her.

Ever since she arrived in Soy, she thought as though she had shed such a feeling. But it was back—or, at least, *trying* to make a comeback.

Talora ignored the feeling, the creeping dread.

She walked back into the house, checked the door as well as the door handle, and made sure to properly close it behind her. She walked upstairs to the guestroom and grabbed an orange BCC sweatshirt from her bag. Once she was dressed in a more comfortable outfit, she walked back downstairs.

Of course, the back door was open—wide open!

"What the hell?" said Talora, as she stepped outside and closed the door with a more forcible tug until the door was completely shut.

She released her hand from the door handle and waited for what she referred to as a hot minute and the whole time during her tense wait, she couldn't help but wonder if the door was going to open as if it had a mind of its own.

It didn't. It was just a door.

And Talora put any doubt to rest.

Weirded out by the back door, Talora walked through the back yard.

Before entering the guesthouse, she came across a worn strip of brown cloth material suspending from a protruded nail on a panel along the doorway. Thinking maybe Dina or whoever had snagged a jacket or even a wool coat on the nail, Talora leaned down and grabbed the strip of clothing from the nail. She couldn't quite tell what kind of material it was, either wool or cotton or something else. It appeared as old as dirt, whatever it was.

Once she rubbed the strange material between both her fingertips, Talora was struck by a momentary dizziness. The feel of the material felt coarse and staticky along her skin, the same feel one would receive while touching the surface of an old analog TV screen. All of a sudden, Talora felt ill. Her fingertips experienced a pinprick sensation.

She dropped the piece of clothing onto the ground. The nausea faded, as if, in an odd way, the material was attached to sickness.

As Talora took a deep breath, she reached for the door handle.

The door opened; however, nobody was on the other side of the door. Talora wasn't able to make contact with the door handle for the door kept moving farther away from her.

"What's up with th doors around here?" asked Talora, as she tried to play off the recent strangeness.

As the door opened entirely, she stood at the doorway of the guesthouse and examined the art studio inside—or what used to be an art studio.

Dusty white sheets were used as coverings throughout the studio and draped over furniture, as well as several easels and unfinished sculptures.

Talora stepped inside the guesthouse and made sure to close the door behind her. It turns out the door wasn't entirely closed to begin with. The door stuck and as with the back door, she had to give it a sturdy tug until it closed all the way.

She wandered around the studio. There were very little curtains covering the windows and natural light poured into the studio, casting out various dust clouds. Talora could only assume that her artwork had been put on hold, especially after starting up her own clothing store. Talora put the suspicions aside and removed a white sheet from one particular easel holding a painting of a woman—whom she assumed was Angie based on the short, spiky, red hair—lying nude on the couch. Her body was fully stretched out across the entire couch. Her right arm holding up her head while her other arm rested along the side of her hip. Talora wondered if the painting was either driven by the imagination of a woman who was channeling a lost—even recently discovered—sexuality or Angie, who could've possibly modeled for Dina. Talora leaned toward the latter.

She placed the white sheet back over the painting and saw a movement in the corner of her eye. Talora turned toward another white sheet that was draped over what looked like a sculpture of some kind. She carefully removed the dusty sheet and before her stood a black cockapoo. The realness of the dog was uncanny and appeared as if it had been stuffed by a taxidermist.

Intrigued by the so-called sculpture, Talora kneeled down and just as she was about to touch the side of its face, the old dog let out a bark!

Startled beyond belief, Talora stumbled backward and knocked over an easel. The sudden crash of the easel hitting the floor caused a chain reaction.

Startled by the sound, the dog ran off toward the door but was greeted by a closed door. Whimpering, the dog pawed at the dog.

Talora caught her breath and regained her composure. She went to let out the dog, but before she did that, she kneeled down and tried to calm the dog.

Immediately, she recognized the dog.

Confusion flooded her.

"Broot?" said Talora, still and shocked. "Is that you boy?"

✝

EVEN if the dog wasn't Broot—Talora had a deep suspicion that it was—she tried to make sense of how the dog ended up in Dina's studio.

Most importantly, *how did he end up in Soy, Missouri?*

That is, if the poor mutt was her old dog, Broot.

Still slightly freaked out, Talora walked Broot to her car and drove to Dina's clothing store La Lueur. All she could think about was Dina and whether or not she was being honest with her. If Dina knew about the dog, then the twenty-five thousand dollar question would be: "Why didn't Dina tell Talora about the dog?" She gave Dina the benefit of the doubt and went to her with a clear conscience.

When Talora arrived at La Lueur, Dina was surprised by her appearance. She handed off the customer to one of the employees, a college girl who was working part time to pick up extra spending money, and pulled Talora to the side.

"Nice place," Talora said, looking around.

"You like it?" said Dina. "I've put a lot of work into it—"

"—Listen, Dina," Talora said over Dina's voice, "you wouldn't believe me if I told you, but. . . " she cleared her throat, ". . . do you know there's a dog at your house?"

Talora was waiting—in fact, hoping—for her aunt to give her an answer like "Yeah," or "I know. That's my dog, Donnie." Or, whatever!

She received no such response. Instead, all Talora got was a long, blank face from Dina.

Dina said over the silence, "A dog? What? You're serious?"

"I found it in your studio."

"What the hell was a dog doing in my studio?"

"I dunno," Talora said, thinking of an excuse to tell Dina as to why she was in her studio. "I thought I heard this noise coming from the guesthouse. I went to check it out. Sure enough, I found a dog in there."

"What kind of a dog was it?" asked Dina.

"A cockapoo."

"Cockapoo?" Inherently, the thought turned her into one of the best detectives in Soy. "Didn't you used to have a cockapoo?"

"I did," Talora said. "And that's what's so spooky about it. He went missing the same time Nathan ran away."

"Yeah," Dina trailed off. "Spooky. So, where is it now?"

"In the car," Talora said, pointing over her shoulder.

"And you think it's your dog—"

"—Broot?"

"Yeah."

"I dunno," she said. " Maybe. I mean, it looks just like him. I mean, it can't be a coincidence, can it?"

"Well. . . "

With a pensive look etched on her face, Dina lowered her head for a moment. Her eyes were wrapped in thought. She looked back up at Talora.

". . . I've heard that some animals can travel a great distance to find their way back home. I think it might have to do with the owner's scent or something."

"Are you sure you're not thinking of cats?"

"I'm pretty sure it's dogs. Back in the day, police used bloodhounds to track people—"

"—Yeah, Dina, but this is a cockapoo," Talora said, playing off her frustration. "All it's good at tracking is another dog's butt hole."

Eventually, after a little convincing, Talora dragged Dina outside to her car, which was parked along the curb in front of the neighboring store, Guilty Café.

Talora opened the back door of the car, grabbed the end of a homemade leash that she made from a stretchy blue band she found in Dina's garage, and ordered the dog outside.

"Is that my workout band?" asked Dina.

"Yes." She saw a hint of anger on Dina's face. "It was either this or rope. I didn't want to use rope because I was afraid it might rub against his skin."

"It's fine," Dina said.

She specifically used that word—*fine.*

She trailed off, "I don't use them anymore."

"Good."

Dina kneeled down and examined the dog.

"It looks old." She glanced up at Talora. "Wasn't Broot old as well?"

Talora followed with a closed-mouth yes, which sounded like a *umm-hmm.*

"And you see the white spot on its back?"

Talora pointed out the heart-shaped spot on the dog's back.

"I see it," Dina said, feeling through the dog's matted hair.

"Can't be a coincidence," Talora said.

"This is weird," Dina uttered.

"I know, right?"

"Well," Dina said, standing back upright, "what are you doing now?"

"I just came by to show you the dog."

"While you're here, you want to check out the merch?"

Talora thought over Dina's offer.

She sealed the deal by telling Talora that she can pick out anything she wants.

"My treat," Dina said.

"What about the dog?" asked Talora.

Dina nodded at Guilty Café. Outside hung a "dog friendly" sign. Next to the entrance was a doggie bowl on the ground. A couple was eating lunch with their German Shepard on the patio. Talora spotted other four-legged creatures walking throughout the café. She heard dogs barking over the sound of a crying baby.

"I know the owner, Marisa," Dina said. "She won't mind watching over the dog for a while."

"Why can't I just bring the dog into your store?" asked Talora.

"Because my store is *not* dog-friendly."

Talora was tempted to follow up with a "Why not?" The two words dangled on the tip of her tongue. However, she spent more time thinking about why Dina wouldn't allow the dog into her store. She had put a lot of money, as well as time and effect into the store. Besides Vladimir—or "Vlad," as she called him before leaving the house—who, except for scooping out little, crusted balls of turd from the litter box, required less responsibility and maintenance, Dina didn't have any other pets inside her house—at least none that Talora was aware of. Each room of the house had different smells to match the paintings and colors on the walls, except for the laundry room, which, of course, smelled of cat turds and realistically, should've been painted the color brown. Talora combed her thoughts and specifically remembered the day she brought Broot, who was just a puppy at the time, to Dina's house. Broot wasn't allowed inside the house and he had to stay in a kennel in the garage overnight: Dina's orders. In fact, Talora remembered she was so broken up about her dog— which would later be her brother's dog—sleeping in a cold garage that she grabbed a sleeping bag, her first, then Nathan after he caught his sister fleeing from the air mattress, and they both snuck downstairs while everybody else was sleeping, and the two of them slept next to Broot.

Unless Dina was one of the greatest poker players west of the Hudson, Talora was convinced that the dog wasn't Dina's.

Surprisingly, the question had hit a nerve with Dina.

More promptly, Dina was tempted to follow up by throwing a term at Talora that only the cliché of a soft-celled, swirly-eyed, hypersensitive, so-called "righteous," sham-bot Millennial would commonly use while haranguing on the Internet: Something along the lines of "Am I being '*dog*-phobic?'"

The two held their tongues.

Dina walked the dog inside Guilty Café while Talora, who was less bothered by not bringing the dog with her, waited outside. A couple of minutes later, Dina returned with a gleeful smile on her face.

"Problem solved," Dina said, holding out her hands.

"She didn't mind?"

"Not at all," Dina said. "Marisa loves dogs more than she does humans. She even has a separate menu for dogs."

"That's cool," Talora said.

"Yeah," Dina said dismissively, "if you're into that sort of thing."

This time, Talora held her tongue.

✠

TALORA spent a good forty-five minutes to an hour trying on various types of outfits and modeling them for not only her number one critic who was Dina, but also for her own reflection in the dressing room mirror.

While Talora was flaunting an autumn squash colored waterfall collar pocket front wrap coat over a nicely fitted black sweater dress, as well as slouchy styling, knee high boots to match the black dress, her eyes crossed the front of the store. She took her eyes off the outfit, then Dina, and witnessed a dark yet, surprisingly, bright figure who was standing on the sidewalk across the street.

Immediately, she stopped modeling for Dina. The childish smile melted from her face. Her demeanor darkened. Both her eyes were pinned on Japhy, who was wearing the same outfit he wore on and off stage, including that same flashy coat, which had a particular way of making everything around it dull and lifeless.

Activity was happening all around him, such as pedestrians walking in close proximity, cars driving by, bicyclists riding by, even a bearded man who was restraining his dog from sniffing Japhy. Yet, despite all of that muted life encompassing and provoking him, his razor sharp eyes never left her. In that moment, Talora thought Japhy was wearing the look of a man who, yes, wanted to kill her.

Thinking maybe he might've been looking at someone else—but *how could he?* *The glass was tinted!*—Talora glanced around the store, praying to spot some washed-up groupie whom he had pity-fucked after a show. She turned her shoulder but saw nobody standing behind her. She looked in front of her but saw nobody, who'd warrant such attention. In other words, she had many props around her. But she was the star of the show!

"Talora?" said Dina, her voice giving off concern. "What's wrong?"

Talora snapped from her trance and turned to Dina.

The only word that she mustered from her lips wasn't a word at all but more or less an utterance of what had the potential of being a word.

"Are you okay?" Dina asked again. "You look like you've seen a ghost."

"Yes," Talora said and tried to find Japhy with her eyes.

He was no longer standing on the sidewalk.

Watching her.

In fact, he was nowhere to be found.

Yet, in Talora's mind, he was everywhere.

"I mean," she stuttered, "no. I just thought I saw someone I knew."

"Who?" Dina owled. "Ex-boyfriend stalking you?"

Talora didn't laugh at Dina's innocent joke. She could hardly bring herself to crack a smile.

"I would if I were a guy," Dina followed up as if she was completing a punch line.

As if a light switch had been turned off inside Talora, her confidence was no longer existent. Her posture was more slouched. Both of her arms appeared limp and heavy as they hung along her sides like cured meat. Even her neck started to arch like a turtle.

One minute, she was glowing, a soon-to-be "Maneater," celestial, unstoppable.

The next, decorated trash.

Even though Talora could feel that sense of panic slowly creeping in, Dina's humor helped remove the tension from the air.

More considerate of Talora's feelings, Dina said as Talora ambled back to the dressing room, "You know, Talora, I was thinking, if you're going to be hanging around in Soy for a little bit longer, if you wanted something to do to maybe pass the time."

"What? You mean, like a job?"

"Well, sort of."

"What do you have any mind? As you can see," Talora modeled her clothes once more but did so in a sloppy, amateur manner, "I'm extremely busy."

"Would you be interested in picking up some extra money?"

"Yeah," she said. "Sure."

Talora's voice went up a couple of octaves.

"I'm clearing out the Victorian style house off Colony Street in order to build a new store, which will be a sister store to La Lueur. The store's going to specialize—or better yet—focused more on eveningwear. Plus, I'm gonna add a bar and lounge on the first floor that way shoppers can enjoy a glass of wine while trying on a fun, flirty dress."

"That actually sounds like a good idea," Talora said.

"The place is old, though," Dina said, "and it needs a lot of renovation."

"So, it's an actual house?"

Dina nodded.

"Three stories," she said. "It was once a bed and breakfast before it was partially destroyed by a tornado. I already have a guy on the job. Name's Morrison, and he's great. But he can use a hand."

"Clearing out a house? That sounds like hard work."

"It's not about hard work, Talora. It's about putting a little joy in the work. Come on. What do you say? And, he's kind of cute too."

"Cute?"

"Yeah. Like an old soul kind of cute. And not only that, I'll pay you."

Talora asked, "How much?"

✝

AFTER they decided on eating a more low-key lunch at one of those home cookin' joints, which was within walking distance from Dina's store, Talora picked up the dog from Guilty Café and followed Dina back to the house where she made a bed in the garage for the dog and left him alone with a bowl of tap water and plenty of food to get him through the evening and then some. As her aunt had advised, Talora changed into more appropriate attire, which she wouldn't mind getting dirty. After all, Dina specifically explained to Talora that the job wasn't at all *Pretty in Pink* and definitely "roll-up-your-sleeves" kind of work. Once she was suited up in blue jeans and an older, smaller, more ragged sky blue sweatshirt that she borrowed from Dina, she rode with her aunt to the three-story Victorian style house that used to be the Beatty Fireside Mansion and parked behind an old rust-colored truck that looked as if it was from a time where television was shown in black and white. Dina showed Talora the front of the house, the porch, as well as the space, which would later be a parking lot. She pointed at certain areas along the roof, as well as gutters that had been repaired, while other areas were still marred by past storms, and painted vivid mental images for Talora, such as a gaudy sign, as well as lighting and a Romanesque sculpture on the front lawn.

Before they walked up the front steps of the porch, they passed a pile of discarded wood and scraps, which appeared waterlogged from rain. Next to the pile was a massive dumpster overflowing with what looked like the guts of the house. Dina made sure to tell her that Morrison was going to take the trash to the dump whenever he could get around to it.

"Looks like you have your work cut out for you," Talora said, her eyes crossing another trash pile in the front yard.

Dina told her to watch her step and emphasize nearby dangers, including broken glass and nails.

"Believe it or not," Dina said in defense, "clearing out the tree that had fallen through the roof was the hardest task. Fortunately, we managed to salvage most of the living room, which will be converted into the lounge-slash-bar area. The way I look at it, it's all downhill from here—or uphill?" Dina didn't fully understand the expression nor did she care to use it. She callously waved it off and forgot that she ever used it. "All of the work we have left is mostly cosmetic. Painting. Adding the bar. Well, not entirely cosmetic. We still have to redo the floors. Open up rooms. This, my dear, this is where *you* come in." She walked Talora to the front door. She pointed at the loose beam along the front steps and told Talora to watch her step. "Oh yeah," she whispered, "plus we have to revamp this whole area." This "*area*," Dina said, as in the front porch. "Morrison needs a hand tearing down a wall."

"Tearing down a wall, seriously?"

"Sure," Dina drawled. "I'll give you goggles, gloves, and all of the gear you need. It'll be fun, girl." Acting like her cautious tour guide, Dina escorted Talora farther into the house, which was stripped of flooring. She constantly pointed out other dangers, as well as where to step and where *not* to step. They stepped into the foyer, making their way around a spiraling staircase.

Immediately, Talora had doubts about helping Dina. She didn't know exactly what it was that had turned her off. Maybe it was the piece of plywood in front of the hallway closet with the caution tape marking the floor like a crime scene.

"Right," Dina said, tracking Talora's eyes toward the taped off area. "*That*," she identified. "Don't ask how that happened?"

Talora paused.

Then, teased, "How did *that* happened?"

Dina sighed.

"You want the long story or the short?"

Talora thought it over.

"Short please," she said.

"Morrison was clearing out the guest bathroom on the second floor when all of a sudden the toilet fell through the floor! The toilet ended up putting a massive hole in the floor."

"Really?"

"Yup."

"What's down there?" Talora asked, creeping closer to the caution tape.

"I haven't been down there, but Morrison says it might've been a wine cellar. Trust me. The floors are next on our list; however, our major priorities right now are to clear out all the walls before we can even think about redoing the floors."

"This place sounds like a deathtrap," Talora said.

"Like I said," Dina said, showing Talora the refinished living room, "it's not *Pretty in Pink*."

Dina showed Talora where the bar was going to be. Then, she walked Talora to every room in the house—or as she put it, every "department."

"Basically," she explained, "it's going to be like a mini-department store with a bar. Each room will have different departments: lingerie, gowns, makeup, etc."

"What are going to do with the other store?" asked Talora.

Dina said, "The plan is to run them both."

"Sounds like a lot of work."

"It's going to be," she said, more optimistically. "When I get burned out, I'll probably hand it off to one of my other employees at La Lueur and focus more on this place."

"Curious," Talora said, as she walked inside what used to be the master bedroom, which was now a gutted room, "what's the name of the store going to be?"

"Right now, *Un Verre* By Design," Dina said. "French for 'A Glass.'"

"*Un Verre*," Talora repeated, as she digested the name. "Not bad."

"The store's going to have a common theme: glass. If you think about it, the shape of a woman's body is similar to a glass that we drink out of. Either it be a wine glass, champagne glass, or even a juice glass, *Un Verre* will highlight all of the different shapes of the woman's body."

"Nice," Talora uttered, as she stood next to the window and peered outside at the street below. She turned her attention back to her aunt and said more thoughtfully, "You think you might be misleading the customer, though?"

"How so?" asked Dina.

"Well, you might draw in more drinkers than shoppers."

"No," Dina argued. "The clothes *will be* the focal point. The bar is going to be what separates my store from other stores. In a way, I'd like to think that the store's going to bring some needed sass to Soy. You know, more character."

"You'll have to get a bar license. Which means you may have to serve food as well."

"I'm working with a chef to create a small menu. I'm thinking more of a tapas style menu. I'm also working with a local artist named, get this, Icepick. Not sure if you've heard of him or not. He's all over social media."

"The name doesn't ring a bell."

"Anyway, he's creating all the logos as well as prints. And he's going to help me with the website as well. He's also working with this glass blower in a small town called Circa to create these life-size sculptures of all sorts of shapely women that will be shaped like a drinking glass. It has almost avant-garde feel to it, very 'out of this world'-New York gala."

"Interesting." Then, she added: "Why don't you drop 'By Design' and keep it 'Un Verre.' It has a better ring to it. Less is more. That's what they say in the marketing biz, right?"

"Well, Talora, your feedback is always appreciated and I will take it in consideration."

"Just sayin'."

A loud *thud* coming from upstairs drew Talora's attention upward.

"That must be Morrison," Dina said, as tiny chips of paint came raining down from the ceiling above. "He was supposed to be installing a new window on the third floor. He should be done already. I tell you what. I'll go grab him upstairs; and if he's ready, you two can start working in the kitchen."

Dina ordered Talora to stay put.

"I'll be right back," she said and walked up to the third floor.

When she returned to the second floor, she was walking with a young man—probably a few years older than Talora, maybe even closer to his thirties—whom she assumed he was this guy, Morrison. In fact, after a short introduction, Talora learned that his name wasn't Morrison. His name was actually Leonard Byrd but was called Morrison by mainly her aunt because he happened to share an uncanny resemblance to Jim Morrison, as in "Jim Morrison of the rock band, *The Doors*."

"I forgot," Dina said over Talora's visual confusion, "he's before your time."

Trying to prove her point, Dina pulled out her smartphone and googled Morrison's look-alike and showed Talora the results. She compared the image from the phone to the flesh and bone standing in front of her.

"I see what you mean," Talora said in agreement. "Yeah. I guess everybody has a twin out there."

"You mean like doppelgängers."

"Dopple-what?"

"Doppelgängers," Morrison said. "They're like twins, but they're not related by blood."

"Are you talking about clones?"

"No," Morrison said. "Doppelgängers."

"I literally have no idea what you're talking about."

Talora laughed first, Morrison followed.

"So," Dina interrupted, "lets put this girl to work, shall we?"

Morrison showed them the way.

He said, "After you."

✠

DOWNSTAIRS in the kitchen, Morrison provided Talora with safety gear, including a pair of goggles to keep debris from hitting her eyes, as well as a pair of gardening gloves, which were the only gloves he could find.

While Dina watched at a safe distance, Morrison ran down the list of do's and don'ts and showed her the ropes on how to properly swing a sledgehammer. Her first attempt was poor and barely even penetrated the dry wall next to the doorway and Morrison was left with no other choice than to step in behind her and in what Dina perceived as an innocent yet slightly flirtatious attempt at a move, adjusted her grip around the handle of the sledgehammer and told her to hold the handle as if she was holding an egg.

"Don't strangle the damn thing," Morrison specified for her. "The downward momentum will do all the work."

Talora did as she was told and drove the sledgehammer through the wall, resulting in a decent-sized hole. She pulled the hammer away from the wall, tearing away a chunk of drywall.

For about three solid hours of tearing away walls and carrying leftover debris to the dumpster outside whenever the kitchen became too full, Talora and Morrison decided to call it quits. Dina had stepped away for a couple of hours to attend to her other business and returned a few minutes before they finished.

Before Talora parted ways with Morrison, he invited her out for a drink. She immediately declined without putting any thought into the invitation.

Dina said it'd be good for her.

Morrison said he'd show her around town.

Talora told him that she'd think about it, which, in other words, meant "heck no."

APPARENTLY, while Dina was away, she bought a new leash, one of those extendable leashes that allowed a dog to move around more, and when she pulled into the driveway, Talora noticed the dog was on the front porch. The other end of the leash was strung around the front column. The dog perked up from its sleeping position as soon as Talora stepped out of the car. The sight of the dog responding to her presence convinced her the dog was Broot, even though she didn't have any proof, except for the spot on its back. All she could do was wonder how he ended up all the way out here in a place that rhymed with toy.

A hot shower after an afternoon of backbreaking labor inspired Talora to reconsider Morrison's invitation. Dina's convincing, as well as a constant usage of the word *cute*, was the icing on the cake. He wasn't at all Talora's type; in fact, they couldn't be farther apart in their personality.

Finally, after going over all of the pros and cons of having a drink with a man whom she had just met and, not to mention, a man whom she was possibly going to be working with—that is, if she continued the work—Talora used Dina's phone to call Morrison. Despite his cool composure over the phone, he was glad to hear Talora's voice. He offered to pick her up. She kindly refused and said that she'd rather met him somewhere. He gave her a name of a place called Jaxxx's, which, at first listen, sounded like Jack's. She didn't spend too much time picking out an outfit. She went casual and wore an outfit that would make her blend in.

When Talora arrived at the dive bar, she was turned off by the name. Immediately at first glance, she thought the place was a strip club—because of the three x's. Turns out it was a dive bar. Inside were all things of a clichéd bar. Capitalism at its finest. Glowing beer signs scattered throughout the bar as if Talora was walking through a spam museum. Names like *Miller*, *Bud*, and *Coors* commonly treated like spiritual totems. In the back were two billiard tables, which were being occupied by two groups, the granola types, who looked as if they weren't going anywhere anytime soon. A younger rowdy crowd of redhats was hanging out by a dartboard. Not too far away from the elephants in the room was one of those modern day "smart" jukeboxes where the patrons chose a song from their "smart" devices. Of course, the song "I Killed The Devil" by Stuffed Animalz happened to be playing as soon as Talora made her way through the bar. The owner Jaxxx, who spelled his name with three x's, was sitting at the end of the bar and keeping an close eye on his toadies, who, at any moment, were ready to act out of line or say something that resulted in the boot by a bouncer named Mouse. Surprisingly, the bar was packed for a Tuesday night. Which made Talora wonder if something else was going on tonight—like a special on drinks or karaoke night or whatever. According to Morrison, who had already reserved a seat—or better yet, "spot"—at the end of the bar for Talora, it was a typical Tuesday night at Jaxx's. To say the least, the residents of Soy, Missouri, liked to drink and weren't too particular about what they liked to drink.

Morrison greeted her over loud music and background chatter and spent the next few minutes screaming what her initial thoughts were on the place but only catching snippets of her answer. He waved down some young, perky bartender named Alicia, whom, after acknowledging Morrison's wave, parted ways with a waitress and was waiting at his command as if she was Rin Tin Tin. Talora gathered that the two of them had a relationship outside that seemingly artificial employee-patron bond where *she* was working him for tips and gratitude and *he* was finding the right angle to get inside her pants.

When Alicia arrived, Talora ordered a cranberry and vodka.

Morrison was drinking what looked like whiskey. All she caught was the name "Jack" when she asked him.

After spending the next few minutes trying to talk over the music, Talora decided to seize the opportunity of grabbing a table that had recently opened up.

Once seated, the drink helped take Talora's mind off the song. For the most part, she mainly asked questions. Morrison did most of the talking, and she was fine with hearing what he had to say about the town. "What's there to do around here?" Talora asked while Morrison pointed around the bar as if he was showing off a guilty pleasure. "You're looking at it." Morrison leaned in closer to Talora and came close to that hookup range. However, it was clear to Morrison that he knew exactly where Talora had drawn the line and went straight to it without any hesitation. "I know," he said, "it doesn't have much of a nightlife. I'm sure for a city girl like yourself it must feel like cultural shock."

He backed off, allowing Talora room to talk freely.

She talked about her love for the small town vibe, the quietness of the countryside; however, she was more curious about what Morrison had to say.

Morrison was a single dad of a six year old girl, who, when asked about her whereabouts, was currently staying with Morrison's mother.

Slight judgment came over Talora as Morrison explained his situation, particularly the one involving a "crazy" ex who had herself a "pill problem" and was a "popper" trying to regain "custody over" *his* "baby girl." Her mind drifted from Morrison's words, leaving her vulnerable inside a negative space.

Talora wanted to ask: "So, why aren't you at home raising your daughter like any normal father?"

Instead, she thought, *you're out grabbing a drink.*

Hopefully, the kid will be in bed by the time you get home.

Except for his days off, Morrison never found much time to see his daughter. Which, somehow, made Talora more ashamed than embarrassed for taking him away from spending valuable time with his daughter. Although it was he, Morrison, who invited her out for drinks. He worked two jobs, one as a so-called "contactor," this sort of Renaissance Man who could repair a car, fix any issue inside a house, build a deck, or even cook a three-course meal. His second job was at one of those big shoebox stores as a freighter/forklift driver who worked a graveyard shift. Tonight happened to be one of his nights off.

When asked how or where he met Dina, Morrison said the two met through a new app called *Get Ur Dun*, which was sort of like a redneck version of Angie's List. She needed help with repairing a leak at La Lueur. Morrison had done such a good job with the leak that Dina had kept his contact information and used him frequently with any other issues she had at her store and even at her house. It was fair to say Morrison was the kind of guy who'd you like to keep handy. And Dina had him in her back pocket.

Despite their city girl-country boy differences, after a couple of more drinks, the two hit it off and for the first time in a long time, Talora felt optimistic about a future in Soy.

After her third drink, she excused herself from the table and passed by a payphone next to the restrooms. For a while, she contemplated calling her parents to inform them that they had nothing to worry about and that she was okay.

She went so far to grab the phone and as she was about to insert a coin into the machine, Morrison walked past her. She immediately backed away from the phone.

"Drinking and dialing," he teased, "bad combo."

"You're right," Talora said and walked back to the table while Morrison excused himself.

☩

SO far, the night flew by without any hitches.

Before she fell into that stranger-danger zone, she parted ways with Morrison on good terms and one-eyed her way back to Dina's.

By the time Talora pulled the car into the driveway and did so in the manner that would catch the eye of a cop on patrol, it was a quarter past eleven. Dina had left a couple of lights on, including the front porch light. Talora chugged a bottle of lukewarm water that she found underneath the passenger seat of the car before heading inside.

Still riding high on a vodka buzz, she refocused and played her own in-head game of pretending as if she had been recently pulled over by a police officer who suspected her of drinking while under the influence of alcohol, and tried her five-star best to walk a straight line along the edge of the driveway. If Talora had been pulled over and was given a sobriety test, she would've failed miserably.

Talora stumbled two times, one of those times she nearly tripped into a bush. She didn't want Dina to see her like this, especially with her being a guest in her house. But she told herself that Dina wasn't a parent; but, most importantly, not her parent.

When Talora stepped inside the house, she headed to the kitchen and grabbed yet another drink of water. Downed the entire glass all in one breath. Dina, who was watching old reruns of *Shark Tank* in the living room, called out to whom she suspected was Talora and Talora, still feeling loose from the buzz, responded with a Shakespearean-like "Yes."

Dina leaned over the head of the couch and asked, "What are you doing?"

"Nothing," she said, straightening her walk.

Her head wasn't spinning as badly as it was in the car; however, Dina's presence reassured her that everything was going to be fine.

Somehow, the topic of the dog was brought up into a one-sided conversation.

With Broot on her mind, Talora was convinced that the dog was Broot and all of a sudden, had made it a nightly mission to prove to her aunt that the dog in the garage was, in fact, her missing dog, Brooty Boy.

"I'm a ninety-nine point nine, nine, nine percent that it's Broot," she slurred. "You'll see."

"I believe you, Talora," Dina said, as if she was talking to a toddler, who was on the verge of throwing a tantrum, and wasn't at all in any mood to contain such an implosion—and explosion.

"No," Talora snapped. "I want to show you—"

She dug out Dina's photo albums from the shelf and as she was about to pull out the photos, Dina eased from the couch in a state of uneasiness.

Talora opened the photo album and flipped to the section where she saw her puppy, Broot.

The entire page was empty.

No photos.

Anxiously, Dina asked, "What happened to all my photos?"

Unable to find the words, Talora opened her mouth in shock.

"Talora? Where did they go?"

"I don't know." She carelessly flipped through the other pages, even bending one of the corners of a photo. "They were right there. I swear!"

"Well," Dina said, "they're not. Where are they?"

She waited to hear an answer from her niece, but all she received was a destroyed young woman who looked as if she was about to melt into tears.

"Talora," Dina said tenderly, "what's going on with you?"

"What d'you mean?"

"I mean, 'What's going on?'" asked Dina.

Again, Talora was unable to find the words.

She set aside the photo albums and told Dina that she needed sleep.

Dina couldn't agree more.

✟

DRENCHING wet with sweat, Talora woke up at nine minutes after two o' clock.

She checked the time and once she realized what time it was, she felt almost upset. She flipped her pillow to the cool side, shut her eyes, and tried to sleep off the hangover. However, her head was splitting in two, as if she had a valley running through the center of her forehead. She couldn't sleep even if she tried. She decided to search for remedies—as she should. She rolled out of bed. Even moving made the pain in her head much worse. She blindly stumbled her way through the night darkness and made it to the bathroom where she ran cool water over her throbbing face. The feel of cool water pressed against her skin lessened the ache in her head; however, the ache was *still* there, chilling like a movie villain.

When she ambled back into the guestroom, she couldn't help but notice that the window was opened all the way. Not once did Talora ever remember opening the window before passing out. She still had on the same clothes she was wearing the night before. Which undermined the whole reason for opening the window. If Talora was so hot—in fact, she was burning up—then it'd only make sense to remove heavy clothing and changed into a cooler, more comfortable outfit? Why open a window?

Talora knew the answer to that question.

And her answer alone made her that much more terrified.

Cautiously, Talora crept toward the window and as she about to close it, she saw a dark figure standing in the backyard. Talora knew that shape. She knew it was him

206

based on the shape, as well as the glimmer in the passing moonlight.

☦

FUELED by questions and yet, at the same time, the alcohol that was still coursing through her veins, Talora marched downstairs and charged through the backdoor. As soon as she stepped outside, she was grabbed by a dark figure. Her first, most basic instinct was one of survival, to get whoever—or whatever—it was who was on her, off her. In one-two combination, she curled both of her arms inward and pushed the figure away and then clawed straight for the eyes. She raked the eyes, her hand falling across heavy clothing covering what felt like a muscular body.

She ran back inside and flipped on the floodlight.

The dark figure, whom she thought was Japhy, was no longer standing on the back patio. He was gone.

Cautiously, she walked to the edge of the back patio and called out his name, "Japhy!" She screamed, "I know you're out here! You coward!"

From behind, she felt yet another presence: Dina.

She turned around and found Dina, half asleep, standing in the doorway.

"Talora," she mumbled, "you know what time it is?"

"I fucking saw him." She checked her arms for marks but couldn't find any. "He grabbed me!" She pointed to the last spot where she saw Japhy last standing. "He was *right* there!"

"Grabbed you! Who?"

"This—this asshole who's been following me."

She raised her voice loud enough for Japhy—or whom she thought was Japhy—to hear her.

"Following you? Talora, are you sure?"

"Yes," she shouted out. "I'm fucking sure."

"Calm down," Dina said, trying to use her hands to calm down Talora. "How concerned do I need to be right now, Talora? Do I need to call the police?"

Talora thought it over.

"Talora, let me call the police—"

"—No," Talora finally said. "That's not necessary."

"Are you sure?"

"Yes." Talora peered out into the night darkness. "He won't come back now that he knows I know what he's up to."

"I'm calling the police—"

"—No," Talora said. "Don't."

Dina looked over Talora and told her to come back inside. She walked Talora back inside the house and closed the door behind her.

✠

TALORA woke up to the faintest smell of smoke.

She rolled out of bed, didn't bother checking the time, and tracked down the smell to the bathroom where she discovered the missing photos in the sink. Each and every one of them was curled and burnt. She knew they were the photos for only one image remained clear to her behind the blackened, bubbled print and that was Dina's face. In the photo, she was a younger and more conservative woman, for the most part that is. From the hazy quality of the photo, it appeared as if the photo was taken around the time Talora used to visit her aunt before they stopped talking. Most importantly, the photo was taken around the time Talora brought a puppy named Broot with her everywhere she traveled.

Slightly numb from the hangover, Talora gathered up all of the burnt photographs from the sink and tossed them in the trash. She ran the faucet and washed out the leftover black flakes and smears along the sink.

✠

MORE composed, Talora walked downstairs. The TV was running in the kitchen; however, Dina was nowhere to be found. She called out Dina's name twice but never receive a response.

As panic started to creep in, Talora started to check each room, including the back of the house. She stepped outside and walked onto the back patio where she found what looked like an old button on the ground. The button was located precisely where she was grabbed. She picked up the button and pocketed it.

When Talora reached the laundry room, which was located in the front of the house, she heard two voices talking outside—one of them, she thought, sounded just like Dina's voice.

She followed the voices to the front porch where she saw her aunt talking to a policeman in the driveway. He was a rather stout man, his face scarred up from a bad case of late adolescent acne. He had a gray mustache looked like as if it was established in 1998. Both his hands were planted on his hips, his thumbs looped over his belt like hooks. She spotted a police car parked in the driveway. Along the side of the car read the word *Sheriff*.

From the casualness of the conversation, she didn't see any reason to panic—at least, not yet. The two appeared as if they knew each other.

Talora decided to crack open the front screen door and eavesdrop on the conversation.

Their voices were muffled. Before the so-called Sheriff parted ways with her aunt, Talora most definitely heard her asking the man if he could keep an eye on things around the house for the next couple of days or so. "Your presence," Dina said, "will scare him away."

Somehow, Dina's words had comforted Talora and a part of her knew that—despite everything that had happened these past couple of days—there was absolutely no reason to get all worked up.

By the time Dina returned, Talora had already jetted back toward the kitchen and fixed herself a Dina's finest brew. Dina wasn't at all surprised to see Talora up so early and considering her inebriated state last night, wearing the same exact clothes that she wore last night.

Although, a part of her had an internal bet going on with herself that young gals Talora's age usually turned into pumpkins after a long night out.

Talora asked before Dina could voice the obvious, "What was that all about?"

"You saw, huh?"

Talora faced Dina and leaned against the side of the countertop. The coffee was much stronger than the day before. After taking a sip, Talora grimaced from its bitterness.

"Too strong?"

"Nope," Talora said, feeling a bubble of nausea in her stomach. "It's exactly what I need right now. So. . . "

"You had me worried last night, Talora—" she said straightforwardly, as she made her way into the kitchen, "—don't flip. I didn't mention your name."

"Trust me," Talora mumbled. "Not in any mood to be *flipping*."

"All I said was that there was this creep hanging outside my house last night and that I," Dina motioned to Talora, "'we' would feel more comfortable if one of Sheriff's deputies kept an eye out for the next couple of days. That's all. . . "

More relieved, Talora took yet another sip of coffee. She came close to spitting it out. Usually, the first was the worst. The second, better. Then, the third, tolerable. However, it tasted as if the coffee was getting worse by the sip.

"Sheriff Tate is a good man," Dina said, as if she was still trying to convince her niece that she was in the right, *not* the wrong, for calling what her rotten generation commonly referred to as pigs. "*Beloved* by our community," she emphasized. "He looks after all of us, Talora. *All* of us."

"Thanks," Talora said softly. "But you didn't need to do that."

"Well, I don't think you gave me any other choice, Talora. To be honest, you scared the shit out of me last night. So, you want to tell me what's really going on? I mean, who the hell is this guy?"

Talora hung her head.

"You'd never understand," she muttered.

Dina stepped forward and faced Talora.

"Then, help me try to understand."

Talora said again, "You wouldn't understand."

"Is that the real reason why you came here," Dina pursued, "because you're running away from someone? If so, from who, Talora?"

Talora's head was pounding again. Clearly, the coffee was not helping at all, nor was her aunt and her grilling. She pinched the bridge of her nose. Then massaged the ache behind her eyes.

As Talora lifted her head upward, she saw a familiar face on TV.

Pacen's face!

Without drawing too much attention to herself, she shifted her weight to one side of her body and canceled out Dina from her partial view.

"The vehicle of Pacen Selassie, also known as DJ Pac-Attack, member of the popular band Stuffed Animalz, was in an abandoned parking lot next to the Panorama Inn in East Harlem, New York. Mr. Selassie was reported missing last—"

Talora darted around Dina and turned off the TV before Dina could listen to the breaking news report. The last words Talora caught before the TV went black was the *explosion, which was captured by one of the hotel—*

"Too much to drink last night?" asked Dina, as she folded her arms over her chest, stood back, and watched Talora and her strange behavior.

Talora asked, "Can I use your computer?"

"Yeah," Dina said. "Sure. Be my guest."

Talora stormed out of the kitchen.

Dina stopped Talora at the doorway by calling out to her.

"Talora," she said, causing Talora to turn her shoulder, "I'm not your mother. But just know that you can tell me whatever you want, that is when you're ready."

Talora nodded.

"I'm not going to judge you." Dina cracked a smile. "Trust me. I'm the last person who should be judging others."

Insulted by the remark, Talora furrowed her brow.

"And what is it that supposed to mean?"

"It means I'm not perfect," Dina said, "and neither are you."

"Okay," Talora said shortly and walked to the office.

Somehow, the sound of Talora's usage of the word and the way it shot out of her mouth like a dart left Dina feeling small as if, no matter what she said to reassure her niece, she was oblivious to what girls went through nowadays, especially in a technology-driven society. Dina didn't have any children, but she could only imagine what it'd be like to have one.

And a small part of her felt no regret.

Not even a sliver.

✠

AS soon as Talora pulled up the web browser on Dina's outdated iMac, she typed in Pacen's name in the search bar.

Several "shocking" headlines from several untrustworthy news sites came up, most of them being click bait and rabbit holes. So far, according to one news site which seemed to be more consistent to what she briefly heard on the TV, investigators didn't have much evidence or details as to Pacen's whereabouts, other than a shaky cell phone video with someone who could possibly pass as Pacen. Basically, all they had was the SUV. But no Pacen.

Frustrated by the lack of information—and even the information she gathered was either distorted for shock value or taken out of context—Talora decided to go on social media sites, which was the worst decision she could've made. All of the hearsay and garbage spewing from the fingers of Stuffed Animalz haters was only adding to her frustration. She came across bogus stories, rumors, alternate facts, and false allegations—one of them being that Pacen groped a so-called "fan" at a concert and that he was getting exactly what he deserved.

"Burn in hell, white boy," wrote username Scream-Queen@404.

Talora read more hateful comments on the Internet and drew her own conclusion that these people—Russian or Chinese bots or algorithms—were sharing or exposing more about themselves than the actual people or persons whom they were hating on.

Talora even read a theory that Pacen left the band and was living incognito in London under the pseudonym Gaffney Wrinkler.

Dina knocked on the doorway and asked Talora if she wanted an egg or whatever. Her choice. Talora's wasn't hungry; in fact, she was starting to feel sick.

"No," Talora said, rubbing the side of her face. "I can grab something to eat later."

"You sure?"

"Yeah."

Talora checked the time and realized it was almost lunch. Yet, Dina wasn't at work.

"Weren't you supposed to go into work today?" asked Talora.

"I was," she said, "but, you know, I didn't want to leave you here alone."

"What?" Talora exclaimed. "No! I don't want you missing out on work because of me. Dina, if you have to go to work, then go. Please, don't let me hold you back—"

"—Do you want to come with me?" asked Dina. "I'll put you to work. Plus, it'll take your mind off whatever it is you're going through."

"What about Morrison?" asked Talora.

"What about him?"

"Does he need help today?"

Talora regretted asking the question as soon as it left her lips. Although the more she thought about spending the day working up a sweat, the more she realized that maybe it was a good idea. "Sweat out the poison," as Pacen used to say.

"I'm sure he does," Dina said over a pause. "Why? Did you want to help out again?"

"Maybe," Talora said. "Yeah. It'll give me something to do."

"I told you it's fun, didn't I? In a way, it's kind of like a rage room."

"Rage room?"

"You know, they have these rooms where people pay to take out all of their frustration on a TV, furniture, even cars."

"Yeah," Talora said. "I think I've heard of those. I didn't know they were called rage rooms, though."

Dina's phone rang. She excused herself, grabbed her phone from the kitchen table, and walked back to the office.

"Speak of the devil," Dina said, showing Talora the name on the screen.

Talora not only couldn't read the name for the name was too small, but also her eyes still hurt.

"Who is it?" whispered Talora.

"Morrison," Dina mouthed.

She answered the call.

"Hey, Mory," she said jubilantly. "Sup?"

While Dina was listening to Morrison, she turned her attention to Talora and started making strange facial expressions.

"Really?" Dina responded. "Well, let me ask her?"

Dina muzzled the phone over her shoulder and nodded at Talora.

"Morrison," she said softly, "wants to know if you can give him a hand today at the new store."

Talora thought it over. The thought alone of losing her mind in Dina's house made her answer easy.

She bobbed her head.

"Yeah," she said, her stomach churning, "why not?"

Talora stood up from the desk while Dina placed the phone up to her face.

"Yes," Dina said over the phone. "She said she can..." she nodded over his response. "...Sounds great." Then, "She'll see you soon... bye."

Dina ended the call.

"How much did you two drink last night?" she asked Talora. "Y'all must've had a good ole time."

"Why?"

"He sounded a little hungover himself."

"Really?" Talora paused. "I don't remember him drinking that much."

She shrugged her shoulders, as if she was shrugging away a dark thought.

✠

TALORA didn't bother to change pants. She threw on another sweatshirt that she borrowed from Dina and left the house with little primping.

On the way to the renovated house, she pulled over on the side of the road to vomit. Afterwards, she felt a hundred times better. Dina told her that, after she finished up at the store, she was going to stop by later that afternoon with a cooler of beverages and sandwiches. Talora was now hungry.

She decided to grab a buttery biscuit at one of those places she swore never to eat at ever again. She managed to hold down the biscuit, as well as the coffee and orange juice.

Once her belly was full, she was looking forward to seeing Morrison again.

When she arrived, Morrison was already there.

Pleased by the sight of Morrison's truck, she carried more pep in her step as she walked up the front porch. Morrison greeted Talora in the foyer. He was acting different, strange. When Talora said "Sup" to him, he mimicked her and said "Sup" back. Talora was bothered by Morrison's demeanor and the words he was using, like following with the word *dog* after sup or using the word *a'ight* or *tight* or *nuttin'* or *chillin'*. These were not Morrison's words, yet they were the words that Talora had grown up hearing. What bothered Talora were his clothes, in particular, that flashy, glittery coat. Talora realized it the same coat that Japhy wore. She knew it wasn't a coincidence. The coat was special, thin and light, stretched all the way down to his ankles, one of its kind. Even Japhy's diehard fans tried to replicate the coat, made their own version of the coat and wore them at Halloween parties, going as their own self-proclaimed "golden god." Even wore that coat at Cosplay events. Morrison didn't strike her as Stuffed Animalz fan.

Talora immediately questioned him.

"What's going on?" she asked. "Why are you wearing that coat?"

With a familiar grin on his face, Morrison reached his hand toward his neck, pinched a handful of flesh underneath his chin, and pulled upward. He kept pulling and pulling and the more he pulled, the more freaked out Talora had become. He ended up pulling off his entire face!

Before Talora, Japhy revealed himself. He held the loose mask of flesh in the air. He even wiggled it around for Talora.

"What the hell did you do to Morrison?" asked Talora, backing away in horror.

"Your buddy, Morrison, is taking a BREAK from work!"

Japhy laughed at the apparent joke.

Talora wasn't laughing at all. Instead, she was looking around the house and searching for nearby weapons and contemplating her next move of attack. To the right of Japhy was a bucket of paint, which could be used as a tool for bludgeoning. In the dining room the sledgehammer was resting against the wall; however, it was too far from her reach and Japhy would be on her before she finished uttering the second syllable of the word *supercalifragilis-ticexpialidocious.*

With his eyes widened in child-like madness, Japhy yelled out, "Catch!"

He threw the wiggly mask of flesh at Talora, who had no other choice than to catch it.

The flesh was scalier than any normal flesh. She could feel the mask moving in both her hands as if, in a way, the flesh was alive.

She glanced down at the whitish-caramel pattered snake coiling around both of her hands.

Startled by the albino ball python, which was extremely docile by nature despite its fiery red eyes, Talora screamed out in horror!

She dropped the snake to the floor; and, in return, the snake slithered away.

Out of options, she ran away from Japhy, who wasn't so thrilled about chasing after her. Instead, Japhy acted as if he was going to take his time with Talora, as if, in a disturbing way, he was toying with her.

"There's nowhere to hide, Talora!" he yelled out, his voice carrying throughout the entire three-story house.

Talora managed to seek cover behind the wobbly island in the kitchen, which she and Morrison hadn't gotten around to tossing in the trash outside. The minor rest had given Talora enough time to plan her next move—which was to basically keep as much distance from herself and Japhy until she managed to sneak outside and run to her car. Her eyes crossed a body in the next room. . .

Morrison!

Japhy wasn't lying.

With a shard of wood protruding from his side, Morrison was sitting against the wall. He was bleeding badly and was drifting in and out of consciousness. As soon as he laid eyes on Talora, he perked back up. The adrenaline had given him enough alertness to motion to his injuries, in particular his left leg, which looked as if it was bending in a way that any normal leg shouldn't bend.

Seeing Morrison and his current state had changed Talora's plan and she told herself that she wasn't leaving without Morrison.

Japhy's footsteps were closer.

Talora decided to steer Japhy away from Morrison by creeping into the next room, which was the living room.

While Japhy crept his way into the kitchen, Talora took cover behind the living room wall, peeked around the corner, and charted out her next position of hiding, which was the hallway closet.

Japhy left the kitchen.

Talora tiptoed to the hallway closet, sneaked inside, and closed the door behind her. In the tense silence, she waited for Japhy to pass. She watched his dark shadow easing across the beam of light underneath the doorway. Japhy's shadow came and went. Then, it came back again. Talora waited in suspense for Japhy to open up the door and grab her. Strangely, he didn't. He kept on walking. Talora listened closely to his footsteps moving farther and farther away. Yet, the shadow below the doorway still remained!

In the darkest of the closet, Talora heard yet another sound.

However, the sound was coming from inside the closet!

She listened closer to the *rustling* sound. She followed the sound to the floor. Then to the albino ball python, which was now slithering up her left leg. With her body shaking, she held the scream tightly inside her chest and at any second, she was ready to explode. She moved her eyes downward to the bottom of the closet door. The shadow was gone. However, she lost track of Japhy's presence.

The snake made its way up her thigh.

Once it reached her waist, Talora couldn't take it any longer.

All in one motion, she grabbed the snake, threw it to the floor, and ran out of the closet.

Japhy was nowhere to be found; in fact, the entire house was silent.

As Talora listened for Japhy, she heard grunts coming from Morrison.

"Talora," Morrison groaned, "help me please. . . "

Talora didn't budge an inch.

"I think my leg is broken," he said, his voice strained.

Again, Talora didn't make a move.

"Talora!" Morrison shouted out.

She could hear the pain in his voice.

He reassured her by telling her that he's gone and that he exited through the backdoor.

Cautiously, Talora crept back toward the kitchen. She grabbed a screwdriver from the kitchen countertop and was ready to use it if necessary.

As soon as Talora stepped into Morrison's direct line of sight, she peered past the living room doorway and saw Japhy kneeling over Morrison.

Japhy's hand was covering Morrison's mouth.

"Why hello, Talora!" Japhy said in Morrison's voice. "Nice to see you again, Talora!"

Once more, Japhy laughed.

He removed his hand from Morrison's mouth and prowled toward Talora.

Holding out the screwdriver in defense, Talora back-pedaled away from Japhy until she reached the foyer. Every now and then, she glanced over her shoulder to see where she was going. Then, when she turned her sights back in front of her, Japhy was three steps closer as if he was able to move triple as fast in blinks.

"Give it up, Talora," Japhy said. "You're mine now—"

"—What the fuck do you want from me?" cried Talora.

Backpedaling away from Japhy, she glanced over her shoulder yet again and saw the caution tape surrounding the sheet of plywood over the floor.

"I want you to suffer until your last breath," Japhy seethed, flexing his hands. His nails extended outward like the talons of a hawk.

"Why?" cried Talora. "What did I ever do to you?"

"What did you do to me?" Japhy repeated hysterically. "You took *everything* away from me!"

Talora backed up to the plywood. She placed her right heel against the corner of the plywood. She stopped and held the screwdriver in front of her, as if it was a knife. She had finally reached the point of no return.

Fight or flight.

Talora chose neither because why exactly?

Because neither *fight* nor *flight* was founded by the very essence that irrefutably separated the humans from the animals. And Talora was tired of the games. The hide and seek bullshit. The cat and mouse bullshit. She was sick and tired of all the bullshit. She felt the warm vibration in her pocket. With her free hand, she pulled out the button and held it in her palm and could see the button shaking as if it was an entity far greater than she'd ever know or understand.

"What you got there?" asked Japhy.

Talora balled her hand into a fist and embraced the energy cast from the button. She felt it calling to her, not the button but a life-force attached to the button, coursing through her body and then past her, peeling back worlds beyond her very own, and opening doorways that were opened by the One whose eye, the one and only eye, the Third Eye, remained an interstellar highway of the great universe, a glowing sapphirine light, hollow and eternal.

"You know, *Japhy*," she said calmly, as the whole tearful act started to wear off, "I never told you this but. . . you're a terrible singer."

Overcome with rage, Japhy suddenly charged at Talora.

At the very last second, Talora kicked the plywood away from her, which, in return, caused the plywood to slide over the floor and reveal the massive hole.

As Japhy was about to tackle Talora, she opened her mind.

And like that, she disappeared into the Void.

Japhy tackled empty air, tripped, and fell into the hole. He managed to grab hold of the sides of the jagged flooring.

Talora suddenly reappeared!

Stunned by the move, she found Japhy hanging below her.

The last words he said to her before he lost his grip were "I win."

She dropped the screwdriver from her hand, then button, which ended up falling into the hole.

Once her hands were free, Talora crawled forward and leaned over the hole to grab him but he already fell. She watched him plummet into the darkness. She never saw him land for it was too dark. However, she heard him crashing heavily to the basement floor below.

The sound of the crash filled Talora with relief and caused her to back away from the hole.

As she was about to check on Morrison's condition, she heard what sounded like a *whimper* coming from below.

She listened closer and heard a familiar voice coming from the floor below.

Japhy was alive; however, he sounded hurt.

He sounded younger.

Talora knew it was a trap—*it had to be*, she thought. He was luring her down into the hole where he'd find an opportunity when Talora wasn't looking and then he'd make his move.

She couldn't help but glance at the hole and the torn strip of coat dangling on a jagged piece of wood. The material was different, older, raggedy, brownish, *not* gold.

Suspicious of the voice, Talora found the door to the basement. She'd be lying if the thought of locking the door, even wedging a piece of lumber against the door and keeping it from opening, then covering up that hole in order to keep him down in the basement forever. Leave him there in the darkness and let him think about his actions for the rest of his meaningless existence. The thought came and went.

Out of curiosity, Talora opened the door and a set of stairs leading into a dark basement was revealed. She walked back to the spot where Japhy had fallen and grabbed the screwdriver. Now, with a weapon in hand,

Talora walked downstairs and switched on a work light that took a couple of seconds to brighten. She spotted the crash once the light fully brightened and highlighted the chaos; and in that chaos, Japhy—or whom she thought was Japhy—cowering in a dark corner of the basement. Part of his coat was ripped. However, it wasn't that same flashy coat that he wore on and off stage; in fact, it looked more like an old brownish blanket, frayed and covered in dirt. The material itself appeared as if it would disintegrate or even turn to dust at first contact. She couldn't see Japhy in his entirety, only a weakened, shorter man who was curled in a fetal position. Except for crying, she couldn't quite tell what he was doing for that old coat was covering his body.

"Playtime is up," Talora said, as she inched her way toward Japhy. She kept the screwdriver close, ready. "I want you to leave me alone or else—"

"—Fuck you," a young voice of angst said from underneath the raggedy coat.

The voice was *not* Japhy's.

The sound of the voice sent a ripple of shock throughout Talora's body.

With the screwdriver loosening in her hand, Talora stepped through the rumble and debris and pulled the coat from Japhy's smaller body. Even the touch was familiar and had that similar staticky, analog TV screen feel to it.

She released the coat. Her jaw slackened with great surprise from the sight of the teenager. Her eyes, as wide as question marks.

"*Nathan?*" said Talora, her voice curling like a question mark. "What?"

Her younger brother, Nathan, turned his shoulder and for a moment, faced his sister. Tears were running down his face. He could hardly make eye contact with her for the shame was too great.

"Jus' leave me 'lone," he cried out.

Talora pulled the rest of the coat from Nathan's body. The pinprick sensation of the coat's material pressed against her hand caused her to drop the coat.

She waggled her hand.

"What—how did you get here?"

Talora kneeled down in front of Nathan, whose face was cringing with rage.

"I said 'Leave me alone!'"

"Nathan," she said, "it's me, your sister."

"Your not my fuckin' sister," he cried, his voice choppy.

"You're telling me this whole time—but how?"

Her eyes fell to that old coat on the floor. She specifically remembered the sensation that she felt when picking up a piece of old, coarse fabric from outside the guesthouse and how it was similar to the sensation that she felt while pulling the coat from her brother's body. She put the clues together, the two memories, three, then four. . .

"You little shit!" Talora barked. "You know the trouble you've gotten yourself into, Nathan?"

"Nice to see you to, *Ta-lora*," Nathan whined.

"Nathan," Talora said, more patiently, "how could you do this to me, to mom and dad?" The disappointment wore off from the very thought of Pacen and was replaced by a greater anger. "And what happened to Pacen, please tell that wasn't you—"

"—Pa' lease," Nathan said with a pout. "That dickhead deserved it. . . "

"Nathan! How can you say that?"

"He's fine."

"Fine? He's dead, Nathan!"

"He's not dead," Nathan drawled. "Well," he paused, a sense of humor coming back to him, "I take that back. He's not alive, either."

"What did you do to Pacen?"

"What did I do?" His body sunk inward, both of his shoulders shrugging in a juvenile "he said-she said" fashion. "I had no control over what those *fangfuckers* were going to do—"

"—Pacen would still be alive if it wasn't for you!"

Nathan rolled his eyes and downplayed the situation.

"He's not dead-dead, if that's what you're talking about."

"You're telling me he was one of them now?"

"Yeah, well, I helped him escape from those lousy blood traders," he clarified. "You should be thanking me!" Then, he said in a more laidback tone, "FYI, if I were you, Lora, I probably wouldn't take the dude out for spaghetti Bolognese anytime soon. *Fun fact*: the garlic might not sit too well on his stomach."

Tempted to strangle her little brother, Talora said from the side of her mouth, "You're an asshole, you know that?"

Brushing off debris, he stood to his feet in a careless way as any young man recovered from injuries.

"I'm the asshole," Nathan shouted at Talora and pointed at himself. "I'm not the one who stuck her big fat nose into her brother's business."

"What you talking about?" asked Talora.

"*You*," Nathan said, the tears flowing again, the rage, "you're the reason why my band is no longer together. *You* are the one who turned all of them against me and made me look like a fool. *You* are the one who destroyed my dreams, Talora! My dreams!" Nathan screamed. "Not yours! They were mine! Mine! And you, you bitch, you took it all away from me by stealing the one band mate who others looked up to! You could've chosen someone else, anyone, even Product—" Nathan thought more about Product and that couch-modeled body for a moment, the rage on-pause, "well, maybe not Product, but anyone else. But you chose Pacen! And it's all YOUR fault!"

"My fault?" Talora said innocently. "I didn't know it was you who was pretending to be some singer named Japhy—"

"—You knew! I know you did!"

"Nathan," Talora said, her voice riddled with defeat, "I didn't know. And I am sorry that I got in the way. I am. But Nathan, you have to understand that I'm not the one to blame here. I apologize for what happened to your band. But what you did, Nathan, with Pacen, how you've kept Mom and Dad in the dark and had them convinced that something awful happened to you, that's irredeemable. Why would you even want to put them through all that pain? For fuck's sake, *Gnat*," Talora yelled back, "Mom and Dad had your ass buried!"

Even more ashamed from his sister's comment, Nathan looked up at her the same way Broot would look at her after having made a boo-boo.

"They did?" said Nathan.

Talora gave him an exaggerated nod.

"Yes."

"I mean I'm still here. I mean," he said and pointed at the coat, "the coat was disguising me. It's not like I'm dead." Nathan was puzzled by the idea of being buried when he could see his own hands before him. "How'd they bury me?"

"They buried an empty casket with your most valuable things inside," Talora said.

"What things?" asked Nathan.

"Comic books," Talora listed. "Your mp3 player, even your Teddy, food for worms."

"Man," Nathan said depressingly, "now I feel really bad."

"Yeah," Talora said sharply, "you should."

She drew her eyes back to the torn coat, then Nathan, whose eyes were laced with a whole world of awfulness.

"Listen, Nathan," Talora said more seriously, "the time for playing 'dress up' is over. D'you ever stop and think that maybe I like you just the way you are, that annoying little brat?" she teased. "You don't need some special coat to be somebody. You are somebody. You're my little brother, Nathan Katz."

"Shut up," Nathan mumbled.

"You *are* Nathan Katz, not Japhy Warthog," she said deliberately.

"It's Warchild!"

Talora couldn't help but laugh at Nathan's defensiveness of his character.

Eventually, the laugh subsided.

Nathan looked in Talora's eyes and spoke the truth.

"I'm sorry, Talora," said Nathan.

Talora hugged Nathan, who broke down in her arms.

"Come on," she said, stroking the back of his head. "Let's go home."

✝

BOTH Talora and Nathan, who was dragging the coat behind him the same way he used to drag around his "blanky," walked back upstairs to the first floor. Nathan had a few bruises on his side, but he could walk on his own.

Once they reached the first floor, they immediately checked on Morrison.

Morrison's eyes bolted open from Talora's presence.

"How bad is it?" asked Talora, as she tended to Morrison.

"How bad does it look?" Morrison returned, as he attempted to sit upright to examine his injuries.

Grimacing from the shot of pain, he was forced to lie back against the wall.

"Rest, Morrison," she said and pulled Morrison's flip phone from his pocket. "I'm going to call for an ambulance."

"An ambulance?" Morrison appeared insulted by the remark. "Fuck that! I can't pay for an ambulance!"

"Don't worry about the money?"

While holding his side, Morrison nodded at Nathan, who was standing behind Talora.

"Where the hell did the kid come from?"

"That's my brother, Nathan. You might remember him as Japhy."

"Japhy?" Morrison said heavily. Even talking caused him greater pain. "Am I supposed to know who that is?"

"You know who he is?"

226

Talora looked into Morrison's eyes.

Morrison had no other choice than to draw his eyes back to Nathan, particularly the coat he was holding in his hand.

In disbelief, he turned to Talora.

"It can't be," he uttered. "But how?"

"It's the coat," she said. "It has this kind of. . . power on people." She turned her shoulder and eyed Nathan. "But it doesn't have the power we share."

Both Talora and Nathan shared eye contact.

The bond, tighter than ever before.

In sudden revelation, she said to Morrison, "You can't tell anyone what happened here. You have to promise me, Morrison. You can't speak a word of this coat, of my brother. You trip and fell into the floor. I found you in the basement. I managed to carry you back upstairs." She opened Morrison's flip phone. "And that's when I called 9-1-1."

She stared into Morrison's eyes and waited for a response.

☦

DINA'S car pulled up in front of the house as soon as the paramedics were pulling out the gurney from the back of the ambulance.

Before Dina could question the two paramedics, Talora was right there to explain everything to Dina. Nearly word-for-word, she told Dina what happened to Morrison, as if she was reading from a script. Dina couldn't have been more devastated by the news. Together, they rushed into the house alongside the paramedics and checked on Morrison while young Nathan watched with melancholy all of the drama unfold from the backseat of Talora's car.

When the paramedics finally arrived at the scene, they asked Morrison what happened. He digested the question and gathered his words. He even shot Talora a look that she'd never forget, one of great indignation and compliance, as if he was guilty yet, at the same time, not guilty, and his injuries, relevant yet irrelevant, were sole contributions of a verse that belonged to a song much greater than anything he had ever heard.

✠

As the paramedics wheeled out Morrison from the house, he pulled Talora close and whispered in her ear, "You owe me one."

Talora kissed Morrison on the forehead and said back, "How about two?"

For the first time throughout Morrison's suffering, he managed to flash a hint of a smile on his face as if the two had a deeper understanding.

The paramedics loaded Morrison into the ambulance.

As Dina was about to step inside the ambulance with Morrison, Talora pulled her aside at the very last second.

"Thanks for everything, Dina," she said, catching Dina off guard.

With a puzzled expression, Dina tilted her head to the side.

"I'm going to take off now," Talora said again.

"Take off—where? Aren't you going to follow us to the hospital?"

"No," she said. "I'm going back home."

"Are you sure?"

Talora nodded.

Behind Dina, the paramedics were securing the gurney to the floor of the ambulance.

"Oh Talora," Dina said sadly and hugged Talora, "I hate to see you go. Of all times—"

"I'll be back. I promise."

Dina faced Talora.

"When people say they'll come back to Soy usually they're lying."

"No," Talora said, not batting an eyelash. "I'm tired of lying."

"Okay. Well, you have my number, right?"

"Yes."

"Okay, well—"

Once more, Talora hugged Dina and held onto her tightly.

Behind the two, the paramedic called out to Dina.

"A'ight," Talora said. "Go on."

"Bye," Dina said, wiping away the tears from her cheeks.

Talora said, "See ya."

"Hopefully sooner than later," Dina said, stepping into the back of the ambulance.

Talora waved goodbye to Dina as the paramedics shut the doors.

Then, she walked back to her car.

Once she stepped inside, Nathan leaned over the center console and asked his sister, "Was that Aunt Dina?"

"Yeah," Talora said pensively. "Why?"

"She's lost a lot of weight," said Nathan.

"Shut up, You," she said, as she teasingly pushed Nathan's head back, started the ignition, and drove away.

Before leaving Soy, Talora decided to drive back to Dina's house and pick up the old dog. Nathan confirmed that the dog was, in fact, Broot.

In a way, Talora didn't want any explanation as to how her dog, Broot, ended up in Soy.

A part of her had her suspicions.

And all fingers pointed at that little shit stain sitting in the passenger seat.

✟

ON the drive home, Talora decided to take a different, more southern route, which took them directly through Kentucky. After an hour of driving through Kentucky, Talora found a rundown area, which looked like a tetanus paradise, along the side of the highway. Part of the building's structure was collapsed by what looked like a storm and from the look of old and rusty car parts scattered behind the closed-in fence behind the building, Talora could only assume that it used to be some kind of car repair or parts dealership. The place was most definitely deserted and happened to be away from a busy highway. She made an abrupt right turn. The sudden movement caused Nathan to wake up from his much-needed sleep.

She drove down a gravel road until she reached the rundown spot.

"What you doing?" asked Nathan.

Talora parked the car and glanced at the coat lying on the backseat in the rear view mirror.

"Talora?"

Talora moved her eyes to Nathan, who had turned the passenger seat into his own recliner by stretching out his feet onto the dashboard. He looked back at his sister as if she had been smoking something.

"I can't drive anymore until you tell me exactly where you found this coat?" Talora asked.

"I was wondering when you were going to ask me," Nathan said quietly.

"Where'd you find it, Nathan?" asked Talora.

Nathan sat up and straightened the seat.

"You wouldn't believe me if I told you—"

"—Right now, Nathan, you can tell me that the President of the United States is a Martian and the only reason why he's pushing the Mars Initiative on Congress is to bring all of his fellows Martians to Earth where they will inevitably take over the human race and turn us into their own hand puppets and you know what? I'd believe it!"

Nathan looked at Talora strangely.

"Nathan," she said with more urgency, "tell me. I deserve the truth."

"Me, Lee, Tom, and Acorn were messing around Hellerman Mall last fall—"

"—Hellerman Mall?" Talora said in a stern manner. "I thought Mom specifically told you not to play there anymore, Nathan! There were two homeless people who murdered there last year! It's only a matter of time before they tear down that place."

"Would you let me finish?"

"Sorry," Talora said, leaning back in her seat.

"Lee was goofing off and throwing rocks at everybody. I tripped over what I thought was a manikin. It was getting dark outside and it was hard to see. I took a closer look and realized it wasn't some manikin."

"What was it?" asked Talora.

"A dead body," he said finally. "But it wasn't human either. Lee handed me a clothing hanger and with the end of the clothing hanger, I pried open its mouth. That's when I saw the fangs. And it looked like it had been dead for some time. I mean, it was old-old. Like some ancient shit. And the smell, Lora, you wouldn't believe the smell?"

"What'd you do with it?"

"Nothing," Nathan said. "We just left it." He turned his shoulder and looked at the coat in the backseat. "I snuck out of the house that night and walked back to Hellerman Mall that night. It was like the coat was drawing me back."

"Well, I think you've proven to me that you're pretty damn good at sneaking around."

"What you mean?"

"Sneaking through the window in Dina's guestroom," Talora said, "trying to scare me."

"What you talking about? I didn't sneak through your window."

"Come on, Gnat," she said. "You did."

"I didn't."

"You're telling me you didn't burn Dina's photographs?"

Nathan glanced at his sister, the growing frustration on her face, and said, "It was me. I did it."

When he spoke, he didn't look her in the eye.

He just didn't.

Talora sighed off her frustration and spotted a gas station not too far away.

"Well," she said, "there's only one thing left to do."

AFTER the argument was finally settled, Talora drove to the gas station, filled an emergency gas can that she carried in the trunk of her Honda Civic, and bought a pack of matches from the convenient store.

Then, she drove back to the rundown building.

While Broot waited in the backseat, Talora and Nathan got out and walked around. It didn't take them long to find a rusty oil drum that looked like the perfect spot to burn the coat.

Once the coat was stuffed inside the oil drum, Talora dowsed it with gasoline and struck a match.

"Are you sure?" Nathan said before his sister dropped the flaming match into the oil drum.

She held the match in her hand and watched it slowly burn toward the tip of her finger.

"Right before you fell into the hole, I was holding one of the buttons from the coat in my hand," she said, zoning out. "Something happened. Something I can't explain. But I do remember the feeling that I felt. It happened so quickly. In the blink of an eye. And in that split second, I felt this darkness come over me as if, for a moment, I could see Death right before me. It was pulling me in, this darkness, and showing me this power, as if I could be something more than human. I never want anyone to harness that power ever again."

"But, I mean, you can literally be anybody you want. Someone who can be a positive influence on the world. The possibilities are endless!"

"You can be anybody you want and you chose to be some six foot five, funky haired guy who was named after a talking octopus in a cartoon primarily watched by stoners who spend their days getting stoned? I'm not judging or anything like that, but, seriously, little bro, you could've aimed higher." She shrugged, as if she was her drop-da-mike moment. "Jus' saying—"

"—Yeah," said Nathan. "So what?"

Right before the flame reached her fingertips, Talora dropped the match into the oil drum. The coat lit up with flames.

As Talora watched the coat burn, she noticed a piece of the coat was missing; in fact, it was the same area of the coat that had ripped against the flooring.

The flame started to change colors, turning fiery orange to pinkish-purple. As the blue fire consumed the entire coat, Talora witnessed these gold flakes shedding from the coat as if the fire was igniting the last bit of the coat's energy, which, for a moment, reshaped and changed colors as well. The coat morphed from a scaly reptilian hide to white silky skin to that same gold coat that Japhy Warchild wore. The coat finally returned back to its original old and raggedy nature. The gold flakes lifted from the blackened burnt coat and became finer, like gold dust floating in the air.

Nathan was left awestruck by the sight of the blue flame, as well as the particles of gold dust floating higher into the air.

Talora was left with even more doubts.

WEALTHY CEO Charley Schultz of Equinoxx Inc. was talking about the speech in New York City when Avanti started to drift from Schultz's words. He followed by making a joke about her former campaign manager, Sonny Mims, and the mutilated state of his body when it was discovered by a drifter outside Tent City.

"His story had *holes*," was Schultz's punch line.

The table of wealthy businessmen burst out in laughter, including the rest of Avanti's staff.

Surrounded by enough money to own an island, Avanti felt the bind released from her body—at least, most of it. For the first time ever since she was seventeen years old, Avanti could finally breath.

Schultz called out the governor's name.

Before he could finish her name "Washington," Avanti interrupted, "Will you excuse me?"

Avanti excused herself from the table, which didn't sit well with the other fat cats in the room.

AVANTI ditched the brunch at Connecticut Senator Daemon Batch's mansion and walked back to the town car where Joel was waiting in the driver's seat.

Vye was next to step inside the town car.

"Avanti," she said in confusion, "you want to tell me what that was all about back there?"

"Did I ever tell you the story about the time I was first bit?" asked Avanti in a trance-like state.

"I thought talking about that sort of thing was a no-no," Vye said.

"I was seventeen years old when I met whom I thought was the love of my life. He was everything I had ever dreamed of. Tall, strikingly handsome, charming, intelligent, *wealthy*, and most importantly, considerate. It was too bad I was underage. But, strangely, my age didn't bother him. He was much older than me; in fact, he said he was thirty-seven, which, I knew, even as a seventeen-year-old girl, was a lie."

She pulled her attention toward the window and looked at the mansion.

"Honestly," she said, "I didn't know how old he was. He may have looked as though he was thirty-seven. But, a part of me knew he was *much* older."

Avanti faced Vye.

"As in centuries older," she said blankly, then moved her attention back outside the tinted window. "After I was 'made,' he told me that I would be *his* for all eternity. We would share a bond, even in death. It wasn't until later I found out that he was filling my head with lies. He said that I was 'his one and only love.' I found out that there were others, hundreds, *thousands* of others. I was left with a broken heart. I thought to myself: I'd never find love that would replace the love I had for him. One day, an extremist organization that went by the name *Sons of Man*—a hate group—found out where he was nesting. Sons of Man had beaten him so badly that, eventually, he ended up shutting himself off from the rest of the world. Unable to recovery from his injuries, he simply disappeared. The moment he died, I felt his presence inside me, still there, thriving. A part of me was glad that he was no longer here. *But* another part of me knew the horror had just begun and that he would haunt me for the rest of my days. For many years, I searched for his remains in hopes to rid the awful curse, this 'signature' that he had bewitched on me. I believe someone out there has beaten me to the punch." Avanti's eyes started to water in both sadness and relief. "My own guardian angel. . ."

"What was his name?" asked Vye. "The vamp who bit you?"

Avanti turned to Vye and said, "His name was Marius Ionescu."

✟

AFTER having been on the road with his sister for over ten hours, Nathan reached the point where he was ready to open up. He turned down the volume on the radio and said to Talora, "There's something I need to tell you, Talora. Something I saw when I put on the coat. This, I dunno, this darkness. Like you spoke of."

Talora paid closer attention to her brother.

"Maybe the experience is different," he said. "Maybe it has something to do with the person who's wearing it. But, for me, it was like I was sharing my consciousness with someone who was sharing his consciousness of hundreds of people. I saw all these images. One of them stood out the most. It was this image of this guy, probably a couple of years older than me. I think he needed my help." He turned to his sister. "Did you see him?"

Talora shook her head.

"No," she said. "Like I said, it was only for a second. So, why do you think he needed your help? Help in what exactly?"

"I dunno," Nathan said. "But, in a way, I could see that he was crying out to me through his actions."

"What was he doing? Who was he?"

"His name was Ajax," Nathan said. "Or Jack. I'm not sure. All I do know is that, when I first put on the coat, I saw all whole bunch of images flash before my eyes and in all of those images, I saw another world, Lora, a world much darker than our own. It sounds insane, I know. But it's real. I know it."

"Insane, Gnat! Really!" Talora said hysterically. "You've been disguised as the lead singer of one of the hottest bands out there—or *once* hottest."

"Thanks," Nathan said, taking the comment as a compliment.

"So," Talora said, "who was this Ajax guy?"

"You sure you really want to know?" asked Nathan.

Talora thought about her next response.

DINA returned to the house after spending a couple of hours at the hospital visiting Morrison.

Mindful of her surroundings, as well as watching her every step, Dina made her way to the hole next to the foyer. She pushed aside the sheet of plywood and examined the dangerous hole in the floor with a flashlight.

Intrigued by her discovery, she shone the flashlight on a piece of cloth hanging from a jagged plank of wood protruding from the hole. Careful not to fall into the hole, she grabbed a measuring tape and extended it outward to about thirty or so inches, then locked it.

With the end of the measuring tape, Dina lifted the piece of old clothing material and as carefully as she could, moved the measuring tape away from the hole in the floor.

Relieved, she retracted the measuring tape and picked up the frayed piece of ancient cloth off the floor. She held the cloth up to her face and couldn't help but think how nice of a scarf it would make for Vladimir.

✠

TALORA and Nathan decided to make a much-needed pit stop at a rest stop once they crossed into New York State. They both went at the same time and planned to met back in front of the water fountain, Talora heading into the women's restroom while Nathan heading into the men's restroom.

As Talora was finishing up in the last stall, she heard a *swooping* noise coming from the outside. She wiped herself clean, flushed the toilet, and stepped outside the stall with a sense that there was someone—or something—else inside the restroom. A slight draft was blowing into the restroom, yet the air condition was no longer running.

Cautiously, Talora walked to the sink to wash her hands under the faucet. As she was about to run the water, she came across a single white rose lying on the edge of the sink. She picked up the angelic white rose and held it underneath her nose. The smell reminded her of home. Immediately, Talora felt as though, despite the creep-factor, she wasn't alone.

A part of her was *finally* at peace.

And optimistic about the future.

"Those who fear him or hold his name in reverence speak his name as though he was no different than a god. And for those unfortunate to find themselves between the grip of his bite, it's the very last word uttered from a dying breath."

— THE CHRONICLES OF KRILLISH

"New Opening"

A ruthless gang of insects, which, on the streets of Leatherwood, had a rap as being a part of one of the most dangerous crime syndicates called "snatchers," was chasing after a well-known crosser of the High Order who went by the name "Tooth Fairy" when all of a sudden a rare canister made from gold slipped from his furry, stick-like finger grip.

The Tooth Fairy recovered the fumble, picked up the precious container, and checked its condition for any damages; first inspecting for any leaks or breaks along the seal and then, once finding none, the crosser continued his daring escape from the wannabe snatchers, who were closing in on his tail. The Tooth Fairy managed to lose the gang in the Tattered Lands once he left the city.

By the skin of his fangs, the Tooth Fairy made it out of Leatherwood and crossed a crumbly, pothole-ridden highway where a rust-covered, overturned sign read "Welcome to Leatherwood: Your *Last Stop*." The Tooth Fairy cut through a red-washed desert and eventually made it to Hill Falls River, which snaked its way around the mountainscapes surrounding the city, and sought cover inside a drain where he spent a couple of hot minutes catching his breath while three emaciated, alien-framed snatchers were lingering on top of a hill.

Once he caught his breath, the Tooth Fairy made his way through the drain. Having to stop several times to tuck and readjust his broad pointy wings, which were folded underneath the worn cloak, in order to squeeze his body through the tight space, the Tooth Fairy ended up crawling through yet a smaller tunnel, which led to a sewer system.

Finally, the Tooth Fairy emerged from the manhole and found himself on Another Street in Another World.

With his cloak worn more securely, the Tooth Fairy cut through the backyard of an older house and counted each and every single footstep he made.

Making sure to not only conceal his dark scaly face, but also the golden container cradled in his arm, the Tooth Fairy exited from the once country-club type neighborhood and walked through the entire night.

Avoiding cars and all human life, the Tooth Fairy trekked through thick woods and prickly vegetation until he reached a small two-story house with a barn settled along the hump of the postcard-like countryside. He snuck onto the owner's property and stole a pickaxe, as well as a shovel from the barn. He made sure to keep the last number in his mind before his detour, which was four thousand and thirty-two steps, which was approximately two miles of walking.

Then, after he grabbed the tools he needed, the Tooth Fairy walked back to the exact spot where he made his last detour and continued counting once more.

The Tooth Fairy ended up walking an extra two thousand steps, which put him in that three-mile mark.

The Tooth Fairy stopped on the number six thousand and some change.

Repeating that number "six thousand" back to himself, the Tooth Fairy dropped the tools on the ground. There, in the dark woods, the Tooth Fairy began to dig. He dug through the warmer side of midnight. Once he finished digging the hole, the Tooth Fairy placed the special container inside. Then, he filled the hole back up with dirt. Which didn't take as long as digging the hole.

After the container was buried, the Tooth Fairy exited the woods and wandered back through the countryside where he spotted a billboard alongside the highway.

The gaudy billboard was promoting a band, *Stuffed Animalz*, which was performing tonight at Fairway Coliseum in Atlanta. The Tooth Fairy wasn't that far from the coliseum and a part of him knew that he still had time, even though it felt as if he didn't.

Guided by an innate hunger, The Tooth Fairy arrived in Atlanta just as Stuffed Animalz was finishing up their final song in a thirty minute-plus encore. It was on the cooler side of midnight, and the Tooth Fairy found himself on another level of exhaustion; however, the worn and hungry crosser powered through the night in hopes of finding his new host.

Once the Tooth Fairy reached the stadium, the band, Stuffed Animalz, was hanging outside their tour bus.

Sure enough, the Tooth Fairy found the right host—The One.

And he called himself Japhy Warchild, the lead singer of the band.

Japhy happened to be sleeping while the Tooth Fairy snuck onto the bus. There, passed out in a bed in the back of the bus, the Tooth Fairy found Japhy's arm flopped over the side of the bed with an empty bottle of Jack Daniels on the floor. The Tooth Fairy tiptoed toward Japhy and got close enough to Japhy to smell his whiskey-flavored breath. The Tooth Fairy opened up his scaly mouth, releasing a bright red light from inside his mouth. The red beam of light shot into Japhy's mouth, causing him to stir from his inebriated state.

Once the red light was drained from the Tooth Fairy, his body suddenly shriveled up like an old plant.

Two weeks later, when drummer of Stuffed Animalz, Tommy Bango, walked onto the tour bus to catch a nap before the concert, he was struck by one of the god-awful smells inside the bus. Tommy tracked the smell to Japhy's bed where underneath he found a shriveled up bat-like creature about the size of a baby with scaly skin and papery folded up wings, which were so crisp and brittle they looked as if they could crack like dried maple leaves in winter from the slightest bungle.

He kept the dead creature all to himself and once the tour had wrapped for the season, transferred it from an ice cooler to an old pickle jar that he had lying around the kitchen and planned never to tell a soul about it.

Except for his wife, that is, who had recently returned home from visiting her mother and two brothers in Thailand.

She could've walked in on her husband doing worst things.

—

"Within An Inch"

I'm sure you already know my name and the story behind the name.

If you don't, then I advise you to stop reading right now, go outside, and enjoy the weather or something. . . well, a'ight then. Don't say I didn't warn you.

Now that we have all that out of the way, let me tell you what actually happened to me with no chase or filter. I'll do my best to keep it all in present tense, so it's easier not only for everybody to understand, but also for myself included.

As I've come to realize these past few hours while lying in one of the most uncomfortable beds with three broken ribs which makes the air feel sharp, a severed spleen, a bruised kidney, a broken wrist, a black eye that's roughly the size of a grapefruit, and enough stitches along the left side of my face and forehead to run a toy train, life is *way* too short. No question.

One day, you're born into the world.

Then, the very next, you can't wait to get the hell out, as if life has become one never-ending after party and you can't wait to call it a night and crash in your bed—at least one nicer than a hospital bed which makes sleeping on a hardwood floor sound doable.

What I've come to learn is that it's in those fine moments between speaking your first word or taking your first step that life offers the tools to survive even though it's those moments that seem like a haze, some *fragmented* memory stolen from the shattered glass of another person's memory. I've always wondered what it'd be like to travel back in time and relive all those fine moments that I took for granted with a greater transparent knowledge, recognize the most crucial events that shaped me, as well as the people who steered me toward my final destination.

Which can only beg the question: Was this my path all along?

Let's rewind and start where my story—my real one, that is—all began.

The location: A Burger King parking lot outside Downtown Atlanta. That's me standing right there, what boomers would call a 'punk' dressed in an oversized Raw Dog T-shirt and black jeans that look two sizes too short.

The short-looking guy I'm buying a pound of red rocks from is Ant, my VP-23 dealer; his real name is Anthony—not sure what his last name is, but I think it rhymes with Scalia. Ant is well known for coming off as your everyday pocket-sized gangster who tries to make up for his *small* size with his *big* mouth. I don't trust Ant, never have. For one, Ant never looks me in the eye; and two, he's always wearing way too much cologne. On the real, though, never ever trust a dude who wears a lot of cologne. It means his trying to cover up something.

Today, Ant's hooking me up with a pound of red rocks; claims it came from, of all places, Seattle, where a vamp's blood is richer than Log Cabin syrup, but I know he's just trying to promote what he calls an ill product.

I call Ant out on his lie, pull out the same exact rock I bought from a hush-hush cat at New Way, who happens to be close pals with Ant's supplier.

I name my price, enforce it. He has no other option than to cave, like the little ant he is. The only reason as to why I still keep coming back to Ant is for certain scenarios such as these. Most of the time, I take whatever Ant can sell, then break it off in eighths and gram bags, scatter it around to blood sniffers and VP-23 junkies—on occasion, cut it with my own blood that I keep on ice—sell it cheap, so that way they can depend on me, pocket the profits, then go home A-okay. Every now and then, I exploit Ant, call him out with a low price and a firm hand but more of a firm hand—balance the scales, if you will. It's a push-and-pull type of relationship. I know, with a product such as this, I can turn it around, sell it to uppity greenbacks at Plymouth, and make four times the profit.

Once I part ways with Ant, I hide the pound of red rocks under the owner's manual inside the glove box of my Mercedes. I've never really been the type who shits where he eats. But I'm starving.

At the very last second, I change my mind and decide to drive into Atlanta.

I'm not too far from Café Pearl, which have these bean burritos that, surprisingly enough, manage to tame the hunger. I usually buy three of them. Eat one. Then save the other two for whenever the hunger returns.

Once I arrive at Pearl, the place is spilling over with the right kind of crowd, hipsters and every flavor of eco-friendly, earth-conscious college kids whose blood is about as bitter as stomach bile. There's a good reason as to why most vamps don't bother with somebody who'd rather enjoy a kale salad opposed to a greasy hamburger. At the last second, I decide to order four burritos, not three.

As I'm waiting on my food, I get a couple of looks from the lounge area. The same looks coming from the same people who claw their way onto the TV or the Internet to talk about how much they care and all about ones like me. But, when they see one—or at least, think they see one—up close and personal, they turn to jello and all of a sudden, they turn into mutes with serious eye problems. Most of the time, they stare, as if they're getting a rare glimpse at an exotic bird. Others struggle to meet my gaze in fear that they may never return. I'm good at hiding myself; and every now and then, especially when the hunger strikes, my mask starts to slip from my face.

The head cashier calls out my name and does so with a slight tremble in her voice.

I grab my order from her shaky hand. The color drains from her face, leaving it pale and ghostly. I've been coming here for the past couple of months to pick up bean burritos. Yet, every time I pick up food, her look is always the same.

I leave Pearl with the bag of food and walk back to my car when I catch them in the corner of my eye.

I immediately sense the danger before my eyes even cross their path.

In a steady glance, I count five of them altogether, all of who are hanging out around my Mercedes. One is peeking through the passenger's window while another one is keeping lookout like the soldier he is. Clearly, they're after my stash. Maybe junkies or even buddies of Ant's who are trying to rip me off. My initial reaction is to beat my chest and protect what belongs to me.

As I'm about to yell at them, hoping the loudness of my voice will scare them off, a sixth man emerges from around the corner.

Immediately, I recognize the masquerade mask on his face.

Then, I realize they're *not* after my stash.

I do a U-turn and take post in an alleyway next to Café Pearl.

As soon as I walk away, I spot a cruiser with a K-9 unit patrolling the street. Over these past couple of years, there's been an uptick in K-9 units. For one, it's much easier to track red rocks, vamp drops, Holy Bombs, Dracula's Blood, or the gazillion types of drugs on the street with werewolf's third cousin. And two, as of lately, it's hard to find a cop—a human cop, that is—who knows when to turn the other cheek on crime. Nowadays, with cop killings on the rise, you couldn't walk too far without finding a cop who's gunning for vamps. I often wonder if they're any different, a member of Sons of Man and an officer of the law. It's fair to say that nothing is black and white anymore. You're either living or you're not.

I peek around the building and watch the gang scatter from the sight of the cruiser.

I wait for a couple of tense minutes until the cruiser eventually drives past my car.

Knowing that Sons of Man may still be hanging around in the shadows and waiting for the right opportunity to ambush me, I take the alleyway in hopes that they'll be gone by the time I reach my car.

I walk around the block and end up stopping at one of Atlanta's oldest record stores. I kill time browsing through old vinyl. My food's starting to get cold and the hunger grips me like a vise. I can't take my eyes off each person in the record store. The veins in their necks or wrist pulse underneath their flesh, that tiny beat calling out to me and causing my mouth to salivate.

With the hunger intensifying, I walk back to my car and ready the car key.

I take yet another alleyway, which leads directly to my car. I make it halfway through the alleyway until I spot a couple of dark figures emerging from behind a set of stairs and shadowy doorways.

I check my six. Two more emerge from the shadows.

Then, in front of me, two more emerge.

I'm completely surrounded.

I count five of them, like before; however, I don't see the other one until it's already too late.

The blood rushes through my veins as I'm blindsided by a baton. I fall to the ground and recover from the daze.

Before I can stand up, I'm hit yet again from behind. The third blow to my ribs knocks the wind out of me. I fall yet again to the ground, shield my face with my arms, and curl my body into a ball.

Each one hovers over my body and starts kicking me. Throughout the fury of swinging arms, as well as snapshots of oncoming brass knuckled fists and bloody white laces, and sinister faces, I witness the same guy with a masquerade mask from earlier standing at the edge of the alleyway.

As I fade in and out of consciousness, another wannabe gangster kneels over my body, sticks his face in my grill, and flashes that elusive *owl eyes* symbol over his face.

Owls eat bats, brutha!

He backs away while the others beat me within an inch of my life.

—

"Compromises"

Ajax?

Ajax?

You awake?

Brass knuckled fists and bloody white laces grip me like violence.

I block out the violence and follow the voice to the one face that I don't want to see right now. She's sitting by my bedside and has a concerned look etched on her face.

I prepare myself for a soon-to-be lecture by mentally searching for a legitimate excuse as to what I was doing downtown, but knowing her, she's already pried through my thoughts and sorted through them like a sock drawer.

Behind her, a three-man entourage is keeping guard by the doorway.

I recognize Avanti's most loyal of loyalists, Joel, who looks as if he eats babies for breakfast, standing among the entourage.

Joel, give us the room?

Yes, ma'am.

Once Joel and the other security guards are gone, Avanti looks at me the way a cop would look at a suspect; and all of a sudden, that dim fluorescent light behind me becomes hotter along the surface of my skin.

How are you feeling?

I want to lash out at her. Question her for even questioning me: What kind of question is that?

But I'm in no condition.

I just got my ass kicked. What'd you think?

Local PD says it might've been a mugging. When they discovered you, they couldn't find any ID or wallet—

—It wasn't a mugging.

Who were they? Did you get a look at their faces?

Since my left arm is wrapped in a cast, I manage to raise my right arm to my face. I form both my thumb and index finger into a perfect circle and then spread out my other three fingers, making my hand look like the 'okay' symbol. I hold the symbol up to my right eye; however, I'm unable to flip the owl symbol upside down due to the IV attached to the back of my hand. Not like I need to do that anyway. She already knows the symbol before I even show her.

Are you sure it was them?

Yeah. Pretty sure. How'd they know who I was anyway?

Maybe they recognize you from the news. You know, with me trying to win back votes from the community, those who have any affiliation with Sons of Man haven't been my greatest supporters lately—

—Stop!

Stop what?

Stop treating me like I'm one of them, Avanti. You may be able to fool them about who you really are. So, just drop the whole act and speak to me like you're speaking to your son.

She looks around the room, as if she's scanning for ears—and eyes.

I've heard there's a brand new technology making waves on the black market. Apparently, it's a device that's able to pick up these certain heat signatures when unprotected skin is exposed to sunlight.

Serious? That's bullshit.

All right. Enough, Ajax. I'm trying to help you out here. I mean what were you thinking? Were you not wearing any sunscreen?

Sunscreen? Who gives a shit about sunscreen?

Avanti asks me if I saw any of them wearing masks.

One.

By any chance, did you see what color it was?

Color? What does it matter what color he was wearing?

It matters.

Red, I think.

She looks away, her eyes glazed over in thought.

Red's pretty high up for an initiation—

—And that's what you think this was, some initiation?

You may not want to hear this, but they targeted you, Ajax. They know who you are—and *what* you are. You think by dressing like this it's supposed to deter people like that? Every argument she starts always begins and ends with my taste in fashion. I know it's all the piercings that really bother her. She backs off for a moment to gather her thoughts, as if she doesn't want to say or do anything more that she may regret. Most of the lower rank members who monitor initiations are yellows or greens. But *not* red.

And I'm sure you don't want anyone finding out what happened. You know, 'cuz that would make things. . . complicated for you and your constituents.

Why are you doing this, Ajax? You know I have responsibilities. You knew how things were going to be when I first signed up for this job. I'm trying to protect you, Ajax, not hurt you. Now, you're putting me in a position where I'm going to have to lie about what happened—

—Lie? Everything you've said to these people is a lie! If you wanted to protect me, then you'd have those mask-wearing fools off the streets a long time ago. Their time is coming. Believe me.

Oh, yeah! And what? You're going to take them on all by yourself? You're lucky they didn't kill you, Ajax! You have to understand that if you get rid of one of these groups, then another one is going to pop up under a different name, a different look, and then, we're back to square one.

Whose side are you own, Avanti? By *not* standing up to these people, you're basically advocating what they're doing to your kind—

—They're your kind too, Ajax. Don't you forget about that?

You're right. They are my kind all thanks to you. It's all I think about! Yet, I want nothing to do with them? I WANT TO FORGET ABOUT THEM! But as much as I want to, I can't!

I had one of my men search your car, Ajax. He said he found contraband inside. Not only that, he found drugs in your glove compartment. You know what I'm talking about, so don't you dare act like you don't. What in the hell were you doing with red rocks, Ajax?

It wasn't mine. I was holding it for a friend.

A friend?

She nearly laughs from the comment.

How can I lie to someone who's a master at telling lies?

Not only that, someone who can see my every thought?

Have you ever seen a greenback on VP-23? They actually think that they can take me in a fight. It's hilarious, that's what it is.

Beating up on innocent kids at your school isn't challenging enough? Now, you're going after junkies from Plymouth in order to do what exactly, level the playing field? Is that it? I thought you were done with all of this nonsense, Ajax.

I am.

Like I haven't heard that one before. When are you ever going to learn? After what happened with that kid at your school, you said you were done fighting. Don't you see what's going on here? This kind of destructive behavior is going to get you killed—

—*Good.*

It's only a matter of time before you start a fight with the wrong person. You thought Sons of Man were tough. There are people out there who make Sons of Man look like pushovers.

FYI, I didn't pick that fight. I was jumped by cowards—

—I don't care, Ajax! You have to be smarter than this!

I'm tired of living like this! All I have is this evil inside me! My emotions get the best of me and I find myself retracing my words. You know the whole time while they were on top of me all I can think about was the *hunger* and how much I wanted to drain each and every one of them. How do you think that would make you look? Because the last thing I'd ever want to do is mess up your political career!

Based on your actions, I'd say you're almost there—

—It's getting worse, you know? These urges to feed. It's gotten to the point where it's all I ever think about.

My confession doesn't sit well with Avanti; however, I can't control the tears anymore. I cry blood.

I just want it to be over. . .

She doesn't even bat an eyelash.

I'm sure you've heard the rumors about me possibly throwing my hat into the 2020 election. The higher-ups have started talking. Word is that they've already given up on next year's election and they're planning on getting behind a younger candidate—me—a supposed dark horse whom they believe will have the best shot at beating Rhodes. That is, if they can't find a way to impeach him from office before the 2020 election.

You're serious? That's five years away!

It's only a matter of time before I start making waves as a potential candidate, Ajax; and you, of all people, know you have to build the momentum sooner than later. And you thought the scrutiny is bad right now. It'll only get worse.

That is, if you choose to run. Right?

Avanti doesn't respond—at least, not with any words.

I find myself mimicking those very self-righteous kids who stare at me from a distance.

Right?

She wipes the tears from my face.

Somehow, I already know what she's going to ask me before it even leaves her mouth.

What if I told you there was a way out of this, a way that would benefit the both of us?

You mean, benefit you.

No.

Her face darkens.

Her eyes sharpen.

The *both* of us. I hate seeing you like this, Ajax. I really do. I can't imagine how it must feel to carry around such a burden. Forgive me, Ajax. Sometimes, I forget that the gene affects you differently. And, if I were given a choice, then I would give you my powers instead of His. But I know, as hard as I try, there are just some wounds I cannot heal.

She touches the crook of my arm just above the cast on my wrist.

The pain slowly vanishes from the bones in my left wrist. I'm able to move around my sweaty wrist inside the cast, as well as the tips of my fingers in my left hand; however, the other pain is *still* there, gnawing at me, throbbing well beyond the bones. I'm able to breath better. I'm even able to see Avanti more clearly out of my left eye, which was once swollen shut.

I catch the tears in the corners of my eyes.

What do I have to do?

Once more, Avanti doesn't even bat an eyelash.

You have to die.

Behind Avanti, I witness a shadow creeping along the side of the wall next to the bathroom. Sitting in the dark corner of the hospital room is Avanti's cryptic aide, Vye. She's wearing all black, a deep black that matches the very shadows that the furniture casts. She removes a pair of sunglasses from her narrow face and leans forward into the pale light, revealing enough of herself for me to identify her. Was she really sitting there this entire time?

What a sneaky bitch.

—

"Slight Fear of Tight Spaces"

One second, it's after dark and I'm *slowly* opening the front door of my house and then, the next, I'm stepping outside into the night darkness. Yet, I'm not walking along the front porch of the house. I'm walking through a dark tunnel in a sewer.

I cover my nose with the wrinkled collar of my shirt to block out the sweaty smells of feces and burnt cabbage. My grip loosens from the sight of a tall, athletic framed-figure walking in front of me, causing the stretched collar to fall from my face. Right then, I don't care about the smell.

With question, I follow the stranger further into the sewers.

Curiosity overwhelms me and forces me to shake my slacked-jaw gape.

After witnessing the reptilian costume, I realize it's a person dressed in a full-body suit of what looks similar to a crocodile or lizard, only it's more slender and humanly designed with not only a short, stubby turtle-like tail opposed to a long tail whipping to and fro, but also two arms that are similar in the shape, as well as size of a human opposed to the small, baby-like arms of a crocodile. Most importantly, the suit is worn as tight as skin. Left in a momentary blip of awe, I can't help but admire how real the costume looks.

Like dreams are known to do, I skip around in time and find myself back in my bedroom sketching a similar creature in my notebook. I can't help but think how eerily familiar the costume looks to that same sketch in my notebook.

I'm back in the dark, smelly sewer.

Walking.

The person glances over his or her shoulder—I'm leaning toward him based on his wide shoulders and toned core. He looks at me with these sharp eyes of a reptile, his head looking more like an iguana rather than a crocodile; his spiky reptilian hair bouncing from side to side in his swivel of a head-turn. The detail alone of the costume and mask is exceptional, especially with that dim, yellowish lighting from the streets above which brings out his sharp cheekbones. The Halloween costume isn't anything close to what you'd find at a Party City, but more so Hollywood-level in its masterful design. Doubts creep in like poison, and I start to believe that it's not a costume or a mask but something else.

My eyes move from the scaly face and move toward a small dark hole at the edge of the tunnel.

All of a sudden, the insides of body churn and everything about me tightens.

—

"Or was it?"

With my face dripping with beads of sweat, I wake up punching and kicking.

Once I find myself back in my old bed, I try to piece together the dream. But it felt so real, like it *actually* happened. The last images I can remember are the pitch-black darkness spreading over the entire neighborhood street, then a mob of pale, emaciated, rabid people viciously attacking me. The more I think about it, I come to a conclusion that these people, like that man-iguana in the sewer, weren't people—at least not people from my world, that is.

I immediately check both my wrists, particular my right wrist.

Another image comes to me.

I see myself wearing a strange watch made up of a gold band and a glass saucer-shaped ball filled with blood.

I was wearing the watch.

But now, not wearing it.

The sight of not wearing a watch makes me relieved. I don't know why I'm relieved, but I feel more at ease knowing it's no longer attached to my wrist.

I roll out of bed and crack open the blinds.

The warmth of sunlight brings about a comfort, which I haven't felt in a long time, even though, at this very moment, time seems all but irrelevant.

I walk to the closed door and as I'm about to reach for the door handle, I take a step forward as if I'm about to walk directly *through* the door.

My big toe stubs the door before the side of my forehead. I'm not sure if I'm still trying to wake up or what, but I don't think much about where such a radical idea would come from.

I open the door and exit my bedroom where I'm welcomed by a hint of cinnamon raisin toast, as well as coffee in the air.

The smells, like the sun, bring about a cartoon-like comfort.

Before heading downstairs, I walk into the hallway bathroom and relieve myself. As I'm about to flush the toilet, I'm drawn to the bathtub.

Forgetting to flush, I walk to the bathtub and look inside. I kneel down and take a closer look at the inside of the tub. I discover a smudge of dry blood caked onto the edge of the drain.

As with the bedroom door, I don't exactly know why I'm drawn to these certain ideas. All I can think about is that maybe it has something to do with my dream.

As I stand back upright, I come across yet another smudge of dry and crusty blood on the floor. Then another one by the doorway, which doesn't look like a smudge at all but more so a drop. I follow another blood drop on the floor next to the top of the landing.

Searching for more blood, I walk downstairs.

I find yet another one in the foyer.

As I'm about to head outside, I hear Tameron's voice behind me. Tameron's standing with her arms planted on her hips at the edge of the kitchen.

Where've you been? I've been calling your name for the past ten minutes.

Ah. . .

The phlegm grinds in the base of my throat. The words feel lost and broken.

. . . I just woke up. What time is it?

Time for school, that's what time it is. Well, don't just stand there. Come on and grab some breakfast. She waves me into the kitchen. You're already running late as it is.

I follow Tameron into the kitchen where a box of Dragon Puffs is sitting on the kitchen table.

Where's Avanti?

Your mother had to leave early this morning for an important meeting. She has an extremely busy schedule today. You know, she's going to be meeting with the Bulldogs later this afternoon. I told your mother to get me an autograph from one player in particular. Not to mention any names but he happens to be the starting power forward.

Okay. I don't keep up with sports. So, I have absolutely no clue who you're talking about.

Someone woke up on the wrong side of the bed.

No. I just have no interest in talking about basketball.

I thought you liked basketball.

Ignoring Tameron, I grab a bowl from the top cabinet, as well as a carton of soymilk from the refrigerator, and take a sit at the table.

Tameron lets me eat in peace and steps out of the kitchen to finish folding a load of clean clothes in the laundry room.

I pour myself a bowl of Dragon Puffs and as I'm trying to piece together the dream I had last night, I draw my attention toward the kitchen countertop where a TV is playing a wildlife show on the *National Geographic* channel.

On the TV, a crocodile is attacking a wildebeest along the Nile River in Africa. As the crocodile takes a chomp out of the wildebeest, I take a bite of my cereal. The chewing strengthens my train of thought.

Then, it all comes back to me.

Or was it?

—

"Call me Detective Robert Washington"

I only take a couple of bites of my cereal before I lose my appetite.

I rush back upstairs to my bedroom. I close the door behind me and search my bedroom for things, items, and artifacts that will help refresh my memory as to what's going on with me, including drawers and my desk. I search underneath my bed but don't find anything that grabs my eye. I check my bookshelf. I even remove a bunch of books from the shelf and skim through the pages to make sure I didn't leave anything behind, a note or whatever.

Lastly, I check the inside of my closet. A white plastic bag lying on the floor grabs me. Inside are bloody clothes. Two flashes of images come at me.

One, I'm in a sketchy alleyway, getting my ass whooped by an anti-vampire hate group known as Sons of Man.

Two, I'm on the street next to an open manhole, getting attacked by a mob of sickly, spiny creatures.

I block out the second set of images—which happened at night—then focus on the first images, which happened in broad daylight.

As I concentrate on the past events, I'm able to get a clearer, crisper view of what happened.

I was jumped by Sons of Man.

And the clothes in my hands are the same exact clothes I was wearing when I was jumped.

I remember bringing home the clothes in a bag from the hospital.

Avanti asked me if she wanted to wash the clothes.

But I said no.

I wanted to keep them as a reminder.

I hear Tameron calling my name several times from downstairs. I place the clothes back into the bag and then close the closet.

Ajax! You're going to be late!

I exit my bedroom and find Tameron standing at the base of the stairs.

This time, both her arms are folded across her chest. Her weight is shifted to one side of her body, and she has the look of a woman who's three foot taps away from being upset.

You know what? I'm not feeling too well. I . . . I was thinking about staying home today.

Uh-ah. No way, mister. Not on my watch.

But I said I don't feel well.

Tough stuff, Ajax. Your mother specifically told me that you couldn't afford to miss any more days of school.

But Tameron, I'm sick!

Sick my butt. I don't want to hear anything of it. You're going to school today whether you like it or not. Now, get yourself ready. And since you're so sick today, I'll drive you to school.

Brent usually picks me up.

Not today, he *ain't*.

Now, I realize, Tameron's upset with me.

—

"Not Quite Right"

Tameron hardly says a word to me during the entire drive.

It's not until Tameron reaches for the radio that I start to freak out. Her hand is *not* her hand. Her hand isn't even human! Instead, her hand is twice the size of any normal human hand. Not only that, her skin is incredibly smooth and scaly— similar to the creature from a dream—or, *Was it some guy dressed in a costume?*

I look at Tameron, who looks no different than she looked two seconds ago. Then, I look back at her hand and it's look like any other normal hand.

You okay?

I try to make sense as to what I just saw but come up as empty as an old paint bucket that's been left to bake in the sun.

Ajax?

Yeah. I come at Tameron harder than I'd like. I sound snappish. So, I try to mellow my tone. Fine.

Something's bothering you, Ajax. I can sense it.

I'm fine.

The heat rises in me. I just want her to shut up and drive.

You know, you can talk to me, right?

It's nothing. I just have a headache. That's all.

You want an Ibuprofen?

No, Tameron. I don't want an Ibuprofen.

Okay. Jus' trying to help.

I switch off the radio and delve deep back into my thoughts.

Was it?

It had to be.

—

"New Way"

Tameron drops me off in front of New Way Academy.

As I grab my bookbag from the backseat, she reminds that I need to be on my best behavior and that my mother pulled a lot of strings to reduce my suspension. I completely forgot about the suspension and what I did to Cory.

Since there are no tardy bells, like any typical high school, I take my time and make sure to avoid him—that is, if he shows up. Knowing Cory, he'd show up at school the very second he was released from the AMC. He was probably wearing his stitches proudly, like it was the latest trend, trying to get warm hugs and likes.

Most of the students have left the courtyard and have already made their way to class, although the remaining stragglers who walk past me look at me with the most sour expressions on their faces, as if I embody the traits of tart candy and just looking at me is no different than tasting me. I pass a couple of students who look more timid than disgusted. I admit that I'm used to the looks.

Outside the courtyard, Brent surprises me from behind. Brent's the last face I want to see right now. I keep walking in hopes that he'll walk the other way, considering his first class is located on the other side of the building. He keeps pace and walks with me. The first name out of his mouth is none other than Cory.

Surprised to see you, brutha.

The word *brutha* has me flinching. All I can think about is that bird-looking vampire hater towering over me.

Owls eat bats.

I snap from my trance.

I heard you messed him up good, man! Who's 'woke' now? You know, it's about time someone finally put that little bald-headed drama queen in his place. I heard he got seventeen stitches.

I'm not supposed to talk about it.

Brent waves off my comment, as if nothing I'm saying is registering.

You shouldn't be ashamed of what you did, Ajax. You did a lot of people a favor—

—And FYI, it was thirteen stitches, not seventeen.

Whatever, Ajax. I'll take any stitches. I'm just glad you're back. You were acting weird the other day.

Weird?

Again, my comment goes in one ear and out the other.

Man, Ajax! I still can't believe you put that friggin' closet-Nazi in the hospital. I heard while he was at the AMC nurses were spitting in his food.

Where'd you hear that?

Tyrone's older sister works at the AMC. She's a nurse practitioner.

He was only there for like a day, Brent. What's the big deal?

All I know, man: your ass is lucky. I wish my mom were governor. I mean, you can practically get away with murder.

Shut the hell up, Brent.

Whoa! Easy, Ajax. Don't push me, man.

Like you're one to talk, Brent. You'd be expelled if it weren't for your dad being the principal.

Not true. He treats me no differently than any other student.

Yeah. Keep telling yourself that.

I arrive at my classroom.

As Brent and I are about to part ways, Brent points out, of all people, Cory, who's standing outside Forensics. He's no longer wearing thirteen stitches on the side of his face; however, the cut left a noticeable scar.

Cory shoots a glance my way and immediately walks into the classroom.

What a bitch?

Dude. I'm not trying to start shit.

What? You agree he's a bitch, right?

Don't you have somewhere to be right now?

That's right. I completely forgot, man. I'll catch up with you later.

In the reflection of the glass, I witness Brent—or at least, someone who looks like Brent—his face all bloody and cut up, his jaw gone, torn off; his body badly maimed, clothes marked with tire tracks; he appears as if he's gotten run over by a truck. With part of his arm dangling along the threads of cartilage, Brent's reflection dawdles away.

I turn away from the window and glance at Brent, who's taking his good easy time to class. He's neither injured nor maimed, as the reflection shows me.

Pushing away the strange thought, I step into the lab, which is already full of students. I take my seat at an empty computer in the very back of the lab and pull out my screen-printing textbook from my bookbag.

After about thirty-minutes into my design, which is made to look like a kind of cut-and-paste type collage of iconic movie monsters as well as slashers, including Freddy Krueger, Chucky, Jason, Michael Myers, Candyman, *The Thing*, Pinhead and those other three from *Hellraiser*, Brundlefly, the zombie in *Day of the Dead*, the mutated, pink-drenched Dr. Edward Pretorius in *From Beyond*, and then last but not least, the 'Slasher of ALL Slashers,' Don Juan, aka 'The Wolf' from the horror flick, *The Effigy*, I pull my eyes away from the screen, hoping it will rid a sudden dizzy spell.

Then, as I continue to tweak the title 'WITCH-HOP' along the top of my design, the dizzy spell returns and forces me to look elsewhere.

Outside the lab, the same reptilian-like creature is walking down the hallway. Mr. Steyer, one of the many bad actors who uses his teaching position as a way to conceal his true identity, makes his rounds around the lab. He stops at each computer to give a few pointers to students. He spends the most time at Awny's computer, and it's pretty clear to those who've been paying the least amount of attention that Mr. Steyer appears closer to Awny than the other students, well, some of them. But I know he has his reasons why he tends to be more available to particularly female students. Mr. Steyer is aware that I'm aware he has two phones. Unless you're a drug dealer, who else carries around two phones? Once I caught Mr. Steyer red-handed—no pun intended—scrolling through porn on his phone. And, from the looks, the girls in the photos were clearly *not* of age.

Knowing that Mr. Steyer is more than likely going to spend even more time on Teagan, another one of his favs who's sitting two computers away from Awny, I take my attention off Mr. Steyer and track down the creature once more, only to find him standing behind the door of the lab, peering inside.

Mr. Steyer stops by and asks how the design is coming along. He even gives me advice on making sure to center the words *witch-hop*. Everything around me starts to amplify, the *tapping* of the keyboards, mouse *clicks*, *talking*, even the kid next to me, Orion, who's *sucking* on a cough drop, the hard candy *hitting* his teeth like a hockey stick to a puck. I can't take it any longer, so I excuse myself from the lab and hurry into the hallway.

I look around the hallway but can't find the creature anywhere in sight.

I walk toward the direction where I last saw him going. I make a pit stop inside the bathroom in order to control myself.

Get yourself together, Ajax.

As I look into the mirror, I notice both my eyes are different. I rub them in hopes that it's all in my mind. A good rubbing will help rid the horror. I crack open my eyes, and they look no different than the eyes on the same reptilian creature. I'm drawn away from the mirror by a noise over my shoulder.

Startled, I check out the strange noise coming from the last stall. I cautiously kneel down and look underneath the stall, only to find a pair of scaly legs and feet similar to a crocodile.

More frustrated than frightened, I storm directly to the last stall and kick open the door.

What the fuck do you want from me?

In the last stall some kid is doing lines of red snow on the top of toilet lid. He looks up at me with wide Holy-Shit eyes.

What the hell, dude? Do you mind?

Sorry. I thought you were someone else.

Close the freakin' door!

He doesn't say anything about my eyes, which prompts me to walk back to the mirror. My eyes appear normal. I leave the bathroom and walk back to class.

By the time lunch arrives, I spend most of the time pacing around New Way, trying my best to avoid Brent. I can't eat. I've completely lost my appetite.

—

"In The Eye of The Bulldog"

Once I'm dismissed from the last class, which is Programming, I C++ my way out of the Technology Building and take a minor detour away from the main courtyard where most of the students chill once school is over and have Tameron meet me at the far side of New Way, away from other students.

I hear the one voice that I don't want to hear behind me just as I'm getting in Tameron's car. He's telling me he can drive me home. But apparently, I make a gesture obvious enough for Tameron to understand that I'm in no mood to be letting Brent drive me home. She makes up a lie about us having to be somewhere soon and we're already running late as it is.

If there's one thing about Brent, it's his uncanny ability to be able to sniff out a lie. You know how dogs and cats have a sixth sense about death? Well, Brent has a sixth sense for bullshit. But I don't care whether or not he's offended. Over the past year at New Way, Brent has turned into a puppet who echoes whatever he hears from the Internet, then passes it off as his own. Nobody sees it, except for me. He's been compromised, manipulated, 'owned,' which is a popular word he tends to use. Even when he talks to me now, he sounds like a crowd talking to me, like thousands of voices and they're all echoing the same thing as if he's incapable of any independent thought.

Thanks to Tameron, I'm able to ditch Brent without any problems; and without thinking, I thank her for having my back in my own inaudible way. We don't talk much during the drive home, and Tameron's fine with the silence. I still feel off, as in I recently woke up from a decent nap, when we arrive back at the house. I go straight to my bedroom. From downstairs, Tameron hollers that she has to step out for a while to run her errands. A part of me wants to tag along with Tameron and is begging not to be alone in an empty house. Another part of me wants to get straight to the bottom of the madness and understand why I still feel as though I'm stuck in a dream.

From my bedroom window, I watch Tameron pull out of the driveway. Then I decide to get in my car and drive to Cory's house. I don't know what I'm doing here—or why I'm here. I park on the street and wait for Cory to arrive. After ten minutes of waiting, I decide to leave. I mean, really, what am I doing?

I reach for the push-button.

Cory arrives at his house.

I open the door, thinking maybe I can catch him before he enters the house. I notice he's left the car running and he appears to be in a hurry. I hang back in the car. He's only inside the house for a few minutes. Then he runs back outside and gets back into his car and drives off. I decide to follow him.

After fifteen minutes of tailing Cory, he finally arrives at his destination: Abernathy Medical Center—the AMC. He already had his stitches taken out—even if he was doing some kind of follow up with a doctor, he wouldn't need to go to a hospital for treatment or evaluation—which begs the question what he's doing at the hospital. He parks his car outside a separate wing, a cancer treatment facility, next to the hospital. *The shaved head!* Why didn't I think of that earlier?

Cory grabs the silvery 'Get Well Soon' balloon from the backseat and walks into the cancer treatment facility.

After some deliberation, I decide to follow him inside. Even as soon as I step inside the building, that part of me takes over the other more scared part. Somehow, I feel as though everything makes sense, as if I'm supposed to be here, as if, in an unexplainable way, me being here has already happened.

I search for Cory and locate him entering a Children's Care Unit. Normally, people like Cory would bring a camera crew with him to show the world that he is a good person and whatnot. The flat, smooth surface of his pockets suggests that he left his phone in his car. I follow Cory down another hallway until he reaches a hospital room where a young girl, who's probably no older than nine years old, is lying in bed. I stand just outside the doorway and watch from behind a cleaning cart. The girl perks up as soon as she sees Cory. The first thing that immediately stands out is their haircut. They're both sharing the same haircut.

It's hard to make out what they're saying. I creep closer and eavesdrop. The girl is Cory's younger sister, Hope, and she's receiving treatment for leukemia.

Next to the bed is a photo of Cory. He's a couple of years younger, I can tell. I've only known Cory a couple of years, and ever since I've known him he's been bald, not like he couldn't grow any hair, which he could. I remember seeing stubs on that waxy dome of his one time.

Cory's sister points at me, resulting in Cory to fully rotate around.

Ajax? What are you doing here?

I just wanted to talk.

I have nothing to say to you.

With a smile on her face, Hope waves at me.

Hello.

I wave back.

Hi.

I didn't know you had a sister.

Yeah. This is Hope.

My name's Ajax.

Cory turns his back to me and whispers something in Hope's ear. He stands up and as he starts walking toward me, I notice the bulldog on Hope's red sweatshirt. I don't know why I'm drawn to the sweatshirt. All I can think about is that Avanti was doing some photo-op with the basketball team later this afternoon.

I follow Cory outside and he suddenly changes his demeanor to the Cory I'm used to knowing. For a moment, he looks as if he wants to hit me.

What the hell you doing here, Ajax? You stalking me?

Do I look like the kind of person who stalks people?

Yeah. He gets too close to my grill, close enough to where he's asking for a punch to the face. You do!

All right. Chill. The truth is I was following you. Listen Cory, I know we're not supposed to be talking to one another. But the real reason why I'm here is to say I'm sorry for what happened.

You? You're sorry? Why are you really here?

I'm here to apologize. The words suddenly get lost in the back of my throat. I never thought I'd turn to plasma, especially in front of Cory, of all people, right? The dude who always got involved in other people's business, who acted as if he genuinely cared about people who didn't look like him whenever he was around people, who'd share a heart-to-heart to someone less fortunate while, at the same time, ridicule them behind his or her back, who made sure to be at the forefront of the crowd or whatever trend, who even pegged himself a 'voice' of the people, even though his hair—or lack thereof—suggested a label far more sinister. Cory Hart rolled with the same tribe who'd tell me that my skin was too light, that I had too many freckles or that my hair was too strawberry blood for a black boy, that both my eyes were goofy-looking and ninety-nine percent of the time, warranted a closer inspection. Why was one the color blue and the other green? Most of the girls who hung around Cory's tight knit, supposed 'all-inclusive' crew were more interested in my appearance, than actually getting to know me.

And for me, that was the hardest fact to swallow.

Despite my grudges with Cory, uttering the word, *apologize*, makes me feel lighter.

Is this a joke? Some prank that Brent put you up to?

No. Honestly, I don't know the reasons why I pushed you. I know, though, when I do find out I'll have to take a hard look in the mirror. But I do know why I'm here.

I look Cory in the eye and make it count.

I'm sorry. For sure.

As he looks me over, Cory digests my apology.

He holds out his hand.

I shake his hand, palm-side only, color-to-color.

Then, he pulls me in for a hug.

I point at Cory's head.

You did that for your sister?

Cory runs his hand over his slick scalp.

Yeah, man. I wanted to show her that not having hair wasn't so weird.

That's nice. I didn't know.

Well, I didn't feel the need to explain myself to people. Some things are best left unexplained. We all have our reasons for the things we do, right?

Yeah. I guess so.

You know why I left Bridgemount High to come to New Way?

No.

During my three years at Bridgemount, I was on the honor roll, played three sports: football, basketball, and baseball. Football season ran into basketball. But it didn't matter. I already had a spot on the team. I was *that* good. But the fact is I had no say in the matter. My father was calling all the shots. Then, one day, he got all over me after we lost against our football rival, East Lake. I snapped. I hit him in front of all the other players. I'll never forget the look on each one of their faces. I was their captain. They looked up to me, and I let them all down. Essentially, that tough, hardheaded guy inside me rebelled and tried to convince myself that I was tougher than my old man and that I finally proved to him that I was not going to be bossed around anymore. After I spent the next couple of days thinking about my actions, I realized I wasn't 'tough' for striking my father. I was weak. I let my emotions get the best of me. More importantly, I let my ego get the best of me. A couple of weeks later, I dropped out of Bridgemount.

If you were that good, then why'd you stop playing sports?

I wasn't pursuing my dream. He shrugs his shoulders, as if the gesture alone is attached to his answer. Besides, I'd rather choose a profession that thrives on helping people, opposed to hurting people.

I reach out my hand and shake Cory's yet again. It's a firm handshake, not at all overpowering, but firm as if we're both matching each other's strength.

—

"A telltale bulge of a pen"

I leave the cancer treatment facility feeling way better about confronting Cory and drive back home.

Tameron should've already been back from her errand run. I give her a call, but her phone goes straight to voicemail. I head upstairs to my bedroom and remove items from both my pockets, including my keys and the thirty-three cents of loose change I superstitiously carry whenever I'm out in public, and toss them on my desk. In my other pocket, I come across a strange object: a black pen with the word *Leatherwood* written on the side. I remove the pen from my pocket. I don't remember carrying a pen nor do I remember even owning such a pen— *What the hell is Leatherwood?* I place the pen next to the black and white speckled Composition notebook on my desk. I'm tempted to open the notebook, to look inside, skim through it, but that part of me is telling me to do it later, that it's too soon, save the best for last. So, I listen to that voice and spend the next couple of hours scrolling through RECOMMENDED videos on YouTube. The bizarre, bold, and shocking titles of videos have me back-tracking through my lightning-fast scroll and giving each one a second survey. One video is about the TOP TEN animals that crocodiles eat, that particular word *crocodile* grabbing most of my attention.

Other words leave me in a state of surrender, words like *blood*, *reptiles*, *lizards*, *midnight*, *watch*, or parodies of the current *Toad Prince* of the United States. I give in to the streaming app, watch each and every meaningless video that, after second and even third viewings, has me more confused about the events that have transpired to-day.

Somewhere between watching a TRAILER for a new show called *Blood and Bones* and a DIY video on *How to Repair a Broken Watch*, I drift for a moment. I wake up from feeling the sudden weight of my head falling into my chest. I snap my head upright and open my eyes. I check the time and two hours have passed! Which is strange because I closed my eyes for what felt like a minute. I turn off the TV and check the driveway for Tameron's car. She's still not back from running errands, so I try her on her phone once more. Voicemail.

That's weird. She always picks up the phone.

I know I'm only supposed to call Avanti for emergencies but I think Tameron being out well past the time she normally spends running errands justifies a call.

Avanti doesn't pick up.

Instead, it's her aide, Vye, who answers the phone. Her voice is muffled for some reason and I only catch something along the lines of my mother being in an important meeting with the mayor of Atlanta.

The sound of Vye's voice triggers an image inside my mind.

All of a sudden, I find myself in the upstairs bathtub. Of all people, Avanti's aide, Vye, is sitting with her legs crossed in a chair next to the bathtub, and she's instruct-ing me to do something to myself.

I shake away the very thought and hang up the phone. It's starting to get dark outside and Tameron's disappearance is making me worried. What if something happened to her? What if she was in a car wreck?

My mind starts to race with all-thoughts negative.

The best remedy to ease the racing mind. . .

Only one idea comes to me.

Yes.

—

"Rhymes with Bleach"

Only a couple minutes into taking my warm bath, I drift off once more. I'm back in the hospital, nursing the same exact injuries that I sustained after I was jumped by Sons of Man in an alleyway.

Even though I can't see anybody in the room, I can sense a presence close by. I focus on the shadowy corner of the room, particularly the dark figure sitting in a chair.

Sure enough, Vye emerges from the shadows. I can't help but draw my eyes toward her hand and the tiny object that she's holding.

The blade glistens in her hand.

Even though I can feel the metal slicing right through me, I know—because Vye knows—that the oxys help numb the pain.

This is me at my most vulnerable moment.

In her words, *my own Command+Alt+Esc—or better yet, delete.*

Of all the ways I imagined going out, I never thought I'd open myself up like this to the outside elements of the world. I'm an open book, the American Dream gone askew, a walking cliché teetering along the crooked lines of controversy, the representative of a thousand generations reduced to ash and limestone, inevitably torn down and rebuilt over and over again until all that remains of once-was is dust along the shoulder of a tired man who's beating an arthritic hand against the drum of extinction. But it's already done—heavy sigh. She's made the final cut.

My modern delete.

As my eyes fall upon the red highways along my forearms, the world around me starts to spin out of control as if, by opening myself up, I'm letting it all inside me, the air, water, and all of it turning to poison in my veins, and it's too much to bear. I've lost all motor functions. The razor blade slips from my ghost of a grip, strikes the edge of the bathtub, and makes a tiny splash in the bloody water.

Tick-tock.

Tick. . . tock. . . tick. . .

I wake up to the sounds of an old clock.

Expecting to see red, I draw my eyes toward the clear water in the bathtub. A heavy weight is lifted from my chest and finally, I can breathe easier just knowing it was all a dream.

The temperature in the room has dropped to the point where it starts to feel as cold as a meat locker. I examine both my arms and don't find any cuts. The once warm blood running from my entire body is gone. Yet, I can still feel traces of it moving along my skin, resulting in a pinprick sensation along the ends of my extremities. With pinpricks dancing along my skin, this invisible blood is no longer lukewarm. Yet, it's cold, like death, and it sends shivers throughout my body; my chest and arms curl inward, pectoral, abdomen muscles spasm.

My heart flutters from the sound of another more resonate, easier *tock*.

I hear someone knocking on the bathroom door.

Is that you, Death—

Before I can hold the rest of my thought, the door *squeaks* open in the greatest horror-movie like creepiness.

I look twice because, at first glance, I don't believe my eyes.

During my dry swallow, my heart feels as if it's climbing up my throat then, after my final *gah-gulp*, falling deep into my belly where it radiates my bowels.

Towering over the bathtub is a seven-foot tall reptile with the pounding stare of an iguana-faced creature ready to rip right through me.

The creature steps closer to me, my eyes going *blink-blink* as if, by doing so, I'm able to get a clearer picture of what exactly I'm dealing with here. Whatever it is, it's not human even though it stands in a way similar to that of a human; and when it speaks my name, its voice is as soft and sonorous as a voice-over actor.

How'd you know my name?

You called me.

Called you—What?!?

Well, not called per se. Forgive me for my use of vocabulary. Let's just say you. . . you reached out to me. Maybe you don't remember.

From the sound of the creature's deep voice, I can tell it's old, as in centuries old.

The creature takes yet another step closer to the bathtub; and now, it's reaching its scaly, clawed hand toward me in what I can only perceive as a threat.

I find an opportunity to escape.

With the adrenaline pumping through whatever blood I have left in my body, I bolt upright and slip from the bathtub before the creature can grab a hold of me. I race from the bathroom and stumble downstairs, occasionally looking over my shoulder. I'm not being chased, yet somehow, I still feel like I am. I look one last time over my shoulder before I run outside and witness the same creature, which appears much taller than seven feet, probably closer to eight or nine, standing under the doorway, its svelte silhouette dark and ominous behind foggy red light.

I open the front door and dart outside.

As soon as I step outside, I immediately wear the cold like a tight, irritating suit; however, my body is still numb from what I believe to be from oxys. I cover up myself with my hands, as if someone's watching, the neighbor perhaps, whoever.

Trying not to expose myself for the whole neighborhood to see, I run down the porch steps and hurry onto the street, which, after one block, becomes darker. The streetlights lining the neighborhood street provide me with a path forward, as if they're being controlled by a dimmer. Eventually, after a couple of steps onto the street, each one of the streetlights goes dark.

A greater *part* of me knows that I've been here before. And the horror soon to come.

I'm left standing, cold and afraid, in the middle of a pitch-black street. Each house, each mailbox, each lawn, each driveway darkens to the point of disappearing into complete and utter darkness, as the dark itself spreads closer and closer to the street until it surrounds me. The only house that I can barely make out is my house, and even it appears as if it's, like the streetlights, dimming. Above, a once bright sky is no more. The stars, snuffed out. The moon, nowhere to be found.

As heavy darkness descends upon me, thousands of tormented voices amplify all around me. Screaming at me. Begging for me to come closer to the darkness. They carry a sick desperation in their voice, a hunger: that's the first thing surfacing through my mind. These people—whoever they may be—sound as if they're solely relying on me to provide them with food and shelter.

I look around and there's nobody on the street but me, and that's when I realize they're coming for me. Lifeless, wobbly arms and spaghetti legs emerge from the ring of darkness. Moaning and screaming, the mob of contorted figures totters into the dim light that encompasses me. I'm more frightened of these tormented things than that creature in the bathroom. It's a bottomless hunger driving them. It's noticeable in their wobble, their gibberish, their screams and cries.

As the mob closes in all around me, I have no other choice than to run away. I make it to the house without getting attacked—or eaten—however, I once came close to them in what felt like another life. They did attack me; however, I managed to escape them but not on my own. I had help.

I close the door behind me and immediately feel the same presence from the bathroom coming from a dark living room.

I knew you'd be back, but never so quickly.

Startled, I track the voice to the creature sitting in the LazyBoy recliner in the corner of the room. Its scaly, lizard-like body bathed in darkness.

Talk about making a statement.

I quickly grab a pillow from the couch and cover myself. I search around for a weapon. I find the closest object I can find, which is a poker from the fireplace.

Quite an impressive list you have here.

For some reason, I already know what *list* it's talking about before I can even wrap my head around how it came to learn of the list.

I step forward.

Behind me, the fireplace suddenly lights up with a mellowing flame!

Startled, I turn around and try to understand how the fire lit up all on its own but can find no other reason, except for the creature in the recliner using a remote control. *Do we even have a remote for the fireplace?* Or is the creature *that* good at creeping me out?

Before I can make sense of what's going on with my body, I'm suddenly distracted by the rustling sound of paper.

Getting struck by an oncoming train with wet concrete filled inside my shoes; leaping from the Mallard Bridge onto a blank canvas which will be later shown in an art gallery; robbing the 24-7 with a water pistol, thus resulting in being shot by the heroic clerk named Haibi who carries a shotgun underneath the counter—

—Enough!

It only gets better.

I watch its arm moving across its fossil-colored underbelly; however, I'm still unable to see what's in its hands for it's too dark.

'*For the longest I can remember,*' it reads, '*I've felt as if I've been living in your shadow, trapped by it, unable to move or breathe. All I wanted was to enjoy the pursuits of any normal sixteen year old. But even that was far from possible.*'

Hey! That's private!

Private, huh?

Yet, it's addressed to—

—Who the hell are you?

I hold the poker in front of me and show this bug breath that I'm not afraid to put out a fire.

The question you should be asking is not who I am but *what* I am.

The creature tosses my journal on the coffee table, which lands open on my note. As it extends its hand outward, I notice something—maybe a device—along its wrist. Before I can get a closer look, it pulls its hand back into the darkness of the living room.

The talking caught me off guard. But, now that I realize it can read, I start to wonder where the creature came from and what it wants from me.

Where'd you get that?

In your bedroom.

What the hell were you doing in my bedroom?

Just piddling around until you came back.

What do you want from me?

It's hard to explain in words and even if I did, I believe it would still go over your head. Not that I'm doubting your intelligence. It's just a lot to take in.

The creature leaned forward in the orange glow of firelight. I'm able to get a closer look at its hand, particularly its wrist, as well as a wristband, which is made out of what looks like pearls.

The beating light from the fireplace hits the iridescent wristband, causing it to change colors at different angles.

But since you asked, I don't think what I have to say will convince you. For this, I'm going to have to show you. . . again.

Show me? Show me what?

As the creature stands up, it hit the top of its spiky head along the ceiling fan. It walks back upstairs.

'Show me what,' I said!

The creature walks to the top of the staircase, stops at the landing, and turns around.

Your options.

Options?

The creature nods toward the bathroom.

Believe me when I say this: time is *not* on your side.

Who—what are you?

Name's Creach.

Like creature?

No. Like Creach.

The creature who goes by the name Creach walks to the bathroom.

Halfway toward the bathroom, Creach stops in front of the railing and looks down at me.

What are you waiting on?

—

"The Blood Watch"

Still trying to make sense as to why I've been seeing Creach throughout the day, I decide to follow the seven-foot tall reptile upstairs.

I make it to the bathroom where Creach is standing over the bathtub. Inside the bathtub is my answer. There, I lie in a pool of blood. I appear to be drifting in and out of consciousness.

From the palish tone of my skin, it appears as if I don't have much longer to live before I'm maggot food. The blood runs from my open veins, which prompts me to check out myself, as in the one standing here, Me. I search for the cuts on my arms once more but don't find any.

I look back up and recognize that old chair next to the bathtub. It is made out of cherry maple wood; and over the years, it has withstood more nicks and scratches than one might endure. The chair talked in creaks whenever you sat in it or put the slightest amount of weight against it and sounded as if it was ready to collapse to a dust pile at any moment. Regardless of its age, as well as its sentimental value, the chair was mostly used as a clothing rack for dirty clothes, including soiled socks and sweaty T-shirts.

All I know is someone was sitting in this exact chair while I was carrying out something awful to my body that I had absolutely no control over. That, I'm sure of. This was *not* me. This was *not* my doing or my final farewell, despite having spoken these shameful words in the past, ones that would most definitely warrant more of a roll-of-the-eye than any need for concern. The fact of the matter: I never would've taken my own life!

But it's already done, Ajax.

Who are you?

That is irrelevant at this point.

Have we met before?

Yes.

How many times?

You don't want to know. But you are here now, as we speak. And I have a good feeling this time around.

I walk past the mirror and spot several strange markings on my shoulders, as well as the back of my neck.

Concealing myself with the pillow, I walk closer to the mirror. The markings are scars, old scars, pink and jagged.

I didn't notice these before.

That's because you're changing.

Stumped by Creach's response, I find myself thinking whether or not I spoke the words out loud. Or, was it my interest in these scars that impelled Creach to elaborate on the current condition of my body?

Changing? What do you mean I'm changing?

With the tip of its claw, Creach picks up my pair of dirty boxers lying on the vanity and looks them over with what appears to be a feeling only a human would feel.

This reminds me. You might want to change into some clothes.

I nod at the boxers.

Can you?

Toss them over?

Yes. Whatta you waiting on?

I'm afraid that's soulistically impossible.

Soul-*what*?

You really think that's a pillow you're holding?

I look down at the pillow and find only my hand covering myself.

And that poker I was holding in my hand, nowhere to be found.

I was just. . .

Yes. That's right. You were, Ajax. At least you *thought* you were. In time, as ironically as it sounds, you will come to realize that everything you once knew about life doesn't exist where I'm taking you.

But how come you can touch things and I can't?

Because I exist. Creach points at my other self clinging to life in the bathtub. He exists. Then, Creach points at me. You don't. At least not in physical form.

Am I dead?

Not dead, but almost. Like I said, you don't have much time.

Till what exactly?

I'll explain it all. Right now, time's ah-wasting. So, make it easier on yourself. Where we're going, it's best you put on some clothes. *Trust* me—

—And where are we going exactly?

I'll show you. Just think of something to wear. We have to go.

That's it? Just think of anything—

Yes. The first thing that pops in your mind.

So I have a mind but no body?

Creach thinks over my remark.

Sure.

You don't sound confident.

Yes. You have a mind. Now, let's—

—Then, you're talking about like something out of *Syntronix*.

I'm unaware of this *Syntronix.*

You know, *The Syntronix.* Everybody knows the movie, *The Syntronix.* Was like one of the greatest science-fiction movies of all time. You know, right hand or left hand? Wizard of Oz? Chiromancy? The lines on our palms that pull us toward the inevitability of, you know. . .

I get nothing from Creach, not even a reaction.

What happens in *The Syntronix* can have real-life consequences to your body outside *The Syntronix*, like, for instance, I look around and find the vanity, say if I submerged my head in a sink full of water and drown my—

—No.

No?

I think I know where you're going with this, but no. The answer is no.

But you didn't let me finish—

—We have to get going. Let's go.

I look down at myself and find myself dressed in the same outfit that I wore to the schoolbook pictures: a white *Mobocracy* T-Shirt over a pair of holey black jeans and the Black Edition of Chuck Taylors. Prior to getting inside the bathtub, I remember removing all of my facial piercings.

I touch my face, my nose first and then my eyebrows, and find each ring and stud attached to my face. Along both my wrists are bands and whatnot; although, one band feels different, as if it doesn't belong to me.

On my left wrist is what I believe to be some kind of watch.

I never wore a watch. Never saw the point in letting time control me.

It's not the kind of watch you're thinking of.

I inspect the strange device on my wrist. It has a gold band. In the center—where normally the clock would sit—is a glass circular enclosure filled with what looks like blood; however, it's not entirely full of blood. It appears as if it's three-fourths full. Which makes me wonder where the other one-fourth had gone? Or, has the blood drained that much since I've been wasting my ghost-breath yapping it up with a seven-foot tall reptile named Creach.

I like to call it the Blood Watch.

Blood Watch?

It's pretty simple. The watch indicates how much life force you have left inside your body. Once the blood runs out, the watch will begin to turn black. And once the watch turns completely black, your body dies. I can't stress this enough: Whatever you do, make sure the watch *never* turns black.

What happens then? You know, when my body dies. . .

You only saw a glimpse of what happens outside. And I know you might not want to hear this now, but you're going to wish you hadn't made that final cut.

Cut? I didn't cut myself. It wasn't me!

But it came from your hand.

I draw my eyes toward the wristband on Creach's wrist. It doesn't look like a watch—at least, none that I've seen in my world—but who knows.

How come your *watch* is different than mine?

This is not a watch.

Then, what is it?

This is a Lazarus Cuff, made from old technology used to make the Tunic of Lazarus.

Lazarus? Like Back-From-The-Dead Lazarus?

Where I come from dead isn't dead.

Dead? Dead is dead. And there's no coming back from the dead.

So you think.

So, what? You're here to save me from death? Is that it?

No. Like I said, I'm here to *show* you.

Show me what?

Your story, Ajax.

—

"Careful What You Wish For"

Creach steps out of the bathroom, and I follow.

I stop at the doorway and look back at my other lifeless self lying in the bathtub one last time before exiting. I'm left transfixed in a somewhat religious awe, as if I'm witnessing right before my eyes what former skeptics would call a spiritual enlightenment.

Remember, time's ah—

—Wasting. Got it.

I push aside the glorified moment and follow Creach downstairs.

The creature opens the door and waits for me to catch up. Then, together, we both exit the house.

Once more, I can't help but stop and turn my eyes back to the top of the landing, hoping to find a sign maybe coming from the bathroom, a clue—whatever!— indicating that I'm doing the right thing by following this seven-foot tall reptilian-like creature to wherever it dwells, which, more than likely, is what I consider to be a fiery place that starts with a capital letter H. Raised to be a Catholic—which, I know, is odd, considering that Avanti, the one whom I see whenever she's not in the public eye, doesn't have one Catholic bone in her body—I can't imagine what other place it'd be. I get nothing, though, no signs or clues, no pull, only a bathroom bathing in a red light that appears to be dimming to the color gray.

To paraphrase Creach, time is no longer ticking but dropping. I glance down at the Blood Watch on my wrist. I slosh around the blood inside the glass ball and can't help but wonder where the blood goes once it drains completely.

I face the neighborhood street, and Creach is nowhere in sight.

Not too far away in the center of the street, a manhole has been slid open.

Immediately, I start thinking more about where Creach is leading me—under the street, for sure—but what exactly waits for me when, or if, we get there.

All of a sudden, Creach's lengthy, scaly arm shoots out from the manhole and articulately waves me closer.

A part of me feels as if the creature's luring me into a trap.

Another part of me feels as if I have nothing else to lose.

I remain convinced of the latter—at least, try to.

Vigilantly, I walk down the steps of the front porch and inch my way onto the street.

As I approach the manhole, the darkness starts to fill the street like a storm of darkness approaching me. The surrounding houses darken. The streetlights dim, then, eventually, burn out. In that dark and unruly storm, I hear growing screams laced with greater agony than hunger. The screams continue to build nearly to the point of becoming deafening.

With nowhere else to go, I decide climb down into the manhole.

I slide the cover over the manhole before the darkness overcomes me.

Below, Creach is waiting for me.

I use the ladder to climb down.

Now are you going to explain to me what that is back there?

Not now.

I stand my ground, not moving until I get more answers.

Once Creach becomes aware of my stillness, it stops, turns around, and walks back to me.

Some call it the In-Between—the Eventide, a place where corrupted souls go to live out an eternity searching for those like you to feast upon. And I'm afraid if you don't come with me, then, eventually, you will join them in eternal darkness.

But there were so many of them.

There are more of them. Lots more. They believe that by consuming another tourist it will release them from the darkness that has bound them.

And will it?

No. You see, Ajax, the ones up there, they had second doubts. For the most part, they weren't ready to die. It wasn't their time. Now, they want out. But it's already too late. Their *pneuma* is trapped in that awful place up there in the world you once knew.

Pneuma?

Think of it as the soul, as you see yourself at this very moment.

I look down at myself, my clothes, my 'pneuma.'

My pneuma, huh? Then, why does it feel like I'm still kind of nervous about what's happening?

As long as you're wearing that Blood Watch on your wrist, you still have ties to your body and your world. Remember, Ajax. Only *you* can save yourself.

Creach attempts to walk away, but I reel Creach back in with another question.

Can they see you? The people of my world?

Only if they look hard enough. Creach holds up the wristband of pearls along his wrist. The Lazarus Cuff allows me to travel more easily through the shadows.

The shadows? What?!?

Creach was right about all of this nonsense going over my head.

Then, how come I can see you?

You can see me because you're dead, Ajax.

The comment alone sends a ripple of anger through my pneuma.

Not yet.

That's the spirit. Creach waves me along. Now, let's go.

But wait! What happens when you take it off? The Cuff?

Creach hangs its head in what appears to be sadness.

I'm afraid the people of your world aren't ready to find out about me or my kind. Creach brings its attention back to me. Its head jerks right in a directional nod. Let's go. I can answer all the questions you have. But we have to move.

Watching my step along the slick, narrow ledge above a still lane of mystery water, I follow Creach through the sewer tunnel. I only get a few steps in before the questions start flaring inside my mind. I look back up at Creach and suddenly realize that I've been here before. My pneuma tingles, and I'm struck by momentary déjà vu.

Of all the people out there, why me? Not like there's anything special about me.

I take my eyes off the ground for a moment, which is a no-no. Before I can find my footing, my heel slips along a slick spot on slimy concrete. My feet fly out from beneath me. I throw out my arms, trying to grab hold of the wall but all I grab is air.

As I fall backward, Creach's arm shoots outward. It happens to grab me with the same hand wearing the Lazarus Cuff. The cuff itself glows with a faint pinkish-white light. I turn my shoulder and realize that I've come inches away from landing in that disease-infested water, which is probably crawling with super bugs yet to be discovered.

Creach pulls me toward the wall.

Syntronix, right? All in the mind, right?

I ignore the very idea of the mind and soul acting like one and make sure to thank Creach for helping me; however, I'm more interested in its hand.

Creach's hand no longer has the scaly appearance of what I first perceived as a reptilian-like hand. Its claw, now fingernails. Its scaly hide, human flesh.

Even Creach's grip feels soft and feminine. I realize the change in Creach's hand had something to do with touching me, my pneuma.

I immediately point out the change in Creach.

Your hand?

Once I find my balance over the ledge, Creach glances down at its hand.

Creach lets go of my arm and becomes awkwardly quiet and for a second, it even struggles to make eye contact with me. Which, I know, is uncharacteristic. When Creach finally finds my eyes, it looks at me as if, in a strange way, it *knows* me.

The Lazarus Cuff allows me to touch you.

I question why Creach is even telling me. The comment sounds more like an excuse. Tell me something I don't already know.

Another thought comes to mind, a cooler thought.

Can I, like, walk through walls and stuff?

Technically, yes.

But your hand, it was like mine. Only more—Are you a she?

I am female. Yes. Does it make any difference what gender I am?

Ah, no. It doesn't—

—Then, are you ready to continue?

Yeah. Sure.

We make it to an intersection in the sewers. Creach makes a right turn. But then, after second-guessing itself, Creach turns back around and makes a left instead.

You sure?

Yes. I'm sure. It's this way. As much as I've traveled through these tunnels, I never get use to them.

I spend the next few moments racking my brain as to how many times Creach has done this sort of thing. So, I ask him—or her.

Forgive my ignorance. But in your world how many days are there in a year?

Three hundred and sixty-five. Well, not counting a leap year, which is three hundred and sixty-six.

Three hundred and sixty-five. So, I dunno. Take how many days there are in a single year and then multiply that by twelve.

Okay. So a lot, huh? And you've met people like me?

You can say that. Well, they aren't nearly as talkative as you.

Believe it or not, I'm more introverted.

I take the comment as a compliment, sort of.

Does time not exist in your world?

Once, yes. It did. So I've read in the *Book Of.*

Book Of what?

The Book Of.

Yeah. Book of what? Never mind.

After the first explosion, it was written that time slowed down so much that it started to reverse—

—Explosion? What explosion?

The explosion happened the same time a bomb was dropped on the southern coast of the island Honshu—in your world, that is.

I remember researching the bomb on the Internet. I know the answer.

You're talking about Hiroshima, right?

That's the one. Then, there was a second explosion—the 'big one,' as everybody calls it. Happened in 1986—your year, that is—the time of Chernobyl.

Surprisingly, even though it was before my time, I remember researching that one, too. I immediately point out that Creach's facts are all wrong.

But wait! After a contamination, the nuclear power station in Chernobyl was contained. What'r you talking about? There was no explosion!

Not in your world, there wasn't.

You mean—

Creach nodded.

But how?

Whether you believe me or not, Ajax, our worlds are connected and whatever happens in your world has a greater ripple effect on ours. Forty-one years passed between the two events; however, during that time between explosions everything has been out of whack. Everything. . . evolved. Or, devolved, one would put it.

Devolved how?

The fact I'm talking to a seven-foot tall reptile that has the body of a lizard or crocodile—can't tell which—only much slender and alien in shape, and the facial appearance similar to that of an iguana (and who, by the way, fun fact: happens to be a chick), makes things clearer to understand.

You're talking about mutation! Aren't you?

That's right, including time itself.

What? Time can't mutant. That defines all laws of nature!

Where we're going, Ajax, there are no laws. There is *no* balance.

The comment alone sticks with me and has me reconsidering my options and for one, spending an eternity in darkness seems, suffice to say, tolerable.

Four seconds in your world could be four minutes, four hours, four days, four months, even as long as four years in my world. Where we're going time is nothing like the way you perceive time.

Trippy.

You haven't seen anything yet.

We come to a stop at the end of a tunnel, which, at first glance, appears to be a dead end. I figure we're lost again, although Creach is convinced that we're on the right track. I mimic her movements as she leans forward; and then, she shows me yet another tunnel, a much smaller tunnel, basically a drainage pipe about the size of an escape tunnel which immediately heightens my claustrophobia.

Immediately, I'm bludgeoned by a fury of racing thoughts.

We have. . . to go through. . . there?

I can hardly even finish a thought.

My throat tightens.

Not a fan of tight spaces, are you? Yeah. Who isn't— —I can't.

Well, I'm afraid you have no other choice, Ajax. The closest entrance is too far away and you don't have time. Trust me on this one. The transitioning takes a while to get used to.

The transitioning? What transitioning? Why are you doing this?

I have a vision of Creach dragging me through that narrow pipe, the Lazarus Cuff on her wrist glowing a pinkish-white color.

Horrified, I shake away the images.

No!

You have to, Ajax.

I can't do it!

Just think of something positive.

I instantly do the one thing I've always been good at it. I rebel.

In a casual manner, Creach kneels down and readies herself to crawl—or better yet—slither through the pipe. I don't follow suit. Instead, I back away. The very thought of being trapped in a tight space causes the fear to spread throughout my entire body—or my pneuma or whatever the hell Creach calls it! I know it's all in my mind, the fear; however, right now never has a feeling felt so strong.

Gripped by fear, I continue to back pedal away.

Creach only gets half of her body into the pipe before she turns her shoulder and finds me backing away.

Ajax, we don't have time! You must come with me!

I shake my head.

No.

Ajax!

I race back to the manhole cover. I climb up the ladder and barely manage to remove the cover from the manhole.

As soon as I climb my way out onto the neighborhood street, they're already on top of me, a mob of hellish fiends desperate to tear me apart. Their screeches only intensify the fear, as if they can smell the fear emitting from the giant pore of my pneuma. I attempt to flee from the alabaster-skinned mob. One of the fiends grabs me from behind and throws me to the ground. Its long, bony, gnarly hand feels slick along my shoulder, as if it sweats slime. The spastic fiend tosses me to the ground, its jaw chomping and exposing layers and layers of jagged teeth. I hit the side of my head along the street.

In a daze, I shield my face from their attack, curl my body into a fetal position, and hope that Creach was wrong about everything.

I wish someone would just pinch me already.

Hold up. . .

Never mind.

—

"Wasn't"

Kicking and punching, I fight off the darkness.

Both my hands and feet connect with the carpeted interior of a trunk.

Outside, I can hear familiar voices.

Yelling my name—*Jackie Boy! Hey, Jack off! Afraid of the dark, are we? What a crybaby? Yeah! Cry for us, you lil' crybaby?*

The voices are younger and coming from what sounds like a group of kids.

This is what you get for kissing my cousin! She said your breath stank! Yeah lil' Stinky, buy yourself a Tick-Tack! Oh! I forgot! You ain't getting out! Yea-yeah, boy! That's right! You're stuck in there for the rest of your pathetic life!

I hear a loud and hollow *thud* above me followed by a couple of less intense *thuds* along the bumper of the car.

The kids walk away, laughing.

Their laughs trail off, leaving me trapped in silence.

Eventually, after all of the kicking and punching, I wear myself out.

To my right, a hazy red light brightens, revealing an umbrella and a dirty pair of butters.

My eyes adjust to the darkness. Only a few inches next to my right shoulder a black beetle is overturned on the floor of the trunk. In similar fashion, the beetle squirms and kicks its tiny little legs in the air, as if it's trying to roll over. After a while, the beetle stops kicking and squirming and eventually, gives up.

In that moment of defeat where the beetle accepts its fate, I accept mine. I'm going to die, eventually, like the beetle; however, I'm not going to die today.

Relieved, yet more determined, I flip the still beetle over on its legs. By doing so, the beetle scurries toward the red light, crawls through the crack in the carpet lining, and escapes from the trunk. I peel away the piece of partial carpet covering the light bulb and punch out the brake light with the tip of the umbrella. Natural daylight fills part of the trunk. I peer through the hole in the rear of the car and spot a lady walking past. I yell out to the lady, stick my hand out of the hole where the brake light used to be, and wave her down.

I pull my hand back into the trunk. The lady is coming this way. I tell her to open the trunk.

She struggles at first, but after a couple attempts, the trunk pops open!

The beam of sunlight blinds me, forcing me to shield my face with my hands.

The walker steps in front of the sunlight; however, her figure is darker, taller, inhuman.

I wake up in my old bed with the splash of sun on the side of my face.

As I sit upright, I look around the bedroom and wonder how I ended up back here. Strangely, I'm drawn to my wrist. I touch my wrist and run my hand along my forearm. I remember wearing a watch on my wrist but can't put an image to the memory.

I roll out of bed.

Once more, my eyes are drawn to my wrist, now both of them.

On instinct, I walk toward the blinds to open them; however, they're already open.

I walk to the door and as I'm about to reach for the door handle, I pause for a moment. Then, open the door. I can smell a hint of cinnamon raisin toast, as well as coffee in the air. The smells, like that sunshine, are comforting.

Before heading downstairs, I walk into the hallway bathroom and relieve myself. As I'm about to pull down my sweats, I'm drawn to the bathtub. I hold it in and check out the bathtub instead. I take a knee next to the tub where I discover a smudge of dry blood caked onto the edge of the drain.

As with the bedroom door, I don't exactly know why I'm drawn to these certain ideas. All I can think is that maybe it has something to do with a dream—or a memory.

Standing upright, I come across yet another smudge of dry blood on the floor. Then, during my exit from the bathroom, I come across yet another smudge underneath the doorway, which doesn't look like a smudge at all but more so a. . .

I follow drops of blood to the top of the landing.

Searching for more blood, I walk downstairs.

I find yet another one in the foyer.

As I'm about to head outside, I can feel someone standing behind me. I turn my shoulder and witness Tameron waiting at the edge of the kitchen. She's holding her arms down by her side and staring at me funny.

Tameron?

I was just going to say something, but I lost my train of thought. Oh, yeah. I was going to make you breakfast. She taps herself on the forehead. Silly poor ole me. You hungry?

Yeah. I'm *starving*.

Well, what are you waiting on? Don't just stand there. Let's go. She waves me into the kitchen. You're already running late as it is.

Late?

Yes. Late for school. And don't give me that excuse that you're not feeling well.

I follow Tameron into the kitchen where a box of Snake Eggs is sitting on the kitchen table. I pick up the cereal box. On the cover is a bowl full of s-patterned oats with white marshmallows in the shape of tiny balls—or eggs?

Where's Avanti?

Your mother had to leave early this morning for an important meeting. She has an extremely busy schedule today. You know, she's going to be meeting with the—

—The Bulldogs. Yeah. I remember.

You do? That's right. I forget how much you like basketball.

I used to, I guess.

You know, Avanti told me you were good. Why'd you stop playing?

I dunno.

Well, surely, there has to be a reason.

Ignoring Tameron, I grab a bowl from the top cabinet, as well as a carton of soymilk from the refrigerator, and take a sit at the table.

Tameron lets me eat in peace and steps out of the kitchen to finish folding a load of clean clothes in the laundry room.

I pour myself a bowl of Snake Eggs and as I'm trying to piece everything together, I draw my attention toward the kitchen countertop where a TV is playing a wildlife show on the *Animal Planet* channel.

On the TV, an iguana is hanging out along a tree branch when, all of sudden, the iguana snatches a grasshopper with its long, rubbery tongue while I take a bite of my cereal.

The crunching sound of Tameron eating from a piece of jelly toast pulls me away from the TV.

As she chews, she turns to me. Globs of grape jelly roll down the side of her chin. She licks up the slippery jelly; however, when Tameron does so, her tongue is inhumanly long, more so like a chameleon rather than an iguana, and it nearly stretches down to the base of her chin. Again, Tameron looks at me funny.

What?

Nothing.

I excuse myself from the table and hurry to the hallway bathroom where, this time, I finally relieve myself.

After I flush the toilet, I notice a strange watch on my wrist—a Blood Watch? I try to remove the watch, but it won't come lose. I'm suddenly turned away from the watch by a *banging-sloshing* noise coming from the water. I put my ear to the wall and hear the sound of water flowing through loose, rusty pipes.

Keeping close to the wall, I track the noise outside into the hallway.

The sound leads me toward the basement door. I follow the sound down into the basement, which, halfway down the steep staircase, appears to be a sewer.

Immediately, I rotate around and walk up the stairs. The door is gone and all that remains is a moldy brick wall.

With nowhere else to go, I decide to walk down into the basement. The farther I walk down the stairs, the more and more the basement starts to look like the sewers. The walls have changed. The air is smelly and musty. Even the stairs I walk on are no longer wood, yet they're made of concrete.

As I reach the bottom of the staircase, I find Tameron standing next to a pipe in the base of the brick wall.

You're running out of time, Ajax.

She taps her wrist, as if she's tapping an invisible watch.

I look down at the Blood Watch. Inside the glass ball only half the blood remains.

Remember, once it turns black—

—Yeah. *I don't know how I know this, but, yeah*, I got it.

The sight of Tameron brings back a wave of memories, making amends with Cory, the Bulldog on his sister's red sweatshirt, meeting Creach, seeing myself in a bathtub full of my own precious blood.

Once more, I look down at the Blood Watch and then both my palms.

All your answers lie at the other end.

Tameron points at the pipe below.

Finally, I make a decision.

I walk to Tameron, get down on both my hands and knees, and crawl through the narrow pipe.

While crawling through thick, clumpy sewage, I glance over my shoulder.

Creach, *not* Tameron, is watching me from outside the pipe.

Keep going, Ajax. You're almost there.

I block out the smell by holding my breath.

Surprise, surprise, I end up breaking a world record for the longest someone's ever held his breath. Who would've thought? I actually miss breathing.

—

"Not in Georgia Anymore"

Just as I'm about to give up after crawling for what feels like miles through hella nastiness, a hazy light materializes at the end of the pipe.

The faster I crawl, the brighter and clearer the light becomes.

The light pushes me forward.

Finally, I reach the light and wind up inside an industrial type room. The surrounding walls look like rusted metal. A mesh of steamy pipes everywhere. I look down, give my outfit a once-over, and what should be clothes covered in all sorts of hella nastiness is, surprisingly enough, clean.

Your pneuma, remember?

I look up and Creach is standing in the shadowy corner of the room.

But how? You were just. . . You can't teleport, can you—

—Teleport, huh? I haven't heard that one before.

But how'd you get here before me? You were just—

—Behind you. Yes. I was. And now, I'm not. The question you should be asking yourself, Ajax, is 'How did you get here?'

I just crawled through. . .

I glance behind me and search for the opening in the pipe but can't find it.

Where'd it go?

You've been here for a while now.

But how?

Like most tourists who have a hard time coping with what happened to them, you drifted into a state of repeat after you nearly got devoured by those slimeballs from the Eventide. Your mind was lost and you've simply been drifting through the same day over and over, surrounding yourself with the present; but most importantly, living out the one particular moment where you felt the most regret. I had no other choice than to step in and help guide you to where you needed to be before your mind was lost forever.

Creach shows me the Lazarus Cuff on her wrist.

Using the Lazarus Cuff, I carried—well, more like dragged you here, into my world. However, while you remained in your state of repeat, in order to reconnect with your pneuma, you had to conquer the one thing that most tourists fail to do—

—My fear.

That's right, Ajax. Your fear.

I was ten years old when a group of kids locked me in the back of a trunk. I thought I was going to die. I remember thinking how much I didn't want to die.

I reckon you were not the same after that day.

Images surface inside me, ones of me kicking kids who looked different than me or punching kids who looked at me differently or even beating kids until they bled.

No. I guess you can say I am—was a bully.

But not anymore.

You know, I never liked doing what I did.

You only did what you had to do in order to grow.

I suppose so.

Ajax, you looked fear straight in the eye and told it who's boss. So, how are you feeling?

Better, I guess.

I look down at the Blood Watch on my wrist, which is half-full. I notice several pinkish scars about the size of toothpicks randomly patterned like wallpaper on both of my arms as well, ones that weren't there before.

Now that we've peeled back the layers, are you ready? You still have a long ways to go. Time is—

—Ah-wasting. Yeah. I got that part.

Creach leaves the rusty room and steps into a surveillance room.

Quietly sitting behind a control board is a slender man who goes by the name Sticks. I'm weirded out yet slightly relieved from his presence. He's a human—a plus for me. And except for the somewhat gaunt appearance, he looks completely normal.

Creach waves at Sticks, who bows his head in a careful, robotic nod.

On one of the monitors, another man—who doesn't look human even though he bares the features of a human—is being chased through a junky river by a pack of what looks like wolves; however, they have twice as many legs as wolves. The action alone is dire enough to warrant a closer look from Sticks.

As he turns around and faces his back toward me, I notice the massive crater in the back of his head.

The hole looks as if it has come from a close-range gunshot.

—

"Stranger in a Strange Land"

I step outside the metallic box-like structure Creach refers to as Outpost #36.

Surrounding the remote building is a barren landscape, desert-like in its dustiness, yet the rocky ground has a darker, almost ashy hue to it. Not too far away is a range of hills and small mountains. I immediately notice a murky, trash-littered river running alongside the outpost. I think about the man in the monitor and how he was being chased by strange beasts.

Creach calls out to me and points to our destination past one particular jagged mountain.

Dark Mountain, huh?

While studying the somewhat beautiful yet ominous mountainscapes, I can't help but notice the red sky, not partially red from the setting or rising of a sun, but full on red-red.

Is the sky normally this red in your world?

How do you mean?

I point up at the red sky.

See. Red.

I don't know what you're talking about.

Hard answer to swallow coming from a know-it-all.

What are you, colorblind?

Yes. As a matter of fact I am.

Really? You mean, you can't see the color of the sky?

Creach doesn't respond to my question. In a way, I feel as if, of all the questions I've asked, questioning Creach's eyesight is off limits.

So, where are we going?

Leatherwood.

Leatherwood, huh? So, is that a—

—Yes. It's a city.

So, what's in—

In the corner of my eye, I spot a *squeaky* rodent no larger than an opossum scurrying toward a gap between two boulders. Normally, I wouldn't think much of it. It's just your ordinary animal more than likely evading a predator, which it probably thinks is Creach, although, I'm not too sure what she eats to survive—and I don't plan on asking either. Or, it's chasing after a mouse or insect or whatever's on the menu. I'd rather be thinking of these common everyday essentials, who's eating who or what's eating what. Or, maybe I breathed in a toxic fume while I was crawling through all that hella nastiness and it's caused me to hallucinate—but then again, how can I breath in a toxic fume when I can't even breath to begin with? I wish any of these ideas were on the table, but that's not at all the case.

I don't know if my mind's messing with me, but I swear the animal that just crawled in that hole looked just like Ms. Culler.

Ms. Culler?

She was my third grade Art teacher. She went missing right before I went to New Way. What the hell am I saying? I dismiss even thinking the idea that my fifth grade Language Arts teacher somehow shrunk down to the size of a marsupial and is now living her so-called chalk-free life in this wasteland of a desert. It was probably an opossum, I tell myself.

Were you close to this Ms. Culler?

I dunno. It was a long time ago. Forget I even brought up her name.

—

"Dark Mountain"

After about a mile of trekking through the rugged landscape, we finally arrive at the base of the mountain; however, after I voice a complaint, Creach informs me that we are not going up the mountain but around it. Which causes my pneuma to tingle in what I can only imagine is a new method of releasing a sigh of relief.

Creach, who's remained rather quiet since we left the outpost, stops halfway up the hill and turns to me.

Let me ask you a question, Ajax—

—Ask me a question? You know I thought I was the one who asks questions around here?

Lately, you've been quiet.

Speak for yourself. I've just been thinking. That's all. I point at the barren landscape, as well as the red sky. It's a lot to take in—

—Why don't you fit in?

What?

In your world—

—I fit in.

But you don't.

But I do.

301

Creach's right, but I'm baffled about how she's right. Somehow, I think it all has to do with what happened in the sewers. The moment Creach grabbed me by the arm everything about her changed; and ever since, she's acted almost as if she's been lugging around a skeleton on her back that seems to be getting heavier and heavier the more we trek.

Which makes me wonder if there's something else she's not telling me, or if it has anything to do with that special cuff on her wrist.

I do what I normally do whenever I feel cornered. I shut off.

Surely, there must be something you enjoy in your world. I noticed you listen to music while drawing characters inside your notebook. Have you ever considered starting your own band?

How would she know these things?

What? How? Have you been watching me?

No.

Then, what makes you think you know so much about me, *Creach*?

Creach holds up her wrinkled palm, as if she's giving me her own version of talk-to-the-hand.

And what's that supposed to mean?

Most shrills would call the ability to see what others cannot a curse. I, on the other hand, consider it, more or less, as a gift.

Shrills?

Me. Shrill. *You.* Human.

So, shrill is a race?

Precisely.

So, you can see what exactly?

I have the ability to see inside anything I can touch. I call it my *sorbere*—a term which was inspired by your world. When I stumbled into your world, I used my *sorbere* to locate you. You may not realize it now but, like I said earlier, you were calling out to me.

I was?

Yes.

And what was I saying to you?

You needed help.

I did?

Yes.

Okay, so, you're talking about telepathy?

Telepathics use the mind. We use our touch.

So when you touched me back in the sewers, you could read my thoughts? Is that it?

Again, Creach gets awkwardly quiet all of a sudden.

Yes. To some degree.

I mean, that's pretty cool. I guess. Avanti, my mom, she has the gift as well. I guess you can say it's kind of like telepathy. Sometimes, it feels as if she knows exactly what I'm thinking, like every now and then, she's poking around up there, trying to understand me. She's not shrill, though. She's what the people of my world call 'vamp,' which is someone you tend to keep your distance from. But, unlike me, she's good at hiding who she really is.

That's the first time I've heard you mention your mother's name—

—A'ight. My turn. So, what's your story? How'd you end up here?

It's a long story, Ajax.

I check the Blood Watch, which appears as if it's below that halfway mark.

I still have enough blood in the watch, which means I'm not dead yet. Right? The least you can do is tell me about yourself. I mean, I'd certainly like to know who's trying to help me.

My name wasn't always Creach. A very long time ago they called me Rapth.

Rapth? Okay. Rapth what?

Just Rapth.

The only response I have is a shrug of my shoulders.

Many centuries ago—which would've been twelve years in your world—this vessel that you're now looking at was dying after being poisoned through Leatherwood's water supply. Tragically, the poisoning killed many of those who lived in Leatherwood, including those of the Rivercry Tribe. The massacre was known as The Great Vanishing.

Rivercry? *Sounds native.*

Who's the Rivercry Tribe?

It is written that they once lived on these sacred lands before The First Migration, which forced them to the Mountains. The leader of the Rivercry, Krillish, is a legend around Leatherwood.

Krillish, huh? Cool name. Who's that?

Krillish is one of the most skilled hunters in Leatherwood, has a bite strong enough to chew through worlds. Even though he doesn't roll with High Order, he is more feared than any member of the High Order. It is written that a member of the High Order whose named was Toofont, was caught deliberately dumping 'corruption' into Leatherwood's main water supply. The corruption was derived from a wicked cocktail of corrupted pneuma, most of those captured from the Eventide. The worst kind of pneuma that has the power to corrode the very life force inside any living thing.

And why'd this Toofont do this?

In the *Chronicles of Krillish*, it is written that the corruption was meant to reduce the overpopulation in Leatherwood. Once High Order found out about this traitor who was working among them, Toofont was stripped of his title in the council and spent the rest of his days in hiding. Like many, I didn't have long before the pneuma of this very body was corrupted and left to perish. As darkness closed in, I was saved by a soul robber named Napone, who stole a pneuma from your world and, in return, sold the pneuma to another shrill, like me, named Pharrow, who then transplanted the pneuma into this vessel—body—you're looking at right now, which, in return, saved me from being swallowed up by the corruption.

So, how did 'Pharrow' transplant a pneuma into your, you know, whatever?

It's not that hard, actually. All you have to do is wait until the pneuma departs its vessel and then grab the pneuma before it wanders away. For instance, in your world, think of it no differently than catching fireflies in a jar.

So, once the pneuma is transplanted into this new body, then what?

The healthy pneuma will rejuvenate the body and mind.

So this Pharrow cat, who's that—

—He was my mate.

And he put someone else's soul into your body?

Yes.

Creach makes it sound as if transplanting souls from my world into creatures like Creach in this world is as common as surgery.

So, what? Where is Pharrow now? He die or something? Or, don't tell me, he got mad-jealous because you were showing off your new 'rejuvenated' body to other, much younger shrills—

—He died. But it was many moons ago.

Oh. Sorry to hear.

It was said that Napone killed and stole the Tunic of Lazarus from a member of the High Order to save this very body from death.

I point at Creach's wrist.

So, how'd you get yours?

Those who work for the High Order are connected to Lazarus.

You work for this High Order, huh?

Creach glances down at the Lazarus Cuff.

Sort of.

Well, do you or don't you?

It's a long story. I'm considered what is known as a crosser.

And what's a crosser?

I thought you'd never ask.

So?

A crosser is someone who's able to cross over into the other worlds, including yours.

And what does a crosser do exactly?

A crosser's job is to prevent one's pneuma from being taken by those of the Eventide. Think of a crosser as what your world would call a tour guide, although a crosser's ultimate goal is to guide the pneuma back to his or her rightful body.

And if a crosser 'you' should fail at guiding me back to my body. . .

I never fail.

More confident, are we. So, how exactly does one become a member of this High Order?

In order to become a member, you must save a lot of pneuma.

Curious, how much? If you had to put a number to it. . .

A lot.

So, you *are* a member of the High Order?

That's an even longer story.

Okay, so the High Order? What is that, like another tribe or something?

They are similar to what your world calls men and women of the cloth.

Like priests?

Similar but far more sinister. They are the Kings of the Jungle.

If they're so sinister, then why do you work for them?

I never said I did.

But you said—

—I'm saying it's complicated.

Complicated. I see.

The High Order remains at the top of the food chain and you will soon learn that the closer you are to the top, the safer you'll be.

Doesn't sound any different than my world.

In your world, you are able to pick and chose your leaders. In my world, there is only the High Order, and they are untouchable. They reside in the highest parts of

Leatherwood, in a golden palace in the skies called Heaven.

Heaven? You're serious? So, how old are you exactly?

I honestly don't know how old I am, but my body is much older than yours. Yet, deep inside my pneuma, I don't feel as if I'm older than you. For all I know, we could be the same age—if that makes any sense.

No. Not really.

So, a shrill, huh? In my world, *shrill* means something completely different.

Is that right?

Yeah. My mom's housekeeper, Tameron, she's known to have a shrill voice when she starts barking orders at me. Talk about nails on a chalkboard.

According to the ancient text, the shrill race is written to be one of the oldest races in my world. It is written that we're able to survive past three hundred years old. But there are those who've survived much longer. After Pharrow died, I had nowhere else to go. Most of the shrills have migrated out of Leatherwood. Being alone in Leatherwood means you have a target on your head. In order to survive, I clanned up and ended up getting involved with a band of scavengers. We did a lot of terrible things. I was trained to kill those who got in my way. I always said it was effects of the *lingering* corruption still left in this old body. It is not me, though, who I am. On the inside. I have these fragments of memory of another life, the life living in your world. And they're getting more vivid as I age.

What do you see in these memories?

Drowning. Creach drifts off. I *see* myself drowning.

What else can you—

—Whatever the case, Ajax, there is no denying what we are by nature.

And what is that?

Animals. We are animals.

I don't know many animals that can speak like you. You seem more human than animal.

Don't let my appearance fool you, Ajax. I'm nothing like you.

We reach the top of another hill. Down in the valley below a city covered in smog resides.

We're here.

Which still leaves me with more questions than answers.

—

"Leatherwood"

Halfway up on South Hill reads the word 'EAT' in bold lettering while the other letters, including the L, H, E, R, W, O, O, D, of the word *Leatherwood* are missing from the sign. Some of the letters were eroded by destructive particle storms that Creach says still pop up every now and then while other letters had been torn down and flattened by radical tribes. It's as if residents of Leatherwood are being reminded of their most basic instincts and never has a simple word like *EAT* carried so much weight—and impending doom.

Reminds me of a place I once knew, only way different. I look again. Well, it doesn't seem that much different.

What place is that?

In my world, it's called Hollywood—well, Los Angeles.

Yes. I've read about it. They call it the City of Angels.

Yeah. *And demons.*

Here, we call Leatherwood 'The City That Came Back From The Dead.'

As much information Creach provides me about the city of Leatherwood, as well as all of the bells and whistles of being a crosser, I'm still confused as to how Creach's world, a world literally underneath my nose, has gone completely unnoticed throughout my sixteen years of existence and I hadn't even heard the faintest utterance about it.

A little advice, Ajax: I wouldn't get too comfortable here. Leatherwood happens to be one of the most dangerous cities in my world. You think Los Angeles has its share of demons. Leatherwood makes Los Angeles look like paradise.

So tell me what exactly is this world that you speak of? Does it have a name? Or, you gonna keep calling it My World—

—Midnight World. Creach stops for a moment and holds out her arm. We call it Midnight World.

Midnight World, huh?

I look down at the skyline of Leatherwood below, the sight of the skyscrapers combined looking like the shape of the bottom mandible of a creature with rotten teeth. In the hub of Leatherwood a sturdier, less crooked skyscraper towers into the dark clouds above. The sky appears different from the way it looked back in the desert and has electricity to it, as if a storm is approaching.

———

"Pit Stop"

As we trek down from hills and into the city, we cut through gutted buildings and try to stay out of the public.

Even though we're headed directly toward a long strip of crowded, noisy bars along a desolate street, Creach can't emphasize enough that we, at all costs, avoid being spotted by the self-indulgent ones inside the bars.

We pass by a mutilated statue of a centaur-looking figure called Bucky Leatherwood. Hardly anything remains of the statue's head and the left side of its face is caved in and appears as if it's been melted.

Who's Bucky Leatherwood?

Bucky Leatherwood is the founder of Leatherwood. The city was named after Bucky Leatherwood here, a notorious *junk* collector, former crosser; however, he didn't work for the High Order.

As Creach is explaining the history of Bucky Leatherwood and his obsessions with my world, in particular,

'America' and 'American culture,' I'm pulled away from the statue by a creature slightly taller than me scurrying away into a recess between two dilapidated buildings. I take a closer look at the spryly creature before it disappears in the shadows. I swear the creature had as many legs as a centipede. Yet, it looked more human the animal. I freak out, knowing that Creach is not the only one who looks different in Midnight World.

What the hell is this place?

I told you. This is Leatherwood.

Creach shows me the way.

More on guard, I follow.

As we make are way around a strip of bars, I can't help but notice two particular establishments, one of them appears to be an outer space-themed bar decorated with outer space memorabilia. For example, the round metal panel with the word NASA mounted above a corridor-like entranceway. Perched next to the entrance is an empty suit of a life-sized astronaut holding a black flag.

I peek through one of the tiny windows. Inside the bar are dozens of monkeys; however, these monkeys appear as if they've experienced decades of mutation. I spot a couple of monkey-looking creatures, as tall as your average human, wearing these modified oxygen masks over their faces, while other monkeys have been altered by gravity—or the lack of gravity—making their postures more gangly and hunchback, their limbs longer and leaner. Some of the monkeys are more like the monkeys I'm used to seeing, and those happened to be the ones flinging projectiles across the bar in what I can only describe as an epic dung fight. As far as the other bar. . .

America?

Outside the bar the massive fossil of a Tyrannosaurus Rex suspends from the glowing America bar sign. The American flag, which appears as if it's been torn to shreds, hangs loosely on the front of the door.

Creach holds out her hand, preventing me from stepping forward for a closer look into the bar's window.

I would especially stay away from that place.

Why?

It's a zombie bar.

Zombie bar? What?

I manage to get just a sneak peek inside the bar where hordes of brain-eating zombies are picking apart what Creach calls a Gobile, which is a cross between a goblin and a frog. The zombies appear as if they're trying to consume the light— or pneuma—a popular zombie appetizer.

You don't want to know what they serve up as their main course. The whole 'you are what you eat' expression is all bullshit. You every heard of the 'A zombie walks into a bar' joke?

No. I haven't.

Suddenly, one zombie in particular removes his serrated teeth from gnawing on a Gobile's square-shaped skull and snaps his head toward me, his jaw nearly swinging from his face from the sudden head turn. Several other zombies follow suit and turn toward the window.

I thought you said I could only be seen by those who were wearing the Lazarus thingy, which means I can't be harmed. Right?

You can't.

Can't what? Be seen or be harmed?

As long as you stay close to me, you'll be fine. Now, let's go.

We leave as soon as the zombie pokes his head from the shredded curtain of the flag. Then, he goes back into the bar and continues to eat.

I try to keep up with Creach.

Can you explain to me why we're being so secretive?

Because.

Why do I get the feeling you're not being completely honest with me?

There are those few who can see you without Lazarus, highly skilled predators who can see beyond the walls that imprison us.

Like that Krillish-cat?

Yes. Like Krillish.

And I take it these highly skilled predators are pretty hostile?

Yes. Like I said, as long as you stay close to me, you'll be fine.

We move through the hellish city using the cover of buildings. It's not until I see a ruthless gang tearing apart what used to be a porky-pig looking dude that I realize the imminent danger of Leatherwood. There are no laws here, nor any police to enforce laws. Only some group called High Order, which, from the streets, looks as if they're untouchable.

After a gang of what looks like human-like scorpions finishes eating, Creach sneaks me over to the latest kill— or what's left of the latest kill. All I can recognize is the snout, as well as the tusks on its fleshy face.

Creach reaches down and grabs a loose brick lying on the ground and with the corner of the brick, gives a good whack against the side of the half man-half bore's mouth. Then pries off one of the lower teeth that had been loosened by the brick. Creach pockets the tooth. She kneels back down after second thought and pries off yet another tooth, this time one of the tusks protruding from its shattered jaw. As with the other tooth, Creach pockets the tusk.

You want to explain to me why in the hell you removed its teeth?

I'll need it for later.

Need it for what?

Creach turns to me.

For you.

We leave Downtown Leatherwood, where most of the action is taking place, and arrive at an even rougher yet eerily suspicious part of the city called SOTO, which stands for Soul Town, the district being so quiet and desolate that I wait for tumbleweed to skip by as they do in old Westerns. We stay off the main streets and cut through several alleyways where dark shadows of what looks like empty buildings offer their share of lurking creatures which Creach calls Gigermites, and the reasons

we're not currently being consumed—*pneuma* included—
is more than likely because the Gigermites have recently
feasted on tourists.

With the notion of being consumed by a Gigermite, I
make sure to stay even closer to Creach as she takes me to
a biker-like bar called Beta.

Looks familiar. So, what are we doing here? I glance
down at the watch and noticed the blood just dipped
down well past the halfway mark. I'm running low.

This will only take a second.

And what's a second in your world?

It won't take long. Promise.

I follow Creach into Beta, which used to be what looks
like a library, and as soon as I step foot inside, the terror
hits me and leaves me in a paralyzed state.

Inside is a cesspool of both man and animal, as if genes
have been mixed up like a blender, some having more
human traits than animal while others more animal.
Most of the action comes from the bar, which looks as if it
used to be the checkout desk. The rowdiness quiets a bit
as soon as Creach makes her presence known. Once hollers and bellows turn to hushed whispers and muzzled
laughs. I can't tell whether or not these creatures fear
Creach or worse, want her dead.

Whatever you do, try not to interact with other tourists. Like you, they don't have much time.

If they don't much time, then why—

—No questions.

Right.

I don't know what Creach is talking about until I spot
a couple of people like me, humans—or better yet, pneumas who have the appearance of your everyday humans.
Never have I felt so glad to see somebody who looks like
me, who has a nose and chin like me. Who talks without
a grunt, gurgle, or hiss. I notice they're sitting next to
other creatures, similar to Creach, wearing Lazarus
thingamajigs.

Sitting next to a guy who looks no older than twenty
years old is a creature with a stubby elegant-like trunk

nose dressed in an oily car mechanic's jumpsuit. The name on the nametag reads: 'Demo.' What stands out the most—except for that elephant-baby-like face—is the necklace around its neck, which looks identical to the Lazarus Cuff.

Creach walks me a freelancer named Azzgul, who's sitting at a table near the bar and playing with a Lazarus ring on his ring finger as if it's an oversized wedding band that doesn't belong to him.

Watch Ajax here while I handle some business.

Azzgul, who doesn't at all possess any of the traits of an animal, looks as if his skin is made of putty and some-one thought it'd be funny to smash and playfully rear-range the features of his face.

With the lingering fear of being consumed by one of these creatures, I watch Creach walk to a booth in the back of the bar where it's more shadowy. She sits across from a strange man wearing a cloak.

I can't help but overhear one of these so-called free-lancers wearing a Lazarus type of earpiece behind me talking about Creach and how she has a price on her head for what she did to Krillish. The name *Krillish* immedi-ately grabs my ghost ear. Then, the name, *Gabriel*, which is apparently the name of a small town outside Leath-erwood. I glance over my shoulder and shoot a glance at a root-looking creature with two beady black eyes sitting at a table with two other brutish figures with horns curled around the sides of their heads parked on either side of the creature they timidly refer to as 'Saggelstache.' I make sure not to make any eye contact or worse, stare at these creatures, especially Saggelstache, who looks as if he could be a real thorn in my side.

I'm drawn back to Creach who's sliding underneath the table the tusk he picked off the dead body in that abandoned building. The cloaked man grabs the tusk from Creach's hand.

Creach stands up from the booth. I turn away just as Creach looks in my direction.

If it isn't another Othersider from the Otherwhere. . .

I turn toward the voice of a hairy Sasquatch-type man with a whole bunch of black eyes and eight arms. He points one of his eight arms at Creach.

Be careful with this one.

Is that so?

Before your pal over there was kicked out of Midnight World, he tried to earn his scales by stealing the kill of the one who goes by the name Krillish. If there's one thing you don't do in Leatherwood is get in Krillish's way. Now, she's trying to repay her debt. So, if I was you, I'd keep an eye on her. She's a sneaky one, she is.

Thanks for the advice.

Hey, othersider, you know what the name Creach means?

I dunno. Creature?

Close. It makes a bottom feeder look like an Orderian—

—Don't listen to Data here. He's just jealous Creach has more saves than he'll ever have.

You want to say what you just said in my good ear, Azzgul.

I look around for the Lazarus device on Spiderman's body but can't find one. All I find is a crinkled photograph of a young woman named Chione in one of his many hands. Which makes me remember what Creach said just a while ago about those who were able to see pneumas with the power of Lazarus.

Name's Data, Data Longlegs.

Creach approaches the table.

Let's go.

Nice seeing you, Creach.

Azzgul.

Creach looks at Data Longlegs and doesn't say a word. Yet, the two have a stare off for a moment. Then, Creach walks away. I follow and do so quickly.

We leave Beta without any confrontation, even though the entire time waiting for Creach to do whatever it is she was doing it felt as if fights occurred on a regular basis inside Beta; and Data Longlegs had his eye—or shall I say, eyes—on Creach.

I don't put much thought into what Data Longlegs said to me; however, I'd be lying if I said was thinking about it.

—

"Opportunists"

Where are we going now?

Black Lake. It's an old tar pit located on the outskirts of Leatherwood. It's the place where your story will be revealed.

Are you sure?

Creach stops walking.

Excuse me.

I saw you hand the tusk to Mr. Lord of the Rings back there.

Creach starts walking again.

With danger lurking close, I have no other choice than to follow Creach.

You must understand that in Midnight World it's good to have friends in high places. When we make it Black Lake, you'll understand everything.

So, who was that guy in the cloak?

Let's just say I was buying you protection. You should be thanking me.

My protection? Protection from what?

Creach points at unlit buildings and the same glowing saber-shaped eyes surfacing behind the dark windows.

From that?

The Gigermites.

Listening to their dog-like 'back-off-or-else' growls throughout the darkness of the buildings, I find myself walking even closer to Creach. Close enough that I nearly ride her heels.

Don't worry. They won't bite.

What exactly are they?

Opportunists.

—

"Dinosaur Juice"

We finally arrive at Black Lake without getting eaten by any Gigermites.

Clearly, the name of the lake was derived from its appearance. Which isn't a lake but a tar pit surrounding by jagged hills and boulders the size of buildings. Even the stingy smell of hot tar irritates my ghost nose and naturally has me waving fumes.

I check the Blood Watch and show Creach how much blood is left. The tiny glass ball is about one-fourths full of blood.

I know. Time can be a little glitchy in SOTO.

What happened here?

This is where it all began. Creach points to the center of the tar pit. This is the site of the first explosion. This is where everything changed.

Creach nods at other so-called crossers like her wearing these different Lazarus devices and standing in a trance around Black Lake with other ghosts like me. Some of them are wearing Lazarus bracelets, earrings, piercings, and other accessories.

Other crossers, like me, bring tourists here to Black Lake to show them their truth. It is the final step before the pneuma is reunited with his or her body.

And what happens after people like me see our truth?

You are shown your truth to help you make your decision.

My decision? Which is?

Whether you want to live or die, Ajax.

What about that other place? You know, the. . . the In—

—The In-Between. Think of your transition as stages. You've already made it past the In-Between. Now, it's what your world calls crunch time—however, in our world, it has a different meaning. *Tell me about it.* Anyway, you have to decide whether you want to stay here in

Midnight World or go back to your world. However, in order to make your decision, you must first see your truth.

Creach pulls out the same tooth from earlier, the one he pried from the dead man-pig in the abandoned building.

What do I have to do?

Creach holds out her other hand.

For some reason, I hear the words of Data Longlegs flooding my mind. How this one—Creach—is quite a sneaky one. I start to wonder whether or not Creach is using me to earn her so-called scales, as the creature from Beta told me.

In your world, you call it a leap of faith.

I glance down at Creach's hand. Then look back at the tar pit.

With the doubts burning right through me, I decide to grab Creach's hand.

In return, Creach hands me the tooth.

What now?

All you have to do is throw it in.

And what happens next?

Nobody really knows what happens. Only you do.

What about you?

This is *your* story, Ajax. Not mine.

I don't think much about the decision.

I toss the tooth into the tar pit.

Nothing happens, at first.

As the tooth finally submerges into the thick tar, pockets of tar bubble. All of a sudden, the entire lake starts to sink.

What's happening?

I turn to Creach, who's standing motionless. Her eyes are rolled back white.

Creach?

I turn back to the tar pit and watch it slowly drain underneath a floor of rocks and boulders.

Eventually, all of the tar is drained from the lake, leaving behind nothing but a massive crater. In the center of the crater is a dark hole, which looks similar to a triangular doorway.

Without saying a word, Creach raises her other arm and points at the hole.

I release my hand from Creach's hand and climb down the rocks until I reach the bottom of the crater. I duck below a jagged rock overhang and without doubting myself, walk straight into the void.

—

"Ghosts"

From my bedroom window, I'm watching Avanti, her mother, Grandma Washington, and my twin sister, Echo, lounging next to the swimming pool.

Immediately, I'm drawn to the baby blue wallpaper on the wall, as well as the bin brimming with childhood toys and the stuffed animals scattered along the bed, which is covered in a green and pale blue alligator-patterned comforter. My hand is the first part of my body that sends me into a state of alarm, then, next, my alligator-themed Pj's.

I walk to the closest mirror I can find, and I'm no longer sixteen. I'm a child, no older than four years old.

I walk back to the window and watch Avanti excuse herself from the swimming pool in the backyard.

I leave my bedroom and walk outside where Avanti is making drinks on the patio. I call out to Grandma Washington but she completely ignores me. It's not until she glances over in my general direction in the similar fashion as a blind person tracking down a presence with unsteady eyes that I come to the bitter conclusion that I'm *not* here, my body that is, even though it feels as if I am present.

Underneath the canopy, Avanti discreetly releases one of her fangs and pricks the end of her fingertip. She drops several drops of blood into grandma's virgin piña colada. She brings the tainted drink over to Grandma Washington, who, after a polite thank you, doesn't waste any time sipping from the cool refreshment.

After Grandma Washington has taken several sips of the virgin piña colada, Avanti suggests that she and Echo go swimming.

Grandma Washington agrees and while holding Echo's hand, enters through the shallow end of the swimming pool. Only a couple of steps into the water, she stops for a moment and grabs her chest. She shakes off the slight discomfort and walks Echo farther into the deep end of the swimming pool while Avanti watches from underneath the shade of the umbrella.

All of a sudden, Grandma Washington grabs her chest once more, this time in great agony. She appears to be experiencing what I've always been told to be a heart attack. Echo, who's *not* wearing any floaters, which seems odd, especially for a four-year-old who can't swim at all, slips from her grandma's weak grip and sinks to the bottom of the pool. Grandma Washington struggles to stay afloat as she tries to swim to the edge of the pool. She ends up sinking to the bottom of the pool, as well. Avanti doesn't jump in to rescue Grandma Washington or my twin sister. Yet, she continues to sit in the lounge chair underneath the umbrella as if nothing is happening!

Finally, after Grandma Washington and Echo have already sunk to the bottom, Avanti stands up from the chair and walks to the pool's ledge and leans over. Creeping closer to the pool for a better angle, I first hear the splash of water, then see the water dripping all over the concrete walkway surrounding the pool. I notice a dark shapeless figure lurking in the shadows cast from the giant umbrella. Wet imprints of elongated feet mark the ground. A tall, dark creature, who appears to be cradling what I can only make out as a purplish speck of light *flickering* like a tiny pulse in one of its gnarly yet somewhat blurry arms, is talking to Avanti. I can't make out what the creature is saying to her, but whatever it is, it has a business-like façade of a two-sided understanding. The dark creature turns in my direction. Which doesn't make the least amount of sense because nobody can see me.

Behind the dark shadows, I witness four pairs of grayish marbled eyes tracking down my gaze.

We make eye contact for a moment.

Only for a moment.

Then, the creature slithers back into the pool the same way one of the alligators on my Pj's would hastily enter a body of water.

I hurry to the edge of the swimming pool and look down at the water, only to find the wavy, lifeless bodies of both Grandma Washington and Echo rising to the surface of the water. In their weightless ascent, their bodies collide, resulting in their lifeless bodies floating face down in the water.

And that's the moment I realize they're gone.

The fence opens behind me!

A slender, graceful woman dressed in all black enters the backyard from the side of the house. At first glance, the strange woman wearing cherry red lipstick looks as if she doesn't exist. Like me, she's just a tourist here for the show. After the minor memory lapse, I realize she's Vye. Of course, Avanti's aide. But *what is she doing here?*

Behind Vye is another woman, who I've never seen before. I hear Vye call her Storm. Throughout my entire childhood, I've heard the name before but each time I've heard the name any further questions I had regarding this so-called person behind the name were reduced to the fits or ramblings of a boy's wild imagination. The young woman, Storm, as she's called, appears to be under some kind of mind control—a spell! Her moves are creepily mechanical. Even when Vye instructs Storm to grab the bird's beak knife next to the wedges of lime from the table and then stab Avanti in the abdomen, she does so robotically.

Carefully studying each stab, Vye folds her arms across her chest. One hand erects upright, fingers curling around her chin in her best Thinking-Man pose.

Again! But harder!

Storm rears back and stabs Avanti in the side.

Vye continues to shape each one of Storm's violent attacks, as if she's a film director directing the most seasoned actor.

Now, the leg. We need to make it look authentic.

Gripping her bloody side, Avanti offers up her right leg while Storm searches for a blunt object.

The umbrella will do.

Storm drops the bloody knife, as instructed, and walks over to the table.

Make sure to turn over the umbrella base.

On command, Storm winds up the umbrella until the shade collapses and then removes the umbrella from the table.

Once the umbrella is removed, Storm kicks over the base with her foot.

No! Use your hands, please.

Storm places the umbrella on the table, kneels down, picks up the base, and then stares at Vye, as if she's waiting for further instruction.

Vye points at an area next to Avanti.

There should do.

Storm carries over the base to the edge of the pool and drops it on the ground. She makes her way back to the umbrella, picks it up again, then, without wasting any time, jabs the upper part of Avanti's shin with the umbrella.

Avanti screams out in pain.

Storm hits Avanti yet again.

All right! Enough!

Nursing her leg, Avanti falls to the ground.

At that moment, as a bloody Avanti lays on the ground and clings to her now broken leg, Storm, who can pass as a soulless corpse with her weapon, the umbrella, gripped in hand, stands right beside a crafty Vye, who's carefully picking over each detail of the scene; and then everything pauses.

Both Grandma Washington and Echo stop bobbing in the water, as well. Even the waves and the tiny ripples in the water come to a pause. I'm stuck in a still horrific freeze frame. Yet, I'm the only one who's able to move.

A dark and wavy figure grows in the corner of my eye, sending a series of hot flashes of panic throughout my body.

Thinking that it's the same mysterious creature from earlier, a greater sense of terror overwhelms me and then, strangely, once I lock eyes with Creach, I can feel my body divorcing all terror. I melt with relief.

Creach surfaces.

Dripping wet, Creach gracefully climbs from the pool and walks up to me. I should be freaked out by the sight of Creach, especially in broad daylight, as any four-year-old should be. But I'm not.

Can you please explain to me what's going on? I don't remember any of this happening.

Yes. You do, Ajax. It's buried. Creach points to the side of her temple. In here. You know what happened. For years, you heard the same lie over and over until that lie became the truth. But not *your* truth.

But I wasn't here. I was. . .

In the corner of my eye, I catch my own reflection in the stainless steel charbroil grille and notice that I'm no longer stuck inside my four-year-old body. Yet, I'm still up there, my younger self that is, standing behind the bedroom window, watching the horror below.

The sight of my younger self frozen in a state of trauma leaves me breathless.

But why? Why would she do this to me?

Everybody has a purpose, Ajax. You just don't know what yours is yet. But, in time, you will.

The scene unfreezes: Avanti returns to nursing her broken right leg while, at the same time, applying pressure to her stab wounds; Vye returns to studying the scene but this time doing so with her arms hanging by her side; Storm appears as if she's still frozen—or still on sleep-mode.

I search for Creach, but she's nowhere around.

Make sure you retrieve their bodies.

Give me a second, will you? Avanti pulls away a handful of blood. I think the bitch went too deep.

As Vye walks over to the table to retrieve the phone, her eyes move toward a small figure standing behind the kitchen window of the neighbor's house.

I have a better idea.

Vye extends the cordless phone toward Avanti.

Touch it.

Avanti reaches for the phone with her clean hand.

The left one.

Once more, Avanti reaches for the phone but this time with her bloody hand, leaving behind a bloody handprint. With her hand still wrapped around the upper part of the phone, Vye immediately pulls away the phone and tosses the phone on the lawn.

Vye instructs Storm to stay put while she walks toward the neighbor's house. I can't help but follow Vye to the neighbor's house. Upon arrival, the neighbor, a woman in her sixties, who the neighborhood kids used to call Dog Lady because she was always walking other neighbor's dogs, opens the backdoor for Vye. Vye enters. I enter, as well. The neighbor closes the door behind her. Immediately, I notice the phone in the neighbor's other hand.

The neighbor faces Vye.

Slack faced, the neighbor holds the phone against her chest.

Do you have the police on the phone?

In that same robot-like movement, the neighbor nods.

You can speak.

Yes. I have the police on the phone.

And what have you told them so far?

I've told them that I heard screaming coming from the house next door.

Is that it?

The neighbor pauses.

Then, *yes.* That's it.

Very good.

Vye opens the door and as she's about to leave, she faces the neighbor.

You never saw me.

I never saw you.

We never talked.

I'm sorry. Furrowing her brow into a deep crease, the neighbor tilts her head in confusion. Who are you?

I'm nobody.

The neighbor starts blinking her eyelids in a seizure-like pace, as if her brain is somehow erasing Vye from her thoughts. Her face returns to normal, showing more expression.

Then, she places the phone back to her ear and closes the door behind her.

I walk with Vye back to the backyard where Avanti has already removed the two bodies from the swimming pool. She's administering CPR on Echo, which, I know, is all act. Echo is beyond resuscitating.

Vye leaves the scene, Storm follows close behind.

When I arrive at the front of the house, I spot two cars, one is a white hatchback, which looks like its wheels are about to fall off, then the other one is a black limo. Storm gets behind the wheel of the hatchback while Vye sits in the backseat. Avanti's bodyguard, Joel, who I've known ever since I can remember, steps out of the driver's side door of the limo and opens the passenger door for me.

I don't say a word to Joel.

Yet, I stop and listen to the sounds of police sirens from a distance.

As I get inside the back of the limo, the police show up at the house. I count at least three cruisers, each one cutting the sirens. Each one of the officers exiting the cruisers looks young and trigger-happy. Storm drives away just in the nick of time. Joel follows suit and drives away as well, and keeps a safe distance from Storm's hatchback while the officers hurry toward the backyard.

Where are we going?

Joel rotates his head toward the rear view mirror. His face is different. He's no longer wearing Joel's face. He's not even a he anymore. He is a she, Creach.

What's going on?

I'm afraid this is for your own good, Ajax.

Where are we going?

You'll see soon enough.

Creach drives out of the suburbs to a rougher section on the outskirts of the city. Storm parks the hatchback in front of the apartment building. Vye gets out first, then Storm.

Having not said a word throughout the entire drive, Creach parks the limo across the street and gets out of the car. By the time Creach makes her way to the back of the limo, she is Joel again. Joel—Creach or whoever—waves me out of the limo. I step out. Joel closes the door behind me.

Are you not coming in?

What is about to happen is for your eyes only, Ajax.

As Joel gets back inside the limo, I walk to the apartment building. I walk up a flight of stairs and from the top of the second floor staircase, watch Storm pull out a key from her front pocket and open up the door to apartment 201— which must be her apartment. Storm enters. Then, Vye. I sneak in behind them right before Storm closes the door behind Vye.

In the gloomy apartment, Vye instructs Storm to close the living room blinds. She does. Then, Vye instructs her to grab three things: first, a blank envelope on the kitchen counter, then a Sharpie, which is lying not too far away, then, finally, the knife from the knife holder. After grabbing all of these items, she brings them back to the kitchen table where she takes a sit. Vye stands to the right of her.

Repeat after me—

Dear Stew.

Vye, who looks as if she's trying to mentally fight off Vye but is too weak, struggles to pick up the pen.

With her hand trembling, she writes *Dear Stew,*

Vye leans over Storm and grabs hold of Storm's writing hand, as if by doing so she somehow manages to lessen the tremble.

Storm only gets through two words, *please* and *forgive*, before I zone out.

I already know what she's going to write before she presses pen to paper. It's a letter addressed to Stew, but its primary intention is for the police after they discover Storm's dead body in the kitchen. I don't know the exact moment when it all goes down, nor do I know how it goes down. For the life of me, I don't know any of these events in the final timeline, but I know them to be true. Stew *never* cheated on Avanti with Storm McBride, and despite what I witnessed back at the house, Storm McBride never attacked Avanti—at least, not Storm McBride, who was capable of thinking for herself without anyone else poking around upstairs. Stew's relationship with Storm McBride was completely platonic. The two knew each other from way back when they practically bumped into each other at every public institution made available by the city. They were close, but not close in a way that would suggest anything sexual or worthy of an affair. Stew kept the relationship secret from Avanti—or least, he thought so—and how he attempted to help Storm during a rough patch in her life but ultimately failed.

I snap hard from the heavy trance, as if I'm yanking myself from someone else's own thoughts.

Storm finishes writing the letter and then picks up the knife.

Right before Storm jams the sharp end of the blade into her throat, I zone out once more. This time, I'm not inside Storm's apartment. I'm lying in the bathtub in my bathroom. It's night, not day. Vye is sitting in a chair next to the bathtub, and she's handing me something sharp.

Once more, I snap from my trance.

By the time I realize what has happened, it's already done. Storm is already dead. Even though her suicide may have appeared as if it was carried out by her own hand, I know that it wasn't.

The sight alone of Storm lying in a puddle of her own blood on the floor triggers only what I can make sense of as a memory. I see myself lying in a bathtub full of blood. Vye's sitting right beside the bathtub, and she's pulling the veins in my arms as if they're strings; the ends of my veins are wrapped around the ends of the sick bitch's fingertips and she's controlling my arms like a puppet. Pushing aside the mad dance, I turn toward the bathroom door, which is open, and peer through the darkness; and for a moment, I witness the dark figure of another woman standing in the darkness of the doorway.

All I can think about is whether or not she watched.

I snap from my trance and turn toward Storm's apartment door, which slams close!

In a fit of rage, I grab the bloody knife from the ground and swing at Vye.

I make sure to aim directly at her throat—the death blow.

Right before impact, my body suddenly recoils in a violent flinch as if Vye's not the one I'm stabbing.

More confused, I look around the back of the limo.

Joel is driving me somewhere, but I don't know where.

It appears to be night outside—at least, it appears to be. I soon realize we're riding through a dark tunnel. Bright flickers of headlights run past the backseat of the car like strobe lights. A geometrically shaped beam from a turning headlight stretches along the entire width of the limo's ceiling and runs across my body like a scanner. The light brings out a couple of pinkish scars along my forearms, ones I haven't seen before. Maybe they were there all along, and I simply wasn't looking close enough. I count at least five of them scattered along both my arms in wallpaper-like pattern. Each razor-thin scar is light pink in color, aged and faded like a year-old stain on one of my favorite, go-to shirts that pays a visit to the washer once a month. It's hardly noticeable, if you're not looking for it; even if you have another pair of eyes to look at it,

more than likely you'll receive the same stupid 'What-am-
I-looking-for?' expression. But when you look up close and
you finally notice it, it's all you see.

As soon as we exit the tunnel, I take my eyes from my
arms and marvel at the vast New York City cityscape before me.

The traffic is congested on the streets, just the way I'd
imagine.

What are we doing in New York City?

There's one last thing you must see before we return.

—

"The Governor's Closet"

Joel parks the limo right behind another limo in front of a
swanky hotel called St. Gabriel, which is bustling with
mobs of reporters, journalists, and a security team, which
is as tight as a snare drum. Reporters travel in packs.
Every now and then, a lone reporter will pick off what
looks like a politician or elected official wearing a tuxedo
that cost more than my entire closet and sock drawer
combined. *Flickers* of camera light shower artificial faces
and toothy smiles.

We're here.

Joel steps out of the limo and opens the door for me.

What am I supposed to do?

All you have to do is follow the crowd.

Joel points to the droves of wealthy New Yorkers jam-
ming up into a crowd of black tuxedos and sparkling
white dresses at the entranceway of the hotel.

And what are you going to do?

I'll be around.

I look down at my outfit, the T-shirt and holey jeans.

I'm not dressed for the part.

Well, that's because you're not invited.

Once more, Joel points to the front of the hotel.

I leave Joel and shoulder my way through the crowds
until I finally reach the main lobby where it's more spread
out.

From behind, I'm greeted by a sneaky young waitress wearing a pair of soles as soft as a wrestler.

Excuse me, sir. Would you care for a hors d'oeuvre?

I'm baffled as to how she can see me.

On her shoulder, the waitress is holding a tray of cucumber slices and crackers covered in tiny black beads, as well as snails, which give off a smell that burns my eyes.

I wave off the waitress.

No thanks.

She doesn't scram from my comment. Yet, she continues to stand there as if she's hard of hearing. I give her the cold shoulder.

I insist.

The waitress takes a step closer toward me and extends her hand, which is no longer her hand but the pale scaly palm of a seven-foot tall reptile named Creach. In Creach's palm, she's holding a napkin with a live rat with a toothpick speared through its squirming body.

What you doing here?

How about a taste? You might like it. . .

Get that thing away from me!

Your loss.

Creach grabs the squeaky rat by its flabby midsection and bites off its head.

Blood squirts from the opening gap in the rat's severed neck.

Yuck!

You don't know what you're missing out, Veggie Boy.

Veggie Boy? I can eat meat, you know?

Sure you do.

I just choose not to.

Well, I can grab] one for your in case you change your mind.

No thanks.

I've heard that the hotel has a rat problem. Bad for guests. Good for me.

By the way, how'd you keep disguising yourself like that? Is that like one of your other superpowers or something?

I have my ways.

So, you want to tell me what exactly I'm doing at some fundraiser—

Before I can finish my train of thought, three vamps talking to the mayor of New York catch my eye. I know them and their queer vibe. Not only that, I can smell them as strongly as I can smell my own self. They give off a certain funkiness, which is often covered up by dabs of cheap cologne.

What do you want first: the good news or the bad?

Bad.

The bad is this particular *monumental* event happens to take place four years after your death.

You mean, I am dead?

Yes. In an oscillating motion, Creach points out the richest cliques in the lobby as if she's showcasing a future without yours truly. Well, at least you are here now, in this timeline.

I thought time didn't exist in Midnight World.

And is that where you think you are?

I mean—

—How did you get here?

I draw a blank.

With my ghost eyes batting in thought, I turn my shoulder and try to pinpoint my point of entrance in the hotel lobby. I was just, you know, in a limo.

Yes. But how did *you* get here, Ajax?

I give up.

I don't remember.

For what's going to happen next, maybe it's best that you don't remember—at least until your story is over.

So, that's it then? There's no going back, is there?

Have you checked your Blood Watch?

I glance down at my wrist.

The Blood Watch is gone—

—Not gone, Ajax. You can't see it because you don't want to see it.

Why?

I'm glad you asked. You have others things to see and right now, you don't need the distraction.

What do I have to see?

For starters, how about this? Once more, Creach directs her attention toward the people—and vamps—in the lobby. Close your eyes.

What?

I said, 'Close your eyes.'

Creach places her knobby, scaly hand over my eyes.

Are they closed?

Finally, I close them.

Yes.

Creach removes her hand.

Now, open them.

I do as Creach commands and open my eyelids, which act like curtains peeling back that fine layer of reality in order to reveal a dead man's party. Standing around me are skeletons dressed in tuxedos and designer dresses. Their fangs are sharp and exposed. Even the once golden-laced, ritzy aesthetics embroidering the lobby is dull and disordered and splattered with blood, which has a brown, soiled appearance from where the oxygen choked out its once movie-red color. Among the crowd of skeletons, I witness one particular figure in a light green dress. The dress suggests that she's a woman; however, she's not as skeletal as the others in the crowd, yet the reddish muscle and tissue, even the veins of her nervous system, still remain intact to her partially exposed skeleton. She turns toward my direction. I can only make out the color in her eyes.

Your world is nothing but a filter and it's time you see it for what it truly is.

What is this? What are you doing? What are you showing me?

I'm not showing you anything. This is *all* you.

Me?

You're finally able to see the faces behind the mask.

I can no longer look at all of the death surrounding me. They turn their black eye sockets toward me and stare at me with voids for eyes.

No! Stop it!

In a fluid motion, Creach runs her hand down my range of vision.

The skeletal faces are gone, replaced by the empty, pale stares of New York's wealthiest elitists who wouldn't dare label themselves as a percentage.

I search for that one particular woman who was covered in all that muscle and tissue in the crowd.

With her back turned, she's walking in the other direction.

A part of me knows it's her.

And another part of me now knows exactly what *I'm* doing here.

What did I just see?

You saw a world without a filter. Now for the real reason why you're here in Manhattan. . .

Walking alongside Creach, we enter a ballroom, which, despite the lobby once teeming with vamps galore, appears, at first glance, stark empty. Then, after I take a closer look at the dark and unlit dining area, I witness hundreds of silhouettes motionlessly sitting at round tables covered in white tablecloths. The silhouettes, as dark as shadows, remain still despite the door abruptly closing behind us, which cancels out all chatter and noise from the lobby. Yet, they just sit there, like film props.

To the left of the dining area, I discover more dark silhouettes dancing on a dim dance floor. The farther I walk into the ballroom, the dimmer the dance floor becomes. Eventually, the dance floor fades to darkness, bringing more light to the stage.

In the center of the stage a single spotlight shines brightly on a podium with a microphone.

Only a few steps in, I notice Creach isn't moving. She, too, remains still and reverent.

Are you not coming?

No. But I won't be far.

Where you going?

I saw a rat near the bar with my name on it.

Nice.

I can't help but glance at the lit podium.

What am I supposed to do?

I'm afraid I can't answer any more questions, Ajax. You already know what to do.

I do—*I think*. But wait a sec!

Creach stops and turns back around.

What do I say?

The faint grayish light dims around Creach until I can no longer see her body standing there.

Creach! What do I say? *Creach!*

Facing the stage, I suddenly feel the heat of the spotlight pressed against my pneuma. The feel alone is familiar. I can actually *feel* the light.

More confident, I walk onto the stage, zigzagging around tables where shadowy figures are sitting still. Each one of them gives off an eerie coldness to them and I can't help but tremble from being so close to their deathly presence.

Finally, after carefully navigating my way through the dimly lit dining area, I arrive at the stage, which is even brighter than before; and when I gaze upon its magnetic lure, my ghost eyes squint from its soft, overpowering glow. I surrender to the bright light and as I approach the podium, I find myself bathing in it.

Once I reach the podium, I catch another dark figure in the corner of my eye. Creach is standing off stage behind the curtain, dipping her head in a nod, as if, in an all-knowing way, she's encouraging me to speak.

I step closer to the podium and as I place both of my ghost hands along the side of the podium, like the spotlight before, I can *feel* the smooth yet bumpiness of the wood on my palms. I direct my eyes forward to the dark audience behind the spotlight and see another figure, this time approaching the front of the stage.

For a moment, I see Avanti's face in the darkness.

I turn to my immediate right.

Speak.

As Avanti darkens to a silhouette, I adjust the mic before me.

The only words that come to me are the last words I wrote in my notebook.

For the longest I can remember, I've felt as if I've been living in your shadow, trapped by it, unable to move or breathe. All I wanted was to enjoy the pursuits of any normal sixteen-year-old. But even that was far from possible.

As much as I want to push the letter to the back of my mind and wish I never wrote it, the spotlight has a peculiar way of fleshing out the words.

So, where am I? I don't know the answer to that question. What I do know is that I did exist—once—during a crucial moment in my life when I wasn't able to form thoughts on my own and my innocence was precious and meant to be cherished, not broken. I had my whole life ahead of me.

I pause and feel the tingle of a new scar surfacing along my skin.

The scar, pink and jagged, forms along the side of my wrist, prompting me to run my finger across it.

Before I can lose myself in the scar, the words force me back to the mic.

I'm in my bedroom writing the words under the hot lamp on my desk.

This is where I've taken myself. To the Dark. To the place of no return. It's not like I had any choice. Right now, it feels as if it's the only choice I have left. Why, you ask. I've tried to put myself out there and show the world what I have to offer. For a moment, I thought I had something inside me, something worth sharing, something that gave me a voice. But the world didn't want to hear my voice. The world wanted absolutely nothing to do with me.

I watch Avanti's shadow silhouette moving closer to the front of the stage.

Sure, I could complain about how nobody gave a shit about me. Or, I can cry about how alone I am. Most importantly, I could point at the world and everybody who treated me wrongly and scream to the top of my lungs: IT'S ALL YOUR FAULT!!! YOU COLD, EMPTY WORLD!!! *You forced my hand!!!*

The truth of the matter. . .

The world didn't give up on me.

I gave up on the world.

I pull myself from the podium; and to the left of me, I find Avanti standing at the bottom of the staircase. She's calling out to me, but her words are going right through me.

I turn the other direction and walk off the stage, the curtains closing right behind me. I walk with Creach into the darkness.

Behind me, a glimmer of light pierces through the darkness.

I hear Avanti screaming out my name.

"Robert!" she cries out.

I can't help but turn toward her voice.

Avanti's standing at the slit of the curtain, half of her face glowing from the beam of the spotlight.

Once she closes the curtain behind her and walks toward me, I lose her in the darkness.

Creach holds out her hand.

Let's go.

I grab Creach's hand, and together we walk into the darkness.

In the darkness, I hear the sound of *banging* over Avanti's voice. The farther we walk, the more her voice lessens. However, the banging intensifies.

Suddenly, I hear two loud, hollower bangs, like a fist pounding on the back of a door.

And like that, a door just so happens to open on its own.

Creach walks me inside a room filled with mirrors.

Where are we?

—

"Mirror, Mirror"

Creach holds out her other hand.

336

Welcome to the Hall of Mirrors.

Creach guides me toward the center of the room. There, I witness dozens of my own reflections in the mirrors covering the entire room.

I can't help but notice one particular reflection, which looks different than the other reflections.

In the reflection, my entire body is covered in pink scars.

I walk to the reflection while Creach stands back.

I stop in front of the mirror, gaze over all of the scars, then look down at my own self and find scars all over my entire body. Even under my shirt.

I have a sudden flashback of Avanti sitting by my bedside in a hospital room. She's leaning over to touch my arm—*There are just some wounds I cannot heal.*

I pull myself back to the mirror, then to Creach, who's standing behind me.

These scars do not and *will not* define who I am. I know who I am. But, in order to survive, I must first learn how to live with these scars.

Creach opens the door, revealing the darkness.

You have reached the end of your story, Ajax. But just remember, your story doesn't have to end here.

Creach steps into the darkness and closes the door behind her.

Wait! Where you going?

Trapped inside the Hall of Mirrors, I can't help but look around at all of my reflections; and now, each one of them is covered in scars.

Searching for the door, I come across a drop of black liquid bubbling over a tiny chip in one of the mirrors. I run the tip of my finger over the black substance, leaving a black smear along the mirror.

I pull away my hand, look closer at the black smudge of a fingerprint left on the mirror, and realize, in that moment, it's tar.

—*How did you get here?*
I draw a blank.

*With my ghost eyes batting in thought, I turn my shoulder
and try to pinpoint my point of entrance in the hotel lobby. I
was just, you know, in a limo.*

Yes, Creach says, *But how did you get here, Ajax?*

I remember standing in front of a tar pit called Black
Lake.

Along the top right hand corner of the mirror yet another bubble of black tar oozes from the tiny chip in the
glass.

With the bottom of my fist, I strike the glass as hard as
I can. More black tar oozes from a larger chip in the
glass. I strike the glass yet again and when I pull my fist
back, it's covered in black tar. The chip has now turned
into a crack that has the potential to spread. I wind back
like a pitcher and punch the glass, causing the glass to
dent into the shape of a spider web but the glass doesn't
break; yet the glass feels thick, almost fibrous when I kiss
it with my fist.

As frustration mounts, I remove the shoe from my foot
and in a heap of rage, throw the shoe at the mirror.

The mirror suddenly shatters!

A stream of black tar floods into the room, knocking
me down to the ground. Before I can find my feet, I'm
already swallowed by blackness.

—

"Exit Poll"

With every muscle in my body tightening, I desperately
punch and kick through the thick, gummy blackness until
I no longer feel any resistance.

Gasping for air, I propel myself upright.

As I catch my breath, I wipe the tar from my eyes and
nose.

Even the eerie, dim light of SOTO seems bright and
blinding.

Creach and Azzgul reach their arms out to me. I grab
hold of their hands and relief washes over me. They both
pull me from the tar pit; and as soon as I feel the weight

of coarse ground against my hands and knees, I realize that something has drastically changed. Each one of my senses is back. My entire body is covered in tar. But I can *see* my body with burning eyes. Even when I take in gulps of air, I can actually *taste* the air. Before, I felt as if I couldn't feel anything at all. I was weightlessly floating around like a leaf forever falling from a tree throughout a strange and slightly primitive world that seemed nothing more than a distorted reflection of my very own world.

Frantic, I run my hands over my arms, then my face.

Why do I feel so—what's happening?

I hear sounds of someone coughing to the far left of me. There, another person, like me but much older, is swimming from Black Lake. The man, who's also covered in black tar, is being helped from the pit by a creature wearing a Lazarus Tie. He, too, appears to be without any clothes. Which reminds me. I look down at myself and wonder where my clothes had gone. Fortunately, the sludgy tar is covering up the areas that I wish not to expose to Creach or Azzgul. I think back to the moment I met Creach when she spoke about the powers of the mind, and try to imagine what my pneuma would look like.

I picture myself in clothes, look down, and nothing has changed.

I forget how self-conscious humans can be about their natural appearance.

Creach grabs a soggy strip of a torn TIRESHOP banner draped over the side of the curb and hands it to me. I cover myself with the raggedy banner.

Thanks.

You're welcome.

Not too long after the naked man emerges, another one surfaces, same situation, only this time much slower. His body bounces upright and then sways from side to side like a buoy. The frail man falls facedown in the tar. Yet another creature, this one sporting the Lazarus device over one of its tentacles, pulls the body from Black Lake.

Creach, what's happening to me?

I will explain it later. Now, we must hurry.

Why? What's going on? Tell me what's happening. . .

Creach tracks down the glowing eyes of a Gigermite surfacing from the darkness of a cave.

I look down at the Blood Watch along my wrist. I wipe away the tar from the glass and try to read it. The more I wipe, the harder it is to read.

We have to leave. Now, Ajax. . .

Creach grabs me by my arm. I notice when she touches me the Lazarus Cuff no longer lights up. Yet, it remains dull and lifeless.

I stand to my feet, staggering at first, then toppling over. Creach pulls me up to my feet and helps keep me balanced. My legs feel numb and mushy like noodles cooked well past al dente. The more weight I put on my legs, the tighter and tinglier they feel. I take a step with Creach's assistance. Then I take another step, but this time without Creach's assistance.

There you go. Now, you're getting the hang of it.

What? What's happening—

—Just try to keep up, Ajax. And, by the way, try to stay alive.

Alive?

—

"Give Me Shelter"

After evading Gigermites, we arrive at Azzgul's rundown apartment, which is located directly across the street from Beta.

The apartment looks as if it once belonged to an old lady whose taste in interior decorating hadn't evolved with the times—my time, that is. It slips my mind how such a mysterious place like Midnight World is neither frozen in time nor capable of adjusting to the time, considering time moves so differently here. The walls are decorated in pink floral wallpaper. On each of the maple bookshelves, the shelves are lined with what looks like trash tossed away from my world: three crushed Pepsi cans that have been stretched out like accordions and given metallic arms and legs; broken animal figurines missing limbs; a rare album sleeve of the *Black* album resting inside a display case. I do, however, come across an old radio, which, despite all of the modern collections along the shelves, would match the Roaring Twenties-vibe I'm feeling throughout the apartment. The furniture is covered in plastic to prevent Azzgul and other creatures from clawing the wool of the couch. To make matters worse, the place reeks of rotten cat food.

Why don't you take a shower while I grab you a pair of clothes?

You take showers?

Of course, we do. After all, we were once like you, Ajax.

Right. So, where's this shower?

Creach guides me toward a bedroom while Azzgul, who hasn't spoken a word since we got here, stands guard by the living room window. I walk into a bedroom, which, despite a teenager-like messiness, appears like any normal bedroom.

As I wait by the edge of the bathroom, which, unlike the bedroom, appears as if I'm going to catch malaria by just looking at it, Creach searches for an outfit for me in Azzgul's closet. I block out the brown stains of what I can I only imagine as being blood or feces or both, splattered over the possible disease-riddled bathtub, as well as the walls. I remind myself that the black tar isn't going to come off with a little bit of elbow grease.

Creach returns with an outfit—more or less, a costume. It's not until Creach hands me the folded red suit that I realize I've seen it before.

This is what Michael Jackson wore in the music video, 'Thriller.' Where did you find this?

As I hold the costume closer to my face, a waft of rot hits me in the face.

One man's trash is another man's—in this case—another creature's treasure.

Before Creach can answer, I already know where Azzgul found the costume.

It once belonged to Azzgul's son. He used to wear it when he hung around the Dog Bar. He's a little bit shorter than you. But it should fit.

I see. I weigh my options: either carry around part of a banner to cover up myself, walk around naked, or, the most likely and more suitable option, wear Michael Jackson's 'Thriller' costume that was probably bought at Party City before it was tossed in the trash. Despite the putrid smell, the sight of the costume brings me a sense of comfort knowing that, even though I may feel as though I'm stuck a place worlds away from my own, I am much closer to home than I realize.

So, where's the glove?

I'm sorry. A glove?

Never mind.

I take the costume into the bathroom.

I also put a towel in there.

You did?

I turn toward the bathroom and find a perfectly folded raggedy-looking black polka-doted towel, which looks as if it's used to clean the dirt stains off rims, resting on the top of a crusty phlegm-stained vanity.

Thanks.

I close the door behind me, place the costume on the cleanest spot I can find, and step into the bathtub. I turn on the faucet, which causes the pipes to clink and clank behind the wall before a burst of brownish-red water spits out. The water—if you can even call it that—smells like sulfur and immediately causes my eyes to burn. Eventually, the water loses its color and returns to somewhat normal. I flip on the shower and wash off the black tar from my body. The water is ice-cold, too, and even when I turn the knob to hot, the water feels as if it's getting colder.

As quickly as I can, I scrub and rinse. I can't help but notice my skin. I start to wonder whether or not it's from the tar. My skin feels harder, coarser, scalier. Even the scars along my body have somewhat sunken and connected to one another, leaving behind these deep, grid-like cracks along my arms. Even the hair along my neck feels much hairier.

Lastly, I draw my eyes to the Blood Watch along my wrist. Once I wash the tar from the glass casing, I notice that the gauge is completely black!

I only spend enough time to partially remove the tar. Then, I jump out of the filthy bathtub and rake away the remaining tar from my body with a towel.

I take a moment in front of a murky mirror covered in scratches and caked in what I can only guess as hardened pus. I check my body for any marks. As I rotate around, I point out two swollen areas, which appear like large knots, running alongside my shoulder blades. I reach one arm around my shoulder and touch one of the areas and it feels incredibly sore. I arch one arm out as if I'm about to do a chicken dance while, at the same time, keeping a close eye on my shoulder blade. The shape of the bone looks rounder and foreign.

I change into my new outfit, which, surprisingly, fits like a glove.

Once I step out of the bathroom, I flinch from the sight of Creach standing in the same position I last left her.

Have you been waiting here this whole time?

I wanted to make sure you were okay. Well, are you okay?

Considering the circumstances, yeah. I guess so.

I show Creach the Blood Watch.

The watch. It's black. I thought you said never let the watch turn black.

Correct.

I am dead, aren't I?

Do you feel dead?

I actually think about my next response.

No. I don't. In fact, I feel the opposite.

343

I roll up the sleeves of my 'Thriller' jacket. Again, I can't help but notice the deeper lines along my scalier skin.

Who were those other people back at Black Lake?

Tourists. People like you, Ajax. People who, you know—

—But I didn't kill myself.

I know you didn't, Ajax.

You know a lot of things, don't you? I'm starting to think maybe you found me for a reason.

And exactly what reason is that?

I dunno yet.

I draw my eyes toward a picture frame on top of a dresser. In the photo I see Azzgul and two other creatures, one, like Azzgul, whose face appears as if a child rearranged the features on his face, and then the other one, a slender and shapely eel-faced creature with purplish-gray skin as slick and shiny as the plastic furniture covers in the living room.

Who's the chick?

That's Azzgul's daughter-in-law, Semi.

I point at the one who looks like Azzgul.

And that's his son, I suppose.

Correct.

So, what's Semi's story?

Semi comes from the shrill race.

The shrill race?

But she looks nothing like you.

I don't look like a shrill because my pneuma is not a shrill.

Your pneuma caused you to look like that?

Over time, this body you're looking at started to *change* after I was saved by Napone. In Midnight World, the air, the water, and all of the resources that your world takes for granted, all of it has a way of tapping deep into your pneuma and fleshing out your true self—

—Mutation.

Apparently, the ancestors of my pneuma had reptile in them. But, like I've said, Ajax, it's not me. Who I am. On the inside.

I glance down at the scars on my scalier arms.

You must realize, Ajax, the stakes are now much more higher than before. In Midnight World, you either survive or you die.

Creach walks toward the window and stares at the glowing Beta sign outside.

The reason why I was so evasive earlier is because there are crossers who'd rather sell a tourist's pneuma to a member of the High Order opposed to earning a position with The Council.

Why?

Survival, Ajax. Just whatever you do, don't die. Azzgul will keep you safe here until the Gigermites lose your scent.

Seriously? So, I'm stuck here?

Not stuck. There is one way you can return to your world—

—I'm all ears.

Become a crosser, get in tight with the High Order. In your world's terms, it won't happen overnight. It may take years.

Years! I can't stay here for years!

It's not like you have any say in the matter, Ajax. It's part of the deal.

Deal? What deal? I never agreed to any deal.

Creach walks out of the bedroom.

Where are you going?

I'm going to sleep, Ajax, as should you.

Sleep? I'll sleep when I'm dead!

Maybe. But I'm cranky when I don't rest. Besides, a 'lady needs her beauty sleep,' am I right? Isn't that what the females say in your world?

I drift off from the sound of the comment. I remember Creach reaching out and grabbing my hand back in the sewers. Her sharp claws were now fingernails. Her scaly hide, human flesh. Even the feel of her grip was soft, feminine. It's not the change in her that I specifically remember. It was the look on her face.

Lost in the comment, I remain speechless as Creach leaves the apartment.

I walk to the window and search for Creach but can't find her.

What feels like only a couple of minutes spent in the 'Thriller' costume and I can already notice the sleeves, as well as the pants and crotch region appear much smaller and tighter, as if, in those couple of minutes or so, it's either the costume that has shrunk several inches or my body is *still* growing. Even those two protrusions along my shoulder blades feel larger and more pointed; and even when I raise my arms over my head, they hurt, not like a sharp, shooting pain, but rather a dull, heavy pain, a growing pain.

My attention is drawn to the bar, Beta, where a flock of business suit-wearing vultures are consuming a weasel-dwarf like creature. One man-vulture in particular is holding a camera and filming the other vultures picking apart the roadkill.

I decide to take Creach's advice and rest in the rickety bed.

I close my eyes.

I can't stop thinking about the comment about Creach being a female.

Then, Creach's expression. . .

—

"Smells Like Chlorine"

I open my eyes!

I roll out of bed and rush to the closet where I dig out a pair of black boots caked with mud. I slip on the boots and exit the bedroom.

Azzgul tries to stop me.

Creach specifically told me to watch over you.

Get out of my way, Azzhole!

I push aside Azzgul, who doesn't put up much of a fight, and hurry outside.

As Creach emphasized earlier, I make sure to stick close to the unlit areas and try not to make myself known.

After scouring the empty streets, I finally spot Creach talking to a disguised figure underneath an amber streetlight. I creep closer and inspect further. I come to the shocking conclusion that the disguised figure is the same cloaked man from Beta; however, he's not any random person who's supposedly giving safe passage for Creach. The man happens to be Avanti's right-hand man.

Joel?

What is he doing here?

As soon as his glossy eyes track mine, Joel pulls the hood back over his head and walks away, leaving Creach alone in the street.

Creach tracks me down.

I'm left with no other choice than to confront Creach.

You lied to me.

I only told you what you needed to hear, Ajax.

I never was leaving, was I?

Creach doesn't answer my question.

Why am I really here, *Creach*?

You made a deal, remember?

I remember. . . Images of lying in a hospital bed flood my thoughts; however, I still can't see the shadowy woman sitting by my bedside, even though I suspect who she might be.

It was all a part of the deal, Ajax. The reason why you can't remember making a deal is because your mother erased it from your mind—or at least, she tried to. But time has a way of exposing the truth. Am I right?

I can remember. Fragments. A flash of anger rushes through my blood. So, what's your deal? What's in it for you, *Creach*? Was I only a job to you? I had a life. Now, it's all gone because of you!

'Two birds, one stone.'

What?

It's an expression from your world.

I know what it is!

My job is to keep you away, Ajax, until the election is over while, at the same time, I'm still trying to buy a ticket back into Midnight World, essentially, redeem myself.

Earn your scales, right? You liar. You never heard me crying for help. You lied to me. *She* sent you. I can't help but think about Creach's so-called 'sorbere' power and wonder if it's all a silly line to make me believe how special she is.

I didn't know who you were at the time.

And what? Now, you do? Besides, why in the hell would you want to come back to this god-forsaken place?

I was reborn here, Ajax. And I will die here.

Then, you belong here.

You're right, Ajax. I do belong here. Leatherwood is my home. This is the only real home I've ever known.

This place is goddamn freak show!

You want to talk about the circus. Your world is too superficial. All you and your fellow members of the human race care about is what you look like or how you act on the outside. Maybe, just maybe one day, when your kind is able to see a living thing for who he or she truly is on the inside, I'll find a way back to your world and hopefully, call it home. But until that time comes, Leatherwood is my home.

So, what? You want to come back to my world because you're scared of what people may think of you. Where I come from, we call that a bullshit ex—

—I'm not scared of what they'll think of me. I'm scared of what they'll do to me if they ever found out who I was. Whether you like or not, Ajax, here, I fit in. At least, I used to. But I'm trying hard to make things right again. Of all people, I'm sure you can understand.

I point at the general direction where I last saw Joel.

And why was Joel here?

He was just checking up on me. Making sure you were safe.

All this time, you betrayed me.

No, Ajax. I saved you. Like it or not, a day will come when you may have to do the same for me.

What did you do that was so bad for such a place like this to cast you out?

Over many moons ago, I got hooked up with scavengers who rolled with this group called Ill-Famy. I was hungry and needed to team up. So, in order to join their nasty tribe, they gave me the specific task of stealing pride of the next civilian who crossed my path. Sure enough, I found a civilian, an easy uprighter wearing heavy disguise, looked suspicious but, if I didn't join up, then I wasn't going to make it alone in Leatherwood. The Ill-Famy hung back while I made a move. The civilian just so happened to be Toofont. Little did I know that Krillish had been stalking Toofont that entire full moon. Unaware that Krillish was about to attack Toofont and avenge those who tragically perished in The Great Vanishing, I jumped in the way and tried to grab hold of Toofont but Toofont ended up escaping into the darkness. Krillish wanted my head for interfering with his business. Krillish figured the worse punishment of all would be to exile me to a world that would enjoy picking me apart. Once the word had gotten out in Leatherwood that it was I who was the one who prevented Krillish from killing the monster behind The Great Vanishing, I could no longer show my face anywhere near Leatherwood. Ever since then, I've been trying to earn my stay.

Creach hangs her head in misery.

Then, she faces me.

Sorry to hear.

There are some wounds that cannot be healed, right?

The words resonant inside me. I start to piece everything together: Avanti, who, surprisingly, hadn't aged a day, standing by the swimming pool and talking to a 'soul robber' that Creach had spoken of while telling me her story about how she managed to survive The Great Vanishing as a result of a soul transplant, essentially, her Great rebirth into the shapely body of an electric eel-

looking nymphet known as a shrill; then, I envision myself
lying in a hospital bed and sitting at my bedside is
Avanti, who's telling me, '*There are just some wounds I cannot heal.*' I can feel her hand touch me on the crook of my
arm. Below my cast, the pain slowly vanishes from the
bones in my left wrist. I'm able to move around my
sweaty wrist inside the cast, as well as the tips of my fingers in my left hand. Despite Avanti's power to heal only
on a surface level, the other pain is *still* there, gnawing at
me, throbbing well beyond the bones. I'm able to breathe
better after suspecting who Creach is and why, of all the
living creatures in the world, Avanti chose Creach to
watch over me.

For years, she had me convinced that it was all an accident. But deep inside, I knew the truth about what
really happened. A part of me didn't want to *know* the
truth, my truth, you know what I mean? She helped me
block it out.

Well, she's a politician, Ajax. And every good politician has a tragedy story.

There must be another reason as to why Avanti is doing all of this, something she's not telling us.

Take my advice, Ajax. Go back to Azzgul's apartment. Rest.

But I can't rest, knowing everything you just told me—
—You have to try.

Creach makes an attempt to walk away.

I still have to earn my stay. Souls to save, remember?

Well, I don't feel saved! I feel imprisoned!

The only prison, Ajax, is the one you make for yourself.

As Creach walks away into the shadows outside the
streetlight, I specifically remember what she told me before entering this chaotic city, about fragments of her
memory that, according to Creach, get more vivid as she
ages, specifically one event, drowning. My deepest suspicion returns to the forefront of my mind. The name hits
me, nearly knocking the wind out of me.

Echo. It is you. . .

Creach suddenly stops from the sound of the name rolling from my lips.

She glances over her pointy shoulder and stares at me. She doesn't speak another word to me. And she doesn't have to. I peer beyond Creach's face and witness an expression, so vague yet so incredibly innocent, pushing through her scaly hide.

Once acknowledging the somewhat religious awe hanging from my face after the epiphany, Creach turns around and disappears in the shadows.

—

"The Lines We Draw/Higher Purpose"

Nathan Katz, who had recently turned seventy years old, was expected to be a grandpa to a baby boy any day now. His daughter, Gila, who was twenty-nine and happened to be a Pisces, like her father, was due by the end of the week, but her OB-GYN told her and her husband, Lekan, that she was entering what she commonly referred to as the "Latent Phase" where Gila's contractions were getting stronger and more regular. Gila's OB-GYN couldn't stress enough that this phase was best experienced at home.

As Nathan did whenever life was about to reveal its certain surprises, he fell into an old habit, which often times turned into a bad habit. Nathan focused on work—and there was plenty of it. Nathan, who had been an architect for over forty years, was currently in the process of building his baby: a new highway called the "You-Way." Privately funded by billionaires across the country, You-Ways were going to be the next big thing in transportation. The ultimate goal was to revitalize the country's infrastructure by eliminating the very roads that had scored the earth and bringing safer, more reliable travel to the skies and reducing the release of carbon emissions.

With a baby boy on his mind, Nathan rescheduled a ten o'clock meeting with Kevin Twine, Director of the Department of Transportation, and decided to step out of the office for a cup of coffee, which would normally be handled by one of his many assistants. However, today, Nathan needed to take the work outside.

As Nathan was leaving his favorite coffee shop, Black Joe's, he was drawn to a crew of construction workers past the flowing aero pods across the beltway. The construction crew, which mostly consisted of dwellers from Midnight World, was assembling one of the Nathan's gazillion docking posts next to the Empire State building, which would be linked up to the web of You-Ways in the sky. The docking post was inspired by the "tractor beams" used in a broad range of science fiction entertainment, including the television series *Star Trek*. Crazy how some of the greatest inventions on earth originate from reading books or watching TV or movies. However, Nathan's attention was drawn to what was happening next to the docking post.

A young woman, probably no older than Gila, extended her hand to a Dweller who had tripped over a support beam lying on the ground.

The dweller, a warthog-like creature with two dull nubs of tusks who, legally speaking, was currently living in New York City under a worker's permit, acknowledged the woman's hand and eventually, after some patience mostly on the woman's part, grabbed hold of her hand. The woman helped up the dweller, who, in return, thanked the woman, who, in return, started up what appeared to be a pleasant conversation with the dweller.

The sight of man and dweller sharing a moment of connection triggered a sudden memory in his head.

Immediately, Nathan couldn't stop thinking about the number 6,000 and the images attached to it. It *wasn't a dream*. It did happen. He recalled the number of footsteps that he took from the point of origin where he made his daring escape from Midnight World.

🍎

Nathan rode a drone to Atlanta, Georgia, where he visited a once upper class neighborhood that was now rundown. Most of the houses were pending foreclosure and if you listened close enough, you could hear the tweets and chirps of birds among the heavy overgrowth of vegetation. Nathan sat down feet away from the exact location that he last remembered.

Nathan found the *exact* manhole and from there, he started walking.

🍎

Six thousand steps later, he arrived at his destination.

The once wooded area was torn down and turned into an entertainment center called The Epicenter.

Making sure to keep track of the number of steps, he forked out twenty dollars for a ticket into The Epicenter. Once Nathan stepped inside, he continued counting. The sounds and sights of roller coasters tempted him to lose his count. He ignored all the bright lights and flashy signs and sweet smells in the air and powered through the super mall. Finally, his six-thousandth step happened to be directly in front of a movie theatre called *The Twin*.

He couldn't help but laugh at the symbolism.

🍎

Later that night, Nathan called his "go-to" guy named Hoyt, who wrangled up a crew of illegal Dwellers. He couldn't emphasize enough to Hoyt that he needed strong—and *quick*—dwellers, ones who were able to work a job twice as fast as typical hired hands. Hoyt had the right crew for Nathan.

Once The Epicenter was closed for the night, Nathan and crew tranquilized the three security guards, two outside the main gates and one surveying the perimeter, and snuck into The Epicenter. Inside, two half scorpion-half spiders, who happened to be brothers, took out another guard in front of the security monitors. Nathan couldn't stress enough not to tie the guard up in a web. The last thing Nathan wanted was to draw any more negative exposure to dwellers. Nathan wiped the monitors clean while the other dwellers got to work. Among the other dwellers were these two brutish bull-like creatures, who were able to carry jackhammers, a miniature excavator, as well as other bulky digging equipment that weighed nearly a ton on their backs. The rest of the dwellers brought their shovels.

Since they only had a couple of hours to work until the tranquilizer darts wore off, the crew didn't waste anytime. They set up work lights in front of The Twin Theatre, planted shop, and got straight to work.

Only an hour in, the crew reached the special container in the dirt. Nathan climbed down the hole with the help of one of many cousins of the notorious desert serpents and a highly evolved alien-like stag beetle and picked up the container carrying a twilight lavender light inside, a purplish light that Nathan had memorized by heart and could very well identify from an entire galaxy of lights.

"You did it, boys. You found her."

🍎

Nathan and the rest of the crew managed to leave before the security guards came to.

The crew was handsomely rewarded with ancient currency, which was cash. Lots and lots of cash.

🍎

After Nathan parted ways with the dwellers, it was already dawn. He surprised his daughter, Gila, with a phone call. She and Lekan were still sleeping, since they lived in the itty-bitty town of Colby, New Mexico, and were three hours behind. Gila managed to make it through the night without going into labor, which, for Nathan, was even better.

Despite having said he was going to visit, Gila was shocked to see her father show up at the house by the time she and Lekan were sitting down for lunch.

That night, Nathan waited for Gila to fall asleep before sneaking into her bedroom. Prior to sleep, Lekan packed the bags just in case. Nathan knew he was running out of time. With the container in his hand, he crept up to Gila in bed, carefully opened the container, and released the pneuma.

At exactly 4:13 AM, Gila's water broke while she was rolling out of bed to use the bathroom. As soon as she called out to Lekan, they both knew it was time.

Only a few minutes after Gila and Lekan arrived at Colby Medical Center, Gila was pushing out a baby.

After the baby was delivered at 8:23 AM, not only were Gila and Lekan surprised by the sex of the baby, but also the entire room—well, maybe, except for one person. Later, Gila's OB-GYN had absolutely no explanation other than blaming it on faulty equipment. As far as blood tests that were conducted during Gila's last visit, her OB-GYN claimed that the tests were ninety-nine percent accurate in determining the sex of a fetus. In Gila's case, she fell into that nearly scientifically impossible one percent.

However, Gila knew that having a baby was probably the last great surprise in life. From a cynic's point-of-view, it was something worth relishing. As far as Lekan's current state of mind, he was more upset than Gila even though he never showed it. All Lekan kept thinking about was redecorating the baby's room. He spent all that extra money on pink paint.

With a weight lifted off his shoulders, Nathan stood in front of the glass outside the hospital's nursery and watched his granddaughter resting comfortably with all the other babies. Lekan moved in beside Nathan.

"Talk about a surprise, huh?" said Lekan, as if he had been thinking of the right line to start up a conversation with his ever-elusive father-in-law.

"Life has a funny way of switching the script, doesn't it?"

"It's weird because, for the past couple of days, I've had his—or her—entire future drawn in my mind. He was going to play basketball like I did when I was younger. Then, after high school, he was going to go to law school. Then, after law school, he would move out of the house, get a job at a decent law firm, and eventually, get married."

"It's only natural for a parent to plan their child's future, Lekan," Nathan said wisely. "I was the same way. As you know, it backfired on me and I'm still left trying to pick up all of the pieces between Gila and I. But as she grows older—your daughter, that is—you will soon realize that the world will open its doors to her and it will show her who she's meant to be in life."

"And what do I do when that happens?" asked Lekan.

Nathan said, "All you have do is close your eyes and hope for the best."

As Nathan touched Lekan's shoulder, he caught a strange woman in the corner of his eye. He moved his eyes away from Lekan and stared at the woman, who was suspiciously dressed in all black. She was wearing a floppy black hat and black sunglasses. For a moment, she turned her head toward Nathan's direction and then walked the other direction. Nathan excused himself and followed the strange woman to the end of the hallway where he lost her around a corner. He searched through a crowd of nurses roaming the hallways. He saw the door to the staircase close but didn't exactly see her enter the staircase. He found the nearest elevator, which wasn't too far from the stairs. In front of the elevator, there was a group of nurses and visitors waiting to ride the elevator. *She wouldn't want to draw any attention to herself,* especially with other people riding the elevator.

Nathan decided to take the stairs.

Once he walked through the door, he leaned over the edge of the railing and peered down through the spiraling staircase. Four flights below him, he saw a dark figure walking down the stairs. He followed, but did so gingerly. He didn't want to aggravate his bum knee.

Nathan lost her once again after he made it to the first floor of the hospital. He searched and eventually found her exiting the hospital.

Once outside, he searched for her and, of course, found her not walking away but sitting on a bench covered in the late-morning shadows towering over the side of the hospital.

In the cool shade, Nathan sat down next to her on the bench. He looked closer at her face, determining her age. What immediately stood out was the heavy makeup worn on her face in order to cover up the spotty skin disease.

"I'm curious," Nathan started, as he turned his eyes toward a younger couple who were passing by, "when they look at you, what do they see?"

"They see the same person you're looking at."

"And is that what you consider yourself, a person?"

"After you lived up to your end of the deal and found a way to destroy the very thing that was keeping the curse alive, the hunger started to settle down two years into my presidency. The curse was—and *still* is—there. But it's fair to say it's not like it once was—"

"—How did you find me?" asked Nathan.

"I can spot your eyes from a mile away, Ajax," she said, removing her sunglasses. The woman was none other than the forty-sixth President of the United States, Avanti Washington.

The comment alone of his mother tracking him through the color of his eyes made him think about the day his eyes started to *change*. He was eighteen years old and about to attend Darmyth when his eyes started to change color; however, neither Nathan nor his ophthalmologist had any explanation whatsoever as to how one eye turned green and the other one blue.

"During my speech at Rosewater Hill, I saw a pair of eyes in the audience. I couldn't help but notice the similarities these particular eyes shared with my son. You know, they say the eyes are the windows of the soul. They are right."

Reflective, Nathan said, "I remember that day like it was yesterday. It was on that day you paved the way for future presidents to come. That was the day you peeled back the curtains and showed the world that we were, in fact, not alone."

I'm standing in a crowd of my peers, wondering what in the hell I'm looking at. To the right of President Washington stands a hairy, short creature who looks as if it's a kid wearing a werewolf costume. But I soon realize it's not a kid.

"You showed the entire world what our past actions have done to our neighbors. And ever since then, people around the entire world have been digging holes in their backyards, trying to locate this 'other' world you mentioned in your speech."

Me and two friends from college buy the last three shovels remaining on the shelves. Nearly every hardware store across the country have sold out of shovels or digging tools. But we manage to find three shovels. While we start digging holes in a soccer field behind the dorm rooms, I stop digging and fall into a deep trance. I can't move at all. I feel paralyzed by the thought of what's waiting on the other side. Alex is asking me what's wrong with me. But I can't speak.

"The speech must've had a powerful impact on you. I see you've made quite a life for yourself. That highway of yours will fail, though. Eventually, man finds a way to destroy what's meant to be good."

Nathan argued, "Given the rise in automobile accidents, I've come to realize how precious life is. Life is worth *living*. That's the sole reason why I wanted to build my highway, to save life, not destroy it. You're wrong about people. People *can* change for the better. I just want to know, Avanti: 'Why'd you kill them?'"

"You know why I did what I did—"

"—I want to hear it coming from your mouth."

"At the time, I needed a tragedy story, Ajax. And believe it or not, it was my tragedy story that landed me in the White House. After the curse started to lift, I realized that it was still there. Those who were close to me noticed and in time, I knew that soon the American people would notice. We all know that a President ages in the White House. So, I aged—or at least, I was made to look as though I aged."

"Violet Odem," Nathan said with hostility, "also known as simply 'Vye.' Yeah. I know all about her. So, what bush is she hiding behind?" Nathan looked around the parking lot. "I have a few words I'd like to say to her."

"You're out of luck. She's no longer with us."

Nathan was at a loss for words.

"One day, we had an argument in the West Wing. Let's just say I came out on top."

"Well, then, I'm glad she got what she deserved."

"It's not merely as bad as what I deserve," Avanti said morosely. "Now, having lived with the idea of what I did to my family, having to wake up every morning to the very thought, that's my hell. Even worse, I get to spend the rest of my existence watching those around me die."

"Such a pity," Nathan said, more cynically. "If I didn't know any better, it almost sounds as if you developed a heart during your time in the oval office."

"Ajax, I never wanted for you to live with this curse. I wanted you to live a fulfilling life and then, at the end, be able to tell the world that you did the best you could, considering the circumstances."

"That's where you're dead wrong, Avanti. I did live a fulfilling life. And the You-Way will be my legacy, *not* yours. It is my gift to the world. Believe it or not, it was Midnight World that showed me my purpose. . . "

After many years of surviving inside Midnight World, I have reverted back to my most primitive existence.

Creach explains to me it's the radiation that is having an effect on my body; however, I'm still convinced it has to do with my bloodline, even though my theory contradicts what Creach said about my pneuma being linked to our ancestors. All insecurity is gone. I no longer worry about what to wear. You know it wasn't long until I out grew that raggedy 'Thriller' costume. At least I'm slightly taller than Creach, which, I believe, is something worth bragging about in front of her. Not to rub it in her face or anything, but, yeah, I also have wings. You dig? She doesn't. I've embraced my new title as 'The Tooth Fairy.' Around Leatherwood, I'm known for being one of the most highly successful members of the High Order with one helluva résumé, including a ninety-nine percent success rate for lives saved. Work hasn't slowed down, but I'm not complaining. The work keeps me busy. Everyday, I find others once like me and show each *flicker*—which, I think, sounds a whole lot better than pneuma—where his or her path went astray in life. It's fair to say I've found a strange pleasure in discovering a flicker's cornerstone. Mostly, I deal with jumpers, shooters, cutters, throwers (those are the ones who throw themselves in front of moving objects like cars or speeding vehicles)—even those who think outside the box when making that final decision to put an end to the suffering. It's the ones who don't think at all that prevent me from sleeping. But I can't help but laugh at the irony and how my entire life I've felt as if I was always late to the party or damned by bad timing, the one who never spoke up at that right moment, yet I held my tongue; and then when it came time to speak, not a single soul was listening.

The only part of my job that helps me sleep easier is knowing that, when the job is done, I saved a flicker from death and reconnected them with the same body they were born in back in the other world. I'd be lying if I said I didn't miss my world, my home, my bed. I wish I was strong enough to fight Vye. Each day, I remind myself that it's the little things, you see, like a bed or clean water or even something you couldn't see, like the smell of an apple pie coming straight out of an oven, that I took for granted during those sixteen years of what I once foolishly called a pathetic life.

But this is my prison now.

And I am bound to it.

"Oh," Avanti said, more casually. "I believe it all right. I've heard a lot about this so-called 'Tooth Fairy.'"

At the peak of my success, Creach becomes one of the many victims from a string of bombs that had gone off throughout Leatherwood. The bomber is said to be another Toofont-fanatic, one who was inspired by The Great Vanishing.

In Creach's final moments, she reveals to me that she is Krillish and that she made up the legend of Krillish in order to give those who lived in Leatherwood a sense of hope. I am left with no other choice than to store Creach's flicker inside the High Chambers in Heaven where the High Order will look after her flicker. However, it is there, during my grievance, that I have another epiphany and realize that the High Order is no different than those corrupted souls from Eventide.

Without members of the High Order watching, I catch them consuming flickers in such a gluttonous manner. Their bottomless need for knowledge of the universe and power has driven them mad. I am no different than a puppet. I'm being used, like Creach was being used, to enrich the very flickers I save, making them brighter and more delectable, in order to later whet the appetite of some fat High Order blowhard who, even if he tried, can't even find his own dick. The flicker is no different than ripe fruit: the riper, the tastier. 'The greater the life the richer the soul': That was once our motto as a crosser. And I've also learned that those 'light baths' the High Order provided to us every full moon are a bunch of bullshit. It's all a production, all lights and camera but not action, all carried out by the letter in order to make us feel more included or 'enlightened,' as they call it. I fear my sister's flicker will soon be consumed by the High Order.

Knowing what is now at stake, I strenuously devise a plan to escape from this awful place. I work a new job: a shooter who shot up a shopping mall during the holiday season when people were buying Christmas gifts. As the cops were closing in to take her down, she turned a gun on herself. Multiple casualties. I do the one thing I said I'd never do: I desert the flicker. But that's the sacrifice. I let one life die in order to save another.

With my plan in full motion, I capture one of the corrupted flickers from the Eventide, bring it back into Midnight World, then release corruption in the High Chambers where all of the flickers are kept in storage. Corruption spreads like a tidal wave to the Walls of Flickers. I locate Creach's flicker just before corruption takes over. Of all the bright colors, her color is easiest to find: *Twilight lavender.* I steal Creach's flicker and I barely escape the Heavens.

"I'm curious, Ajax. What flipped the switch inside you? Was it a memory? Something you experienced?"

Immediately, Nathan went back to the moment he saw a young woman helping up a dweller from the ground.

"It was something an old friend once told me."

Nathan recalled what Creach had said to him a long, *long* time ago.

Maybe, just maybe one day, when your kind is able to see a living thing for who he or she truly is on the inside, I'll find a way back to your world and hopefully, call it home. But until that time comes, Leatherwood is my home.

"That reminds me," Avanti said, pulling out a wrinkled, black and white speckled Composition book from her gator-skinned purse. "I thought you might want your journal. You know, for keepsake."

Avanti handed Nathan Ajax's old journal.

Surprised, Nathan held the journal in his old, papery-skinned hands.

"I completely forgot about this," he said softly.

Nathan flipped to one sketch in particular, a sketch of a seven-foot tall reptile named Creach.

"So," Avanti said expressionlessly, as she pulled Nathan from his trance. "I see you're a grandpa now."

"Yeah," he said, finding Avanti's words. "That's right."

"Impressive."

"To be honest," Nathan said, "I never thought I lived to see the day."

"*So*," Avanti said, her voice rising, "are you going to tell me what they named your granddaughter?"

"I was the one who actually suggested the name."

"So, what did they name her?" asked Avanti.

"Echo," he said, graciously wearing Ajax's smile. "Her name is Echo."